EXCHANGE ALLEY

EXCHANGE ALLEY

MICHAEL WALSH

WARNER BOOKS

A Time Warner Company

For my friends

Warner Books, Inc., 1271 Avenue of the Americas, New York, NY 10020
Ⓦ A Time Warner Company

Printed in the United States of America
First Printing: July 1997
10 9 8 7 6 5 4 3 2 1

Library of Congress Cataloging-in-Publication Data

Walsh, Michael (Michael Alan)
Exchange alley / Michael Alan
p. cm.
ISBN 0-446-52069-1
I. Title.
PS3573.A472242E96 1997
813'.54—dc20   96-42029
CIP

Book design by Giorgetta B. McRee

Entia non sunt multiplicanda praeter necessitatem.
(Beings ought not to be multiplied except out of necessity.)
—Occam's Razor

BRIEFINGS

And the angel of the Lord said to her: "You are pregnant, and will bear a son; and you shall call his name Ishmael because the Lord has heard your affliction. And he will be a man of the wild; his hand against all, and the hand of all against him, and in the presence of all his brothers shall he dwell."
— Genesis 16:11–12

Hear, O heavens, and give ear, O earth: for the Lord hath spoken, I have nourished and brought up children, and they have rebelled against me.
— Isaiah 1:2

Eichmann was the product of two thousand years of Christian history, the whole end of which is the destruction of the Jews. . . . He did, in fact, just carry out orders—a matter of importance to us—but the main thing is that he carried out mankind's will with regard to the Jewish people.
— Yeshayahu Leibowitz

The work of intelligence agents often takes place under abnormal conditions. Therefore they should be resilient and strong in spirit, and possess an iron will in order to overcome all the difficulties and privations of their difficult way. An agent should be a pure person despite his having to be everywhere where the sores of the present-day society are especially evident, remembering that he serves the great idea of the people.
— from the Official KGB Handbook

We believe our people are the Agency's most important resource. We seek the best and work to make them better. We subordinate our desire for public recognition to the need for confidentiality. We strive for continuing professional improvement. We give unfailing loyalty to each other and to our common purpose.
— Central Intelligence Agency Credo

I have and always had the full sanction of the U.S. Embassy, Moscow USSR, and hence the U.S. government.

—Lee Harvey Oswald, letter to Secretary of the Navy John B. Connally, January 30, 1962

Three shots were fired at President Kennedy's motorcade in downtown Dallas.

—UPI reporter Merriman Smith, 12:34 P.M., November 22, 1963

Part One
GENESIS

Prologue
Bethesda, Maryland
Summer, 1964

It was very hot in the attic room. The quarters were small, about three meters square. The door was covered with a metal screen. There was one window, locked and papered over, high up on the pitched ceiling; too high for him to look out, even standing on the bed. The bare gunmetal military cot stood in the middle of the room and was bolted to the floor. It had no sheets or blankets and one filthy pillow. There was a chamber pot in the corner, but no sink, and no running water. The only light was a single bright, bare bulb in the center of the room.

Wake-up was at 6:00 A.M.; lights out at 10:00 P.M. They made him razor himself with cold water, no soap or shaving cream. Once a week, but never on the same day, he was permitted a shower, to which he was led blindfolded and handcuffed; the cuffs stayed on throughout. Each day, he got to eat a small bowl of watery soup and some tea. He was not allowed to brush his teeth. Sometimes he would have visitors, whom he received blindfolded. But most days would pass without any human contact at all, unless you counted the creep who brought him his meals and, if he felt like it, emptied the chamber pot.

Still, things could be worse. He could, for example, be a prisoner of KGB instead of the CIA. His Soviet colleagues' interrogation methods were not a pretty sight. They smashed you in the face and squeezed your nuts, they beat you with rubber hoses, they strangled you with a belt, they kicked in your ribs with hobnail boots, they pulled a plastic sack over your head and suffocated you, they shot you full of dope, they hung you from meat hooks, shoved bottles up your behind and crushed them. The worst was when they put you bare-assed on a chamber pot and then heated it from below; there was a rat in the chamber pot, and the only way out for him was up and through you. At least there was no rat in his chamber pot.

Yuri Ivanovich Nosenko, the prisoner who did not officially exist, was thirty-seven years old. Soviet Naval Intelligence had recruited him when he was a student at the State Institute of International Relations in Moscow; by 1953 he was working for the MVD, the KGB's precursor. There were those who uncharitably attributed his recruitment and rapid rise in the service to his father's position as minister for shipbuilding under Khrushchev, but he preferred to believe it was his excellent grades in Marxist-Leninist theory that had first attracted attention.

Nosenko showed up on CIA's door in Geneva in June of 1962. At that time, he was the chief security officer for the Soviet delegation to the disarmament talks in the Swiss lakeside city. A private word to an American diplomat brought Pete Bagley running in from Bern. Bagley, a Soviet specialist, arranged a meeting at a safe house outside Geneva, where they were joined by George Kisevalter, a Russian-born agent who had already dealt with Popov and Penkovsky and was considered the best man for handling Soviet defectors. Nosenko told them he was a major in the KGB. As proof of his bona fides, he gave up a minor Soviet agent, a correspondent for Radio Moscow working for CIA who had been re-doubled by KGB, and exposed a couple of British agents who had switched sides. He told them that the columnist Joseph Alsop, a good friend of President Kennedy, was queer and that KGB had the photos to prove it. He said there were forty-two microphones hidden in the walls of the American embassy on Tchaikovsky Street in Moscow; later, CIA managed to find forty of them, tucked away in bamboo tubes built into the walls and located behind the radiators to shield them from metal detectors.

In January 1964 Nosenko returned to Geneva and, as arranged with Kisevalter previously, sent a cable signed ALEX to a CIA asset in New York. That was the signal he had something to say. Traveling separately for security purposes, Kisevalter and Bagley were on the next planes.

They met Nosenko under the marquee of the ABC Theater in Geneva and took him to a safe house. After several meetings, he informed them that he had suddenly been ordered back to Moscow and wanted to defect immediately. After some discussion, Bagley offered a fifty-thousand-dollar fee, a ten-thousand-dollar bonus for information already received, and a working contract at twenty-five thousand dollars a year.

The next day, February 4, he was given forged American papers and driven across the border into West Germany; in Frankfurt, he met with David Murphy, chief of the Soviet Russia Division, who repeated Bagley's assurances. Murphy added one more detail: that Nosenko would be expected to pass a lie detector test. A week later Nosenko flew aboard a military aircraft from Frankfurt to Andrews Air Force Base in Maryland and was transported to a nearby safe house. The first thing they did was flutter him. The second thing was tell him he had flunked.

They stripped him naked and a tall, pale, balding doctor conducted a lingering, painful inspection of his bodily cavities. Then someone pulled a T-shirt over his chest and wriggled a pair of underpants up his legs and around his loins, followed by a pair of overalls and slippers. A blindfold was knotted over his eyes and somebody slapped on a pair of cuffs. He was quickly hustled out, dragged up several flights of stairs and deposited in an airless attic. They removed the blindfold and slammed the door.

And here he was, God only knew how long later.

The door to his room opened. "Good morning, Yurochka," said a man he had not seen before. "My name is Norman. How are you feeling?"

"*Yeb tvoju v dushu mat'*!" cursed Nosenko as one of the guards bound his hands and feet and tied him to his chair.

"Now, now," said Norman, replying in Russian. "We'll have none of that kind of language in here. This is America." The man was well dressed and he had clean fingernails. Despite the meanness of the surroundings, he looked as comfortable as if he were in his own living room.

"I want to see McCone," said the prisoner, in English.

"Not much chance of that, I'm afraid," answered Norman. "What would you say if the situation were reversed and I told you I wanted to see KGB chairman Semichastny? I wouldn't get very far, would I? The

DCI has no time to waste on small fry. That's why he's asked me to have a little chat with you."

The interrogator lit a cigarette. "Now then, to the business at hand. We're having a problem and I want to go over it with you one more time. Because some of the things you've been telling us just aren't true. Such as that baloney about your being a major in 1962 and a lieutenant colonel now. Which was, as you're well aware, a slight exaggeration— *Captain* Nosenko."

"You've seen my papers," said Nosenko. "You know that when I was working the Cherepanov case I was carrying an internal Soviet travel document that gave me the temporary rank of lieutenant colonel. Besides, why are we wasting our time with this stuff? You know why I'm here. I want to testify before the Warren Commission. About Oswald."

"You already have. Remember the statements you gave the FBI just after you arrived, on February 26 and March 3? Without asking us, Hoover's already sent them over to the commission. We wish he hadn't done that—at least not until we can decide whether you're for real or not—but nobody tells the J. Edgar what to do. Not even the president of the United States."

"You are trying to cause war between our countries," spat Nosenko.

"Oh not at all, not at all," said the man called Norman. "It seems to us, rather, that it's your side that has been acting, shall we say, provocatively lately. We haven't made any attempts on the life of Secretary Khrushchev, have we?"

"Nobody's perfect," said Nosenko, eyeing the cigarette jealously.

"Ah, but you seemed perfect when we first met you. You really did. Pete Bagley went to the mat for you, don't you know, and you broke his heart. Together, we're going to try to mend it, Yuri Ivanovich."

The interrogator shuffled some papers. "You know what really bothers me?" he continued. "What really bothers me is just how lucky we were to meet you. I mean, of all the gin joints in the world, you have to walk into ours."

"What do you mean?" Nosenko was confused. He had never seen *Casablanca*.

"I mean that I simply find it extraordinary that you should have always been in all the right places at all the right times in the Oswald case." The man was waving his cigarette around in the air for emphasis. "Look at it from our point of view, Yuri Ivanovich. Here the president is killed by a marine who had defected to the Soviet Union and then redefected to our country. Along comes a man from the Soviet Union, who claims to be an intelligence officer and says his service has never been in touch with this Oswald and knows nothing about him. But—just by the sheerest million-to-one-shot coincidence—this same man tells us that he can be certain because he himself has been in charge of the noncontact at every step of the way. Sort of taxes the credulity, doesn't it?"

Nosenko was silent.

"Look, we can't very well instruct our Moscow chief of station to ask Chairman Semichastny if you're telling the truth. But of the thousands of KGB men around the world, you're the only one who had direct supervision of the Oswald case—not once, but three times. You handled his case for the Second Directorate when he first landed in Moscow in 1959; you handled the case again last year when he applied for a Soviet visa from Mexico City; and you put together the whole dossier for Kremlin review right after the assassination. How many KGB men could say as much? We are unbelievably lucky, and I do mean unbelievably."

"But it's true," said Nosenko. "I was in charge of the file. I wrote part of it. I know what's in it. That's what I want to tell you about. There are things you need to know."

Norman referred to some notes. "I'm going to read part of an FBI memo about you, Yuri. It's about the report you prepared for your superiors after the assassination. It says, and I quote, 'Nosenko recalled that ... from the date of Oswald's arrival in the USSR until his departure from the USSR, the KGB had no personal contact with Oswald and had not attempted to utilize him in any manner.' In other words, you had no interest in this American defector, not even for propaganda purposes. I find that hard to believe."

Nosenko drew a deep breath, trying to catch some of the smoke in his lungs. "We thought Oswald was one of yours," he said. "He was crazy enough."

"What do you mean?"

"I mean he was dangerous. He was red-flag trouble. KGB took one look at him when he arrived in the fall of 1959 and made the decision to stay away."

This statement brought a hearty laugh. "Stay away from a marine who had served at Atsugi? Who stated publicly that he wanted to give you radar secrets? Who said that he 'might know something of special interest'? And then six months later the U-2 comes down? You expect me to believe this?"

"Just like you expect me to believe that when he came back the CIA had no interest in him either?" replied Nosenko. "A defector who spent two and a half years in the Soviet Union? Who returns to the United States and continues to claim he is Marxist-Leninist? Who agitates on behalf of Castro's Cuba? I can't help it whether you believe me or not. I'm telling you the truth. Anyway, if you thought we were running him, why did you let him back in? You haven't always been so friendly to Americans who leave your country for ours, *pravda*? 'Better dead than Red,' I think you say."

Norman rose from his chair and approached Nosenko; for a moment, Nosenko thought he was going to slug him. Instead, the interrogator lowered his face to Nosenko's level and spoke directly at him through gritted teeth. "I know you're lying," he said. "And I'm going to get you to admit it if it takes the rest of my life, and yours.

"Here's what I think: that when you first came to us in Geneva two years ago it was already part of a KGB setup, that even back then your side was planning a liquidation. But hitting the Principal Enemy's chief executive is pretty serious stuff, isn't it? So you bide your time and you poke and you prod—in Berlin, in Cuba, in Laos, in Vietnam, in every goddamn place you can think of—until Khrushchev figures our guy is a pushover, a patsy who won't fight back and doesn't deserve to live, and that Mother Russia's got just the nut for the job. That's what happened, Yuri Ivanovich, and that's what you're going to say."

Norman stood up straight. Suddenly his tone changed. "I've got some good news for you. You'll be getting out of here soon."

"It's about time," said Nosenko with relief.

"Don't get your hopes up; you're just being moved. But we think you'll like the bucolic setting. We call it the Farm."

Nosenko swallowed hard. Everybody in Moscow Center knew about the Farm: the CIA's supposedly secret training facility in rural Virginia.

"One last thing," said his interlocutor, referring to another piece of paper. "On November 16, 1959, Oswald was interviewed by a reporter named Priscilla Johnson in her hotel room. You assumed she was a spy, of course, so you bugged her. This is what he told her:

"'I am here because I am a Marxist. For the last two years, I have wanted to do this one thing. At the age of fifteen, after watching the way workers are treated in New York, and Negroes in the South, I was looking for a key to my environment. Then I discovered socialist literature. I knew that if I stayed in the United States I would become either a worker exploited for capitalist profit, or an exploiter. Or, since there are many in that category, I'd be one of the unemployed.

"'I just turn thumbs down on everything, on it all. I want to give the people of the United States something to think about.'

"Well, he certainly did that," said the CIA man. "Around here, we're very deep in thought."

Chapter One
Ramapo, New York
Thursday, October 18, 1990; noon

Bob and them found it just over there." The woman smacked her lips in recollection. She was only about forty, but she looked sixty. One of her front teeth was missing, and the others were crooked and yellow. Her hair hung in greasy strands around her forehead, and there was a large mole on her left cheek. Her hands were wrinkled and gnarled. Arthritis, thought Byrne, and bad nutrition. Life was tough in the country. Almost as tough as it was in town. "We live out here pretty much by our lonesomes," she said. "Like it that way."

Lieutenant Francis X. Byrne of the New York City Police Department asked the woman for her name. Jean, Jean Brandmelder. He wrote it down as she spelled it out. Byrne followed the woman through the clearing in the woods. Even though it was mid-October, the weather was still warm; hot, even. "Bob and them was out hunting this morning, early," Jean explained. "But really it was the dogs. They all of a sudden set to barkin' and Jimmy—that's my son Jimmy right there—went over to see what's all the fuss about." Another smack of the lips. Byrne took notes as he walked and hoped he would be able to read them later. The nuns always said his handwriting sucked, and the nuns were always right.

"Bob and them" were standing near the body. Bob was Mr. Brandmelder. He was a big, heavy-set, older man with a weak handshake and the outsized girth that comes from a rigorous diet of McDonald's, Coke and Cheez Doodles, one of the rural widebodies; Byrne thought he looked and sounded just like Andy Devine. Or maybe, with enough eye shadow, just Divine. Over his shoulder, Bob was carrying a shotgun, broken to show it was unloaded. On his face, he wore a gap-toothed grin. "Howdy," said Bob as Byrne approached. He was pointing. "Over there." He had a slight accent of indeterminate origin.

At first Byrne thought Brandmelder was indicating Jimmy. The son, about eighteen, was a sallow, rat-faced kid—looks obviously ran in the family—with a nasty glint in his eyes. A normal teenager would be horrified by what he had just found, but not Jimmy. He, too, was smiling. He shuffled his feet and spat on the ground by way of greeting. "Hey," he said. Next to him stood his buddy, Billy Walters, a mean-looking dirty blond with a wispy mustache and a tattoo of a girl straddling a dagger.

A dull hum rose from the hard, packed ground: flies. There hadn't been much rain lately, and there were no apparent tracks or footprints.

On the surrounding hills the trees were nearing their autumnal foliage peak, but Byrne found nothing in the scenery to admire. He hated coming up here to the Rockland County boondocks, upstate, across the Hudson and a world away from New York City. The Ramapo hills were alien territory, a largely inaccessible hill country populated by folks who were all more closely related to each other than the law allowed—a little slice of Appalachia on the border between New Jersey and New York State, just sixty miles from midtown. Anything could happen here, and anything did. It was the perfect place for a dump job like this.

Plus his ex-wife, Mary Claire, was living over in Nyack, nursing her bitterness and cashing his alimony check every month, which was how he knew she was still alive.

Byrne bent down to look at the body, snapping on a pair of rubber gloves and beginning his examination. The homicide detective was thirty-three years old, young for his rank. At five feet ten inches and one hundred and seventy-five pounds, he was about average size for a cop, and although he was waging a vigorous counterattack in the gym as often as possible, he could feel his body already starting to slide. Still, at least he had his hair, which was something not every guy his age could claim, and there was no gray in his light brown locks. Looking at him in his off-the-rack gray suit, one would never guess that he spent most of his time communing with dear, recently departed total strangers; he might be mistaken for a middle manager in a struggling business, the kind of guy you saw on the subway, wondered what he did, and felt vaguely sorry for. Only his eyes, blue, hard, cold and indifferent, hinted at his unpredictable, explosive temper.

Byrne contemplated the nameless victim, and felt the little thrill he always got when staring into the face of death. He had graduated from Fordham University and few had expected him to follow his father into the department—it was such an Irish-American cliché—but here he was, right where he wanted to be. Not because of the human tragedy, or to protect the innocent, or to satisfy society's need for justice or any of that blather. Not even out of a sense of revenge for his dad, who had been killed in the line of duty when Byrne was still a boy. He had become a cop because murder fascinated him.

"First we didn't know what it was," someone said, and Byrne turned to look for the speaker. It was Jimmy, the son. "The sun was just comin' up real bright, and with the light right in my eyes well, hell, I thought it was a damn possum." He looked down at the body. "It bein' so white an' all."

The state cops who had found the abandoned BMW 318i with diplomatic license plates had had the good sense to leave the crime scene alone. The corpse lay as it had been discovered, on its side near the base of a tree, the face turned away and partially covered by shoulder-length sandy hair. The body was entirely naked and bent slightly at the waist, the knees pulled up toward the chin; assume the position, thought Byrne to himself: the fetal position. The skin was milky white, gradually fading in death to a pale gray. The buttocks were smooth and hairless, as were the arms and legs. "Give me some room, please," said Byrne.

Thank God it wasn't a popper. All cops hated those exploding human sausages that had been left to stew in their own juice and then erupted when you looked at them cross-eyed. He had one a few months ago, a young black or Hispanic woman—it was hard to tell, given the state of decomposition—who had been raped, brained with a boulder and buried in a shallow grave at the north end of Central Park; for some reason, no one had felt the necessity to report her disappearance for several days. When Byrne and his Crime Scene Unit tried to move the body, her stomach came apart in their hands and the intestines slithered out. It took him a week to get the smell out of his nostrils.

The whine of the forensic photographer's camera was intrusive. It felt like they were making a snuff film. The camera, an Olympia 35mm with a 50mm lens shooting Kodak Tri-X color film, fired again as Byrne sketched the scene in his notebook. "I think this guy's ready for his close-up," said Vinnie Mancuso, an investigator attached to the medical examiner's office, as he set up the next shot.

The corpse held its jackknifed position as Byrne rolled the body over. By the looks of things, the victim had been dead eight to twelve hours; rigor mortis had begun to set in, and the skin's lividity was fixed, or would have been: there was almost no blood left in the body, and none on the ground, which indicated that the killing had taken place else-where.

"Muthafucka!" exclaimed Mancuso, who had thought he'd seen every-thing and probably had and yet was still taken by surprise. For even in the welter of dried blood and butchered flesh it was clear that the body was that of a man whose entire manhood was missing, the penis and tes-ticles excised by a sharp, scalpel-like instrument. Byrne guessed he had been alive at the time. What was the point of cutting somebody's dick off unless he was still around to enjoy the experience? For some reason, the image of an Aztec executioner, ripping the beating heart from a vic-tim's chest and exhibiting it to him just as he died, came to Byrne. Thank God the Aztecs weren't around anymore; they'd probably be pouring over the border from Mexico, opening restaurants, driving gypsy cabs and performing virgin sacrifices in the Bronx—if they could find any virgins. Who said New York never got any breaks?

Gently, Byrne brushed the hair back from the face, which might have been handsome once, when it was a face. One bullet, fired from behind, had exited through the right side of the head in the occipital-parietal area, blowing out the side of the skull and a good deal of the brain; at least one other shot, apparently from the front, had smashed through the bridgework. The eyes were pale blue and sightless. The throat was cut through the right carotid artery.

The facial expression, however, was untouched by the carnage. Was it still a pathetic fallacy to ascribe emotion to an inanimate object that once had been a human being? No matter how horrible the manner of their deaths, the deceased often had a peaceful look upon their faces, as if they were only sleeping, but this victim was extraordinary: not just peaceful, but at peace, like a saint who had just joyously embraced his martyrdom.

Now for the distasteful part. He knelt, spread the dead man's buttocks apart and dropped an object into a large evidence bag. It was a polished ebony dildo with a silver tip, about seven inches long.

"Wonder what the good sisters would say about this baby," said Mancuso, who was widely regarded as having both a vile sense of humor and an encyclopedic knowledge of restaurants. Mancuso was from the Bronx, but a branch of the family had owned a restaurant in New Orleans, and he always knew where to eat; hell, the man could even find food in New Jersey. "They'd probably take a shine to it. Did I ever tell you about Sister Ann Miriam, the one I had back in eighth grade? We used to call her Sister Sam, and a couple of the kids swore that underneath her habit she . . ."

Byrne wasn't listening to Vincent Mancuso's Catholic school reminiscences. He was looking at the markings on the dildo. Cyrillic, but whether Greek or Russian or even Bulgarian he could not tell. Not for the first time, he wished he had paid more attention to his language studies in college. Maybe if he had, he'd be in the FBI like his brother. The way New York was getting, it was like the Tower of Babel on the streets. Nobody committed crimes in English anymore.

The Brandmelders and Billy were standing silently nearby; Jean's mouth was working, but she was saying nothing. She might have been chewing gum, or tobacco. The others stared at their feet. "You ought to see the car," said Jimmy. Byrne sighed: these fag killings were always so messy.

"Let's take a look at it," Byrne said to Mancuso, and together they headed over to the BMW, which had been left on the road, a rude foreign intruder in Chevy Impala heaven. It was a new two-door coupe, black with light gray interior. "German car, ain't it?" said Jimmy. "We're German. *Brandmelder*. Means 'fire alarm.'" He seemed proud of his knowledge.

Byrne, however, wasn't interested in Jimmy's ethnic derivation right now. "I want a double-check on the registration," he ordered. "And I want prints on this vehicle, inside and out; make sure Aprahamian runs 'em through every AFIS system he can think of, full liaison with the FBI. And everybody keeps their mitts off the car, okay?" One of the two members of the Bronx-based Crime Scene Unit who had made the journey north with him—his name was Andersen—went running back to the squad car to do the detective's bidding.

The vehicle was immaculately clean inside, if you didn't count the bloodstains on the driver's side. No trash, no old newspapers in the back seat, no candy bar wrappings on the floor, no old stained Styrofoam coffee cups. Just a car phone, and nothing else.

"Let's also get the blood type off this mess, gentlemen," commanded Byrne, continuing to make notes. It seemed clear that the stains, while extensive, were not arterial bleeding. If the victim's throat had been cut while he was in the car, the gouts sprayed forth by the pumping heart would have covered the windshield and been spritzed all around the interior of the vehicle. These stains, on the other hand, were pretty much confined to the seat, as if he had bled heavily while driving. Driving where? Surely not all the way up here, unless he had stopped along the way to change into his birthday suit, cut his own throat and shoot himself in the head several times before continuing on to his final destination.

Mancuso had disappeared under the front seat but came up empty-handed. The only thing in the vehicle appeared to be the keys, which sat in the ignition awaiting their owner's return. They were going to have a long wait.

"Check the glove compartment, Vinnie," said Byrne.

Mancuso popped it open. "Nothing here, Frankie," he said.

"Gotta be," commanded Byrne. "Always is. Pennies, nickels, dimes, quarters, cassettes, Kleenex, Kotex, old maps, a woman's panties, something. Look some more. Nobody's this neat."

Again, Mancuso came up empty-handed and shrugged. "See for yourself, boss," he said. "No registration, no rental agreement, no insurance card, nothin'. And sure as hell no gal's panties. In fact, no panties of any kind."

At that moment, Andersen returned. "Lieutenant," he said, "DMV says the vehicle is registered to the Danish consulate general on Second Avenue in Manhattan. The principal driver is listed as one Edwin A. Paine of 442 Little West Twelfth Street, New York, New York."

"Twelfth Street? What's a Village fruitcake doing with an embassy

car?" asked Byrne. "Call BCI and see if this boy rings a bell." If Paine
had ever been arrested, the Bureau of Criminal Identification would have
his New York State Inquiry Identification System number. And if Paine
had a NYSIIS number, the Photo Unit would have a picture of him on
file.

Byrne peered into the empty auto and then climbed into the back
seat. "Lemme have a look," he said. He ran his hands between where the
seats met the back rests, where folks usually stuffed their seat belts, and
down the sides. Nada, not even an old pen. Byrne was fishing around in
the side compartments of the BMW, just below the windows on the
driver's side, when he felt something.

"Uh, Lieutenant?" said Andersen, who was still standing there. "That
address? It's not Twelfth Street, it's Little West Twelfth Street. They're
not the same street, sir."

"Just a minute." He didn't need a lesson in the arcana of Greenwich
Village geography at this moment. He could get that from his art-dealer
girlfriend Doreen the next time he stayed over.

"Nobody lives on Little West Twelfth Street, is all," persisted the patrolman. "It's the meat-packing district. Where the sex clubs are now."

The object was crumpled, but even before he looked at it he could tell
by the paper's thick texture that it was a photograph. Byrne climbed out
of the car and into the sunlight, where he could get a good look.

"The slaughterhouse district," insisted Andersen. "My dad used to
work there."

It was a back-and-white snapshot of two women, with their arms
thrown casually around each other's shoulders. They were both wearing
smiles, sweaters and out-of-date hairdos, which were being tousled by
the wind. One of them, the movie-star pretty lady on the left with the
flashing eyes, he did not recognize, but the other, plainer one he certainly did. She was young, she was fresh, and she most definitely was his
mother, Irene Byrne, of Woodside, Queens, New York. He put the picture in his pocket, as unobtrusively as possible, and hoped no one would
notice.

"Body bag," he said.

Chapter Two
One Police Plaza, Lower Manhattan
Thursday, October 18, 1990; 2:00 P.M.

Is it as bad as we thought?" asked J. Arness White, captain of detectives, a big, broad-shouldered man who not only happened to be Byrne's boss but, as the *New York Times* never tired of pointing out, also happened to be black.

In the warm mid-October weather, White was decked out in his trademark summer tan suit, which he wore with beige Florsheims that he had bought recently on a visit home to Houston, Texas; he was not about to let a little thing like the calendar tell him how to dress. At six feet two, White walked tall and he talked as tall as he walked, just like his daddy and three years in the marines had taught him to; his daddy, Erasmus J., had been a *Gunsmoke* fan and named his eldest son, the third of his six children who had lived, after the actor who played Marshal Dillon. ("Don't forget he was the Thing in *The Thing*, too," his daddy would remind him. "And that Thing could really kick ass.") Not surprisingly, everybody called him Matt, and nobody crossed him.

Byrne was sitting across the desk from his boss. "Maybe worse," he answered, trying to decide where to begin.

Byrne and White had worked together for more than a decade, when a young Irish-American patrolman from Queens had graduated into the Robbery Identification Program, one of the mandatory training grounds for aspiring detectives, and had become friends with the black man from Texas. Matt White could smell a burglar in the act of thinking about a crime and he taught Frankie everything he knew, honing the younger man's instincts according to the White Code of Conduct: Never trust nobody, and that goes double for your mama. Which, translated, meant that you couldn't go wrong assuming everyone had something to hide, no matter how close they were to you, and it was your job to find out what it was. It made for good cops and bad relationships, but so be it.

White and Byrne had risen together through the ranks double-time, with White always one step ahead. They made an ideal odd couple: White aloof, cool, rational; Byrne mercurial, hot-headed and intuitive. Even after they had both gotten their gold detective's shields and passed the civil service exam for sergeant, Matt continued to play rabbi to Frankie, which was a cause for some wonderment. The uncharitable whispered that White was simply bowing to departmental tradition, which dictated that all cops, whether black, Italian or Jewish, were at heart Irishmen, and it didn't hurt to have a real one by his side. Especially the son of a departmental hero who had been killed in the line of duty.

Only once had Matt White ever lost his temper, which, as everybody knew, was how he got his departmental nickname. And which was why, as only Matt and Frankie knew, White and Byrne, they took care of each other.

Byrne had been the catcher on a robbery report in lower Park Slope and he and White drove over to Fourth Avenue to check things out. A pretty Puerto Rican girl named Rosa Montez told them that her common-law husband, Enrique Marcon, had stolen some jewelry she had brought over from San Juan and was trying to pawn it or sell it somewhere in downtown Brooklyn for money to buy drugs. Byrne was openly skeptical that a few cubic zirconiums could bring anything more than a nickel bag but Matt shushed him, spoke kindly to the girl and told her they'd get her jewelry back for her. She held Matt's hands, tears in her eyes. "Ee' wa' my mama's," she said. "She bring i' f'om Espain. Ee' mean' a lot doo her, and now i' mean a la'doo me." Byrne thought it was a waste of time—"It's just a couple of spic junkies, for Chrissakes, who gives a fuck"—but Matt knew better.

"You have to treat everybody with respect, Frankie," Matt lectured him as they returned to their car. "Otherwise, how can you expect them to treat you? Maybe you forgot the lesson of the potato famine, you harp-playin', paddy-drinkin' mackerel snapper." Byrne got the point. They drove up Flatbush Avenue, shaking down the fences, looking for Enrique, but no street action, no Enrique, no nothing. They went back to see if Rosa had any other ideas.

Marcon, however, had seen them drive up and had hidden behind the stoop of the house next door. As soon as they left, he had started in on Rosa with an ice pick and that's the way Matt and Frankie found them, Rosa and Ricki, she in his arms like a reverse Pietà, punctured and bloody and dead. Byrne drew his pistol and was about to arrest Marcon when, without a word, Matt took out his .38 and shot Enrique twice in the head. "RIP, motherfucker," he said, firing his pistol point-blank. "Gimme the gun, Matt," said Frankie, but White wasn't finished. He stood over Enrique's prostrate form and emptied the remaining four rounds into it. "The gun, Matt," said Frankie softly. White handed Byrne the spent revolver and never used it or another word of profanity again. Byrne's report indicated that the arresting officers had been threatened with deadly force and that White had fired in self-defense. But the precinct detectives knew the truth, and after that, Matt was the King of the RIP, the angel of death.

The King had personally handed Byrne the case that morning, when the news came in from the state police. "This one looks like it's right up your alley," he had said. "A diplomat, maybe. NYSP'd much rather we handled it. And for obvious reasons I'd much rather *you* handled it than anybody else around here."

"Jeez, Matt, you're still sore about last week. I can't help it if you suck at squash."

"Watch your mouth. You know I don't cotton to talk like that around here. You think this is a movie set or something? You think all black cops talk ghetto trash?"

"No, sir."

"You got something against African Americans?"

"Not much, sir!" They went through this all the time.

"Are you aware that your commanding officer happens to be black?"

"Yes, sir."

"And are you further aware that everybody named White happens to be black, and that conversely everybody named Black happens to be white?"

"Yes sir, I am."

"Good. My daddy taught me that. Don't you never forget it."

White's deep bass voice—Byrne was sure Paul Robeson must have been his real father—snapped him back to attention. "Well, Lieutenant?

Do I have to wait until my hair straightens before you finally open your mouth?" The fastidious captain kept both his hair and his fingernails closely cropped, buffing the latter and oiling the former.

"The car is registered to the Danish consulate general in the name of one Edwin A. Paine," said Byrne. "He comes up blank with BCI, and the consulate told me when I called that there's nobody there by that name. I'm on my way over there now to play show and tell with the consul general. Furthermore, the driver's address is listed on Little West Twelfth Street, which checks out as a gay S&M place called the Rambone."

"Uh-oh," muttered the captain. A box of cigars stood to one side of the polished, ultraclean desk. On special occasions, White even smoked one, or pretended to.

"... and sure enough, we found a love aid inserted into a bodily cavity, to go along with a throat that was cut from ear to ear. Not to mention considerable cranial damage caused by gunshots. So as of right now we got a technical John Doe, resident of a basically nonresident area, who was driving a nonexistent diplomat's car, murdered by a person or persons unknown at an unknown location at a time to be determined by Sy Sheinberg, who's conducting the autopsy tomorrow morning." Byrne put a hopeful smile on his face. "In other words, your basic piece of cake."

The captain pondered this intelligence. "Ugly," he said at last. "Uglier than my mother-in-law sitting on the throne in my bathroom on Saturday morning with her hair in curlers readin' the latest issue of *Guns and Ammo*. And here's where it gets worse." He stood up and started pacing around his office. "While you were up there in Ramapo, I got a phone call from the FBI in Washington," he confided. "We're talking drums along the Hudson *and* the Potomac."

"What do you mean?" asked Byrne.

"They want this case to have our top priority," said White, and Byrne found himself wondering how he was going to explain to Doreen that their fall foliage weekend in western New England was now on hold. "Which of course means your top priority."

"Then why don't they take it themselves?" asked Byrne. He hated the FBI and its ham-fisted, meddling crew of Notre Dame frat boys, as his boss well knew.

White took a deep breath. "Because they don't want to raise a ruckus if they can avoid it. You're probably wondering how this particular stiff got to be on the A-list so quick. Me too. I hate to psych you out, Frankie, but your report's already earmarked for the commissioner, the mayor, the governor, the FBI and even the CIA. Heck, maybe even the White House. Plus everybody wants it yesterday. So do I. We can't have representatives of foreign governments getting chopped up on our watch no matter how much monkey business they've been up to. So tread firmly but lightly, and if it's as dirty as it looks, keep as much of it out of the papers as you possibly can. You've got all the liaison resources you'll need; just ask. And get it over with as quickly as possible. Like you did with that Bolivian guy."

"Coloredo," supplied Byrne. Two years earlier, the Bolivian ambassador to the United Nations had gone up in smoke, along with his family, as his car tooled down Second Avenue. Byrne and his partner, Detective Sergeant Gino Andretti, had traced the bomb to a Colombian munitions factory in Queens, a household operation that was producing ordnance for half the South American gangs in the city. It had been a revenge killing, made inevitable when the ambassador had welshed on a drug deal and had foolishly supposed his official standing would afford him some protection from the Medellins. All that came out in public, however, was a story about a heroic diplomat who dared defy the cartels and paid for his virtue with his life. The Bolivians were grateful, the State Department was grateful and Matt White was especially grateful: Byrne had been promoted to lieutenant, one of the youngest in the department's history, shortly thereafter.

"Furthermore, for the very reasons of discretion I just outlined," said White, "you're flying solo on this one. Eyes only to me, and I do mean these baby browns, starting with your Unusual Occurrence Report and right through your Fives." The captain pointed to eyes that, as usual, were perpetually shaded by sunglasses, even indoors. "And if Malecki or Finnegan wants to know what you're up to, you refer them to me, understand?" Malecki and Finnegan were White's two deputies, pale, resentful Starbucks and Stubbs to his dark Ahab. "Anyway, Andretti's got enough to do with the work you two already have. How's your mama?"

The segue took him by surprise until he remembered the confidential report he had filed overnight on his run-in with a prowler at his mother's apartment in Queens. "She's okay," said Byrne, although in truth he was not so sure. His mother's neighborhood was getting worse every day, and the episode last night had put his nerves on edge. "I think I scared him off."

"Well, you never know. And she's your mama, the only one you got. Don't you never forget that. But this ain't the nineteenth century anymore, and you can't just go around taking potshots at anybody who pisses you off. You're the best detective I got, but try to control that Irish temper of yours, will you? There's going to come a time when I won't be able to shield your fat Hibernian butt anymore."

Byrne ignored the homily but silently accepted the criticism. How could he not? The captain was indeed covering his ass on this one. Unauthorized discharge of a firearm—his second offense—was serious business; he was lucky he wasn't back on administrative leave, just like last time, or, worse, pounding a beat. Fortunately, the guy had disappeared into the night.

"So," said White, stretching and rising, "if you want to keep that rep from getting into the newspapers and forwarded to the Civilian Complaint Review Board, I suggest you get on the case asap. I think you catch my drift. And remember that no matter who this guy was, right now he's just another homicide victim in a city that gets two thousand of his brothers and sisters a year. And you're a homicide detective. So go detect something."

Byrne took the hint and got up to leave.

"And Frankie, one other thing," said White, just before he closed the door. Byrne could feel White's eyes upon him, sunglasses or no sunglasses. "I know that, in this city especially, the victim is always presumed to be a saint. But when you've been in the business as long as I have, you know that in the end everybody gets what's coming to him. This guy was in the wrong place at the wrong time for the right reason, and it's your job to find out why. What have I always told you? That the most uncomplicated explanation usually turns out to be the correct one. It's that simple."

Byrne wasn't so sure about that, which is why he hadn't mentioned the photograph.

Chapter Three
Midtown Manhattan
Thursday, October 18, 1990; 3:00 P.M.

M r. Pilgersen will see you now."

The tall, blonde Danish secretary was gorgeous, like all Danes. As he was ushered into the consul general's office, Byrne wondered what they put in their gene pool to keep it so clean.

Consuls general, Byrne knew, generally did two things: they hustled trade and they ran spies. These jobs were often complementary. Aside from the United Nations, New York City lacked Washington's diplomatic cachet, but it was still home to one of the largest populations of intelligence agents on earth. Where there were spies there must be secrets, and the Big Apple had plenty of those—commercial and industrial secrets, trade policy secrets and plain old political secrets. Through the FBI and the Intelligence Division of the New York City Police Department and its Office of Special Investigations, the Americans spied on the Soviets. With the KGB, the GRU and their representatives at the United Nations, the Soviets spied on the Americans. Meanwhile, the Europeans spied on each other and the Israelis spied on everybody.

Byrne's mind was still on the pretty secretary, or executive assistant, or whatever secretaries were calling themselves these days to improve their self-esteem, when he found himself shaking hands with Nils Pilgersen. Were her eyes blue? Was she wearing a bra? What was that perfume? "Please sit down, Lieutenant Byrne," the consul was saying. His peremptory tone brought him back to reality, and Byrne sat. "How can I help you?"

"Well, for starters," he began, "you can clear up a little mystery for me." His tone was firm but friendly.

"A pleasure, Lieutenant." Pilgersen's manner indicated that he was a man who was generally very pleased, or at least contented, with himself.

"I believe you're already aware that a man was found murdered upstate this morning, and that a car with diplomatic tags was found near the body."

"Is that right?" said Pilgersen. "I think Miss Bentsen mentioned something about that to me, but I'm not sure I see how—"

"Well, sir," Byrne said, not waiting for the obligatory disclaimer, "we've run a check on the vehicle and it appears that it was registered to the consulate in the name of one of your employees, a Mr. Edwin A. Paine. Ring a bell?"

Now Pilgersen looked him straight in the eye. "You must be mistaken," he said. "We have no one here by that name."

"But—" objected Byrne.

"I suggest you reconfirm your information," said Pilgersen. "Surely you don't expect me to believe that the New York State Department of Motor Vehicles never makes a mistake."

He had a point there. "They're quite sure, Mr. Pilgersen."

"That may be so," said Pilgersen, "but the fact remains that there is no Edwin Paine employed by the Danish government, either here or at our UN mission."

"Then how do you explain the fact that his car has diplomatic plates identifying it as Danish?" inquired Byrne.

"I'm sure I don't know its significance," said Pilgersen implacably, and started making little flapping motions with his hands, as if he were shooing away a particularly pesky fly. "Therefore I'm afraid that unless you can convince me otherwise, our interview, like all good things, must come to an end."

Byrne disliked getting the high hat, especially from foreigners. "Maybe these will help jog your memory," he said, passing a couple of Mancuso's crime-scene photographs across the clean desk.

Pilgersen had the opportunity to view the body fore and aft, and there was a separate shot of the love aid that they had extracted from the corpse. "Good God," exclaimed the consul. Like most Scandinavians, he pronounced the word as if it had an umlaut: *güd*.

"Do you recognize this man?" asked Byrne.

Instead of answering, Pilgersen jabbed at his intercom with one practiced fat finger. "Miss Bentsen," he ordered. Five seconds later the door

opened and in she walked. "This is Lieutenant Byrne," said Pilgersen by
way of introduction.

"Hello," she said. "I'm Ingrid." In the Scandinavian fashion, she didn't
pronounce the final *d*, and so it came out sounding like *Ing-ree. "Taler de
Dansk?"*

"I'm quite sure the lieutenant is innocent of any knowledge of Danish,
Miss Bentsen," said Pilgersen, handing the photos to his assistant.

"Just kidding," she said, just before she sucked in her breath in a single
quick gasp and brought her hand up to her wide mouth.

Pilgersen nodded gravely in Byrne's direction. "It is, of course, very
difficult to speak with certainty based on these photographs," he said,
"but it would appear that this man may indeed be familiar to us. I'm
sorry, Lieutenant, to have been so abrupt with you at first, but you understand that in cases like this, where there is a possibility of international repercussions, the best policy is always to err on the side of
caution."

"Spoken like a true diplomat," said Byrne. "So you do recognize this
individual?"

"The body appears to—and please note for the record that at this
point I am only saying that it appears to—bear a resemblance to a member of my staff." He seemed agitated, but diplomatically so.

"And that would be?" prompted Byrne.

"That would be Egil Ekdahl," said the secretary, Ingrid. Like many
Nordics, she had a tawny, almost golden cast to her skin.

"Yes," agreed Pilgersen, "Mr. Egil Ekdahl, our associate cultural attaché."

"Can you spell that for me, please?" asked Byrne, and Pilgersen did. "I
would be very grateful if you could come down to the medical examiner's
office this afternoon to take a look and help us make sure. If you're squea-
mish, you can view the body over closed-circuit TV." That was the way
they were handling IDs now; it was amazing how many stiffs went flying
when the nearest and dearest started indulging their grief.

"Of course, my dear lieutenant, I would be happy to," replied Pilgersen.
"Well, perhaps *happy* is not exactly the correct word to describe my emotions regarding this most unpleasant situation, but you will have to forgive
my sometimes unidiomatic command of your language. Will you please

excuse me and Miss Bentsen for a moment while we speak in Danish? Thank you."

The pair babbled away in a guttural tongue for a few moments. "You may go now, Miss Bentsen," said Pilgersen finally, in English. The secretary shut the door so quietly that for a moment Byrne thought she was still in the room.

"I need to know all about this Mr. Ekdahl—or Mr. Paine, or whoever he is," said Byrne, bluntly. He hated when people spoke foreign languages in front of him; his mother, who was born in Poland but never spoke anything but English at home, had always told him that it was rude. "I need to find out whether he went looking for his fate or it came looking for him. And I'd like to begin with the issue of his name."

To his surprise, the consul let out a deep sigh, as if he were glad a long-running charade was suddenly over. "Lieutenant Byrne, you are a man of the world," he began.

"Not of your world, Mr. Pilgersen."

"Our worlds are perhaps not as different as you think."

"I don't get to Oslo very often. Or Stockholm." He wasn't sure if either one of those cities was in Denmark, but they must be close.

The consul general ignored his ignorance. "That's not at all what I mean. What I mean is simply that we've both seen something of life, perhaps even of the darker side of life, and we haven't flinched."

"In my line of work, you flinch, you're dead."

"Well put, Lieutenant Byrne, well put. Let me start again." His voice fell a decibel level. "Mr. Ekdahl, while an exemplary diplomat in every respect—and I would like to emphasize the word *every*—had, or so I am given to understand, a private life that, shall we say, he preferred to keep private, a private life that may have sometimes led him down a path that would not be, as it were, to everybody's taste. Especially in this country," he added as an afterthought.

"So . . . ?" asked Byrne, not quite sure where this particular track was leading. "What kind of private life? One involving castration and the creative use of dildos?"

Pilgersen blushed like a schoolgirl at the words; some man of the world, thought Byrne. "Well, I don't of course have any firsthand knowledge of these things myself, if you know what I mean, but I believe that Mr. Ekdahl was a man of sophisticated sensibilities."

"Sexual sensibilities, you mean," interjected Byrne.

"Er, yes, and from time to time he exhibited certain, um, predilections in, er, establishments where his, ah, sensibilities could be indulged and attended to with the utmost, um, discretion." Pilgersen's hands suddenly rushed for each other and, mating, bounced up and down on his spotless teak desk. "It would not surprise me at all that, for security purposes, he might have used a nom de plume, so to speak, although this particular name of Paine is unknown to me."

"What is its significance, do you suppose?" asked Byrne.

"That, too, I am unaware of," said Pilgersen.

"And do you always let your personnel run around under false names?"

"Actually, Lieutenant," confessed Pilgersen, his voice falling, "although I was frankly unaware of this particular name, there was a private understanding which Mr. Ekdahl and I had regarding security. I didn't want him getting into any difficulties that could, could—come back to trouble him at his place of employment."

"Exactly which kind of predilections are we talking about here?" asked Byrne, referring to his notes to make sure he had spelled it correctly; it was not a word he heard very often in interviews. "And what kind of establishments?" Sometimes he was deliberately obtuse, and other times it just came naturally.

"I hope you understand that I'm not entirely at liberty, nor am I under any obligation, to discuss the personal lives of my staff with you, Lieutenant," said Pilgersen. "Suffice it to say that Mr. Ekdahl was a young man and like all young men he sometimes lived dangerously and thought he would live forever."

"So he thought he was God. What else can you tell me about the deceased?" asked Byrne. "What did he do around here, for example?"

Pilgersen settled back in his capacious leather chair; Byrne could tell at a glance that it wasn't Naugahyde. He seemed grateful to steer the conversation away from sex and back to business. "Mr. Ekdahl's duties, like those of any consular cultural attaché, largely concern, or, alas, *concerned*, the promotion of Danish culture in the United States—Danish art, music, theater, things like that."

Byrne didn't know Denmark had a culture beyond Victor Borge and Hans Christian Andersen. He permitted himself a small sarcasm: "Was that a big job?"

"Oh, yes, indeed." The irony sailed over Pilgersen's head like a fly ball into the right-field seats at Yankee Stadium. "We Danes are tired of being thought of as just another indistinguishable chunk of socialized Scandinavia, with pretty girls, workers on permanent psychological sick leave and an exaggerated affinity for alcohol—a 'white bread' country, as you Americans say. Mr. Ekdahl's task was the promulgation and furtherance of Danish culture in the United States."

Byrne had a sudden inspiration. "Did you ever see that William Castle movie—what was it called?—about the Danish guy in Solvang, California—I hear there's a lot of Danes there—who was really a she? Or maybe it was a girl who was really a he, I forget. Anyway, the same he/she played both the brother and the sister until in the end it turns out that—"

"I'm a busy man, Lieutenant," admonished Pilgersen. "I don't have time for the cinema."

"Sorry," apologized Byrne. "How long had Ekdahl been working here?"

"Almost a year. He came to us in November, I think—let me see, I can tell you exactly." Pilgersen rummaged in a desk drawer, but Byrne was sitting too far away to see what was in it. "I'm just looking for last year's diary—ah, here it is." He flipped through the leather-bound Filofax expertly. "Yes, it was November 22, 1989. I remember now because his flight was delayed, and so he arrived on a Tuesday instead of a Monday."

"The day JFK died," said Byrne.

"Surely your late president was killed many years before 1989," objected Pilgersen.

Byrne snapped out of his reverie. "Right," he said. "It was in 1963. But that date tends to stick in the mind of any American old enough to remember where they were when they heard the news. Even though I was only six, I remember my father crying—"

"I'm sorry," said Pilgersen brusquely; he had detected the nostalgia in Byrne's voice and was seeking to preempt any wallowing. He turned his flippers palms up and shrugged. "But that was a long time ago."

"Yes," agreed Byrne. "It was a long time ago. So . . . what kind of a guy was this Mr. Ekdahl?"

"Mr. Ekdahl is, or was, a fine young man," said Pilgersen, "a rising star in our consular service and an outstanding emissary of my government. I don't mind telling you privately that he was being groomed for bigger and better things. I remember asking him just after he settled here what he liked best about New York. Do you know what he said? 'The intellectual climate.' Those were his exact words."

Byrne had to laugh. "Pardon me for saying this, Mr. Pilgersen, but a dildo up your bum doesn't seem to have much to do with the intellectual climate."

Pilgersen shrugged. Foreigners, Byrne decided, were just not the same as you and me, even if their skin color was. He had never spent any time in Europe, but from his experience with Europeans, he would rather take his chances with Americans of any shade than with a "white" European. Good guys or bad, Americans of every race could be counted on to react to the same set of stimuli in more or less the same way. Europeans, however, were another matter entirely. You never knew what the hell they were going to say, or do.

"Did Ekdahl have any enemies?" asked Byrne. "Anyone ever make any threats against him or the consulate?"

"One of the advantages of being Danish," said Pilgersen, "is that aside from the omnipresent Germans one has very few natural enemies. We Scandinavians try to wend our way through the thickets of East-West relations by giving as little offense as possible. So I don't believe for a moment that this murder was politically motivated in any way."

"Then was there anything unusual about his manner or movements over the past few days? Any unexplained absences, for example? A phone call that upset him? His mommy make him come home early one night? Any detail, however small, that you can remember would be very helpful."

"He was away for a week or so last month—on holiday in Europe," said Pilgersen. "But I can't be expected to be held, how do you say in English, accountable for the activities of my staffers when they are off duty, now can I?"

"But no one worried when Ekdahl didn't show up for work yesterday?" asked Byrne.

"I allow my staff a certain degree of latitude, Lieutenant."

"I'm sure you do," said Byrne. "But the fact remains that your gift of liberty gave Mr. Ekdahl death." The man was getting under his skin. "Much as it may surprise you, we really do try to solve these murders in New York."

"I'm glad to hear that, Lieutenant," said Pilgersen, unruffled. "Because

I can assure you my government will be extremely interested in a speedy and expeditious resolution to this case."

"And not just yours," said Byrne, watching to see what effect his words were having. "Mine, too. For some reason, Washington is taking a great deal of interest in this case, and if there's one thing I don't like it's people looking over my shoulder while I'm working. What is it about Mr. Ekdahl that's got everybody so damn interested?"

Pilgersen's poker face remained in place. "Diplomatic murder goes to the very heart of the international social compact, Lieutenant. I would hope you would extend the same diligence to any foreign government."

"And I would," replied Byrne. "And yet there's something going on here I don't quite understand yet. I realize that even sophisticated European sensibilities can sometimes get out of hand, and that what starts out all in good fun can get a little crazy. But look at these pictures again. What this murder most reminds me of is a kind of human sacrifice, like an early Christian martyr. The expression on his face is . . . well, beatific."

"Indeed, Lieutenant, indeed." Impulsively, Pilgersen stabbed for the buzzer on the office intercom again. "Miss Bentsen," he said, "could you please clear an hour in my schedule this afternoon?" He looked at Byrne expectantly, as if waiting for applause. "So that I might meet you later at the morgue to make a positive identification."

"It won't be pleasant," said Byrne. "I think you'll find that in person it's a lot worse than it looks in these pictures."

"I think I can maintain my composure," said Pilgersen. "What else do you need?"

"Ekdahl's medical and dental records would help," said Byrne. "His dossier, too. You can black out whatever you need to for security purposes, but I'd appreciate it if it wasn't too much, because I'll need his personal history: where he was born, name of parents and next of kin, stuff like that. A list of friends and contacts, where he liked to go to eat, hobbies. You know what I mean."

Pilgersen shook his head at the wonder of it all. "I'll get my staff on it right away. Our files are models of comprehensiveness, Lieutenant, and I can assure you that you'll know his favorite flavor of ice cream by the time you're through."

"I'll also need photos of Ekdahl: passport, ID cards, candids, whatever you've got. You never know what's going to help. One time I was working a homicide, and you know what cracked it for me? A dog collar that the husband had taken off the family Saint Bernard and wrapped around his girlfriend's throat when he strangled her during sex. The wife had another one at home just like it."

"Amazing." Pilgersen didn't really seem to be amazed. He rummaged around in a drawer, came up with a copy of Ekdahl's passport photo and handed it to Byrne. "I'll see what else we can find."

"Yeah, you just never fuckin' know. Excuse me, sir." The vulgarity was deliberate.

Pilgersen remained unruffled by Byrne's crudeness. "Don't worry," he said, "I've heard words like that before. We have them in Danish, too. They're almost the same."

"You speak any other languages?" asked Byrne, taking advantage of the opening. "I always think it's so great when a guy can speak two or three languages. I took French in school myself, and my mom speaks Polish and a little German, but none of it stuck." Byrne chuckled. "Use it or lose it, like they say."

"I speak French, German, Italian and Russian," Pilgersen volunteered.

"In addition to English and Danish," added Byrne. "Russian, you say?"

"Our diplomatic service requires fluency in the five basic European languages. Those would be German, French, Italian and English—and Russian," replied Pilgersen. "Very few people speak Danish outside Denmark, so we Danes need to learn the other fellow's tongue. We're very much like our fellow Scandinavians in that respect. Hungarians, too. Linguists to a man. Or to a fault. Your mother speaks Polish? Isn't that a bit unusual?"

"For an American, you mean?" asked Byrne. "She was born in Poland, came over here as a young woman."

"Really? I never would have guessed." For the first time, Byrne seemed to be defeating Pilgersen's expectations of him. "You Americans are such, such . . ."

"Mongrels?" suggested Byrne.

"Internationalists," corrected Pilgersen. "Within each of yourselves, you contain the whole world."

"*E pluribus unum*, and all that jazz," said Byrne. "Just out of curiosity, what languages did Ekdahl speak?"

"The same as I," replied Pilgersen.

"Russian, too?"

"Yes, of course," said Pilgersen. "He is, or was, a very good linguist. Very *güd.*" That sound again, like a cow mooing.

"Thank you very much for your time, Mr. Pilgersen," said Byrne, rising. "Let's plan to meet at the medical examiner's office at, say, five?"

"Five o'clock will be fine. And I'll let you know as soon as I've gathered what you need." Pilgersen started to get up, in order to usher him out.

"One more thing," said Byrne, as if he had just remembered. "Do either of these women look familiar to you?" He casually tossed the photo he had found in Ekdahl's car onto the diplomat's desk.

Pilgersen gave it only a cursory glance and shook his head. "No," he said, returning it, and Byrne believed him.

Byrne was halfway out the door when he stopped. "I just remembered the name of that movie," he said.

"Movie?" asked Pilgersen.

"The transvestite one. The one I was talking about earlier? It's called *Homicidal.* You ought to check it out. I mean, you being Danish and all."

"I'll do that, Lieutenant," Pilgersen assured him. "Just as soon as I am able."

He could see the blonde secretary bending deliciously over a filing cabinet in the anteroom. Her skirt was tight across her appealingly round backside. She sensed that he was looking, turned and gave him a playful little smile as he closed Pilgersen's office door behind him. He pointed a finger at her, an imaginary gun that went off with an imaginary bang.

"I'm preparing the information you requested," she told him, "and Mr. Pilgersen has asked me to get it to you personally."

"I appreciate that," said Byrne. "Why don't I just come by and pick it up whenever it's ready?"

Her voice fell to a conspiratorial whisper. "I'm afraid that won't be possible. The consul general has said that while he is more than willing to cooperate with you in every way, in the interests of security you must not be seen collecting this dossier from us directly. I'm to give it to you myself, off-premises. *Vil De ikke besøge mig imorgen?*"

"Say what?" It appeared she enjoyed torturing him.

"Sorry." She giggled. "That means, could we possibly meet tomorrow?"

"Where?"

"Do you know the Hunt Club? It's that new place on East Fifty-third

Street between Park and Lex." Park and Lex; it was amazing how quickly even Danes could become New Yorkers.

"Right. Fifty-third between Park and Lex."

"There's no sign, so I'll wait outside. Besides, they might not let you in."

"You'd be surprised the places a smile, a shoeshine, a badge and a .38 can get you into. What time?"

"Shall we say nine o'clock? There won't be much happening before nine, and even that might be a little early."

"Make it ten, if you want."

"Ten it is, then," she said, and turned back to her work. "Don't forget your dancing shoes. I love to fox-trot."

Chapter Four
Hell's Kitchen
Thursday, October 18, 1990; 11:00 P.M.

The murder was the lead story on all five local New York City television stations that evening. "Tonight on *Eyewitness News*: a naked and mutilated body is found dead upstate, and police are following clues that may lead them down diplomatic corridors in Manhattan and Washington," said a sober, stern-faced, standard-issue Asian-American anchorwoman in her best how-can-things-like-this-happen-here-but-aren't-you-glad-they-do-as-long-as-they're-not-happening-to-you? manner, introducing the videotape. Outside One Police Plaza, a reporter was talking quietly and earnestly into a microphone, as if he were broadcasting a golf match and someone was lining up a difficult putt.

"We don't have many details as yet, Keisha, but police are saying"—for no syntactical reason, he emphasized the word *are*—"that the body of an unidentified white male was discovered near Ramapo in Rockland County at about eight o'clock this morning by a group of local men who had gone hunting." He looked serious, but delighted to be there on such a good story, what with a white victim and all.

Some film showed the clearing where the corpse had been found. "The nude body was found with its throat cut, and had been shot several times in the head, execution style, as well." It seemed to delight one and all that the body was unclothed when found, as if that somehow made its death saucy. The reporter's voice-over continued with some aimless empty footage of grass and trees, a quick glimpse of the abandoned BMW, a view of the Brandmelder house, some old tires and a refrigerator lying in the yard, and then Jimmy Brandmelder's homely face filled the screen. He looked uneasy. "Well, we heard the dogs barkin' and Billy and me went to take a look and we saw him jus' lyin' there dead."

"How did you feel?" asked the reporter, who had rushed back to the city in time to drop off his tape and get downtown for his stand-up.

"Scared." Jimmy giggled nervously. Behind him, the viewer could make out a rusted but formerly green 1976 Plymouth up on cinder blocks. All of its wheels and one of the doors were missing and the seats were ripped out. "Excited."

The reporter's face suddenly intruded. "The extensive mutilation will make identification extremely difficult, but one possible clue to the victim's identity is a late-model BMW found abandoned nearby. The vehicle bears diplomatic license plates, which indicate it is registered to the Danish consulate in Manhattan, and we've been told that police are investigating the possibility that the victim may have been a diplomat, attached either to the consulate or to the Danish mission to the United Nations."

Cut to a shot of Pilgersen, studiously ignoring the cameras as he went up the steps to his office at 885 Second Avenue after returning from the morgue. Reporters were shouting questions at him—"Anybody missing lately?" was one—but he said nothing, waving them away with a dismissive flap of his fat hand. The camera followed his stately procession up to the door of the consulate and happily recorded its commentless closing.

Then to Byrne, standing in the plaza outside police headquarters. Behind him, in the distance, loomed Brooklyn Bridge. "We are working in full cooperation with the Rockland County authorities and the New York State Police," said Byrne, his rank and name superimposed by the Chyron generator in the studio. "At this time we have no suspects, but the investigation is continuing." His face betrayed no emotion. It wasn't supposed to. He knew the drill.

So did the reporters. "Has the victim been identified yet?" one of the other television reporters shouted. "That information is unavailable at this time," Byrne said. His accent was pure Sunnyside, the heart of Irish Queens: *Dat information iz un'vailable at dis toyme.*

The reporters, however, spoke fluent Queens, and Byrne's answer threw them into a frenzy. "Could this be a Mob hit?" "What about an act of terrorism?" "Is there any evidence of foreign involvement?" "Will the FBI be called in?" The questions came in waves, but Byrne wasn't answering them any more than Pilgersen had.

"Have the next of kin been notified?" Byrne always marveled at the dumb things reporters could ask. "At the present time," he concluded imperturbably, with the obligatory one-answer-fits-all, "we are making every attempt to positively identify the victim."

Byrne brushed away further questions and started to leave, but the newshounds were persistent. "Lieutenant Byrne, if the body really is that of a diplomat, what would be the political implications of such a murder? Isn't this going to make foreign governments even more wary of sending their people to New York?" The reporter, an earnest young man with an embarrassing mustache, made sure he got into the picture with the famous homicide detective.

"I do not want to speculate on that or anything else at this time, but you can be assured that all available leads will be followed up and every pertinent bit of information will be thoroughly investigated," said Byrne, a past master of the passive voice, as all cops were. "That's all for now," he told the pack, holding up his hand for emphasis. "When we find out more, you'll be the first to know. Trust me."

The reporter again: "As you can see, Keisha, the police aren't saying much. But sources tell *Eyewitness News* that the case has been given the highest priority, possibly as a result of pressure from the State Department in Washington. And the fact that Detective Byrne, who as you recall handled the spectacular Jaime Coloredo assassination case two years ago, is in charge of the investigation is another strong indication that the diplomatic community may be involved. Time will tell." The reporter looked earnestly into the camera. "This is Mike McIhatton reporting for Channel 7, *Eyewitness News.*"

The anchorwoman moved on to a fire in the Bronx that had killed a thirty-eight-year-old grandmother and three small children, all of whom had different last names. Her tone did not change, nor did her somber expression. Coverage on the other channels was nearly identical, the news readers each faking regret over this senseless and tragic waste of human life. Thank God there was always a cute item to follow. On Channel 7 it was about the wedding of two three-hundred-pounders in Sioux City, Iowa, who were married by a two-hundred-and-ninety-five-pound justice of the peace; after the ceremony, all three were stuck in an elevator for an hour and a half, and the groom had to be treated for heart palpitations at a local hospital, where the honeymoon was now being celebrated. There was a shot of the bride on a hospital bed near her husband, snacking and smoking a cigarette.

Byrne decided he didn't look too bad, considering that he never photographed well. He supposed he could be warmer on the tube, although next to that dead fish Pilgersen he looked positively chummy. Doreen, whose downtown art world routinely encompassed celebrity buyers and sellers, would not be impressed by today's minor brush with celebrity. His mother would care more, but then mothers were supposed to. Considering that Irene Byrne spent most of her waking hours watching television, it was a special proof of her son's continued existence on the only medium she really trusted. Whether she cared about his continued existence was another matter. As much as he loved her, he had never been any good at confronting his mother. Now he was going to have to. Even if she was the only person in the world he was afraid of.

It was rare for him to have a chance to watch the late news, the daily urban diary of fires, private plane crashes, bank robberies, jewel thefts, random shootings, drug arrests, rapes, muggings and murders. For five minutes each evening, either before or after the stories about Madonna and Michael Jackson, calamity in all its multitudinous forms filled the small screen, its resultant misery writ large on the face of the victims, who were taking the decline of urban America on the chin.

But Doreen was attending a function tonight, a party he would have had no desire to attend even were he invited, which he was not. Doreen moved in a fast crowd and there were times and places when Byrne as her boyfriend simply did not exist. He tried not to take it personally, but having a cop at a party where cocaine might possibly be imbibed, or where some specially solicited, good-looking women might be present who just might be available later for the going rate of two hundred dollars an hour—well, inviting a cop to such a party would be considered gauche. He could respect that. It wasn't his job to stop all the crime in New York.

And so he was home, in his bachelor walkup at 736 Tenth Avenue, right above the old Sunbrite bar. The neighborhood was run-down and seedy, a series of drab four- and five-story tenements. Nowadays the real estate brokers and yuppies were trying to call it Clinton, but to Byrne and several generations of Irishmen it was and always would be Hell's Kitchen, the toughest neighborhood in Manhattan. There was none of the shabby romance of Little Italy or even the piquancy of the Lower East Side about Hell's Kitchen; its dreary avenues and desolate side streets proclaimed their former proximity to the elevated railroad tracks that used to run down the middle of Ninth Avenue, and the old Hudson River Railroad freight tracks on Eleventh Avenue—Death Avenue to its denizens. The inhabitants had always been among the lowest of the low: first German and Irish, later Italian and Puerto Rican. From the Thirties to the Sixties west of Eighth Avenue, this was the area in which cops feared to tread, and for long stretches of the nineteenth century, they simply avoided it and left the murderous poor to their own devices. At the turn of the century parts of it had been a middle-class black neighborhood, but the opening of Harlem had allowed the Irish slums to encroach from the south and west. By any name, Hell's Kitchen was a pit and probably always would be.

The Sunbrite, though, had a special connotation. It was where Mickey Featherstone, Jimmy Coonan and Eddie "The Butcher" Cummiskey, the pride of the Westies, once passed around a milk carton containing a victim's genitals and laughed their asses off. Three dickheads chortling at a dick where once real studs like Owney Madden and Mad Dog Coll had roamed. At least if the Westies were still around he would have some companionship, even if it was bad; now he had only the beer in the refrigerator and the tube. Idly, he reached for the Manhattan telephone directory while a commercial was on, searching for inspiration, and looked under the letter *P*.

Byrne never assumed any name was simply a random alias. The most vivid imagination couldn't top some of the names you found in the phone book. There was Anil Shitole, U Phuket, Gustav Prick and dozens more. There used to be an ongoing contest among the detectives to see who could come up with the most unintentionally obscene name, but with the influx of Asians and Indians in the past decade, there were now just too damn many candidates. Once the immigrants saw the humor in their surnames and started changing them the challenge would be back. U Phuket, indeed.

There was no Edwin Paine, Edward Paine, Eddie Paine or E. Paine; a call to 411 proved there was no unlisted Paine, either. There was a Peter Paine, DDS, but that was unlikely to be his man. He turned his attention to the letter *E*. Edelstein, Sidney. Edwards, C., M.D. Eisenach, Franz. There it was: Ekdahl, E., over on East Seventy-seventh Street. He cross-referenced the address with the city directory he kept at home, but at first glance there was nothing unusual about the parade of names in the building: Davis, Moody, Goldstein, Van Zandt—the usual New York City ethnic soup. At least he knew Ekdahl existed, unlike Paine.

He flipped through the cable channels on the remote control. CNN was boring its audience with footage from the latest bus accident in Bangladesh, while ESPN was running highlights from a bodybuilding contest. HBO and Cinemax had the umpteenth reruns of movies nobody wanted to see in the first place: early Tom Cruise—he must have been about fourteen when he made that picture—and a stupefying Clint Eastwood vehicle about stealing a Russian plane. Right: *that* was believable. Channel J, the public-access station, sometimes had some diverting programming, but he was bored with Robin Byrd and the ads for the escort agencies that alternated with clips from old black-and-white stag films of the fifties.

Against all odds, however, somebody was saying something interesting on C-SPAN.

"A whole new generation of Soviet defectors will be expected to ante up far more than in the past." The man being interviewed was a retired CIA officer named Donald Jameson, and he looked appropriately grave. "The answers we're going to get will be brought out by individuals who have realized you can't claim political asylum anymore, but if you bring over a fat enough file you can make a deal. It's the last valuable capital they have."

The interviewer pondered this intelligence for a moment. "What exactly are you saying?" he asked.

Jameson replied: "What I mean is that no longer can a Soviet defector expect to be welcomed here just by virtue of being a defector. The Yurchenko case was such an embarrassment for all concerned that the CIA and the FBI are taking a much longer look at the bona fides of walk-ons these days."

"Walk-ons?"

"Agents with whom we have not had a previous relationship, who show up unexpectedly on our doorstep, full of promises. What I'm saying is that from now on they're going to have to come across with the goods, in the form of hard intelligence—files, documents, photographs—that would otherwise be unobtainable."

The interviewer seemed worried. "Isn't that dangerous? I mean, defecting has always been hazardous, but how do you expect a KGB agent to smuggle files and photographs out of the Soviet Union when they are so closely watched? Wouldn't that be terribly risky?"

"That's their problem," said Jameson.

Chapter Five
Hell's Kitchen
Friday, October 19, 1990; 6:00 A.M.

In his dream, Byrne was running as fast as he could, running toward a voice whose owner he could not see, but whose presence he could feel.

"What is it, Francis?" said the voice. "Hurry and tell me."

There was a stitch in his side, but he kept running because he was afraid—afraid of what had happened and afraid that if he stopped, the voice would stop too, and then he would be all alone, forever.

"Come on, boy," said the voice again, a man's voice, deep and rich and resonant with masculinity and authority. "Hurry up."

The pain was greater now, but he was trying to ignore it. If he could just keep moving one leg in front of the other; this running couldn't last forever, and when it stopped, the pain would stop.

"I can't anymore," he heard himself saying. "I'm tired."

"Yes, you can," said the voice, sternly. "Try harder. Be a man."

He was running down a long corridor, a dark tunnel, the one he and Tommy and the other guys had been playing in: tunnels of water lines and sewer pipes and steam vents that were like a subterranean world beneath the streets of Queens. Once in a while a workman would leave a manhole cover ajar, and then he and Tommy and some of the other kids in the neighborhood would get a crowbar and pry it off and scramble down inside. It was more fun than stickball.

A rivulet of water ran down the middle of the sewers, and you tried not to step in it because for sure it was gross and you could get the crud, but the tunnel was wide enough that even the klutziest kid could straddle the water and scoot right along. At first they didn't go very far, never venturing too distant from the light cast by the open manhole cover, but after a while, everybody got braver, and sometimes they went really far, past the point where the tunnels converged, and they could hear the cars rumbling above them, and they were sure they had to be near Manhattan by now.

No matter how far they went, though, they never went so far that they couldn't see the light. Even on a cloudy day, the light from the manhole shone like a beacon. Nobody wanted to admit that they were scared of the dark or anything, but not even Tommy, who was the bravest of the bunch, would ever let the manhole's light entirely out of his sight. That's why they always had Johnny Zinka or one of the other guys who weren't quite full-fledged members of the gang guarding the manhole cover, to yell in case any Sanitation Department workers came by and tried to put it back in place, which wasn't very likely because those guys were always goofing off, talking to the girls in the neighborhood. Once, he overheard Mrs. Duffy gossiping that Jennifer Doran had gotten knocked up by one of them back behind McGuffin's garage, although everybody else always assumed it was that punky Shanahan kid back from college. In fact, once your eyes got used to it and you realized that it wasn't pitch dark underground, you could even see stuff. Like Coke cans and cigarette butts and sneakers and old waterlogged magazines that never turned out to be *Playboy* but sometimes were *National Geographic*, which was almost as good. Or like the pair of panties he, Francis, had found once, right beneath the storm drain, and of course they all sniffed them to see if they could smell anything. Like the gun Tommy had just found.

"Run, Francis," the disembodied voice was saying. "Hurry up. They're going to make me leave soon."

The gun was lying in a pool of yucky water, but Francis reached right in and pulled it out. It wasn't as slimy as he thought it would be, but it was rusty and old and didn't look very safe. Nobody could tell if it was loaded or not, and there was great debate. "It is too loaded," said Francis, who knew that the first rule of firearm safety was The Gun Is Always Loaded, even if it wasn't. "Betcha."

"You always were a chicken," said Tommy, and pulled the trigger.

The noise was overpowering. When Francis opened his eyes, the first thing he saw was little Timmy Kelly bawling. Nobody liked Timmy Kelly because he was a crybaby, but this time Francis could forgive him because there was blood pouring out of both of his ears and his nose, something Timmy hadn't even noticed yet because he was so busy screaming.

"Francis, I have to go now," said the voice.

Billy Costine was sitting down, right in the middle of the water, and Francis thought he looked like one of those monkeys in the cartoons, the kind that saw, heard and spoke no evil. His hands were clapped to the sides of his head, his eyes were shut and his mouth was moving, but he wasn't making any sound, at least any sound Francis could hear, but maybe that wasn't surprising, because Francis still couldn't hear anything. He wondered if he was deaf.

Tony Gandolfo was already running back the way they had come, because Tony Gandolfo really was a chicken. Tony liked to pretend he was a tough guy, tougher than any cop's kid, and his dad had taught him a couple of cuss words of Italian, like *baci mi* and *va fan cuolo* and stuff like that, which he liked to use because he thought they made him sound like a mobster. But now he was running away.

"You'd better hurry if you want to say good-bye," said the voice inside his head, growing fainter.

He was half sitting, half lying against one of the tunnel's sides. From this position, he could see everybody and everything, from Tony's disappearing butt to Timmy's blood to Billy's mouth, which was still moving and still, as far as Francis could tell, not making any noise.

The other thing he could see was Tommy, who wasn't doing anything, just lying there and basically not moving. "Tommy," said Francis's lips, "you okay?"

"I can't wait anymore, son," said the voice. "They're going to be mad at me if I don't leave on time."

He tugged at Tommy's arm, trying to roll him over, but he was a big kid, heavy, and now he was heavier than ever. "Come on, Tom," he commanded. "Come on, man." But he knew it was no use because Francis had been right and the gun was loaded, and it was an old gun and it wasn't very safe because after all those months in the pisswater it had rusted, and there was probably shit in the barrel and when Tommy had pulled the trigger he was aiming down the tunnel, away from everybody, just in case, but it didn't matter because the barrel was clogged and something blew when he fired and whatever it was it blew right back at Tommy, a piece of metal or something, and it blew right through his right eyeball and, in this dream, that was that.

"It's your fault," cried Billy Costine. "You bet him. You killed your own brother."

He was running now as fast as he could, the light of the manhole cover in plain sight, looking up at the sky, reaching out for the pair of outstretched hands that waited there to pull him up, to hoist him aloft, to bring him to safety. "I'm almost there," he heard himself saying. "Don't go yet."

"Good boy," said the hands. "I knew you'd make it."

He felt himself rising into the sky, out of the darkness of the sewer and into the daylight, and just like that his father's arms were around him, and he was hugging him tight, but there were others with him as well, other men, big men like his dad, and they were impatient and were saying, let's go, Bob, let's go, we're out of time, we have to go now, hurry up for Chrissakes, and they pulled him away.

"Good boy, Francis," his dad was saying. It didn't seem strange at all that half his father's head was missing.

"Good-bye, Daddy," he said. There wasn't time to tell him what had happened, or to say I love you.

Chapter Six
One Police Plaza
Friday, October 19, 1990; 10:00 A.M.

Francis," said Captain Malecki, "would you please come here?" For a superior officer, Malecki was awfully polite.

"Can it wait, Jack?" asked Byrne. "I'm kinda in a hurry."

"No, Francis, as a matter of fact it can't," came the reply. Malecki always called him Francis, just like Doreen did. "Something's come up."

John Tadeusz Malecki was a big, hawk-featured Pole from Hamtramck, Michigan. He had come to New York and the force straight out of Notre Dame—how the FBI had missed him Byrne would never understand—but he had always wanted to be a cop and for Malecki there was no police department like the New York City Police Department. In the same way that stockbrokers, journalists, television executives and Mafia capos dreamed of making it in New York, so did this Polish Michigander, who even pronounced his surname the Polish way: *Ma-wets-ski*. He hated being called a Polack, and anyone who referred to him that way to his face was always invited, politely, to step outside. After a couple of examples had been made, the men got the message. Captain Malecki was a Polish American.

There was little love lost among Malecki, White and Bill Finnegan. All three had been competing for the top job when White leapfrogged over his two Caucasian competitors. That in itself was enough to create animosity, but privately Byrne suspected Malecki of anti-black sentiments—almost inevitable, considering where he came from—while about Finnegan's racism there could be no doubt. If White ever did make commissioner, which with the rumors that Richard "Moby Dick" Flanagan was about to get axed by the mayor over that botched mosque raid in Brooklyn was a distinct possibility, Byrne couldn't decide who would be a worse successor, the stiff-necked Malecki or Finnegan, a dedicated apparatchik whose people had been on one urban force or another, and probably on the take, since the Dead Rabbit Gang roamed Broadway.

"Really, Jack, I'm gone. On my way to an autopsy."

"The stiff will be just as dead in half an hour," replied Malecki in a tone of finality. "I need you to take a statement, and we're short-handed this morning. Don't worry, it's the usual urban pathology." He shook his head. "Really, I don't understand how the inner-city population continues to thrive given the predilection for homicide among our disadvantaged brothers and sisters. And how any mother can murder her own son is utterly beyond me." Malecki, the only practicing Catholic Byrne knew—maybe the only one left in New York outside of the Cardinal—had six children of his own.

Reluctantly, Byrne gave up. As Malecki guided him to a desk, he descried a large black woman, age indeterminate, who sat handcuffed in the metal chair upholstered in ripped green imitation leather. She was talking to herself in a low voice.

"Francis, I'd like you to meet Ms. Goins. Albertha, this is Lieutenant Francis Byrne." Albertha looked up at him with dull, glazed eyes, and kept up her sotto voce interior monologue. "Don't worry, she's already waived her right to counsel," said Malecki as he departed. "Take it away, Father Byrne."

Byrne sat down at the desk and glanced at the arrest report; just a couple of paragraphs were all he needed to get the general idea.

"Hello, Ms. Goins," he greeted her.

"I'm awfully sorry about it," she said.

"I'm sure you are—may I call you Albertha?"

"Sho' you can, honey."

"Let's see, your baby is named Isaiah?"

"You mean was," she said. "He was my baby. Okay?"

"Your baby Isaiah is dead?"

"Yes, sir, he dead."

"Can you tell me how it happened?"

"Yes, sir, I can. He done died."

"How old was he?"

"Three, I thinks. Sometimes it be hard to keep track."

"And where is the baby's father?"

"He work at the hospital."

"Which hospital?"

"Wingdale."

"You mean the state mental hospital in the Harlem Valley?"

"Wingdale's what I call it. Sometimes I takes the bus, sometimes the train. Goes right from Grand Central, but be careful to change at Brewster North. Get off at Brewster and yo' ass is gonna wait or walk."

"Why were you in Wingdale?"

"I tried to kill myself."

"It says here you mutilated yourself."

" 'Zat mean cut?"

"Yes."

"I guess so."

"It says here that on several occasions you slashed yourself with a knife, that you tried to cut off your breasts. Is that right?"

"I guess so. I was tired of men always grabbin' me."

"And that after baby Isaiah was born you stuck a broken Coke bottle into your vagina and chopped up your insides pretty good. Why did you do that?"

"I was sick of havin' babies."

"Why did you keep having babies?"

"They feels good goin' in, not so good coming out."

"Who was the father?"

"Some nigger."

"He was a black man?"

"Oh, yeah, he black all right."

"What was his name?"

"Amos, I think. He the janitor."

"You think?"

"It was dark. They turns the lights off at ten o'clock sharp and you has to be in bed. Tha's jes' where I was, too, in bed."

"With Amos?"

"You got it."

"How did he come to be in bed with you?"

"Oh, yeah, he come all right. That's how you gets a baby. Man put he thing inside yo' thing, he come and you gets a baby. I know. I've had babies."

"It says here you're the mother of six. And where are the others now?"

"I don't know. They gone. State done took 'em."

"To put them in foster homes?"

"I guess so."

"How did you get baby Isaiah back?"

"Judge done give him back to he real mama. He say I got rights."

"When was this?"

"About two weeks ago."

"Where was baby Isaiah before that?"

"With some white folks."

"And was baby Isaiah happy in his foster home?"

"I guess so. He called them white folks mommy and daddy."

"And why did the judge take baby Isaiah away from them?"

"Because I'm he real mama."

"Your psychiatric report says you're mentally unstable, and that in the opinion of the social workers, baby Isaiah's life was going to be in danger if he were taken away from his foster parents and given back to you."

"Tha's bullshit. Ain't no white bitch he mama."

"Did you ask for baby Isaiah to come to live with you?"

"No."

"Who did?"

"My lawyer, Mr. Howell. He say I got rights too."

"And so Mr. Howell petitioned the court for the return of your child?"

"Say what?"

"The lawyer asked the judge to give you back your baby?"

"He did."

"And so baby Isaiah came to live with you on West 138th Street?"

"Tha's where my sister Delia live. I don't got no place a my own yet. I'm on the list."

"Tell me about baby Isaiah."

"He was a frisky little puppy. Gonna be a basketball player for sure. Tha's why I named him Isaiah."

"After Isiah Thomas?"

"You got it."

"How do you mean frisky?"

"Always gettin' into shit, is what. He done wrecked one of my nice dresses when he throwed it out the window."

"Weren't there any guardrails on the windows?"

"You kiddin'?"

"And your apartment was on the fourth floor?"

"Not my apartment. Delia's."

"Albertha, I want you to tell me exactly what happened to baby Isaiah. You were angry with him this afternoon, weren't you?"

"I was."

"Why?"

"He done broke Delia's nice new lamp."

"And what happened?"

"Baby Isaiah knocked it over, and it smashed all to shit. I knowed that Delia was gonna be mad when she got home."

"So you whupped Baby Isaiah?"

"I had to. Tha's how you teach them babies to behave. Tha's how you show them love."

"What else did you do?"

"I tied him up."

"What did you tie him up with?"

"The lamp cord. It was loose."

"Tell me how you tied him up."

"I put the cord around his neck."

"Around his neck? Why?"

"He was cryin' something awful and I tole him to shut up but sometimes baby Isaiah he jes' don't listen, okay?"

"And did he stop fussing?"

"Not right away."

"So what did you do?"

"I pulled the cord real tight."

"Then what happened?"

"He started to choke and was makin' an awful sound."

"What did you do then?"

"I took the cord and tied one end to the leg of a chair near the window."

"The other end was still around baby Isaiah's neck?"

"Yes."

"And then?"

"I throwed him out the window, just like he done to my dress." Albertha blinked back tears from the memory. "I sure am real sorry. I loved little baby Isaiah."

"I'm sure you did, Albertha."

"I was jes' tryin' to take care of him."

"I don't think killing him was the best way to do that."

"But he better off now. He don't suffer no more. And ain't that all what this world is about, Mr. Policeman? Sufferin'?"

For the first time in the interview, Albertha started to cry. "I loved that little baby too much," she wailed. "I jes' loved him to death."

Chapter Seven
520 First Avenue, Manhattan
Friday, October 19, 1990; 11:00 A.M.

D r. Sheinberg's waiting, Frankie," Mancuso was saying as he came in the door. "So come on into the lab and let's see what's on the slab."

Seymour Sheinberg, M.D., was one of the city medical examiners. Though his headline-grabbing chief, Barry Sonnenschein, got most of the glory, Sheinberg, Byrne thought, was the best. He was a tall, ascetic, bearded man, less than a generation removed from the shtetl—his father had been a cantor in Breslau, before the Nazis rendered the profession moot and the postwar boundaries had transformed Breslau into Wroclaw, Poland—and nearing retirement, but he was fond of red wine, brown women and black humor. Jesus, thought Byrne, if some of his autopsy-room jokes ever got out, every ethnic group in town would be on their ass in a New York minute. But if you couldn't make a joke here among the dead, the best-behaved and least sensitive audience in the world, where the hell could you?

"Sorry to hold you up, Sy," apologized Byrne. "Had to take a statement. Mother who killed her kid."

"He probably deserved it," said Sheinberg, only half-listening as he busied himself with his preparations for the autopsy.

"He was only three, Sy," protested Byrne.

"That doesn't mean he might not have deserved it later," retorted Sheinberg. "It's what a good detective down South asks about any murder victim: Did he *need* killing? Some folks just do, whether sooner or later."

The body was stretched out on a metal autopsy table with holes in it to allow fluids and water to drain off. There was a tag on its big toe.

Index Number__24 _____ M.E. Case Number ____678____

The City of New York
Office of Chief Medical Examiner

Compartment Number: 122   Name: Edwin Paine/Egil Ekdahl
Place of Death: Unknown   Date: Oct. 19, 1990

Back to Be Completed If Autopsy Performed

"Well, I can tell you one thing right now," said Sheinberg, referring to the abattoir that was the corpse's groin, "his mohel better have a good insurance policy. This is the worst excuse for a circumcision I've ever seen." He switched on the overhead microphone that would record every detail of his examination.

In the morgue, the body was only marginally less frightful than when

Mancuso and Byrne first encountered it. The hands had been wrapped in paper bags to preserve any hair or fibers that might have lodged under the fingernails—plastic bags can cause condensation that leads to destruction of evidence—or even small pieces of skin that might have been ripped off an assailant during a struggle. The dildo extracted from the corpse lay alongside, encased in a plastic evidence bag. Otherwise nothing had changed. The man looked like a white wax doll after a child had finished bashing it against a wall.

It was part of a homicide detective's job to be present when the victim was undergoing the legally mandatory postmortem examination and, under the circumstances, it seemed the least he could do. Lawyers sat down across a desk to interview their clients, to glean the particulars of their case, to mount an attack or plan a defense. Here, the dead were your clients, and their bodies were the best witnesses not only to what had killed them—that was usually fairly obvious—but, very often, to the identity of their murderer as well. It was amazing, reflected Byrne, how often the corpse, in all its apparent helplessness, had the last laugh on the perp: a torn scrap of clothing material here, a scraping of epidermis there; a hair on the lapel, the blood type of secretions, bite marks, pieces of rug fiber. The dead body was awash in clues to its demise, if only you knew how and where to look. Reflexively, Byrne glanced up at the Latin inscription found on the walls of autopsy rooms everywhere: *HIC EST LOCUS UBI MORS GAUDET SUCCURSO VITAE.* This is the place where Death is happy to come to the aid of Life.

"Three shots to the head for this sweetheart," said Sheinberg. "Two fired from the rear, one from the front, all at close range; look at those powder burns. Only a head holds powder burns like these little starfishies. And then there's his secondary ear-to-ear smile. We'll know which came first after we pop his top."

Sheinberg hit the play button on the twin-decked ghetto blaster he always kept in his examining room and got busy. The music was by Mozart. "*Eine Kleine Nachtmusik,*" said the pathologist. "It helps me relax. Of course, I'm not as relaxed as this fellow here." Carefully, he removed the paper bags from the corpse's hands. "His fingertips have been filed off, too," he said. "If he was ever printed, it probably won't do us a damn bit of good. Aprahamian will be able to get some partials off him, but I wouldn't hold out too much hope; this is a professional job, the way a doctor or someone who knows something about medicine might have done it. Either somebody really disliked this boy, or somebody's trying to hide something, or both."

"Then why did they leave his car parked nearby?" inquired Mancuso. "I mean, that wasn't very smart."

Sheinberg took a deep breath. "Ah," he said. "The pot cries out to the kettle as the voice of Mancuso is heard in the land. It's a good thing for society that criminals usually aren't very bright or we'd never solve any of these cases. Unless, of course, they want them solved."

"You got a point there, Doc," admitted Mancuso.

"Indeed I do, my friend," replied Sheinberg. "Now, if there are no further inquiries from the peanut gallery, let's open him up and see what made him stop ticking."

Sheinberg bent over the corpse's torso, studying it as if it were the Talmud. Long, slim fingers were attached to wide-palmed hands, and as his wrists snaked out from beneath his lab coat's sleeves, Byrne could see the last few digits of the faded concentration camp number tattooed on his forearm, a legacy of his time in Theresienstadt. "He shaved, or was shaved, just before he was killed," he decided. "Not just his face, his whole body. And how about this?" On the left shoulder there was a small crude tattoo of a crouching leopard, its teeth bared in a fearsome growl. Sheinberg whistled softly to himself as Mancuso moved in with his camera for a close shot.

"What's that all about?" asked Byrne as the motor whirred.

"Tell you later when I've had a chance to think about it," said the doctor.

With an almost erotic delicacy, the pathologist swabbed and cleaned the damaged pelvic region. "Well, looky looky," he said, indicating a wound of entrance low in the abdomen whose existence had been obscured by the more dramatic wounds to the genitals. After some brief surgery Sheinberg reached into the viscera and extracted a bullet, which he put on the evidence tray. Byrne glanced at it curiously.

You got used to the chop shop after a while, the detective mused, as Sheinberg went about his grisly task. He had been there many times, taking that last long walk with the victims before their bodies were ripped apart in the law's search for admissible evidence. Some rookies tended to barf during the craniotomy—that's what the emergency bucket in the corner was for—but even the most tender sensibilities eventually hard-ened in the face of so much legally sanctioned carnage. Whatever had happened to the victims in their last moments, what was about to hap-pen to their remains was even worse. The good news was, they were be-yond feeling it.

Sheinberg took a scalpel and made a long Y-shaped incision across the chest, the tail of the Y extending down below the sternum. There was al-most no blood.

"Running on empty," said the doctor, reaching for the electric saw. Its whine always made the hairs on the back of Byrne's neck stiffen. "Looks like he was drained before they dumped him."

"There was plenty of blood in the car," said Mancuso.

"Not enough, Vinnie," interjected Byrne. "Do you know how much blood there is in a human body? Five thousand cc's—five liters—in an adult male. Women have about a liter less."

"How much is five liters in real money?" asked Mancuso.

"More than a gallon," replied Sheinberg. "You spill that much blood, you're not driving the car, you're swimming in it. My guess is that some-body slit his throat and siphoned him off in a bathtub or shower room, someplace with plenty of running water. Either just before or just after he died; I'll tell you later."

With a sickening crack the saw sliced through the ribs until the entire breastplate sprang free of its moorings. Sheinberg reached in, pulled out the chest and set it on a stainless-steel gurney nearby. With an easy, fluid motion the doctor then removed the internal organs—the linked heart, lungs, liver, stomach and other viscera known as the organ tree—and placed the assemblage in one of the sinks.

"Nothing in the reserve tank, either," observed the doctor from across the room, exploring the contents of the stomach. "No last supper for this little angel." Sheinberg continued his examination as Byrne took notes. "Heart slightly enlarged, but otherwise looks good; I would say he was something of an athlete. Liver's in good shape, ditto the spleen. Guy's as healthy as an ox. Except, of course, he's dead."

Sheinberg worked over the intestines for a while, then examined the corpse's rectal area. "Shit," he exclaimed.

"What the hell you expect, Doc?" said Mancuso.

"Quiet on the firing line," said Sheinberg, humming softly; Mozart was the doctor's favorite. "Frankie, do you remember the guy with the gerbil up his ass?" asked Sheinberg, who was famous for his detailed memory of every autopsy. "They brought the boyfriend up on manslaughter charges, later dismissed."

"I know you can indict a ham sandwich," said Mancuso. "But a gerbil?"

"Wasn't my case, Sy," said Byrne. "But I've heard of stuff like that."

"It seems," continued Sheinberg, forgetting the body in front of him for a moment as he spun his tale, "that this guy got a gerbil up his tush, and it killed him."

"How the hell does a gerbil get up your ass?" asked Mancuso. "Does it jump out of the crapper when you're on the throne and head for pay-dirt?"

"Those are the shit-eating alligators that live in the sewers, Vinnie," said Byrne. "Gerbils can't swim."

"You think I'm joking," said Sheinberg. "Well, screw you both. I'm not. The guy really did have a gerbil up his hind end, which gnawed through his sigmoid and descending colon and made it practically to the transverse before the damn thing suffocated and he bled to death. Amazing, really, what some people will do for kicks."

Mancuso looked at Sheinberg. "Are you shitting me, Doc?" he asked.

"Of course not, you moron," replied Sheinberg. "Gay men have been coming into doctors' offices for decades, sporting various foreign objects from, and in, unlikely places. It used to be your basic foodstuffs—carrots, cucumbers, sausages, lubricated with a little vegetable oil or egg whites. Then came more serious things, like pens and pencils and lipstick applicators, working up to Coke bottles, whiskey glasses, flashlights, lightbulbs. And now they're into small, furry animals. Takes all kinds, I guess."

"I still don't understand how the gerbil gets up there," objected Mancuso. "That would have to be one shitfaced gerbil, you ask me."

Sheinberg shook his head. "The way they get the gerbil in is through a length of PVC pipe, the kind you use in modern plumbing, with a diameter according to your taste and physical capability. Some of the guys turning up in emergency rooms these days have rectums so stretched from fist-fucking that they can literally shove a baseball bat up their ass, K-Y jelly or no K-Y jelly, and don't think I haven't seen a few of those designated hitters wander in here over the past ten years. Anyway, they stick this pipe in their butts and induce the gerbil—"

Byrne broke out laughing. " 'Induce the gerbil,' " he repeated. "Jeez, Sy, sometimes you really kill me."

"Whatta they do, shove a firecracker up the gerbil's ass to make him run?" asked Mancuso.

"No, they shove a little teeny piece of PVC pipe up his ass, with an even tinier gerbil inside it, and so on ad infinitum," said Sheinberg. "How the hell do I know? The point is, they do."

"How come you never hear about that stuff on Gay Pride Day?" asked Mancuso. "And what if it's a female gerbil? Do they have just as much fun with a girl gerbil?"

"No wonder they won't let them march in the St. Patrick's Day Parade," said Byrne. "Hell, I wouldn't either, not with gerbils up their ass."

"Every group has its dirty little secret," said Sheinberg, "and when that group cultivates an air of victimization, the secret is often secreter, and dirtier, than most."

"If you ask me," said Mancuso, "gerbils are about as dirty as they come."

"That one sure was," said Sheinberg, returning to his examination. "By the way, Frankie, you guessed right about his being alive when they hacked off his schwanz." Sheinberg wiped his bloody gloves on his apron. "Thought you'd like to know."

The photographer started to make another wisecrack, but Sheinberg cut him off with the buzz of the saw again. He was opening the skull. Even Mancuso had nothing to say. No matter how many times you saw this part, it never got any easier.

The doctor traced the circumference of the head with the saw, slicing through the thick cranial bone, opening the head the way he'd open a soft-boiled egg. When he finished cutting, he popped the top of the skull up with a small lever. Sheinberg reached behind the corpse's ears and began to peel the scalp forward across the face. The face was now literally inside out. It looked like the most disgusting Halloween mask in the world.

With the skin out of the way, Sheinberg reached inside the head and with one motion removed the brain, like a magician pulling a rabbit out of a hat.

"It's a boy!" said Mancuso. "Congratulations, Frankie."

"No, it's a brain," answered Sheinberg, "and if you had one, you might be able to tell the difference."

Sheinberg spent some time with the damaged brain, weighing, slicing, probing, tracing the bullet paths. "Inside the head, a gunshot takes on a life of its own," he explained. "It scoots around the interior of the noggin like a pinball on speed. It makes my job very difficult. Especially when the hitman uses a .22, as he or she did here. One of those babies gets inside your head, it really goes to town. It's the Little Egypt of ordnance: it zigs, it zags, it crawls on its belly like a reptile. That's why the Mafia uses .22s. Maximum damage with a minimum of firepower. No fuss, lots of muss."

Byrne listened to the liturgy according to Sheinberg. He'd heard it before, and he knew that it was meant to be greeted with applause from the audience after the great Seymour Sheinberg, M.D., finished amazing the hoi polloi with his deductive brilliance. For it was true that Sheinberg knew every move that a bullet could make even before the bullet made it. "Do you think this could be a Mob job?" he asked.

Sheinberg shrugged, as if to say, How should I know? He stripped off his gloves and washed his hands.

"The head shot—the first head shot, I mean—wasn't the fatal wound," said the surgeon as he dried off. "Oh, there was significant damage to the cerebellum, the occipital and the parietal lobes. It's a four-plus wound, nonsurvivable. But it says here this man was already dead from his leaky chops."

"You mean his cut throat," said Byrne. "What else?"

"The other shots definitely look postmortem. Somebody wanted to make sure this boy's physician, dentist and mommy would have a hard time identifying him. The paths are a bit confusing, but I think I've got them sussed out. It'll all be in my report."

"Don't forget the gut shot," said Byrne, indicating the slug on the tray.

"Right," said Sheinberg, reaching for the object and scrutinizing it closely.

"Why you would shoot a guy in the belly after you'd already cut his throat is beyond me," said Byrne. "Which means, I suppose, that it's also possible that the abdomen shot was the first wound. Could he have survived it?"

"Doubtful," said the pathologist. "It's probably a fatal all by its little old self. It just would have taken longer. And unless you're Superman, or insane, the pain would have been unbearable. A throat-cutting would have been merciful."

"Which brings us back to square one: which is the fatal wound and, if he was dead or dying anyway, why were the others inflicted?" asked Byrne.

"Good point," said Sheinberg. "Because the funny thing is, the bullet in the abdomen came from a different gun—a .38, it looks to me."

"Let me have a look at that," said Byrne, examining the missile closely. He could tell at a glance that it was a Smith and Wesson .38 Special, a well-balanced and accurate cartridge popular with match shooters, the military, the FBI and the police; like most cops, he used them himself. Judging by the extent of cranial damage the .22s, he guessed, would turn out to be Remington Fire Balls, which have even more explosive force than .357 Magnums, especially at close range. "So there was a total of four shots, from two different weapons—which of course implies two killers—plus the cut throat and the missing peter. Why do you suppose they hacked off his weenie?"

"'Weenie' is not the precise medical term, Francis," said Sheinberg, "but let it stand for now."

"I mean," continued Byrne, "that's an argument in favor of the Mob. Cutting off a guy's pud is the way the Mafia deals with squealers. But they usually stuff it down his throat, whereas we can't find this guy's missing johnson."

"Don't forget the damage to the rectal area," said Sheinberg. "Some time before or just after death, this man was violated anally with a sharp object. And I assume this is the instrument in question right here." He picked up the dildo.

"Well," said Mancuso, "it beats gerbils. At least you don't have to feed it."

Sheinberg examined the implement with interest. "Nice piece of workmanship," he remarked. "My late uncle Harry the jeweler would have approved. As the good book says: 'Thou hast also taken thy fair jewels of my gold and of my silver, which I had given thee, and madest to thyself images of men, and didst commit whoredom with them.' Ezekiel 16:17. Which leads me to the obvious suggestion that if you want to find out what happened to this poor bugger, maybe you're better off skipping Little Italy and instead making a foray to some of the more, shall we say, exotic night spots that Fun City has to offer."

"Such as?" asked Byrne.

"Do I look like a fairy godfather to you? Read *Screw* or the *Voice*. Now this guy, on the other hand . . ."

"And the tattoo and the writing on the dildo?" interjected Byrne.

" 'The Writing on the Dildo.' Sounds pretty apocalyptic, doesn't it, in a fractured-fairytales-for-grown-ups kind of way," said Sheinberg. "It's in Russian."

Byrne suddenly had an idea. "What about Little Odessa, Sy?" he asked the pathologist. "We've been talking about the Mob here, but maybe we have the wrong Mafia. What if the Brighton Beach gang did this guy?"

Now there was a nasty thought. Byrne hated Brighton Beach. Some of the detectives thought the chinks were clannish and secretive, but they were positively chatty Cathays next to what was called, in deference to local ethnic sensibilities, the Russian mob. Not only were more and more of them arriving every day, they were being welcomed ashore by members of Congress. It didn't matter that a goodly portion of them were not political or religious refugees at all, but simply criminals that even the KGB had no further use for and was glad to get rid of. Or, worse, were criminals that the KGB still very much had a use for, and was only too happy to smuggle into the U.S. under the cover of quotas for the Soviet Jews. Which is why no detective enjoyed a case that ended in Brighton Beach. There were never any happy endings there.

"That notion had occurred to me," agreed Sheinberg, hefting up the dildo and pretending it was a throwing knife. "Except that the inscription on this baby has got to be somebody's idea of a joke."

"As long as you're translating, maestro," prodded Byrne.

"I'm a little rusty, as you know," replied Sheinberg, "but I'll give it a whirl." He studied the instrument, his face a pantomime show of puzzlement, effort, remembrance and, finally, amusement. Byrne was aware that from the minute he saw the writing Sheinberg knew what it said, but he indulged the pathologist his love of drama.

"You're not going to believe this," the doctor said at last. "Near as I can make out, and allowing for differences in idiom, it says 'Mother's little helper.' "

"Muthafucka," said Mancuso.

"You're right," said Byrne. "I don't believe it."

Chapter Eight
The Upper East Side and Greenwich Village
Sunday, October 14, 1990; 7:00 A.M.

On Sunday morning Egil Ekdahl rises as usual, precisely at seven. He is a man of regular if not to say rigid personal habits, no matter what indulgence he has been permitting himself the night before. Although he has just returned from Europe, he shows no signs of jet lag. He is tanned, toned and fit, the incarnation of Juvenal's bromide. He prefers to quote the Latin original from the *Satires* in its entirety: *Orandum est ut sit mens sana in corpore sano.* You should pray to have a sound mind in a sound body.

Ekdahl is enjoying his time in New York. Yes, it is dirty and uncivilized and in many other ways appalling, but the city—Manhattan—offers certain blandishments, fillips, to a man with his refined and specialized tastes, attractions he can't find quite as easily elsewhere, and that makes it more than worth the filthy streets and the vulgar populace.

Before he steps into the shower, Ekdahl admires himself, naked, in the mirror. His mother always told him he favored his father, and here he stands, nearly six feet tall and starting to fill out, wearing his hair rather unfashionably long to cover the faint beginnings of a receding hairline; sometimes he pulls it back in a ponytail. His light blue eyes are pale and clear, his features regular; there is a malleability, a mutability, about his face that comes in handy in his field. Persons of both sexes find him attractive.

After luxuriating in the hot spray until thoroughly soaked, he spreads the shaving gel across his face, chest, arms and legs and rubs it in vigorously. He takes a fresh straight razor—he has seven, and hones one anew with a leather strop each day—and shaves himself with it, all over, including his groin area, carefully avoiding that which his mother taught him long ago should be left alone, until his skin is as soft and smooth as a girl's; unconsciously, he caresses his chest and bottom. Ekdahl does not like safety razors.

He also detests body hair of any kind, especially on women. It repulses him when a woman has even a single hair growing out of her nipples, or if her pubic growth is too luxuriant or her forearms too hairy, or if she has a tuft at the small of her back or, worst of all, the hint of a mustache. Sometimes when a girl doesn't measure up he shaves her himself. It is playful and sensuous and he finds that if he couches his request in erotic terms she will usually let him do whatever he wants to her. He is an artist with a razor.

Stepping from the stall, he towels himself vigorously, enjoying the feel of the material's rough fiber against his sensitive skin.

Ekdahl opens his closet and apprises his wardrobe carefully. He is fastidious about his clothes. At work, he favors single-breasted double-vents, worn with plain white Sea Island cotton shirts, just like the ones James Bond always demanded, and French cuffs. Bally shoes and conservative Italian silk ties complete the ensemble. This morning, though, there will be no Savile Row suit. Instead, Ekdahl dons a pair of tight but otherwise faded and nondescript Levi 501s and a pink polo shirt, over which he throws a light green windbreaker. A blue Mets cap, under which he tucks his tresses, beat-up Reeboks and a pair of sunglasses complete the ensemble. Briefly, he strikes a quick pose. He will pass, especially in the Village.

If Ekdahl is fastidious about his grooming and his clothes, he is equally selective about his furnishings. They are few, but choice, for Ekdahl really does believe, and experience has taught him, that less is more. The Bang and Olafsen speakers, the high-definition television, the stereo hi-fi VCR with surround sound and Dolby, and the BMW in the four-hundred-dollar-a-month garage beneath his building make him appear to be practically a caricature of the Eurotrash yuppie; his bedroom, meanwhile, is artless Scandinavian simplicity itself. A more private possession, his pornography collection, his close friends, if he had any close friends, would admit is particularly fine.

Ekdahl speaks idiomatic American easily and as well as his other languages, but he prefers to keep his normal linguistic identity European. It gives him a certain distinction in cachet-mad, insecure, Eurocentric, Wasp-Jewish New York. He has always marveled at this. In New York, a city of immigrants, you can hear twenty different languages on the street every day, but most of them are boogaloo tongues that nobody cares about, much less wants to learn: Korean, Urdu, Hindi, Gujarati, Hausa, Ibo, Farsi, Tagalog, the Chinese dialects and sub-languages and, of course, various Central and South American variations on Spanish, not to mention the Creole patois of the Haitians. But speak a civilized language—preferably French—and monolingual New York society is at your feet, praising your intelligence and marveling at your sophistication. Ekdahl finds it amusing, especially since language ability has nothing to do with either.

The classical radio station is playing an aria from a Tchaikovsky opera as he laces up his shoes.

> I love you,
> Love you immeasurably.
> I cannot imagine life without you.
> I am ready right now to perform a heroic deed
> Of unprecedented prowess for your sake.
> Oh, darling, confide in me!

sings the baritone, for some reason in English. Ekdahl, an opera fan, recognizes it immediately as Prince Yeletsky's second-act aria from *Pique Dame*, in a very poor English translation. *The Queen of Spades*, as it is also known, is his favorite: an opera about passion, obsession and desperation. The desperate deeds that men do for the love and admiration of a woman. It seems appropriate to his morning's reverie, and to his day's purpose.

Promptly at 8:00 A.M., Ekdahl leaves his apartment building on East Seventy-seventh Street, not far from the river, and heads for the Lexington Avenue line, going downtown on the number 6 train to Brooklyn Bridge. He is not one of those snobs who brag that they only take taxis and haven't been on the IRT since they were in high school.

The New York City subway system is cleaner than it used to be. He had been expecting *The Taking of Pelham 1, 2, 3*, but the graffiti is largely gone from the trains, at least from those running through white neighborhoods. But the advertisements, some of them in Spanish, are aimed at the lowest stratum of ridership: cures for hemorrhoids, AIDS hotlines, abortion clinics, secretarial schools. One in particular has become his favorite: "TORN EARLOBE?" it shouts, as if that injury were the most common thing in the world. How do you tear your earlobe? Ekdahl wonders, and then decides it must refer to the charming practice among the city's "youths" of pulling expensive earrings right off the lobes of the ladies without bothering to unfasten the clasp.

Ekdahl lets his eyes wander around the car. It is strictly against New York etiquette to make eye contact with a fellow passenger, but the crowd this Sunday morning is listless, languid, indolent. A couple of white punks in black leather and faux-British Mohawk haircuts, on their way home from a night of club-hopping, sit with their elbows on their knees, staring dully at the dirty floor. An enormous black woman sprawls serenely across a bench, her mouth open, breathing heavily. At the far end, a jogger is stretching her hamstrings. Ekdahl appraises her legs expertly, following the curve of her thighs up to her shorts. He stops admiring only when she turns to glare at him. A woman always knows when she's being watched, and only in America does she not appreciate it, until she is so old, ugly and fat that no one will look at her anymore.

Ekdahl stays on the train to Astor Place. There are only a handful of homeless in the big, handsome station, newly renovated to reflect the neighborhood's toney origins (the beaver friezes Ekdahl finds particularly piquant) but up on the street it is another story. The place looks like Lagos. The sidewalk in the no-man's-land between Eighth Street and Saint Mark's Place—between the East and West Villages—is littered with junk, mostly old clothes and back issues of *Time, Better Homes and Gardens* and *Playboy*. Ekdahl has long wondered why the police, whose precinct house is right across the street, don't do something, but a man explained to him once at a cocktail party that the vendors, by offering reading material for sale, are protected by the First Amendment. In that case, he retorted, they ought to amend the amendment. Where do you think you are? asked the man. The Soviet Union?

At the corner of Eighth and Greene there is a little coffee shop called Franco's. Ekdahl takes a seat in one of the booths and waits. He looks at his watch. It is precisely 8:36 A.M. He is twenty-four minutes early. He likes being early for appointments.

There are about ten other diners, if this kind of face-feeding can be called dining, mostly little old ladies from the neighborhood, pecking at their cheap breakfasts while waiting to die. Behind a long counter, the Puerto Rican waitresses shout unintelligible orders to the black cook, who appears to understand them perfectly. There is an emergency exit at the back that leads through the kitchen and out onto Greene Street. But the only way in is through the front, a clumsy double entryway that empties first into a small glass-enclosed vestibule and then into the restaurant.

"Yes?" It is not so much a question as a demand. It sounds like "Jess?" Ekdahl glances quickly at the plastic-covered menu, spattered with pancake batter and dried egg yolk, and orders some toast.

"Coffee?" The waitress is clearly resentful that he is not ordering more.

"No, thanks." He never drinks coffee.

The waitress—not bad, actually, if a little heavy in the hips—grunts, turns and walks toward the counter, with Ekdahl's eyes following the sweep and sway of her behind. It is true, what the old men say: every woman is beautiful, in some part.

Now he spies the man he is to meet coming through the door. Rawlston is stocky, almost heavyset, but well turned out in a blue blazer, tan slacks and brown Bass Weejuns. He wears a light blue Arrow shirt with an open collar. He has a suntan. He looks like a salesman at a West Side Oldsmobile dealership.

"Mr. Paine?" the big man addresses the room without embarrassment. In person, Rawlston looks older than Ekdahl has expected, although they are nearly the same age.

"Over here," Ekdahl replies. They shake hands perfunctorily as the newcomer settles into the narrow booth. "Murray Dutz," says Ekdahl, introducing himself.

"Who?" Rawlston is already confused.

"The name is Murray Dutz."

"Where's Paine?" asks Rawlston.

"It doesn't matter what I call myself," replies Ekdahl. "It's the thought that counts." For the occasion, he has selected a way of speaking that combines the hint of a southern inflection with a hard-edged, Brooklyn approach to consonants: the accent of the white working-class "Yats" of New Orleans. It was one of the dialects he had studied in school.

"Whatever." Rawlston shrugs, shifting his bulk uneasily in the small red booth. He hates this kind of New York City restaurant, with its plastic booths and cheap Formica tabletops, jabbering cooks and moody waitresses. He thought he had left this kind of dining behind years ago.

Ekdahl observes the man's discomfort and savors it. He knows exactly what he is doing bringing a large man like Rawlston to Franco's and squeezing him in one of the tiny booths. First, it will be hard for a man his size to get out quickly; second, it is the last place any of Ekdahl's acquaintances would be likely to encounter them; and third, it is so banally public that just by sitting there he is hiding in plain sight. Ekdahl's train of thought is temporarily interrupted by a pair of pretty legs walking east on Eighth Street.

John Rawlston looks across the table at the man he has been sent to meet. He isn't quite sure what is supposed to happen, or why he is even there. Ordinarily, they send a runner for a spec meeting like this, but his orders have been clear. He is to head from Ozone Park to the Village for a meeting with a Mr. Paine, find out what he's selling, size him up and report back. Sounded easy enough, but the lack of qualifying detail bothers him. Only the presence of his piece under his left armpit gives him some measure of comfort. In his experience, it was always the dumbest situations that were the most dangerous. Coldly, he assesses this man named Dutz, who is gazing back at him with a frank—a little too frank, in his opinion—blue-eyed stare. The guy gives him the creeps. Rawlston decides Paine, or Dutz or whoever, is a fag.

"Mr. Rawlston," Ekdahl says without preamble, "I've asked for this meeting to make you and yours what I consider to be a very attractive offer for something I believe can be of considerable use, and is of considerable interest, to your organization."

Rawlston doesn't like the way Dutz emphasizes the word *attractive*, but it might just be the funny accent. "I hear it's some kind of file," he says.

"It is indeed," agrees Ekdahl. "A secret file of considerable importance about a man and an event that changed the course of history. A file that some folks in this country would give their eyeteeth to see. A file that's worth a fortune to at least two governments, several of your least favorite federal agencies and your business associates in Chicago, Tampa and New Orleans."

"Wanna get a little more specific?" asks Rawlston.

In response, Ekdahl's voice falls nearly to a whisper. "Are you familiar with the names Golitsin and Nosenko? What do the events of November 22, 1963, and their aftermath mean to you? I have reason to believe, Mr. Rawlston, that they have a very special meaning not only to members of your organization but to you personally."

"I don't know what you're talking about," Rawlston says, looking around the room.

"Say, you're not being followed, are you?" asks Ekdahl theatrically. The place is nearly empty except for a few old dears finishing their breakfasts, and a guy in a business suit at the counter who arrived about ten minutes ago and is calmly devouring an omelette; Ekdahl has had his eye on him since he walked in. This is not the kind of place that gets many suits. "Sometimes you ginzos ain't so hot, security-wise. If any of this ever got out no place in this great land of ours would be safe for me. They would chase my butt from Selma to Seattle and back again."

"I guess that's your problem," says Rawlston.

Ekdahl settles back in the booth, appearing relaxed. "You see, John, I'm from New Orleans. Born and bred, on a dumpy little street just off Canal in the French Quarter called Exchange Alley that back then probably had more bars, pool halls and poontang per square foot than any other street in the Quarter. It's been cleaned up now, make it safer for the tourists, they said. So now we got beer in plastic cups 'stead of hookers, but what the hell. Anyway, in 1985 I joined the United States Marine Corps figurin' I'd see something of the world. Did basic at MCRD in San Diego, took some tests and the next thing you know I'm drawing guard duty at the embassy of the United States of America in Moscow, USSR."

Ekdahl leans forward, dropping his voice. "While I was there, certain events occurred which you may have read about in the newspapers. I will mention only the name Franklin Doubletree, sergeant, USMC. Do you remember? Nice-lookin' guy, couldn't lay off the dames? Horniest sumbitch I ever did see, and let me tell you I seen some in the marines. Anyhow, the good Sergeant Doubletree and some other marines got themselves caught in a 'honey trap.' To put it bluntly, they were screwing some Soviet gals who turned out to be KGB swallows. The first thing they teach you when you draw embassy duty is you don't fuck with the locals in any wise. Well, ol' Franklin did and he got his self, and us, into a hell of a mess. 'Course they court-martialed his ass faster'n you could say Geronimo, but the damage was done. Missing classified papers, bugs planted both in the embassy and in Spaso House—where the ambassador lives—that type of thing."

"What does this have to do with, you know, the thing we're talking about?" Instinctively, Rawlston glances around and Ekdahl notices that the businessman is doing too much listening and not enough eating.

"Well, let's just say that I met a girl in Moscow too, but unlike Franklin I didn't get caught," continues Ekdahl. "And let's just say that I liked her so much that I let her talk me into working for her side. Or at least I made her think she did. Let's say that, technically, I guess I still am. And, finally, let's say that I want to quit and come home. And you're the guy who's going to help me get out, alive, well and well-off."

Although Ekdahl doesn't smoke, Dutz is the kind of man who would, so he produces a cigarette, taps it a couple of times against the Formica and lights up. "I don't know how much you know about the spook business, John, but not every marine is what he appears to be. Just as not every CIA or FBI agent is what he appears to be. Or every member of the Bergin Hunt and Fish Club, for that matter. Some marines, the smart ones, work for Naval Intelligence. Like me."

Rawlston shifts uneasily in the booth. "I thought you said you were working for the Russians."

Ekdahl laughs. "Nobody says you have to work just one job anymore, buddy. So in order to make my exit from the service of various governments as graceful as possible, not to mention remunerative, I have managed to get my hands on certain documents which I and my lady friend are offering to your people for the nice round sum of five million dollars, after which Murray Dutz disappears and everybody's happy. What I have is nothing less than the KGB file on another U.S. marine, one who defected to the Soviets, married a Russian girl who may or may not have been involved with Soviet intelligence, returned to this country and shot and killed the president of the United States. His name was Lee Harvey Oswald, and everything the Russkies know about him is in this file. I gather there's enough in there to blow the Warren Report right out of the water and get half the CIA and the FBI brought up on charges of sedition, if only you know how to read it. Me, my Russian ain't too good, but that's what I'm told, and on very good authority, too." He taps some ashes onto the floor.

"Most people think the Warren Report is bullshit anyway," says Rawlston. "If they even remember what it is. So who cares about the commie version?"

Ekdahl blows a smoke ring in the man's face in reply. "Look at it this way, John. Nobody has ever seen the KGB file on Oswald. During the Warren Commission's investigation, the Russkies gave up a couple of documents here and there, but beyond assuring us they didn't have the slightest idea what had happened, that's about all they did. One of the reasons this thing has dragged on for nearly thirty years is that we don't have all the pieces of the puzzle, and when you don't have all the pieces, well, you can invent the most fantastic shapes to fill in the blanks. The party that gets its hands on the Oswald file is going to be able to eliminate a lot of cocka-mamie theories. Because here's the truth: What he did in the Soviet Union. What they did to him. The precise nature of his relationship with Naval Intelligence, the FBI and the CIA. Not to mention the GRU and the KGB. The reasons behind his defection, how he was handled within Russia, his real role in the assassination, at least as they see it. Which means that fin-gers may finally start pointing in some right directions. Pipers are going to have to be paid. And balls are going to have to be squeezed."

Rawlston seems unimpressed. "Not my balls."

Ekdahl shakes his head at the man's thickness. "Do you have any idea how valuable this material is? If Oswald was a CIA or Naval Intelligence plant, sent to infiltrate the Soviet Union—and if he later returned and shot Kennedy—then the CIA had de facto complicity in the president's death. If, on the other hand, Oswald was turned—'doubled'—by the Soviets and was sent back to kill Kennedy . . . well, John, we were a hell of a lot closer to World War III in 1963 than anybody knew at the time. Even closer than during the Cuban Missile Crisis. Lyndon Johnson sure as hell thought so."

"That was a long time ago. Nobody cares anymore."

"*Au contraire*, John. The CIA cares; they have never entirely come clean with the American people, not to the Warren Commission—where, of course, they had a former DCI named Allen Dulles sitting on the panel and taking care of business—not to the FBI, not even to succeeding presidents. Hell, they probably haven't even come clean to themselves. And the KGB sure as hell cares. The old Soviet Union is on its last legs, John, in case you haven't noticed. Any country where the men can all be bribed and the girls can all be bought hasn't got much goin' for it in my book. It's just a matter of time. And nobody can predict what the hell's going to happen when the Soviet Union finally does crash and burn. A prostrate, defenseless Russia, a shattered, renegade KGB, proof positive of Soviet complicity in Kennedy's death . . . jeez, it's a dream come true for our side. The perfect reason for taking them out now, one way or another. Who could blame us? *Laissez les bons temps rouler!*"

"But what has this got to do with my people?"

"You know about Sam Giancana and Johnny Rosselli and Santos Traf-ficante and Carlos Marcello and Jacob Rubenstein, aka Jack Ruby, Lone Nut II. You know how deep they were in it. And you know most of them are dead, one way or the other. You know how many bullets somebody put into Giancana? Seven. One in the back of the head, one in the mouth and five in a semicircle under his chin; death to snitches. That shut ol' Mooney up but good. And his pal Rosselli . . . I hear they had to cut off his legs to fit him into that oil drum. Damn!"

Ekdahl looks up, to see if his words are having any effect. "So I figured you guys might have more interest in this stuff than anybody. Certainly, you can pay. And at five mil it's a bargain; imagine what the concessions from the FBI alone will be worth to you when you dangle this baby in front of their fat Irish gobs. And you can back the CIA off your drug operations, too. No more Pizza Connection bullshit; you'll have a free hand. Hell, you'll make back your money in a week."

"And have the feds jump down our throats."

"I doubt it. What are they going to do? I guarantee you'll have 'em by the short hairs. Just as soon as you come up with the cash, deposited in the proper Zurich bank account." Ekdahl rubs his hands together and calls for the check. "I'm afraid that's about it for today, buddy. Sorry you didn't get anything to eat. And here I was buying, too."

Rawlston stays silent while the girl sullenly slaps the bill down on the table and clears the plates. "We'll have to meet again," he says quietly as Ekdahl grabs the tab and throws some money on the table. "I can't authorize this on my own. Besides, how do we know you're telling the truth?"

"John, have you ever heard of the island of knights and knaves?"

"What?"

"It's a game that logicians like to play. There's this island, see, out in the middle of nowhere, on which live two kinds of people: those who always tell the truth and those who always lie. Your job is to tell them apart by asking the right kinds of questions. Well, the secret world is a little like the island of knights and knaves. Let's assume for the moment that one side—let's call it the CIA—always tells the truth. The other side—we'll call them the KGB, but that's just arbitrary, because morally they're basically the same outfit—always lies. Okay, then if the Russians are knaves and they always lie, then logically it stands to reason that when you ask them if they ever had any interest in Oswald—if they ever talked with him, or recruited him—and they say no, they're lying, right?"

"I guess so."

"Now let's suppose some normal humans get shipwrecked on the island.

They're just regular joes like us: sometimes they tell the truth and sometimes they lie their asses off. The problem is that they're physically indistinguishable from the knights and knaves. Now it's your job to sort out the
knights, knaves and humans, and the only way you can do it is by asking
questions and then using the old noodle to figure out who's who in the zoo.
Next, let's assume that, from time to time, the knights and knaves switch
sides. That is, the truth-tellers, every one of them, are now liars and vice
versa. Now you've got to figure not only who's who, but who's who at any
given moment. And you have no idea how long each moment is, only that
you know they're of irregular lengths. Not so simple anymore, huh?"

"Guess not."

"Well, it gets even more complicated. Let's now assume that when the
knights and knaves switch sides, they don't all do it. That is, some of them
switch and some of them don't. Some knights becomes knaves; some
knaves knights. They're still opposites, though. And they're still morally
consistent; that is, they either always lie or they always tell the truth. But
now black is white, white is black, up is down, down is up and everybody's
confused. Am I right?"

"Well, if you put it that way."

"And don't forget you've got your civilian population caught in the middle, sometimes good, sometimes bad, always human. And the hell of it is
this: that by switching sides unpredictably, what do the knights and knaves,
taken as a group, resemble but normal humans? Wheedling, cajoling, begging, insinuating, misleading and generally bullshitting whenever it serves
their purpose. That's the hell of it, John; the truth is contained in the art-
fulness of the lie. It's a fun-house hall of mirrors, an E-ticket ride straight
to hell. My world and welcome to it."

Ekdahl roots around in his briefcase as if to retrieve something. The
double-action Colt King Cobra .357 Magnum lies nestled at the bottom.
The handgun is a beauty, with a special wooden stock direct from the Colt
Custom Shop and a six-inch barrel finished in Ultimate Stainless, a high-
sheen buff that makes it look as though it is made out of nickel plating. At
ten yards, it can put five Norma 158-grain full-jacket rounds into a two-
and-a-half-inch shot group in jig time, and with a velocity of 1,262 feet per
second there are few targets that can walk away from that kind of punishment. Experienced range shooters sometimes dismissed it as a poor man's
Python, but it is nearly the same gun at half the price, the same gun that

Jack Ruby used to shoot Oswald, a one-shot kill that at close range had destroyed the man's insides. You had to admire a gun like that. Ekdahl knows good value when he sees it.

The Cobra, however, he leaves in its lair. Closer to hand is the Walther PPK .38 autoloader with the 3.2-inch barrel and six-shot magazine, the American-made version of the famous German pistol. It weighs only twenty-one ounces, and even with the silencer it fits inside the waistband of his trousers with ease, like a second dick. Ekdahl carries it everywhere he goes; he feels naked without it.

He finds the folder he is looking for. "You *were* followed," he says quietly.

"What? Who?" Rawlston feels himself starting to sweat.

"If we're going to do business together, you're really going to have to be more careful. No wonder the FBI is kicking your butt."

Ekdahl stands up quickly and eases himself out of the booth smoothly. "I'll call you in a couple of days to set up our meeting with the big guy," he says to Rawlston. "In the meantime, I hope you like to dance." He places the folder on the table. It is marked simply AEFOXTROT.

Smooth as Astaire, Ekdahl scoops up his briefcase and glides in one motion over to the man at the counter and taps him on the shoulder. "Did you know," he practically whispers, "some people believe you can see the image of his killer in a dead man's eyes?"

The man starts to say What the? but his sentence is cut short by a single gunshot, spit from the silenced Walther, which has been planted just under his left nipple. The bullet enters below the breastbone and continues upward at an angle, exploding the heart. The man flinches once, his mouth working, still trying to get the *f* out, but no sound emerges except a short, sharp gurgle because he is already dead and doesn't know it, and then his head comes down on the counter with a deafening crash, launching his half-eaten ham-and-Swiss omelette onto the floor. His face hits the Formica so hard it breaks his nose and sends a gout of fresh blood spurting, but his eyes are rolling up in his head and he isn't twitching. To all appearances, it is a sudden, massive, fatal heart attack. These things happen in the best places.

"Oh my God!" yells Ekdahl. "Oh my God! Oh God Oh God Oh God." He is screaming and moaning in equal parts, his voice pitched half an octave higher than normal. "Somebody, please help please help oh my God oh shit help."

The little old ladies munching their bagels are just now starting to react—"Get a doctor," one of them is saying—as the kitchen boys come running to see what is the matter, and one of them later tells police that all he can remember clearly is some fairy shrieking, it all happened so fast. All other memories have been obliterated by the sight of the dead man.

"Call an ambulance! Call 911!" Ekdahl shouts at the busboy, who flushes, turns and runs for the phone. The waitress remains frozen at the counter and the ladies just sit there, hoping it is all a bad dream or at least some bad nova. Ekdahl totters briefly, as if about to break down, then suddenly lurches for the rear exit.

Outside, hardly anyone takes notice of a man doffing a cap and windbreaker and stripping off his jeans in a Greene Street doorway, to reveal a pink short-sleeved shirt and a pair of summer shorts underneath. This is New York; everybody does whatever he feels like in the streets, whenever he wants. The Eighth Street BMT station is just a short block away.

Chapter Nine
Brooklyn
Sunday, October 14, 1990; 10:00 A.M.

From Eighth Street, Ekdahl takes the R train all the way to Coney Island; it used to be the way the N train went, but for some obscure reason the two lines switched routes several years back. He remembers trivia like this; you never know when it, like Joe DiMaggio's batting average during World War II, will come in handy.

Ekdahl is proud of his knowledge of the New York City subway system, so proud he hardly ever uses his car. Few natives know it as well as he does. Ekdahl makes it a point of pride never to help anyone on the subway.

The brakes scream at each stop in counterpoint to the conductor's announcement of the station. Today's conductor is something of a comedian; at Canal Street, for example, he affects a Charley Chan accent. It's a good thing he's black, thinks Ekdahl, or they'd have him up on insensitivity charges faster than you could say nigger in a woodpile. The train lurches to a start again and rattles down the tracks. He finds its rhythmic wiggle soothing, like being in his mother's arms.

Ekdahl remembers very little about his early childhood, except for this:

He is five, and living in the United States. One day, a strange woman comes to his home. She is smiling as she approaches. "Give me a kiss," she says. "I'm your mother."

He is standing outside the house in Bethesda. His other mother, a thin-lipped woman named Edith O'Brien, is inside doing the ironing. She did the ironing every day at eleven o'clock in the morning, when her favorite soaps came on television. Even so, she has the senses of an eagle, and from within the darkened doorway she cries out, "Who is it, Johnny?" Johnny was what she always called him; he thought it was his real name. Probably she could hear the muffled running of the engine of the car from which his new mother has emerged.

His new mother is a well-dressed woman, the most beautiful lady he has ever seen, or could ever imagine. She smells of perfume and flowers and cigarettes, and her long, dark hair is being tossed about playfully by the breeze, as if God himself is tousling it. She seems terribly grown up, but not old like Edith. She bends to kiss him, but he pulls back. "Come on, darling, don't you know your own mother?" she asks. Her voice is smooth and musical, with an accent he has never heard before.

His new mother reaches out, grasps him firmly by the shoulders and pulls him toward her. She kisses him hard on the lips. It is not unpleasant. She kisses him again.

Ma O'Brien has appeared. She has taken one look at the woman kissing him, expelled her breath in a short violent puff and headed back inside. He hears his old mother dialing the heavy black telephone.

"My darling, I'm so sorry," his new mother says, and hugs him.

"Sorry for what?" he hears himself saying again, seventeen years later.

"You say something, man?"

His reverie has been interrupted by a Negro sitting beside him. The man is wearing unlaced running shoes and a backward baseball cap, from under which peek a set of cornrows. "No," says Ekdahl. "I don't believe I did." He does not much like Negroes. They make him nervous.

"Yes you did, motherfucker, you said something. You said you were sorry. Sorry for what? What you done?"

Ekdahl smiles his winningest, whitest smile. "I guess I was just having a little daydream."

"Yeah, you dreamin', all right," said the man. "I been watchin' you, and you practically asleep at the switch. Good thing ol' Rufus ain't no mugger, else I woulda snatched your wallet 'fore you could say jack shit."

"Good thing," agrees Ekdahl.

"Hey, I can dig it," says the man. "I was having myself a motherfuckin' wet dream about that ho' over there." From behind his dark glasses, the man's eyes caress a well-dressed blonde sitting across the aisle. She is wearing tennis clothes and is reading *New York* magazine. He smacks his lips and gives himself an imaginary high five. Ekdahl finds himself wishing that he was better at separating hostile inflections from humorous ones in black American speech.

"I hear you, my man," says Ekdahl, suddenly friendly and confidential. "Wouldn't mind a piece of that myself. But I hear that once you've had black you never go back."

The black man laughs loudly, and a few heads turn to see if there's trouble brewing. White men confronting black men on the New York City subway make every rider nervous. Another high five, this one returned by Ekdahl. The riders relax; everything is cool. The blonde looks up and smiles. She is not one of those New York females who think even an implied compliment is a fighting word or an act of political provocation. The white guy gives her the creeps, but the brother is not bad at all.

Ekdahl pays no attention to her. His mother is talking to him again.

"For everything that's happened. Our separation." She lowers her voice. "The way you're being raised. Everything. I know you blame me, but it's not really my fault. There wasn't anything I could do. But now I've found you and we won't be separated ever again." She hugs him fiercely, and then turns to say something to one of the men in the car. "I hope your father can see you someday. I know he'd be proud of you. I know he is proud of you."

Ekdahl just looks at her. Already at this age, most of his emotions have been beaten out of him. He hardly ever cries.

"My father . . . " he starts to say, but the words won't come. One time Dad O'Brien came home drunk and called him a commie brat bastard and nearly killed him, hit him across the head so fast he never saw the blow coming and so hard he still has the scar on his side, the scar he got when he went crashing into the sharp corner of the coffee table; and he kept hitting him until his mom intervened shouting something about killing him and needing the money, and little Johnny finally was able to run out the front door and down the block where he hid out with one of his friends until darkness fell and it was safe to creep back into the house because by now Dad was surely sleeping it off, and he was.

"Is a very brave man," his mother replies, holding him ever tighter. "Someday you'll know how brave." Ekdahl feels her hot, salty, stinging tears running down his left cheek. They burn, but they do not hurt. "Mother's going to take you home with her. Where you belong. Run inside and get your things." The sound of the car's engine is very loud in his ears. "Now run!"

Instinctively, he obeys.

Mom O'Brien is hanging up the telephone and reaching for him at the same time. "Where do you think you're going?" she shouts and lunges. The receiver falls to the floor.

Johnny avoids her grasp and achieves the safety of his room, slamming the door behind him. He hears a noise, as when Dad opens a bottle of champagne, but much louder. He scoops up a few favorite toys, stuffs them in a rucksack that had been a Christmas present from one of his many uncles and comes back into the living room.

Mom O'Brien is lying quietly on the sofa. Her mouth is open but she is not breathing. She has a new, wine-red beauty mark in the center of her forehead. Her arms are thrown back, her skirt pulled up slightly. He has never seen her like this before.

The telephone is back on the hook. The television is still on. "Is she sleeping?" Ekdahl asks his new mother.

"Yes, darling." She takes the rucksack from his hand. "I'm going to take care of you now," she promises. Another kiss. "Just as you will always take care of me."

Ekdahl closes the door behind him very gently. He doesn't want to wake Mom O'Brien. She gets very angry when her afternoon nap is disturbed. "Where are we going, Mother?" he asks.

But his mother does not answer, for the R train has halted. The doors are opening and the conductor is calling out the final stop. The Negro is gone, and the yuppie tennis player. He is the last person on the train, getting off at the last stop.

Only a few Puerto Ricans are Indian-summering on the poor man's Lido. At Nathan's, a handful of old black men are working over the broiling grills, their sweat one of the famous hot dog place's secret ingredients. A few Jews and Italians from the old neighborhood sit on the boardwalk, noshing on wieners, staring out to sea and into the past.

Ekdahl walks briskly east, to Brighton Beach. Brighton Beach Boulevard itself is deep in shade, courtesy of the elevated train tracks that bifurcate it. On the avenue, the newly arrived Russian Jews are wandering around, selling their cheap Soviet books, wearing their cheap Soviet clothes and eating their cheap Soviet food in places like the Restaurant Moskva, after which they go for walks along the boardwalk because it reminds them of their cheap Soviet seaside resorts, where their less fortunate fellows eat their cheap Soviet ice cream and dream of a new life in expensive America.

The sun is shining as he turns left onto Brighton Fourth Street and stops before a small, bedraggled Cape Cod on the east side of the street. The nameplate on the door reads N. MEDVED. The house is on the wrong side of the tracks, on the north side, but out of and away from the shadows of the D train that rattles past on its way to its own Coney Island terminus.

With his key, he unlocks the door and slips inside. There is no air-conditioning, and the sea breeze is still today, but the dark room is a welcome refuge from the heat outside. It is always dark in here. A woman is there to greet him. "*Dobraye utra, Mat'*," he says. In Russian: "Good morning, Mother."

"Ivan Yuriyevich." She smiles and embraces him. "Vanya." It pleases him to hear his real name in her mouth, now that they are together again.

Chapter Ten
Little Italy
Sunday, October 14, 1990; noon

Y ou wanna tell me what happened?"

Even though the sun says midday, it is dark inside the apartment at 247 Mulberry Street, and Rawlston's eyes are still getting used to the gloom. Outside, the streets of New York are warm, but the living room with the drawn shades is kept cool. The don likes it that way, so he won't sweat so bad in the double-breasted Brioni suits he wears. The boss hates stains under the armpits of his suits. It shows no class.

"This was a simple job yesterday, a simple fuckin' job. I wasn't askin' for no trouble. All's I wanted you to do was check the guy out. Did I say to start shootin'?"

"I didn't," replies Philip Sacco, aka John Rawlston.

"Don't contradict me, you know what I mean." Across the sparsely furnished room looms the considerable bulk of Angelo Genna, ensconced royally on the sofa. Sacco has to admit he looks great in his $2,300 threads and hand-painted floral tie; the Gucci socks are a nice touch, too. One thing you had to say about Genna, the man had taste in clothes. Italian taste, maybe, but taste nonetheless. "I'm askin' yuz again, what the fuck happened?"

"Yeah, he's askin' ya nice, Phil." That would be Joey Aiello, standing, as always, beside the boss somewhere in the darkness. The consigliere emerges from the shadows and takes up his customary position right behind the boss. He is a tall, gaunt man, a made man since 1956, made when he was only twenty-three, and he is Angelo Genna's best friend in the whole wide world.

"We had a little talk, just like you said. How was I supposed to know what the guy was up to? Hell, I didn't even know he was packin' until he popped that guy at the counter."

"And just who the fuck was that, may I ask?" the don wants to know.

"Beats me. I didn't even hardly notice him until he got dusted."

Genna puts his hands together, his fingers pointing skyward, as if he were praying, although Sacco knows the only God the boss really believes in is himself. "No good," he says after some contemplation. "It's no good. But more worse than that is, you fucked up. What'd I say to you? I said go find out information what's going on with this cocksucker." His tone is taking on a threatening edge. "I was makin' you an errand boy. High-priced errand boy—hey, what do we pay this guy anyway?—just like those asshole lawyers I got, Muck and Fuck I call 'em. When Joey told me what he gave those fucking guys, in two and a half years, gave 'em a fucking mill, and I said to him 'What the fuck you talking about? What the fuck, are yuz nuts?' So when Joey tells me what I'm givin' you, which he will as soon as I let him open his fucking mouth, which I won't at the present time, and when I find out that it's more than two dollars and fifty-two cents a month, which it probably is, that's when I'm going to start calling you somethin' else, Suck, maybe, as in you suck. Muck, Fuck and Suck, the three blind assholes. How much is it, Joey? I would be a billionaire if I was looking to be a selfish boss. So Phil, I'm askin' yuz again, what the fuck happened?" The don strikes a pose, as pleased with himself as if he had just delivered Hamlet's soliloquy.

Sacco takes a deep breath and begins. "I showed up and the guy was already there. Nice lookin', prob'ly queer. Tight blue jeans, little fruity windbreaker—"

Sacco's narrative is briefly interrupted as Aiello transfers his weight onto one leg, raises the other and farts. "Like that you mean?" he inquires.

"Cut the shit, Joey," commands Genna. "Keep talkin'."

"Mets cap—"

"Musta been a faggot," remarks Aiello. "Only queers root for da Mets."

"Whatever." Sacco shrugs. "It was a Mets cap, is all. Anyway, he tells me his name isn't Paine, it's Dutz, and he's got something for sale that he thinks we might be interested in."

"God save us from guys that thinks," says Genna, and starts praying again.

"Apparently he's got access to a Russian file on the prick that shot Kennedy, and he thinks we might be interested in it."

"Yeah, what's his name, Oswald." Genna chuckles softly. "Lee Harvey Fuckin' Oswald. I remember that from my Brooklyn boyhood."

"Whatever," continues Sacco. "He says he was a marine who served in Moscow. I couldn't follow some of the things he said too good, but well, the bottom line is he's got his hands on something about this Oswald guy and the price is five big ones."

"Five thousand bucks is a lot of money for a piece a paper," comments Aiello.

"That's five million."

"Fuck me!"

"Payable to a Swiss bank account, so either he's got a hell of a lot of chutzpah or this file must be some pretty hot shit." Sacco pauses. "That's about it."

"So what's in it for us?" inquires Genna. "For our five big ones?"

"He says we can get the FBI off our back, and maybe even the CIA, too, vis-à-vis the Pizza Connection and stuff like that," replies Sacco. "Says we'll make our money back in a week."

"Vis-à-vis," repeats Aiello. "I love it when you talk like that. It's like you went to college."

Genna ignores his consigliere. "How?"

"How is that the outfit what has this Oswald file can pretty much call the tune, on account of everybody wants to know what's in it. FBI don't know, ditto the CIA. I mean, if you just look at this from the point of view of family business alone, if the Russkie file shows that Marcello ordered a hit, well, we can put his family out of business tomorrow. You know, do a favor for the FBI and make life easy for ourselves. And surely that's worth five mil, in peace a mind if nothin' else."

"What else did he say?" Genna is thinking. He is doing a lot of that these days, what with the feds breathing down his neck.

"That's about it. He said he'd be in touch. He also gave me this. I gather it's a kind of sampler." Sacco takes the folder out of his briefcase and puts it on the coffee table in front of Genna. A half-eaten tuna sandwich and a glass of beer bear mute witness to an interrupted lunch.

Genna rises from the couch and begins leafing through the folder. "Looks like more boring government bullshit to me, is what it looks like. Hey, Joey, you think they got one a these on me?"

"You bet, boss. If they don't, they ain't doin' their job right, and you sure as hell ain't doin' yours, neither."

"Fuck this." Genna throws the file back onto the table and paces around the room. "I don't give a shit about this right now. You know I hate to read. And what I still want to know is, who the hell the guy at the counter was, and why did Mr. Dutz or Mr. Putz or whatever his name is whack him."

"Jesus, these fags really enjoy their work," offers Aiello. "Can't make up their minds whether to fuck a guy or kill him. Personally, they scare the shit out of me. Any guy doesn't like pussy, well . . . " His voice trails off, as if he is stunned at the very thought.

"Hey, I don't know if he really was a fag or not, he just dressed kind of Christopher Street funny, but he talked straight enough and that piece he had was all right. He just glided right up to the poor sorry son of a bitch and capped him, then he started screaming and carrying on."

"Yeah, so's everybody in the joint can make him," says Aiello.

"You was being tailed," decides Genna.

Sacco doesn't know whom to answer first. He chooses the consigliere. "No, that's just it. He looked like half the other people on the street in the Village, and besides, nobody was watching him, they was looking at the dead guy. He's a pro, you ask me."

"Tailed," repeats the don, ominously. "A pro, maybe, but whose pro? We got another fuckin' situation here." Genna shrugs his broad shoulders, indicating the meeting is over. Sacco is halfway to his feet when the boss speaks again.

"It's always some fuckin' situation or another. And guess what, Phil, it's your fuckin' situation. I wanna meet with Dutz or Futz on Wednesday, and before that I wanna know what's this Foxtrot shit, and who that asshole at the counter was. And if he's not for real"—he pauses, then repeats his words for emphasis—"and if he's not for real, I will personally sever his motherfucking head. As in dead and I do mean dead and disappeared, permanent. Now get outta here." He dismisses Sacco with a wave of his pinky ring, to which is attached his right hand.

"You know what else I really want?" asks Genna, who looks longingly in the direction of the kitchen. Sacco stops for moment, and then realizes the question is not meant for him.

"You see this sandwich? This tuna sandwich?" the don says, addressing his lunch; a Medici prince contemplating the skull of Yorick. "That's all I

want—a good tuna sandwich. You can't fuckin' get them anymore." The
town is going to hell, and there is not a damn thing he can do about it.

Chapter Eleven
Brighton Beach, Brooklyn
Sunday, October 14, 1990; evening

Ivan Yuriyevich Didenko, which is Ekdahl's real name, killed his first
man at the age of thirteen.

It happened in Paris. He and Mother were walking back to their
hotel, the Université, on a bleak winter's Sunday evening when she stopped
to inspect something in a gallery window, one of those "primitive" paintings that Paris is plagued with. It was an African village scene, with a tribal
chief in full regalia holding court to an admiring band of natives. The shop
was closed, as were all the others, and there was no one else on the Rue
Jacob.

Mother stopped to look and admire. She started to say something, and
Ivan began to listen, but all at once he was on the ground, in the gutter,
felled by the force of a tremendous blow to the head. He tried to get up,
but his legs wouldn't obey, and then he heard Mother's muffled scream and
saw her heels dragging along the sidewalk. He put his hand to his head and
it came away sticky. There was no pain.

He had found his feet and was up now, running. Down one of the side
streets—it might have been the Rue des Saint-Pères—he saw Mother on
the ground, kicking weakly. There was a shape, a man, on top of her.
Mother's shoes were off, her skirts hiked high, and one of her stockings was

torn. As he neared, he saw that her blouse had been ripped open, and her breasts were exposed to the weather. One of the man's hands was grasping at them; the other was over her mouth. The man's pants were down around his ankles, his backside was bare, and he was raping his mother.

Ivan watched for a moment, transfixed. The Paris pavement was damp and dirty, and it smelled of piss and dog shit, as Paris streets do.

The man's hips were pumping furiously; he was concentrating so fiercely on his task that he was oblivious to everything around him. Mother was putting up only token resistance, if that; at first, Ivan thought she was unconscious or dead, but then he saw her fists balling and thumping uselessly against the man's back. Even this pitiful counterattack was too much, however, and as he watched, the rapist propped his upper body up on his forearms, as if he was doing a half push-up, and struck his mother in the face hard, knocking her head to one side. Blood dribbled from the corner of her mouth, and she was still. The man slid both hands underneath her for support, and once more his hips began their rhythmic thrusting.

Ivan was glad he had worn his long hair up that day, out of the way. Carefully, he removed the necktie that Mother always made him wear on Sunday, wrapped both ends of it around his wrists and grasped it firmly in both hands. He was sorry he was going to have to ruin it, possibly his white blouson as well, and hoped Mother would not be too angry. He crossed one hand over the other, making sure there was still plenty of slack. With a cat's leap he straddled the man's waist, slipped the makeshift garrote around the man's neck and pulled his hands briskly apart.

The man's head snapped back and up. In one motion, Ivan tightened the noose by circling his right hand over his left several times. The man's feet shot straight out, seeking a purchase on the ground, but his arms were pinioned beneath Mother, and already the blood vessels in his head had begun to close and he was gasping for air.

Ivan brought both his knees together and with a little leap came down with his full weight onto the man's spine. He could hear the man groan, and he felt something give. The fight was starting to go out of the man now. For a moment, Ivan considered striking him, but he dared not risk letting go until he was sure he was dead. As he looked down he could see Mother beginning to awake.

Vanya pulled the rapist's head toward him, arching the man's back as he pulled and twisted. The man's arms sprang free from beneath Mother's dead weight, but they flapped uselessly at his side, and after his spinal cord snapped they stopped moving altogether. Even when the body went limp he kept up his hold, counting to sixty, counting very slowly even when the dead man's sphincter relaxed and he was suddenly splattered in feces. As Vanya released his grip the man's head flopped straight down, bouncing once off Mother's bare chest.

Ivan stood up and rolled the man off his mother and onto the sidewalk. He was calm as he coddled the man in his lap like a baby, twisting his head until he heard a sharp report, and then he knew the man was dead for certain and couldn't hurt Mother anymore. He helped her to her feet. Mother's clothes were torn and dirty, but her cloak was long, and Ivan was able to cover her nakedness. If anyone saw them now, it would look like she was drunk, had slipped and fallen and banged her head. Or perhaps that she was a prostitute, and a john had beaten her. Either way, no one would care.

"We must do something with the body," Mother gasped.

Vanya rolled the man toward the street. The corpse was wiry, but not heavy. There was a black Citroen parked at the curb, an old one, the kind that looked like a cross between a beetle and a tank. Without much difficulty, Ivan shoved the body under the car, positioning the man's head in front of one of the rear wheels, so that it would be crushed when the owner pulled the automobile away from the curb.

During the battle he had been vaguely conscious of a stirring below, in that forbidden place, brought on by the confluent proximity of his mother's breasts, the rapist's backside and the violent struggle. He could feel that his underwear was damp, drenched in a sticky, viscous liquid. "What's happening to me, Mother?" he cried in fright. "Am I dying?"

Mother was there with him, kneeling before him, ministering to him. "No, my darling," she said. "You are not dying. You are living." Her touch was soft and, in the half-darkness, her eyes gleamed and her hands glistened. "I knew this day would come, my Vanya," she said. "Today you are indeed become my son. Today, like your father, you are a man." He was no longer cold.

Far from it: he has been warmed by the memory, sitting here in the darkened living room of the house on Brighton Fourth Street. The sofa is old and well-sprung and it gives obligingly under his weight.

"*Chai*, Ivan Yuriyevich?" Mother asks. She is still beautiful, just as beautiful as the day he first saw her. As she walks across the room toward him, bearing the tea, he notes approvingly that her figure retains its full complement of curves.

"Vanya," she says, "there is blood on your shirt." The few droplets would have been invisible to anyone else, but a woman can always smell blood. She puts her hand on his chest. "Are you hurt?"

"No, Mother," he tells her.

"Is he dead?" She always knows.

"Yes, Mother." His eyes drop and he blushes. Mother is always so proud of him.

"But you have his blood on you," she says, setting the samovar down in front of him. "Take off your shirt and let me wash it." Obediently, he removes his pink polo shirt and hands it to Mother. "Your shorts, too." She looks at him now, as naked as the day she bore him, and runs her hands across his chest. She hands him one of her long robes and he puts it on. They drink their tea in silence.

"Tell me about my father," he says at last.

"Your father was a very brave man. This I tell you always. A very brave man, who suffered much. And loved much." She smiles. "You look so much like him. His body was beautiful, like yours. He was strong and very brave, like you, my son, Ivan Yuriyevich." She strokes his hair gently. "And now you are all I have to remind me of him," she says, and kisses him lightly on the forehead.

"Now that I have found you again, I would find him too," says Ekdahl. "I want to see him. I want to know him." There is urgency in his voice.

But she is not answering these questions; she never does. "Did you bring it?" she asks.

"Yes, Mother," he answers. He can hear the reassuring hum of the washing machine in the next room.

"Let me see it," she commands, as she takes him by the hand and leads him into her bedroom. Her cloak slips from her shoulders and drops to the floor.

"It's right here," Ekdahl says. "Right here in my briefcase, where I always keep it." He reaches in and removes the object his mother loves and needs so much. Since his father she has not known a man. The Helper, carved from pure ebony, was originally purchased at a bazaar in Mali by a Munich-based half-Turkish film producer with whom Ekdahl had done business, and was presented to him as a gift. Ekdahl has had the thing capped with silver plate and, because of its special function, has had it inscribed in handsome calligraphy across its ample and accommodating length.

"Bring it here."

Now he is holding Mother in his arms, caressing her, feeling the warmth and firmness of her figure. She is so beautiful; there can never be a woman as lovely as Mother. It is quiet in the small house near the ocean. Mother is lying on the bed. She looks up at him and smiles. Tenderly, he bends his head low, guiding the instrument to its destination. Mother closes her eyes and sighs.

She is holding his free hand with one of her own, maintaining the Helper deep within her body, in the secret place that had given him birth. Her body is starting to shake. She kisses him, this time passionately, just as she had on that wonderful day in Paris, the day he became a man. The day that had never come again, no matter how many times he killed.

"I love you," murmurs Mother, sleepily. Her voice is beginning to drift, her consciousness slipping away. How beautiful she is! He has known women, and he has known men, but there is only one Mother. He would kill anyone who came between them. She would too. "*Ya lyublyu vas, Mat'*," whispers Ekdahl.

Chapter Twelve
The Upper East Side
Friday, October 19, 1990; 4:00 P.M.

The yellow tape across the door of Ekdahl's apartment on East Seventy-seventh Street reads CRIME SCENE: DO NOT ENTER. BY ORDER OF

NYPD. Byrne disregarded it. He could. He was in charge of the investigation.

Experience had taught Byrne that if you wanted to get inside the head of someone then you had to go where they went, see what they saw, smell what they smelled, touch what they touched. Just as you never knew how big Saint Peter's really was until you went to Rome and saw it for yourself, so also could you never chart a victim's fate until you put yourself in his shoes, following his path to destruction as if it were a signposted Stations of the Cross.

The building stood near the intersection of York Avenue in one of Manhattan's best neighborhoods. In the New York snob's scheme of things, the more desirable part of the East Side was the streets north of Sixtieth and west of Third Avenue, but once you got this far east, almost to the river, the pecking order reversed itself and the closer you were to Sutton Place and York Avenue the better. Ekdahl may have had outlandish tastes in his private life, Byrne reflected, but you could certainly never prove it by his uptown address. The only drawback with the location, in Byrne's book, was that this far east it was a long walk to the subway, but he expected that a man like Ekdahl probably disdained public transportation anyway.

He knew from the flat's floorplan, which he had picked up from the super, a sullen Hungarian named Kovacs, that it was not large, consisting of a short entryway, living room, dining area, small kitchen, bedroom and bath. As he turned the key in the lock and opened the door to 33-C, the interior was pitch black and Byrne fumbled for the switch that he knew ought to be just inside the entrance. Where the hell was it? His groping hand, skimming the wall, finally found the light mechanism, but the damn thing didn't seem to work. Maybe the electricity had already been turned off, but Con Ed wasn't that efficient. Maybe the man was just too cheap to replace the bulb. He left the front door open as he stepped inside, hoping he wouldn't bark his shins against any exotic Nordic furniture.

It was very quiet on the thirty-third floor, the only sound the dull white ambient noise that rose from the Friday afternoon traffic below. Even at this height he could hear the rude urban beast tirelessly groaning and singing, whistling and spitting, shrieking and humming. Byrne stopped for a moment, waiting for his pupils to widen. He stood in the

foyer, trying to pick up some vibration, however faint, of its former inhabitant.

At first, it appeared that the living room was completely empty, as if
the furniture had already been moved out. There seemed to be nothing in
it, no tables, chairs, carpets or any of the normal accoutrements of life.
Although the apartment faced Queensward, commanding a prized view
of the East River, the windows had been covered over with a heavy
opaque material that admitted no outside light. Finally, he descried the
sole item of furniture, rising dimly in the center of the room like the
black monolith from Kubrick's *2001*. It was a large wooden cabinet about
the height of a man. Byrne tried to open it, but it was secured by a dead-
bolt.

The light switch in the bathroom functioned normally. The room was
spotless, done up in chic black and white: black tub and sink, white walls
and toilet. There were no visible traces of blood in the tub or shower;
wherever Ekdahl had gotten done, it probably wasn't here. Byrne opened
the medicine cabinet: European toiletries, some facial scrub, some skin
lotion, some hair gel—and an impressive assortment of fresh razors.
Straight razors, too, six in all, each one honed to a hair-splitting edge.

He tried the kitchen next. The cabinet shelves stood empty, and the refrigerator was bare. Talk about a lonely guy, thought Byrne as he returned
to the darkened living room.

His improving eyesight picked up a thin crack of light just barely visible beneath a doorway. That would be the bedroom. Before he went in,
he walked around the perimeter of the living room, to make sure he
hadn't missed anything. He hadn't. Then he pushed open the bedroom
door, which was much heavier and more solid than the pasteboard portal
he had been expecting, and he might have wondered why Ekdahl would
go to the trouble of installing a special door, when suddenly he staggered
back, every thought driven from his mind.

The light hit him with the force of a supernova. His wide-open pupils
raced to shut themselves, sending red concentric after-images shooting
along his optic nerves and straight to his brain. Defensively, he retreated
into the darkness for a moment, trying to regain his equilibrium. Although half-blinded, he could see that the bedroom's windows were also
sealed and the walls were painted bright white, which only intensified the
radiance of the light—a lone, bare, impossibly bright floodlight sus-

pended from the ceiling. It was this light, more akin to a halogen street-lamp or something used to illuminate night games at Yankee Stadium than to a normal ceiling fixture, in which he was now bathed.

Still reeling from the shock, Byrne stumbled back into the bedroom. Shielding his eyes with his right hand, he tried to take inventory. Like the living room, this chamber was nearly devoid of furnishings. The only thing in it was tucked away into the far corner and lying on the floor: a sheetless, pillowless straw pallet. Except for a lone built-in closet along one wall, the room was otherwise empty.

He slid one of the doors aside. How many suits did a man need? One for every day of the week, maybe every day of the month, brushed and pressed to a fault; in Ekdahl's wardrobe, apparently, no sport coats need apply. Byrne noticed that each wooden hanger bore the logo of a different international hotel. Here the Amigo in Brussels, there the Savoy in London; here the Mark Hopkins in San Francisco, there the Imperial in Tokyo. A row of shirts, uniformly white, uniformly pressed. The ties were hung neatly on two sets of racks. The shoes, at least ten pairs, were regimented on the floor. The drawers held a pair of blue jeans and a couple of casual shirts, but no underwear.

He went through the suit pockets one by one. There was nothing in them, not even pocket lint. Byrne patted down the interior jacket pockets as well, with the same result. He felt something in one of the pants pockets, which he assumed was a stray coin, but it turned out to be, of all things, a subway token.

The closet had two sliding panels; when one was opened, it covered up the other. Byrne closed the open panel and slid its companion sideways to the left. There, hung at the end of the row of suits, and kept just as neatly, were seven or eight dresses, along with a handful of skirts, blouses and blazers. A complete woman's external wardrobe. Taken in toto, the closet looked like it belonged in the bedroom of a young urban professional couple, but Byrne had no evidence that Ekdahl was married, and doubted he was the marrying kind. So whose clothes were these?

There was nothing left to do but to inspect the crude bedding. No mystery writer or Hollywood script doctor would admit it, but it was amazing what cops found hidden in pillows and between the sheets. Not just rubbers, which were plentiful, and weapons, which were legion—everything from zip guns to Uzis, from pocketknives to stilettos—but

other equally useful stuff like books, newspapers, cash, checks, bank re-
ceipts (some people apparently loved counting their money in bed), and
foodstuffs, which ranged from simple crumbs, bread crusts and cheese
rinds to entire cans of noodle soup.

So he was only half surprised when he came upon a small metal key
wedged into the straw, half-recessed and nearly invisible. Gingerly, he left
the solar luster of the bedroom and made his way back to the living
room. His eyes were adjusting once more to the changed conditions, and
so he felt for the ridges of the key like a blind man, trying to match them
up with the cabinet's lock. After fumbling for a while, he slipped the key
in; it fit perfectly. With a slight tug, he pulled open the double doors.

By the light streaming from the open bedroom door he could see that
the interior contained a large television set of European manufacture. A
remote-control device lay next to it. Beneath was a single drawer. He slid
it open and found a large manila envelope that, upon his opening it,
proved to contain a catalogue and a videotape. Sitting on the floor, he
flipped the catalogue open at random. The headline caught his eye.

AMAZING MICROVIDEO!

Just when you thought you've seen it all! Here's your chance to get
an inside look at a hot, wet pussy! This amazing new medical probe
places you right smack dab in the middle of a vagina! Imagine wit-
nessing massive ejaculations from loaded, throbbing dicks—they'll
be shooting right at you! Be a part of the woman's convulsive,
creamy orgasm. You even get to look the camera man right in the
eye! This is like nothing you've ever seen before. Your swollen dick
will be pounding with pleasure & you will be getting off fast and
hard! 120 mins $29.95.

None of the merchandise on offer was to be purchased by minors
under the age of eighteen, read a warning on the cover. But for discrimi-
nating adults, the list of available titles included *Up My Ass, Down My
Throat; Tiny-Titted Transsexuals; Lesbian Russian Teenagers; Tongue My Tool; Girls
Who Take It Up the Ass; Guys Who Eat Pussy & Suck Cock, Too; Lactating Hermaphrodites;* and *She-Males Who Eat Cum.*

Inside, there were pictures of girls with impossibly huge breasts, so big they looked like a pair of dirigibles grafted onto the woman's chest. There was their male equivalent, Long Dan Silver, a man whose phallus was so humongous Byrne wondered how he managed to get it into his pants, much less into a girl. There were men with two penises—Byrne could hardly believe this one, but there were the photos, plain as day—having sex with two women simultaneously. There was a whole series of videos devoted to Napoleon the Dwarf Man, a big-dicked midget who apparently had no problem getting girls to go down on him, although it was probably easier for him to go up on them.

But the weirdest thing was the transsexuals—she-males, he-shes, chicks with dicks. Some of them even had names: Suleika, who looked like an animated wax doll, and Sinead, who was depicted in the promo stills as having sex with a man and a woman at the same time. One picture showed him/her squirting milk from his/her small breasts while a man sucked his/her cock. Talk about being your own best friend. He wondered if the transsexuals could come. He wondered why, if they were half man and half woman, they dressed up like women, with hair and makeup just so. If their most important appendage seemed to be indisputably male, didn't that really make them men? And if so, why didn't they just put on a loose-fitting shirt and tie and go to work like everybody else? He wondered where they bought their clothes.

What did you give a she-male for Christmas? A jock? A bra? A lifetime subscription to *Tiny-Titted Transsexuals*? Byrne thanked the good Lord he didn't have to worry about that bit of social protocol. Dori was usually satisfied with some l'Air du Temps. He picked up the videotape, which was unmarked, and looked around in frustration for the VCR. It took him a few moments to figure out that it was part of the television set, cleverly incorporated into the design. You had to press a button and it emerged from its camouflaged hiding place in the base of the set like some science-fiction contraption.

The remote control was something NASA might use to launch the space shuttle; it had funny little buttons with those annoying pictographs that apparently made sense to everybody on planet Earth except Americans. Byrne found the TV's on button (miraculously, it came on), popped the tape in the player, heard a satisfying whir of machinery and sat down on the floor to watch as the screen flickered to life.

Chapter Thirteen
Midtown Manhattan
Friday, October 19, 1990; 10:00 P.M.

Ingrid was right: there was no sign in front of the Hunt Club, just a house number. The building was a typical Manhattan brownstone, indistinguishable from its fellows on the north side of the street. The buildings came in a couple of different colors—faded brown here, discolored gray there—and each was similar in size and shape and price; if there was anything here for less than two million dollars, Byrne would like to see it. The only thing that distinguished the building that housed the club from its neighbors was the steady stream of people going in and out. It looked like a crack house for white people.

And what white people. He had never seen so many beautiful women in his life. Eurotrash all—whether real or faux—they arrived in taxis and limos, skirts soaring as they exited the cabs; he half expected a helicopter to land and disgorge a new complement, fresh off the boat from cruising the Greek islands. Byrne wondered briefly how much the annual cost of their health club memberships and cocaine dependencies added up to. Probably the budget of a small country.

There was no sign of Ingrid. There were plenty of gorgeous blondes, even a few unescorted ones, but none tarried very long on the sidewalk. A supercilious doorman with a long ponytail and an earring in his left lobe gave them only a cursory glance and a surly nod as they whisked by in a puff of Nina Ricci glamour. The men were just as good-looking. Every one of them appeared to be a male model–cum–bodybuilder; Byrne wondered what they did for a living that permitted them twelve hours a day to work on their bods and another twelve hours to snort coke and get laid. Europeans just had more time and more money, he decided.

From his vantage across the street, Byrne had a ringside seat of the human comedy. Dispassionately, he despised these people. They weren't real New Yorkers; hell, they weren't even real Americans. They all had funny faces and funnier accents and bank accounts in funny currencies whose notes had different colors and came in different sizes and whose coins were too damn heavy. They lived in co-ops and condos and they never rode the subway; to them, New York was the hundred and fifty blocks of Manhattan south of Ninety-sixth Street, the Midtown Tunnel, the Long Island Expressway, the Van Wyck, Kennedy Airport and the Hamptons. The city's other seven million people were faceless nonentities; Brooklyn, aside from the Heights, was terra incognita; Queens was a mysterious land of middle-class minorities; the Bronx was a war zone; and Staten Island was part of New Jersey, wherever that was.

That wasn't his New York. Byrne's city was a nocturnal land of cops versus bad guys who came in all shapes, sizes and colors. His New York was a city where South American drug gangs emptied whole houses in Queens, and cut the throats of sleeping infants and raped the women after they were dead. His New York was black twenty-eight-year-old grandmothers tied up by muggers in their living rooms and set on fire in front of three little children who didn't bother to tell the neighbors until they got hungry. His New York was teenage Hispanic live-in lovers who got tired of hearing their babies cry and chopped them up with machetes and fed them to the family dog. His New York was fat guineas waking up dead in the trunks of cars, Irish punks who stuck knives in little old ladies for their Social Security checks. His New York was a never-ending riot of spear chuckers, jungle bunnies, slopes, gooks, chinks, japs, harps, micks, griks, dagos, greaseballs, goombahs, ginzos, krauts, heinies, frogs, sheenies, hebes, kikes, spics, ricans, doms, sheep-suckers, chicken-fuckers and various other wiseguys, scumbags, scungilis and lowlifes. His poor, tortured city that he loved so much—so much more than these awful people did. For a moment, he felt in the mood for a spontaneous drug bust, just to remind them where they were: in his town and on his turf.

He snapped to attention at the sight of Ingrid standing across the street, looking straight at him. Byrne jaywalked over to her. In the evening, away from the office, she looked much younger.

"Hi," he said.

"Hello, Lieutenant," she said. "Thank you for coming."

"No problem."

She took him by the arm. "Would you like to go in?" she asked. "I think even with those clothes they might admit us."

They swept past the doorman, who gave Byrne a distinct frown of disapproval but backed off when he spied Ingrid. Byrne knew his mismatched dark-green blazer, blue slacks and brown shoes—brown shoes, Jesus!—positively screamed *off-duty cop*, but he didn't care because he was inside, deep in the heart of the Other New York.

Well, at least it wasn't the Happy Land Social Club. The place looked more like a private home than a club, a preferred residence whose owners had suddenly been called away on business to Paris or Milan or Athens.

" . . . want to drink?" Ingrid was asking.

"Hmmm?" he said.

"I said, what do you want to drink?" she repeated.

"I'm on duty."

"Lieutenant, you're on duty precisely as long as it takes for me to give you the file you requested. After that, you're off."

"And just where is this famous file?"

"Do you think I'd carry it with me?"

"Why not?"

"Because where would I put it?"

She had a point there. Ingrid was wearing a black shift, her blonde hair falling naturally on either side of her symmetrical, aquiline face. She was not wearing a bra, and Byrne wasn't entirely sure she was wearing underpants; there was certainly no panty line visible when he admired her behind as they walked up the stairs to the second floor. Her legs were bare in the warm weather, and cleanly shaven. She was carrying a small black silk handbag. No place to hide a file.

"I don't know," he replied. "I'd have to frisk you." Her nose was a little too big, he concluded after studying her long and hard for any defects, but otherwise no problem.

She gave him a look and ordered him a Johnny Walker Black, neat, and a vodka orange for herself.

"How'd you guess my tipple?" he inquired as he drained his glass.

"Your reputation precedes you." She laughed appealingly.

Before Byrne could say anything, she took him by the hand and led him up another flight of stairs. "Let's dance," she ordered.

"No, thanks," he declined. "I'm just a heading-for-middle-age white guy trying to wait out rap music until it goes the way of disco."

But Ingrid was not taking no for an answer. "I told you to bring your dancing shoes," she insisted. "You know what they say: girls just want to have fun."

The third floor was the dance floor. At least it was dark, had a hard-wood floor, and there were loud, pounding noises being played over an invisible sound system. After a moment, Byrne began to make out the words.

"Bitch! Muthafucka!"

"BITCH! Muthafucka!"

"BITCH! MUTHAFUCKA!"

"Nice lyrics," said Byrne as they swung out onto the crowded dance floor. "Noel Coward must be pissing his pants." But Ingrid didn't seem to hear him. Knowing he looked ridiculous, Byrne started to dance, but after just a few minutes he began to run out of breath. That was the trouble with the damn music today, he thought as the room started to swim. In his day, no self-respecting song except "Hey Jude" lasted more than three minutes; now these extended versions went on for ten or fifteen minutes at a time, and then segued immediately into another, inter-changeable, mechanical-rhythm-sectioned song. No wonder these people spent all day in health clubs, just so they could be in shape to dance at night. Or maybe it was vice versa.

" . . . music?" shouted Ingrid.

"What?" said Byrne, as loudly as he could.

"I said, do you like the music?"

Byrne pulled Ingrid close to him. "No," he hollered between breaths. "I hate it."

Ingrid was so close she was practically biting his ear. "You're not old enough to be so square." She laughed.

"I'm older than I was when I came in here," he said, as she swirled away.

Byrne may have been sucking wind, but Ingrid was gliding smoothly and sexily across the floor. Byrne had always thought Europeans lacked rhythm, and certainly Ingrid for all her charms couldn't hold a candle to some of the boogie girls Sy had introduced him to uptown, but he had to admit that for a white babe she handled herself dance-wise rather well. He also noticed that while Ingrid was beautiful, she would have to share the title of best-looking woman on the dance floor with at least ten other women. This must be where models go between shoots, he thought as yet another twenty-two-year-old goddess slid past him. He knew he was as invisible to them as the planet Pluto.

Ingrid was back, bumping her tush against his; that, apparently, was what the lyrics demanded they do, not that he could understand them. She bumped, stepped away, circled him with a smile, then bumped again. He found himself enjoying the experience, and wished he had been a little more diligent in getting back to the gym. Tomorrow, he promised himself; those kids in unlaced sneakers got younger and faster every year.

Byrne was holding on, waiting for the bell or the towel, when there was a break in the music and Ingrid took him by the hand and maneuvered him to a seat in the far corner. After the heat of the dance floor, it was welcomingly cool.

"Another drink?" she asked.

"Not right now," gasped Byrne, but she was already gone—how did she move so damn fast?—across the room, shouting at the bartender over the din. And then she was back, nestling against him in the dark nook. Suddenly, a feeling of intense animal well-being flooded over Byrne. His other weakness was coming to the fore.

She saw his guard drop. "Can I ask you a question?" She looked at him, and even in the dark he could feel the penetrating blue of her eyes. "You don't have to answer if you don't want to."

"Shoot."

"How did you get this case? Egil's, I mean. They found his body upstate, so why aren't the police there handling it?"

"Ordinarily they would, but when the victim is a city resident and a diplomat at that, they usually ask us for help."

"And you're only too happy to oblige."

"Of course," said Byrne. "We aim to please."

"I'll be the judge of that," she said, and fell silent. You could hardly hear over the music, anyway.

"Did you ever go out with him?" Byrne asked during a brief lull in the entertainment.

"Yes. Egil was a very nice man, Lieutenant. We all liked him a lot."

"Did you sleep with him?" His boldness surprised even him. "I've heard that in Europe, if a girl likes a man, she sleeps with him."

"So they say," she replied. "But that doesn't mean we're all sex-crazed sluts. It's just that we're not as hung up about sex as you Americans are."

"What about AIDS?" asked Byrne.

"What about it?" Ingrid seemed puzzled.

"Don't you worry?"

"Not very often. First of all, I don't sleep with that many guys. Second, there are such things as condoms. And third, I'm not really into Haitians, Africans, American blacks, Puerto Ricans, gays or inner-city bisexual IV drug users. Look around. Do you see any of them here?"

Byrne had to admit that, as far as he could tell, he didn't.

"There aren't any, that's why. And we don't want them." Ingrid was warming to the subject now, her eyes flashing even in the dark. "We have our own world here, and we don't want any part of yours. That's what killed Egil, Lieutenant. Your world."

Her sudden vehemence took him by surprise. "Call me Frankie. As long as I'm off duty."

She was looking right at him now. "Frankie," she said, "do you know a single heterosexual white person who's contracted AIDS other than through a blood transfusion?"

Byrne had to admit he didn't. He didn't even know any transfusion cases. "But I've read about them," he replied lamely.

"And I've read about Elvis sightings at the Burger King in Butte, Montana." She paused. "I'm not saying you shouldn't be careful, women even more than men. But Jesus Christ, you can't go through life . . ." He lost the rest of her words over George Michael.

The music was again too loud for conversation; besides, the talk about AIDS had spoiled the mood. Not that he had really contemplated cheating on Doreen, but you never really had to cross Temptation Bridge until you came to it. Ingrid had pulled away from him a little and was lost in her thoughts. He wondered if she daydreamed in Danish. He wished he could say something in her language, just to catch her by surprise, but then realized in this din, no matter what he said would either emerge unintelligible or come out something like "Please hold my cheese sandwich, I've just been struck by lightning."

"Do you want to go downstairs?" he asked. "It's quieter there and we can talk."

"Why not?" she said. Obviously, he had flunked his dancing test.

They got up to leave. A husky man with bad skin and a dark complexion spotted Ingrid as she rose and rushed over. She greeted him coolly and they began to jabber in German or Danish, Byrne couldn't tell which. The big guy sounded pissed off.

"Frankie, this is Gunther." She pronounced it something like *Goon-ter*.

"Hi," said Byrne, extending his hand.

The big man ignored it. "Hallo," Gunther said, without looking at him, and then relaunched his monologue. Byrne took the opportunity to size him up.

He smelled like a skunk. Jeez, if these Euros thought they were so sophisticated, why the hell couldn't they get a little propinquity to a bar of soap or some deodorant? He heard somewhere that many European girls didn't shave their armpits or their legs. Legs, maybe, but pits . . . if there was ever anything that got a guy to half-mast asap, it was a pair of hairy pits. Surely in a thousand years of civilization they had mastered the use of the razor by now.

The man was big, standing at least two inches taller than Byrne and outweighing him by, he guessed, fifty pounds. Gunther wore his brown hair short except for a rat's tail that snaked down from the back of his head. He wore a tan sport coat with yellow checks, purple slacks, white socks and sandals. And Ingrid had the gall to make a crack about his wardrobe. No kid in Byrne's old neighborhood would have lasted two minutes on the street with clothes or a haircut like that.

Ingrid kissed the big man good-bye on his forehead and took Byrne's hand as they headed for the stairs. "Gunther is a film producer from Munich," she was saying as they went down. He could hear her now. "He works at Bavaria Studios."

"What language were you speaking? Was that German?"

"Yes. Nobody speaks Danish except another Dane."

"Why did you learn German?"

She stopped on a stair and turned back to look at him. "When you live in Denmark," Ingrid said, "you learn German in self-defense."

Byrne changed the subject as they began walking again. "Have you ever been in the movies?" he asked. "You're pretty enough."

"Thank you but I'm not; my nose is too big. I did do some acting when I was younger."

Byrne wondered just how old she thought she was. That was the problem with being with someone in her twenties; she thought last year was ancient history, and five years ago was before Christ. The next thing you

knew, she'd be talking about her high-school boyfriend, and what a trau-
matic experience it was when they broke up.

They were back at the second-floor bar. Byrne noticed that the pre-
vailing motif was that of the chase. There were murals of fox hunts, wild-
boar hunts, bear hunts; one whole wall was given over to a depiction of
the Rape of the Sabines. The human comedy again: kill or be killed, eat
or be eaten, molest or be molested. Social Darwinism at its finest. He
looked at Ingrid, ordering another round of drinks, and wondered who
was doing the chasing here.

They were face to face at the bar. "Who is Edwin Paine?" he asked, as
casually as he could.

"That was a name Egil sometimes used privately," she answered without hesitation.

"Why didn't you tell me that when I called yesterday?" He was sure it
was she with whom he had spoken on the telephone.

"How was I to know who you were?" she asked. "Anybody can call up
and say he's a cop. Anyway, Egil liked being mysterious sometimes.
Maybe he thought he was a secret agent or something." She laughed and
moved closer, elevating his pulse rate even higher than her dancing had.

"But why 'Paine'?" he pursued. "Or maybe it was really 'Pain,' as in
hurt?"

She spoke to him as if to a small, not very bright child. "No," she said,
"it was Paine as in Tom Paine. Don't you even read your own history
books?"

"Not since Sister Mary Veronica ditched her wimple, came out of the
closet and joined a lesbian commune in Tampa," said Byrne. "But that
still doesn't tell me why he used it."

"Did you ever try to make restaurant reservations under the name of
Egil Ekdahl?" she said, and he had to admit she had a point. "Besides, I
suppose he felt it was more diplomatic, no pun intended, to use another
name when he was on one of his pub-crawling expeditions."

"Is that what you call them?" said Byrne. "Did you know that he gave
as his address an S&M club in the meat-packing district?"

"Have you been over there yet to find out why?"

"It's next on my to-do list," said Byrne. "As a matter of fact, it was a
choice of this or the Rambone on my social schedule tonight."

"You don't look like that kind of boy to me," said Ingrid. He wondered how she knew—and how much she knew—about the Rambone.

"But I did go over to Ekdahl's apartment this afternoon, and what do you think I found?"

"I give up," she said. "Furniture?"

On a hunch, he showed her the photograph. "This." It was only a white lie.

"She's pretty," she said, pointing to his mother's companion. "Who are they?"

Strike two. "That's what I was hoping you could tell me."

Ingrid shrugged and looked idly around the room. "Guess what else?" asked Byrne. "A bunch of your clothes. And not much else. What's with that place, anyway?"

"Poor Frankie," she said, and reached across the table to pat his hand. "You don't have the slightest idea what you're talking about, do you?" He was about to ask her what she meant, but she had already risen. "Would you excuse me for a moment? I have to pee." She smiled and, quickly, kissed him on the cheek.

These Euros, scoffed Byrne after she had left. "I have to pee." No American girl would talk like that. Didn't they have any sense of decorum?

Someone tapped him on the shoulder. Byrne turned to his right and found a young woman staring at his feet. Was it his imagination, or did there seem to be an unusually high ratio of women to men in the place? Not that he was complaining. "Excuse me," she said, "but do you realize what a dork you look like in those shoes?" She laughed and addressed her friends. "We're going to have to find a new place, guys," she said as they cracked up. "But if you bring the coke," she breathed in his ear, "you can park your footwear under my bed anytime." Byrne smiled and tried not to let his embarrassment show.

Now a voice was booming in his left ear: "You're doing great with the ladies tonight, my friend," Byrne thought it said. It belonged to Gunther. Goon-ter.

"What?" said Byrne, turning to face him.

"I said you're doing great with my lady tonight."

"Pardon?" said Byrne, but the big German had already shoved him. Byrne was glad that, just in case, he had his shield and his piece.

"I said," the man began, and pushed him again, harder this time. "Perhaps you have already forgotten what happened in Moscow." Byrne had no idea what the guy meant, although it was clear he had been drinking. He decided it was time to gain control of the situation; he'd had it with this Euro horseshit.

"I heard what you said, pal. Now I want to know what you mean."

Gunther hesitated at this display of intransigence on Byrne's part, which gave the cop the opportunity to drive a left into the big man's midsection. He followed with a right to the jaw, the blow doubled in force by the downward and forward motion of Gunther's head. Gunther straightened up and then sat down hard, his breath expelling in a single gush as he hit the floor. He was sitting there stunned, a small puddle of urine spreading under his pants, with Byrne standing over him, ready to bring the point of his shoe up hard under the man's chin should he try to get up, and half hoping he would, when Ingrid came back.

Jesus Christ, thought Byrne, she goes to the ladies' room and the next thing you know . . .

"It's all right," she said to the bouncer, who had come running. He was big enough for Byrne to cool off immediately, the tattoos on his exposed biceps rippling. Ingrid looked at Gunther on the floor and addressed Byrne. "Was he giving you a hard time, darling? He can be such a brute." She said something to Gunther in German and several people at the bar started to laugh. "Come on, big boy," she said, "take me home. This place is getting boring." The girl who had made fun of him, Byrne noticed, was now looking at him with new respect. Typical female, he thought: no matter how "liberated," they all still found male violence sexually exciting.

Expertly, Ingrid maneuvered Byrne down the stairs, out the door and onto the street. "What the hell was that all about?" Byrne asked as she hailed a cab.

"He's very jealous when he's drunk," she said, opening the door and climbing into the back seat. Definitely no panties. She gave the Pakistani driver an address on East Forty-seventh Street. "I told him you were my new boyfriend," she said, and slipped her hand into his. "And that you are much better in bed than he is.

"It's the first building on the right, the one with the awning," she told the cabbie as they turned off Second Avenue and onto her street. "Here." She threw a five spot into the front seat and opened her door. "Well, are you coming up?" By the light of the streetlamps, she looked very beautiful, even with her big nose. "It's waiting for you."

Chapter Fourteen
Midtown Manhattan
Friday, October 19, 1990; 11:00 P.M.

Byrne wasn't sure what he had been expecting, but even so he was surprised at how ordinary Ingrid's apartment was. He had imagined that the dwellings of single Scandinavian gals would be huge lofts furnished in chrome and glass or elegant East Side brownstone floor-throughs. But Ingrid's place was a normal third-floor walkup in a nondescript small brick building. The walls were painted a bland off-white, and the furniture was standard Conran's. Framed posters from the Whitney and the Met hung on the walls, and a few cheap Belgian Oriental rugs covered the floors. It was neat, clean and comfortable, but not homey. It looked like a motel.

"Nice place you got here," he said, perfunctorily.

She gave him a look. "No it isn't," she said. "It's a dump. Anyway, it's just temporary. And I'm hardly ever here." She kicked off her shoes and padded over to the liquor cabinet in her bare feet. "Take off your jacket," she commanded. "You look hot. Also ridiculous. Drink?" she inquired.

"Not right now, thanks," said Byrne, who'd already had enough. Everybody thought that because he was Irish he could drink, but he really wasn't as good at it as Mancuso and certainly not as good as Sheinberg.

"Sure?" She had a glass in one hand and the bottle in the other, and looked about to pour.

"Well, okay." He promised himself he'd sip it slowly.

"You don't have to just stand there, you know," Ingrid informed him. "Find a seat and sit in it."

Byrne took his whiskey and sat down on the sofa, where Ingrid joined him. They clinked glasses.

"No, you're not doing it right," she suddenly complained.

"Doing what right?"

"Toasting. Don't look away when you touch glasses. You have to look into the other person's eyes. Otherwise it's rude. Try again."

Once more they raised their glasses to each other. This time Byrne looked her right in the eye.

"You have lovely blue eyes," she said to him, beating him to it, and he looked away. "Don't be shy!" she said playfully and, setting her drink on the table, reached out and grasped his free hand. Her fingers stroked his palm. Byrne put his drink down.

"Look, Ingrid," began Byrne, "I know we're making progress fighting crime in New York City and soon even your old granny'll be taking midnight strolls in Central Park, but right now there's still bad guys to catch. I'm having a nice time, but you haven't given me the file and as much as I enjoy your company, I'm starting to lose my famous Irish patience, which immediately precedes me losing my famous Irish temper, which believe me is something you don't want to see."

"Ooooo," she mock-shivered. "I bet you're hot when you're mad," she said. "I bet you do really nasty things, like beat up suspects. I bet," she whispered, "you even beat your girlfriend sometimes, when you're having sex. And I bet she likes it, too."

"We're not here to talk about me," Byrne reminded her uneasily. "We're here to talk about your boyfriend Mr. Ekdahl."

"I didn't say he was my boyfriend," protested Ingrid.

"But you did sleep with him?" pursued Byrne.

"I didn't say that, either," she corrected. "Why don't you pay attention to the words I use?"

Byrne wasn't going to fight her about it. "Anyway, wasn't Ekdahl really queer?"

"What makes you think that?" she asked.

"Straight guys are not usually found giving out addresses of gay clubs as their primary residence."

"Frankie," she said, "sometimes young people like Egil come here from Europe and they go a little crazy in the big, bad city. He was only twenty-four, hardly old enough to drink in your country, and all of a sudden he's presented with all these, how do you call them, alternative lifestyle choices. Who are we to say whether he was gay or not? I don't think he knew himself. And now he'll never know, will he?"

"I guess not," said Byrne. "And my job is to find out why not."

"You know," she went on, "Egil had a real romantic streak. Apparently his father died, or abandoned him and his mother when he was small. Egil cared a great deal for his mother. He used to talk about her all the time. One of his dreams was to get her over here to join him."

"Speaking of whom," said Byrne, "where is his mother? We like to notify the family when possible."

"I don't know," said Ingrid. "Back in Denmark somewhere, I suppose."

"That ought to be in the file, right?" he said, finishing his drink and getting to his feet. "Which I'd be very grateful if you could give me now."

She sighed. "You're probably right," she said. "The only problem is, I don't have it yet."

"What kind of shit is this?" exploded Byrne, almost knocking over his glass. "What am I doing here then? What have I been doing the whole night, except making a fool of myself on the dance floor and having to punch out some kraut who thinks I'm drilling you. You're a fun date, but I think my mother's calling me and I have to go home now." He got up to leave.

"Wait." She was still sitting on the couch. "It's coming."

"What, it's got legs?"

"As a matter of fact, yes. So if you'll try to be a little less excitably Irish and wait a few minutes, you'll get all you need, I promise you. Now sit."

He sat, wondering what the hell was going on.

"Perhaps you'd like to ask me a few more questions while we're waiting." She leaned back, her hands in her lap, looking very proper.

"Then stop playing games with me and tell me something I don't already know," Byrne said. "Tell me why he used a false name! Tell me why he gave the Rambone Club as his address! Tell me why somebody cut off his dick and shoved a dildo up his ass! Tell me something about this man that will help me find his killer. Jesus, you people certainly are pretty damn casual about the death of a co-worker!"

If she felt ashamed of her lack of feeling, she didn't let it show. "We're not an emotional people, Lieutenant," said Ingrid. "That doesn't mean we don't experience pain."

"As in 'pain'?" he asked. "Or 'Paine'?"

She shrugged. "Maybe now I should tell you what he was like in bed. I can't answer all your questions, but I might be able to help a little."

"Start helping."

She paused, uneasily. "I told you he was nice," she began. "But in bed he could be not so nice. Sometimes he would get kind of rough." Her eyes flashed and she started breathing more deeply. "He had a problem, how you say, getting it up, and so he needed a little extra excitement."

Byrne looked at the attractive, poised, intelligent woman sitting across from him. Funny, she didn't look like a pervert. "What kind of excitement?" he asked. "Did he ever hit you?" he inquired.

"Only when I asked him to," she said.

That wasn't exactly the answer he had been expecting. "Why didn't you report him to Pilgersen?"

"Why? It was nobody's business but ours. After all, we're consenting adults. It's just that he made me a little nervous the way he used that, you know, thing."

"The dildo, you mean," he supplied. "Was it always the same one, or did he have a collection?"

"The same one. It was made of ebony." Byrne's mind raced back to the Ramapo field. "With a silver tip. He even had a pet name for it."

"Don't tell me," said Byrne. "Mother's Little Helper."

She didn't seem at all surprised that he knew. "It was his little joke," she said.

"Did he ever hurt you? With it?"

"You know how when you're making love sometimes things can get carried away."

"You people have a funny way of making love."

"Oh, don't be such a square," she said with exasperation. "Sometimes I find your Puritan morality absolutely intolerable." She stood up and went to the window.

"Look at this city!" she exclaimed. "Look at this country! The place is going to hell, and what do you Americans care about? You don't care that the streets are falling apart or that half the city isn't safe at any time of day or night, or that your schools suck and your kids are stupid and your health care system makes doctors rich and people sick. All you care about is who's fucking whom, and how. Well, fuck you!"

"Are you finished?" Byrne inquired politely. She glared at him from across the room, her chest heaving. "If you hate it here so much why don't you go back to Stockholm or wherever you came from?"

"You see what I mean?" she shouted in exasperation. "You don't even know where Stockholm is! It's in Sweden. Can you name one single place in Denmark?"

Byrne thought for a moment. "Oslo?" he finally said.

The tension broke, and Ingrid started to laugh. "God, you're stupid," she said, and sat down again. Affectionately, she ran her hand through Byrne's hair. "Oslo's in Norway. Where I'm originally from."

"I thought you were Danish," objected Byrne, confused.

"As if you could tell the difference," said Ingrid. "I was born in Norway, in a city called Drammen." She took a deep breath, filling out her dress spectacularly. "It's not a very big place by American standards, only about sixty thousand people, but for us that's a fairly sizable town. People in Drammen have an inferiority complex, though. The city is too close to Oslo, and so they think of themselves as second-best or, worse, irrelevant."

"I bet you never had that problem, Miss Bentsen," said Byrne.

"That's not my real name, you know." She was full of surprises tonight. "It's Kyrkjebø." It sounded like *Shushuba*, the way she said it. "My father came from a working-class family from one of the valleys. But he was smart and he was ambitious and so he was able to get an education and work his way, how you say, up the ladder."

"Doing what?" asked Byrne.

"He was, is, a doctor. He works twelve hours a day, seven days a week, and he'll probably keep on working that way until the day he dies." There was a trace of bitterness in her voice. "That's why my mother left him. To us, there are more important things in life than just getting money. But that's all you Americans ever think about, isn't it? Money, money, money." She folded her arms across her chest and frowned at him.

Byrne decided it was time to change the subject. "I repeat," he said, "if you dislike America and Americans so much, how come you stay?"

She leaned forward. "Because, despite everything, I like it here." Byrne felt her tongue flick briefly into his ear. "Even if it's lonely sometimes." Then her open mouth was upon him and her darting tongue was playing hide and seek with his, and his hands were all over her, grasping her ripe, braless breasts—they filled his hands as if scientifically calibrated to the exact dimensions of his grasp—and down the back of her backless dress, right to her hips and by God she really wasn't wearing any panties until all at once she straightened up and smoothed her skirt.

"Good evening, Mr. Pilgersen," she said.

Chapter Fifteen
Midtown Manhattan
Friday, October 19, 1990; 11:15 P.M.

Good evening, Ms. Bentsen. And to you, Lieutenant," said Pilgersen. "Ordinarily, I discourage my staff from fraternizing with the locals, but in this case I am forced to make an exception."

Byrne had no idea how the man had gotten into the apartment. He must have been here all along, watching the show. He disentangled himself from Ingrid's embrace and managed to straighten his tie.

"You look fine, Lieutenant," said Pilgersen. He was not smiling. "You as well, Miss Bentsen, as always. The reasons I have made an exception are twofold." As he got to his feet, Byrne was trying to decide whether the man was just foreign, or a pompous ass. "Reason number one is that Ms. Bentsen volunteered to act as the liaison between our government and the New York City Police Department." Byrne glanced over at Ingrid, but her face betrayed no emotion. Beneath the fabric of her dress, her nipples were erect. The consul caught him looking.

"I can assure you, Lieutenant Byrne," he said, "that her affection just now was reasonably sincere. She thinks you are, er, how do you say here, cute." He smiled and went on. "And reason number two"—Byrne was now sure he was a pompous ass—"is that the unfortunate demise of our Mr. Ekdahl is a matter of great interest and extreme delicacy and urgency." The consul general finally took a breath. "Extreme delicacy."

"I get the picture," said Byrne, impatiently.

"So let me say by way of preamble that this conversation we are having has never happened. Anything that I may say to you in the course of this evening I never said. Anything that I may show to you, I never showed you. Your police records will indicate that the consul general of Denmark was polite but for reasons of security unable to be very helpful in your investigation. Do I make myself clear?"

"What's the big deal?"

"In order to answer that question, I'm going to have to ask you to ac-company me to my office. Don't worry, it isn't far." He opened a door off the hallway—Byrne had thought it was bathroom or a closet—and the next thing he knew they were inside the darkened consulate. Now he knew why he hadn't heard Pilgersen come in: the man was already home.

Pilgersen switched on a light. "I expect you to keep this knowledge to yourself. But I have no worries on that score." They were in a small con-ference room; one wall was mirrored, and the other three were adorned with photos of scenic Denmark. Pilgersen indicated a chair and Byrne sat down. Ingrid had disappeared.

"I've asked Ingrid to retrieve Mr. Ekdahl's file," he began, "but I'm afraid you're going to be disappointed. It's very jejune."

"Pardon?" said Byrne.

"Jejune. Thin. Insubstantial. Intellectually unsatisfying. J-e-j-u-n-e. Some people mistakenly think it has something to do with youth, a mis-reading of *june* for the French *jeune*. Instead, it derives from the Latin word for 'fasting.' " He bounced his hands on his desk.

"Thanks for the vocabulary lesson," said Byrne.

"Usually the files on our staff associates are much more complete. In fact, Lieutenant Byrne, I am counting on you to help me add to this dossier."

"Mr. Pilgersen," said Byrne, "I'm happy to help you in any way I legally and ethically can, but frankly I've already wasted far too much time screwing around with you and Miss Congeniality. Once I get what I need, I'll be on my merry way, trying to find out who killed Ekdahl and to bring that man, woman or group of people to justice. That may sound naive and silly to you sophisticated Europeans, but that's the way we do it in America and the last time I looked, New York City was still part of the U S of A. Which means that, diplomatic immunity or no diplomatic immunity, you're in my sandbox now."

Pilgersen didn't seem to take his outburst personally. "Your crude playground metaphors and policeman's bravado don't interest me, Lieu-tenant," he retorted. "Believe me, I have at least as much interest in re-solving this affair as you do. We are looking at a situation that could be potentially very embarrassing to my government; my job is to ensure that no such embarrassment occurs, at least publicly. So you see we are on the same side, in the sense that it is to both our advantages to get to the bottom of this as quickly as possible. That's why I've asked you here tonight. I hope you will excuse the small episode in that appalling night spot, but it was a necessary diversion for security purposes. Thank you, Ingrid."

She placed a small folder on the desk. "I told you, there wasn't much," said Pilgersen, and looked at Ingrid as if she were somehow responsible. "But until an hour ago I didn't know why." He handed the file to Byrne. "Go ahead, open it."

The consul was right. A cable from the Danish Foreign Ministry to Pilgersen advising him of Ekdahl's appointment in New York. What appeared to be a brief curriculum vitae of Ekdahl, also written in Danish. Some papers and letters whose purpose he couldn't quite make out at first glance. Not much else. "Help me out here," requested Byrne.

"What do you want to know?"

"Full name."

"Lars Egil Ekdahl."

"Date of birth?"

"14 August 1966."

"Place of birth?"

"According to this, Fredericia, Denmark."

"Where is that, more or less?"

"Near Middelfart."

Byrne put down his notebook. "Come on," he said.

"That is the proper name of the place. We can't help it if you Anglo-Saxons find some of our words amusing. *Fart* in Danish comes from the word meaning 'to travel.' "

"It means to make headway, as in a railroad journey," offered Ingrid. "But quickly."

"I'm not Anglo-Saxon," said Byrne. "I'm Irish. Well, half. So where's this Fredericka . . . "

"Fredericia." Pilgersen spelled it.

"And Middelfart?"

"West of Copenhagen. Middelfart is on the island of Fyn; Fredericia is on the Jutland peninsula. Copenhagen itself is actually our eastern-most city; it's very close to Sweden. Look at a map sometime, Lieutenant."

"I promise I will, real soon," said Byrne earnestly. "But let's quit fart-ing around. What else is on his résumé?"

Ingrid giggled but her boss missed the pun. Pilgersen's sense of humor was so impaired he could almost be German. "Not much," said Pilgersen, studying the document as if he had never seen it before in his life. "There's a brief summation of his education and a recapitulation of his employment history. Nothing remarkable here, except for one thing."

"The suspense is killing me."

"The names of his parents."

"Which are?" It was like pulling teeth with these people.

Pilgersen flushed and hesitated. "The names you see here, Arne and Gunilla Ekdahl, are not important."

Byrne was tiring rapidly of the game. "And why not?" he asked.

"Because, as of late this afternoon, I have confirmed that they do not exist. Or, rather, that they no longer exist. Mr. and Mrs. Ekdahl were killed in an automobile accident in Cyprus two years ago. Along with, I should add, their daughter Dorothea and their sons Ole and Lars Egil. The whole family, it seems, was wiped out when their car collided with a vehicle being driven by an Egyptian businessman named Ali Mah-moud. Mr. Mahmoud was carrying a can of petrol in the boot of his car, and both vehicles burst into flames shortly after impact. Very little of the bodies was recoverable. I believe the mandibles were instrumental in making the identifications."

"So Ekdahl really isn't Ekdahl at all," said Byrne. "Just as he really isn't Paine, either. But if he wasn't Ekdahl and he wasn't Paine, then who the hell was he?"

"That's what we're all here to find out," said Pilgersen. "I assure you, I am as surprised as you are. Obviously he was posted to this mission under such deep cover that not even I was informed."

"Is that normal for a cultural attaché?" asked Byrne.

"I hardly think so."

"And thus it may be correct to suggest that Ekdahl was not a really a cultural attaché at all."

"One could certainly draw that conclusion." Pilgersen bit his lip. "We are in the realm of national security here," he said. "Surely, you are aware that all governments post intelligence people under diplomatic cover, usually in some innocuous post like the second secretary for trade. Mr.

Ekdahl's rather elevated security clearance did raise certain questions in my mind, but I have been a diplomat long enough to know not to ask any questions. Deniability is very important in my field."

"Mr. Pilgersen," said Byrne, "you told me the other day that Ekdahl spoke Russian."

"Among his other languages, yes," said the consul.

"Would it be possible, then, that he was sent here undercover to keep an eye on the Soviets? I can't imagine, no offense, that being a cultural attaché is such a big job. And I'm just guessing because I'm not up to date on your country's relationship with the USSR, but presumably you try to keep tabs on what the Russians are up to, if only in self-defense."

"That is correct," agreed Pilgersen. "Although you should not necessarily conclude that it was the Soviets who were his special object of interest. Not every nation views the world through the bipolar lenses of the United States. It could just as easily have been the Italians or the French or the Germans or other members of the European Community. There is considerable opposition in my country to some of the provisions of the treaty now being negotiated, and I would not be at all surprised if it were to be rejected when it comes to a vote a year or so hence. We take the EC negotiations very seriously; a unified Europe is not something that everyone holds as self-evidently good."

"I can't imagine why not," said Byrne, who couldn't have cared less. He was much more interested in the remaining few documents in the file. "What is this?" he asked

Pilgersen looked at the piece of paper he was indicating. "That," he said, "is what is ringing alarm bells in Copenhagen."

Byrne studied the document. It appeared to be a letter written, he supposed, in Danish on stationery whose letterhead read something like WENCO—WENETA HANDELSBOLAG, addressed to "Amerikanska Ambassador," and signed by somebody named Dir. Wenström. He copied the opening down in his notebook: De "Farliga" Organisationerna.

"I wonder if you might be so kind as to translate this for me and let me have a copy," said Byrne.

"I'm not sure I can do the latter," said Pilgersen, "for reasons that will soon be clear to you."

Byrne suddenly stood up, his cop's senses on alert. "What kind of

room is this?" he asked. "I mean, what goes on in here?" He caught Pilgersen and Ingrid looking at each other.

"It's a conference room," said Pilgersen.

Byrne was walking around now. His eyes scanned the corners of the
ceiling until he found what he was looking for. "It's much more than a
conference room, isn't it, Mr. Pilgersen?" Byrne reached down and un-
holstered his .38. With one smooth motion he brought it up to eye level
and trained it on the eye of the camera hidden in the smoke alarm. "I
wonder how long it takes the goon squad to get here," he said.

Ten seconds later the doors burst open and four men with semi-
automatic weapons came crashing through. Pilgersen rose and shouted
something at them in Danish.

"I've always wanted to see one of these," said Byrne, strolling around
the room with nonchalance. "I mean, I've read about them in novels and
seen them in the movies, but to be right here in a real one, geez, it's an
honor. Where is it, Mr. Pilgersen?"

"Down and to your right, Lieutenant."

Byrne found the recessed button near the bottom of the mirror and
pushed it. A large screen slid slowly toward the ceiling, revealing a rec-
tangular picture window that looked into the next room. That room was,
as Byrne had suspected, filled with electronic surveillance gear of all
kinds: tape recorders, video screens, loudspeakers, monitors, radios,
multichannel satellite television reception, the works. It looked like a
showroom at the KGB Wiz.

"Nice rig you got here," said Byrne. "Bet the ladies love it."

"I thought you might be impressed," said Pilgersen, and he flicked a
switch on a remote control that had suddenly materialized in his hand.
"And I think you'll find it very amusing as well." The monitors suddenly
came alive. On each, Ingrid was flicking her tongue in Byrne's ear and
kissing him.

"Aw, shit," said Byrne.

"Wait, it gets better," said Pilgersen.

On the screens, Ingrid slipped out of her black dress and, naked,
helped Byrne undress. Byrne couldn't help but admire her body even as
he wondered how the hell they managed that trick.

"It's called morphing, Lieutenant," said Pilgersen, answering his un-
spoken question. Byrne looked over at Ingrid but again her face betrayed

no emotion. "Instant computer morphing. It's the very latest thing. All
we need is one good full body shot of you and one facial close-up, and
by combining the elements of your image with preexisting digital stock
we can simulate any kind of action we want so vividly even your own
mother wouldn't know it wasn't really you. Imagine, for example, what
this bit would look like on the evening news."

"They can tell it's a fake."

"I don't think so. The opening footage of your ear and Ms. Bentsen's
tongue is very real, and after seeing that, who's going to question the rest
of the sequence? And even if they eventually did find out, your reputation would have been long since ruined. Furthermore, we can do anything we want. For example, if the previous film was a little too racy for
your straitlaced American television, we can fashion something more appropriate to the level of taste in this country and, I gather, your own personal predilections."

Again Ingrid's tongue flicked into Byrne's ear. But in this version he
drew back and slugged her, knocking her off the sofa.

Byrne jumped to his feet, his heart pounding.

"I think the lieutenant has seen enough, Ulf," said Pilgersen, and the
film stopped. "Art imitates life, Lieutenant. And that's not all. We can
have you saving small children from kidnappers, or we can have you dealing drugs on a street corner in the Bronx. We can have you heroically
pulling a young girl out of the river or raping a woman in her living
room. And everything can be downloaded onto a cheap videocassette
and sent directly to the local television stations and to your superiors.
Primitive peoples used to be afraid of the camera because they thought
it would steal their souls. Well, they were right. It just took a little while.
Vive le microchip. Long live the Japanese."

"What do you want?" asked Byrne.

"Your cooperation."

"Which means?"

"Which means you're working for us now. After all, the camera doesn't
lie. Isn't that right, Special Agent Byrne?"

"It sure is." The familiar voice came from behind Byrne and to his
left.

"Hey, Tom," he said, turning to look at his brother.

Chapter Sixteen
Midtown Manhattan
Friday, October 19, 1990; 11:30 P.M.

Jeez, I'm sorry about this, Frankie, but there really wasn't much choice," his brother was saying. "We've got a great big fucking problem on our hands and I'm afraid you're going to be part of the solution. Gimme your gun. I know how easily you lose that Irish temper of yours and I'd sure hate to end up like Joey Hanrahan."

Byrne set his .38 on the table gingerly. "Okay, Tommy," he said. "We'll play it your way, for now."

"Thanks, buddy." Tom Byrne put the pistol in the band of his trousers, lit a cigarette and inhaled deeply. "Just like old times, huh? Little Frankie, a day late and a dollar short." He looked around the room. "Everybody out except the consul general and Ingrid. And I mean now. Go home; the show's over." Quickly, the place emptied.

Special Agent Thomas A. Byrne of the Federal Bureau of Investigation took a drag on his Marlboro. "How d'you like my little honey over there? Nice piece of ass, huh?"

"Don't be so crude, Tommy," objected Byrne.

"Please, Agent Byrne," remonstrated Pilgersen. "May I remind you of our agreement."

"I'm havin' a little reunion with my kid brother," barked Tom. "So why don't you shut the fuck up and mind your own business or I'll have your lard ass transferred to Senegal and you can watch the jungle bunnies gobble up every blonde in the joint."

"Get to the point, Tom," said Byrne. "I haven't got all day."

"What's the matter, Doreen calling you?" his brother snapped. "I never did understand what you see in that little gook." He turned to Ingrid. "Did he tell you about Doreen? She's Frankie's cute little half-breed girlfriend. He likes 'em funny-looking, don't you, Frankie? What is she, a war baby love child that somebody left behind after a night of chitty-chitty bang-bang in a Saigon whorehouse?"

"You always were an asshole, Tom," said Byrne, who didn't care to hear Tom's opinion of Doreen.

"Well, looking at that little home movie we just saw, I wonder who's the asshole now?" Tom looked at Pilgersen. "Okay, fatso, tell my dear brother what this is all about."

Pilgersen rubbed his flippers together as he considered his remarks. "You see, Lieutenant," he began, "it seems that your charming brother also has a particular interest in the Ekdahl case, which somewhat parallels our own. It also seems that this incident has aroused interest at the upper levels of your government as well and Agent Byrne has been dispatched from Washington in order to—"

"I'll take it from here," snarled Tom. "Jeez, Frankie, some guys just can't seem to get to the point even if you put a gun to their heads." He trained Byrne's pistol on the consul for emphasis and encouragement. "Ekdahl and I were working together," said Tom. "I need to know who killed him tout de suite, and that's where you come in. You're the one with the local badge and the up-front authority, and so from now on consider me your shadow. Whither thou goest, so goeth I. You and me are partners."

"If you want my help, why not just ask?" said Byrne. "Why the charades?" He looked reproachfully at Ingrid.

"Insurance, Francisco, insurance. I know you and I haven't always seen eye to eye, and I know that you're not particularly likely to share information with me out of the goodness of your heart. So I needed to find a little encouragement for you. And that's where Ingrid came in. I'm sorry we couldn't have allowed your interrogation to go a little farther, but I didn't want you in too deep if you know what I mean. Blood may be thicker than water, but blackmail's thicker, and more reliable, than both of 'em."

Pilgersen opened his mouth. "You were right about Mr. Ekdahl's not being a normal cultural attaché. In fact, I must now confess that he wasn't a cultural attaché at all. I myself only learned the true nature of his mission today, and I will reveal some of its particulars to you with the understanding that nothing we say in here is to leave this room, or that videotape you just saw most assuredly will."

"Get on with it," barked Tom, impatiently.

"Very well, Agent Byrne, very well." Byrne marveled how the man could remain so unflustered; must be the diplomatic training. "Lieutenant, are you familiar with the Soviet concept of 'illegals'?"

"Can't say that I am," said Byrne.

"An illegal is a Soviet agent who appears to be a bona fide representative of another country's diplomatic corps, but who in fact is working for the Soviets—who in fact *is* a Soviet. In Moscow, the KGB has a whole program dedicated to producing and training illegals—it's a division of the First Chief Directorate known at Moscow Center as Directorate S or Illegal S—and their results have been, to say the least, impressive. Obviously, the amount of information such an agent is privy to, and the amount of disinformation he can disseminate, is considerable. It usually takes years after the agent is introduced into the country for him or her to work his way up the diplomatic hierarchy and into a position of authority, but the program's success rate has been substantial."

"And Ekdahl, or whoever he really was, was trying to find such a mole?" asked Byrne.

"In a manner of speaking," said Pilgersen. "The problem is, he also was one."

"Which is why he's dead," interjected Tom. "The question is, who greased him? Here I'm working with this guy on a sensitive operation, and it turns out that not only is he under cover but under double cover—he's a Soviet illegal pretending to be a Danish diplomat pretending to be an intelligence officer looking for Soviet illegals—and all of a sudden he turns up dead in some shitkicker's backyard."

"Looks to me like the prime suspects are sitting right here in this office," said Byrne. "Mr. Pilgersen? Ingrid? Or maybe the Russians found out his cover was blown and whacked him themselves?"

Pilgersen threw up his hands in mock horror. "My dear lieutenant!" he exclaimed. "Surely you don't mean to suggest . . . ? But I have something here to assuage your suspicions. This letter"—he waved the piece of paper that had caught Byrne's eye earlier—"may be of some significance. I have this evening received confirmation of its authenticity."

"You want to tell me now what it's all about?" demanded Byrne.

"Well, it's rather odd," said Pilgersen. "It dates from 1964, February

21, to be exact, and is postmarked Nässjö, Sweden. Roughly translated from the Swedish it says, 'Have you thought that our world is a great community of organizations.' Note there is no question mark at the end of that sentence. Further: 'There are a great number of idealistic organizations, there are professional organizations, there are political organizations, there are organizations within the business world, et cetera. Practically everyone in our world now belongs to one or several organizations. And the organizations have significant power in our world— one can well call them a third power in our world.' "

Tom Byrne rolled his eyes impatiently, but Pilgersen continued reading.

" 'What I want to show you, with the enclosed picture, is the clenched right hand, upright, slightly leaning toward the shoulder, the thumb at an angle over the fingers. It requires training, for the member, to execute this organization's sign.' "

"Sort of like the Green Hornet," cracked Tom.

Again, Pilgersen chose to ignore him. " 'I have seen this sign made, but I cannot recall where, as well as writing paper with this emblem. He wants to show with this sign, all is clear'—another way to translate this phrase, *allt är klart*, might be 'the job is finished'—'but help me now. If you can get hold of this organization, which has this sign, you have come to the solution to that terrible crime, which happened in November 1963, in your part of the world. I have traveled much, you can certainly search out this organization in our world, I wish you great success and sign, Wennström.' "

"The picture to which he refers, Lieutenant," said Pilgersen, "is that of Lee Harvey Oswald, giving the clenched-fist salute shortly after his arrest by the Dallas police." Pilgersen sat back, as if that explained everything.

His brother took over the explanation. "This particular document exists in only two places," he said. "One is CIA, to which it was forwarded by the ambassador and immediately classified as secret. The other is the KGB. CIA released the document in 1976 under the Freedom of Information Act—what a pain in the ass that thing is—but in a bowdlerized form, with various names blacked out for security reasons. This letter, as you can plainly see, has no such censor markings. Which leads to the conclusion that it could only have come from the KGB file."

"That doesn't necessarily follow," objected Byrne. "Wennström could have sent it to dozens of people."

"But he didn't," replied Tom. "CIA traced it six ways from Sunday, the way they did with all the nutball missives that flooded the Agency after the assassination. In March of '64 the Langley homeboys sent a memo to the Chief of Station, Western Europe, and told him that their files contained only one reference to anybody named Wennström, a Johan Artur Wennström who was sentenced to ten months in jail in Sweden for espionage. They also came up with three more folks with that surname in the Nässjö telephone book, as well as a listing for the Wenco-Weneta Trade Company, which exported household furnishings. At our behest, Swedish intelligence put Wennström's feet to the fire and got him to say where he sent the letter."

"So some Swedish meatball had a theory, so what?" asked Byrne.

"You're missing the point," said Tom. "It's not so much *what* he said, it's *that* he said it. And to whom he said it. And now, where what he said has popped up."

"We believe, your brother and I," interjected Pilgersen, "that what Mr. Ekdahl was trying to do was nothing less than to purvey the KGB file on Lee Harvey Oswald."

"Which up to now has been strictly the property of Dzerzhinsky Square," added Tom. "But this piece of paper tells us that the Oswald file really is on the loose. That's why I was working with Ekdahl, trying to make sure he really had it, or could get his hands on it, and of course to obtain it for our side. And now he's gone, and with him the secret of the file's whereabouts. That's why everyone's so hysterical."

"So you're telling me that not only was Ekdahl really a Russian agent, he was a *rogue* Russian agent?" asked Byrne. The case was getting more confusing by the minute. "If your theory is correct, it means that the file is missing and the Russkies will want it back as soon as they realize it's gone."

"Which means we'd better find it before they do," said Tom.

"What makes you think they haven't found it already?" asked Byrne. "Maybe that's why he's dead."

"Yes, but who are 'they'?" responded Tom. "We don't know for sure that it was the Russians. It could have been anybody to whom he was trying to peddle it. Which is where you come in, Frankie. Lead us to Ekdahl's killer and you'll lead us to the file. The thanks of a grateful nation will be yours." He glanced at Ingrid. "And maybe more."

"We need you, Lieutenant," pleaded Pilgersen.

"What do you mean 'we'?" Tom suddenly snapped. "I don't know about you, Frankie," said Tom, "but I've had just about enough from this guy." He leaned over toward his brother. "Plus you know what, I think he's maybe been getting a little piece of Ingrid on the side when I'm not looking. Whaddaya think?" Tom read the same suspicion in Byrne's eyes. "My sentiments exactly, brother," he said.

Pilgersen had no idea what he was talking about. "Excuse me?" he said, but those were his last words because Tom had pulled out his brother's .38 and shot him once, through the heart. Pilgersen fell heavily, his large body collapsing to the floor like an inflatable doll whose plug had just been pulled.

"Jesus Christ!" exclaimed Byrne, jumping to his feet. Tom put his hand on Byrne's shoulder and sat him back down again.

"New York's gettin' to be a tough town, ain't it, Frankie?" said Tom. "How come there's never a cop around when you need one?"

Byrne looked over at Ingrid, who was sitting silently. If she felt any emotion at the death of her boss, she did not show it. Byrne knew he ought to arrest his brother for murder right now, and her as an accessory, but how could he? He was unarmed, and Tom held the murder weapon, which unfortunately was his service revolver.

"Frankie, you sit tight for a minute. Don't worry, this room is soundproof. Nobody heard a thing. Ingrid, give me a hand."

Ingrid rose quickly and fetched a large plastic garbage bag, which she lay out beside the body. Tom rolled Pilgersen's heavy corpse onto it while she washed down the blood on the marble floor, and together they dragged the late consul general into the next room and shut the door.

"We'll come back for him later," said Tom. He turned to Byrne. "Here's your heater. It's done its job." Byrne slipped the still-warm pistol back into his ankle holster and stood up. "I don't know about you, Frankie, but all this violence has got me working up an appetite. What do you say to some dinner? I know a good Chink place up the street that's open all night. And spare me my Miranda rights until you've heard what I have to say, okay?"

Chapter Seventeen
Midtown Manhattan
Friday, October 19, 1990; midnight

Byrne, his brother and Ingrid walked in silence up Second Avenue. They found the Ye Kwan Wok near the corner of Fifty-fifth Street and settled into a booth. The joint was practically deserted, which suited Tom Byrne just fine.

"Look, Frankie," he said, "I know you're sore, and maybe you can run me in for homicide right now if you want to and maybe, given that it's your bullet in Pilgersen's black heart, you can't, but I'm relying on you to at least hear me out before you go doing anything rash. You've known me all your life, so you know I can be a liar and a bastard, but this time I'm telling the truth, and you're just going to have to believe me. Plus, Ingrid will back up everything I say. Right, darling?"

She nodded silently.

"The first thing you need to know is, Pilgersen was full of it. Sure, he was cordial, mannerly and well-spoken, but in every other way he was a thoroughly rotten and nasty individual. It was time for him to go."

"Anything to drink?" It was the Chinese waiter.

"Beers," said Tom. "T'sing Taos. And the usual, for three."

"T'ree T'sing Tao, usual," repeated the waiter, and vanished, scooping up the unwanted menus as he departed.

"Aren't the Danes going to be a little pissed off that you just unilaterally recalled their consul general?" asked Byrne.

"On the contrary," said his brother, "this operation has their complete approval. By taking out Pilgersen, we've just spared them a whole shitload of embarrassment, and I wouldn't be surprised if you and I are in line for a medal one of these days. Privately, of course."

"What do you mean, embarrassment?" asked Byrne.

"A lot of what Pilgersen said," began Tom, "was true. The Russkies do have a well-developed program of illegals, who penetrate the Western diplomatic corps. The one thing he forgot to mention was that he, Pilgersen, was the real illegal. You can imagine how much Copenhagen is enjoying that little revelation. And boy, did he do some damage. Whenever the Soviets needed something done discreetly, they came to Pilgersen. He was especially adept at finding safe houses for various new kids the Russians were importing, and he could provide them with covers, new identities, false passports, the works. Made our job of keeping tabs on the KGB reinforcements at the embassy in Washington and at the UN a real pain. As you saw, Pilgersen also was equipped to handle the most sensitive kinds of communications and blackmail operations. You were in good hands with Nils Pilgersen, and I'm ashamed to say that it took us years to catch on to the crafty son of a bitch. But who ever suspects a Dane?" Tom whistled softly in admiration.

"How did you finally nail him?" Byrne was curious.

"The Oswald thing," replied Tom. "Ekdahl led us to him. It's true, the file's on the loose and we're after it. But let me tell you who else is standing on line to get at it: us, by whom I mean various agencies of the U. S. government, not just the FBI; the Russians, who want it returned pronto, thank you very much; not to mention the Mob, to whom we understand it's already been offered; hell, maybe even Lady Bird Johnson. Round up all the folks who had something to gain by Kennedy's or Oswald's death—CIA, FBI, Naval Intelligence, the Cubans, the Mafia—and you can bet that each of them is pretty darn anxious to know what's in the KGB file. Which, of course, is why the Russians have been so chary about releasing any of it. They've got the ace in the hole, or at least they did until recently. And now they want it back, big time."

"I don't get it," objected Byrne. "Why kill Pilgersen? Wasn't he helping you on this one? And if he was dirty, why not try to double him and run him yourself?" Byrne looked over at Ingrid, whose face was a mask of indifference. "What if he killed Ekdahl? In that case, you've just shot your prime suspect. Besides, you're putting yourself at risk, Tom, and much as I'd love to run you in, I'd still like to know why you did it before I bust you. I'm going to have to explain this to Mom, you know."

"A number of reasons, Frankie," answered Tom. "Number one, as a service to the Danes. Number two, we can't let this knowledge about the file out; it's strictly need-to-know and Pilgersen obviously couldn't be trusted. And three was personal: I didn't like the way he put his hands on my girl. Anyway, Pilgersen had outlived his usefulness, which was to hook me up with you." He opened his briefcase and produced a videotape, and Byrne suddenly recalled the tape he had watched in Ekdahl's apartment; he still couldn't believe what he had seen. "Your little show," Tom said. "Because Pilgersen was right about one thing, and that was Ekdahl's pursuit of the Oswald file—the Nalim, in Russian. We couldn't take the chance that Pilgersen might actually beat us to it, in which case the file, all seven or eight fat volumes of it, would be back in Moscow so fast it'd make your head spin. And then where would we be?"

"So he killed Ekdahl," said Francis, "to retrieve the file for the Russians."

"I don't think so," said Tom. "We've had the late, great Mr. P. under twenty-four-hour surveillance for the past two weeks, ever since I came back from Moscow. Unfortunately, we did not have Ekdahl under same. He was my responsibility, and I blew it. Which is why this case has taken on a personal aspect as far as I'm concerned."

"So who the hell was this Ekdahl guy?" asked Byrne. "Was he a patriotic Dane, working undercover, who just happened to stumble onto the Oswald thing in the course of his investigation of Pilgersen, which is why the consul was trying to frame him as a Soviet illegal? Was he a Russian agent, doing his duty? Or was he free-lancing? If you were working with him, you ought to know."

"You're right," said Tom. "I ought to know. But I don't. And that's where Ingrid comes in. She knew him better than anyone. And if I were you, Frankie, I'd get her on my side to help you clear the case. Not that that should be too difficult—working with her, I mean." It occurred to Byrne that they were talking about her as if she were not there. "I'm rooting for you. Because if you don't clear this one, and pretty damn quick, this little video goes to the commissioner, Captain White, the TV stations and the *Times*, along with a note about what really happened to Joey Hanrahan." Tom's eyes were hard, as hard as his fists had been when they were young.

"Who's Joey Hanrahan?" asked Ingrid.

Hanrahan was a two-bit thug who hung around Tenth Avenue bars with remnants of the Westie gang. The Westies had essentially disappeared as a force in 1987 when Mickey Featherstone turned rat and sent

Jimmy Coonan to jail for life, but there were still plenty of punks in the neighborhood and Hanrahan was one of them. Mary Claire had just left him, after the business with Tom, and here he was, unable to believe that his marriage was over and that he was living by choice in Hell's Kitchen. So Byrne was in a black Irish mood when Hanrahan, fueled by liquor, rolled out of the shadows and into his path one night. "I don't like yer fookin' face," he said, throwing a punch that caught Byrne just below the right ear, temporarily stunning him. Reflexively, the detective drew his pistol and identified himself as a police officer, but Hanrahan was past caring, out of his mind, really, screaming obscenities into the night and howling at the moon with beery bravado. Byrne stood his ground as a succession of bottles whizzed by, but when he saw his assailant reaching into his pocket, he fired. It turned out that Hanrahan had been groping for a shiv, a homemade pig-sticker that he habitually carried, but it still looked bad, shooting a drunk, even if in self-defense, and Byrne, the hero of the Coloredo case, was quietly put on administrative leave until the fuss died down. "Never mind," said Byrne.

What the official inquiry showed, but which information thank God had been suppressed, was that there were two drunks that night, as Byrne's blood test so clearly showed. But Tom knew. Tom always knew. "I'm not kidding, pal," he said. "I'm exposed on this one as well. And if I go down, you go with me. Brothers in arms to the end."

"What do you mean, you're exposed?" asked Byrne, as if he didn't know.

"It's a long story, Frankie," he said. "Maybe later. Maybe never."

"How do I know I can trust you?" objected Byrne. "How do I know I can trust Ingrid? I mean, after this evening . . ."

"Oh, she's kosher, aren't you, babe?" said Tom, giving the woman's arm an affectionate squeeze. "My Danish princess."

"Yes, Lieutenant, I'm kosher." She answered him instead of Tom.

"So tonight was just an act?" he asked.

Tom spoke for her. "She did tell you she used to be an actress, didn't she?" he said, and gave her another nuzzle. This time Ingrid returned the gesture of affection, slipping her arm into his and hugging him close.

The waiter reappeared, bearing fried dumplings, hacked chicken with sesame sauce, some won ton soup and three T'sing Tao beers.

"I really wish you hadn't said those nasty things about Doreen," Byrne told Tom. "You wouldn't have the guts to say that to her face. She'd beat the crap out of you."

"You ought to know," said Tom.

"Is she really Vietnamese?" asked Ingrid.

"No, she's Japanese," answered Byrne. "Well, half-Japanese. Her mother was Japanese, and her father was an American serviceman. She never met him. She came to the U.S. when she was a teenager, to study."

"What's her name?" asked Ingrid. "I mean her full name."

"Doreen Grace Watanabe, but professionally she goes by Dori Grace. She's an art dealer."

"Purveyor of pretentious, expensive bullshit to the stars," said Tom with a snort. He quickly downed his beer and signaled for another. Like an auctioneer at Christie's, the waiter caught the hint of a hand movement and deduced its import immediately.

"I thought the Russians were pretty much clean on the Kennedy assassination," said Byrne, redirecting the conversation.

"That's what they wanted us to think," replied Tom. "But who really knows? That's why the file is potentially so explosive. What I do know is that if the Oswald file really is running around loose, then I've gotta have it. And God help anybody who gets in my way; I'd run over my own mother."

"He would, too," Byrne promised Ingrid. "They hate each other."

Ingrid reached across the table and took his hand. "Listen to your brother, Francis," she said. "This is serious."

"Damn right it is," agreed Tom. "You see, the Warren Commission concluded, among other things, that Oswald had had no dealings with the KGB during his years in the Soviet Union. The CIA claimed that he had never worked for them either, ditto the FBI. That's three secret or semisecret agencies, at least two of which have a guilty conscience and something to hide. By the way, do you know how old Oswald was when he died?"

Byrne didn't have the slightest idea, and said so.

"Twenty-four," said his brother. "Twenty-four, just like Ekdahl. Here he was, a hick kid from New Orleans, with a mother who lived most of her life just this side of Tobacco Road, who had one full brother and one half-brother, who never knew his father, who tried to join the Marine Corps when he was still underage, who defected to the Soviet Union, married a Russian girl and came back dragging dossiers three times the size of the Manhattan phone book from both Moscow and Washington; Jesus, you should see this guy's 201 over at Langley."

"So what?" asked Francis, who was bored by this ancient history. "Are you saying he did it or he didn't do it? Don't tell me you're one of those kooks who claims a firing squad emerged from the manholes at Dealey Plaza. Anyway, who cares who killed John F. Kennedy? He's just as dead, no matter who pulled the trigger."

"Look," said Tom, "Hoover was only too quick and happy to tell Johnson that Oswald was the guy. Except that LBJ never quite believed it. He went to his grave thinking the Russians or maybe the Cubans had whacked Kennedy, or at least had something to do with it. But what was his alternative? Start World War III? Far easier to blame it on a climate of right-wing hatred in Dallas, and on a lone nut, and hope that everybody forgets he was a Communist. Easier than going on television and telling the American people that their beloved young president had just been taken out on orders from Moscow. That would have made the Cuban Missile Crisis look like a day at the beach. Or maybe *On the Beach*."

"But who cares now?" asked Byrne. "The Soviet Union is liberalizing under Gorbachev; the Cold War is practically over."

"Maybe," said his brother. "Maybe, although you'll get an argument from CIA on that one; half the Company thinks the whole glasnost-perestroika movement is a commie plot. Anyway, let's not debate the assassination. The point is, the damn thing is still too hot to handle, and it's in everybody's best interest to make sure it stays deep-sixed. And I mean permanently."

"You mean," asked Byrne, "you want it, only to cover it up?"

"Damn right we do!" Tom seemed exasperated. "The thing is too explosive to see the light of day. Because no matter what's in it, somebody is going to look bad." Tom lit a cigarette; it didn't matter that they were sitting in the no-smoking section. "Let's go through the possibilities: One, Oswald was a CIA agent, rogue or otherwise. The Agency looks bad. Two, Oswald was a KGB agent. The CIA and the Soviets look bad, not to mention my own beloved FBI, which blew it big time. Three, none of the above, which means he either had no connections—not fucking likely for a kid with his résumé—or he was working with the Mafia.

Which makes the FBI really look dumb, especially since Special Agent Hosty was on Oswald's case well before November 23."

"And since Hoover always maintained that the Mafia didn't exist," observed Byrne. "Guess he never visited New York City."

"Unlike us," agreed Tom. "But thanks to my, er, impeccable connections within the consulate"—yet another squeeze, this one closer to a fondle—"the Federal Bureau of Investigation learned that Pilgersen had gotten the wind up and was preparing to implicate Ekdahl as the illegal to divert suspicion from himself. The way I see it, Pilgersen figured Ekdahl for a chump. Which is why he set up a meeting with the Mob. Or rather, set him up."

Orange-flavored beef, General Tang's chicken and some spicy shrimp in Szechuan sauce now made their appearance on the table, along with another round of beers.

"What meeting?" asked Byrne.

"Remember that homicide down in the Village a couple of days ago? The one in the coffee shop?"

"Vaguely. Wasn't mine."

"You ought to because you guys haven't cleared that one, and I know how much you hate it when a well-dressed white guy gets greased in front of a dozen witnesses and you can't even come up with a usual-suspects arrest. Well, lemme tell you, that got our attention down at the Bureau because the guy who got capped was one of ours."

"Why didn't you tell me?" exclaimed Byrne. "That never came out."

"No, and it never will, either," said Tom. "But it was a damn good man we lost in Marty Pavone."

"Why didn't you press NYPD for action?"

"Couldn't, Frankie. Pavone was undercover, and we couldn't afford to expose him, even posthumously, because the operation is ongoing."

"Genna?" Byrne asked his brother.

"You got it."

"But what's that got to do with Ekdahl?"

"Pilgersen knows that Ekdahl's got the file, so he confronts him, tells him he knows what he's up to, and offers to help him out in exchange for a piece of the action. Ekdahl has no choice but to pretend to cooperate, because he doesn't dare tip his hand. So Pilgersen sets him up with a Genna family thug named Rawlston."

"'Rawlston' doesn't sound very Italian to me."

"Oh, he is all right, a young hothead with impeccable family connections. 'John Rawlston' was the illegitimate son of Johnny Rosselli and his girlfriend, the one she conceived in late 1964 and gave up for adoption. The guy had a sense of humor, I guess, because he used his father's old alias. Even funnier, he used dad's real name, Filippo Sacco, as his own. Personally, I find such filial piety touching."

"That doesn't explain how you knew about the meeting to have your man Pavone there," objected Byrne.

"Because what Pilgersen and Genna didn't know was that Sacco was ours," said Tom. "Our man in the Ravenite Social Club. He never forgave the goombahs for murdering his father—they chopped Rosselli up, stuffed him inside an oil drum and dumped it in Dumfoundling Bay in Florida—and he's been hot for revenge ever since. Imagine our surprise, then, when the Ravenite wiretaps turned up some chatter about the Oswald file. So we wired Sacco, and sent Pavone downtown as a backup, just to keep an eye on things."

"But something went wrong," said Byrne.

"Tell me about it. Pavone tailed 'Rawlston' to this coffee shop in the Village. Witnesses said there were two men sitting together in a booth talking, and then one of them all of a sudden walks up to the counter and pops Pavone, who was sitting there having his breakfast. Didn't even have a chance to finish his omelette."

"What makes you so sure it was Ekdahl?"

"It was him all right: we have his voice on the tape. Ekdahl was negotiating with Rawlston when he got spooked by the tail, figured he was made, got up, smoked Pavone and disappeared out the door."

"If that's true," said Byrne, "then he was a much more formidable character than we thought. Did Rawlston know Pavone was a tail?"

"I don't think so. I was trying my best to protect him, because you hate to see an asset like him blown. But somebody blew him, bad, and then later they blew him away."

The light came on in Byrne's head. "You mean the rubout Wednesday afternoon on Carmine Street," said Byrne.

"One and the same. I lose my best mole, right after he meets with Ekdahl and then with the Teflon Don himself. Which can only mean that somebody fingered him. They cut him up but good, the way the Mob always does to a stoolie. They slit his throat from ear to ear."

"Which is the same thing that happened to Ekdahl," said Byrne.

"Yeah, you figure it out, Sherlock," said Tom. "If you ask me, the Mob took care of him too, the same day."

"Which means Genna might have the Oswald file?" asked Byrne.

"Not necessarily. I think Genna decided Ekdahl was more trouble than he was worth, and that was that. Unfortunately, Sacco's wire went dead halfway through the meeting at which he was killed, so we don't know for sure. But just look at the timing: it all fits."

"I wonder," said Byrne.

"Wonder all you want," said Tom, brushing aside his brother's skepticism. "It's one possible explanation for the events of the past fortnight. But it's plausible." He drummed his fingers on the tabletop. "It may even have the added advantage of being true. The point is, what have we got?" Tom continued. "Trouble, right here in Hudson River City."

"Let's forget about who killed Ekdahl for the moment," suggested Byrne. "Why are we so sure Pilgersen didn't already have the file?" He was starting to wish for the simplicity of a Bronx multiple.

"He didn't," replied Tom. "We've looked pretty carefully, and besides, Ingrid has been watching him. Not even any pillow talk, right?"

Ingrid was reading the remains of her sesame noodles as if they were chicken entrails.

"Then let's look at some alternative explanations," insisted Byrne. "The Mafia thing is certainly possible, but it's a little neat. Plus it doesn't explain who drove the car to Ramapo, why there weren't any traces of another vehicle, and how the bloodstains got all over the front seat. You know that I believe the fuck-up theory of human behavior is always much more plausible than conspiracy. What if the mess on Carmine Street has nothing to do with Ekdahl? It's not beyond the realm of possibility that Genna found out about Sacco and whacked him; it wouldn't be the first time you've failed to cover your assets. And let's suppose that, given Ekdahl's idea of sexual fun and games, it's equally possible that his death might just be what it looks like: an unrelated, and most likely gay, sex killing." He drained the last dregs of his beer. "Let's consider another possibility: the Russian mafia. Sy Sheinberg raised this one this morning. The body had a Soviet-style tattoo on the arm, and there were Cyrillic markings on the dildo, too. What if Ekdahl was somehow involved with the Russian mob, about whom we don't know shit? And finally, one more possibility: you killed him, Tommy. You've admitted you were working with him to get your hands on the file, and that you'd run over Mom to get it. Plus we've all just seen your penchant for violence."

"Runs in the family," muttered Tom.

"What if you killed Ekdahl, and are just blowing smoke up my ass about the Mob to cover your behind? Or to get me to help you get Genna? Or," Byrne went on, "let's look at Ingrid here. Have you ever seen a likelier suspect than her? A beautiful girl, having an affair with one brother, throwing herself at the other one. What if you're both lying to me and *she's* the real Soviet illegal? What if Pilgersen, knowing of your relationship, was blaming Ekdahl to you in order to keep her suspicions allayed until he could prove it? I mean, he wasn't exactly planning to get shot tonight, was he? What if you're both in this together?"

"You're full of what-ifs, aren't you?" said Tom.

"What-ifs, and what-abouts," said Byrne. "As in what about this?" He took the crumpled photograph he had found in Ekdahl's car from his wallet and put it on the table in front of his brother. "Explain that."

Tom studied the picture for only a moment and handed it back to Byrne. "It's Mom," he said, "years ago, when she was young. I don't know who the other gal is."

"That's your mother?" asked Ingrid incredulously. "You didn't tell me."

"A picture of our mother, which I found in Ekdahl's car," amplified Byrne. "In fact, it was the only thing I found in the car, except a lot of blood. Now what the hell would Ekdahl be doing with a picture of Irene Byrne?"

"Why don't you ask her?"

"I'm going to," said Byrne, although he had been hoping to avoid having to.

"Yeah, well, pal, I don't envy you," said Tom. "I'd rather go head to head with Genna than Irene any day. Let's get the check and get out of here. I've had enough excitement for one night." He leaned over and kissed Ingrid. "Almost."

"What I can't grasp right now," said Byrne, "is this: Is Ekdahl the good guy or the bad guy? Is he a sinner or a saint?"

Tom got up. "Sometimes even bad people can be agents of goodness," he said. "Or maybe he's just human, like the rest of us, capable of good and evil on the same day, sometimes even before breakfast. Take it from me, Ekdahl was no angel. But as of today, what we both care about, and we're both looking for, is what, not who, really killed Ekdahl: the file."

Byrne shook his head. "Maybe, Tom, but I still have to find out who because that's what I get paid for. I don't give a rat's ass about Oswald, the CIA, the KGB or the FBI. And now I got another homicide on my hands, one to which I am a material witness, and in which I, alas, am also implicated, thanks to you. So what's to prevent me from taking you downtown and making you sing? The way I see it, I kill two birds with one stone: at some embarrassment to myself, I solve the Pilgersen murder, get a leg up on the Ekdahl case, and get rid of you, all in one fell swoop. I mean, what would you do if you were me?"

In response, Tom held out his wrists. "It's 'if you were I,' Frankie," he corrected. "Cuff me, Lieutenant, if you like, although I wouldn't forget that video if I were you. It's pretty easy for Ingrid to hail a taxi to Kennedy and be gone tomorrow if she feels like it, and you could spend a lot of time in the can with me while they look for her body. Or you can use your head and get with the program."

Byrne found himself admiring his brother's grammar; he was, after all, a Harvard man, although much of the time you'd never know it. He yawned. "I'd better get some sleep if I'm ever going to figure this out."

"Everything all right? Dessert, coffee, everything all right?" It was the waiter, who had materialized. "Coffee, dessert?"

"No, thanks," said Tom Byrne.

"Coffee, dessert?" repeated the waiter, expectantly.

"The check, Wong," said Tom sternly, and Wong toddled off. "And I'd better go to the john before I take a leak on the floor. Pay up, will you? Here's my share." He slapped some money down on the table. It was an unusual gesture, coming from his brother. Tom must be feeling expansive, thought Byrne. He must be expecting to get laid.

"Are you staying with Doreen tonight?" Ingrid asked Byrne after Tom had left.

"No." He didn't feel like going into details. "I'm at my own place on Tenth Avenue."

"Is she pretty?"

"I think so."

"What does Tom think?"

"I try to keep her as far away from Tom as possible." That was one way to look at it.

"Why? Did he make a pass at her?" She stared at him. "I bet he did."

Byrne chose not to answer, turning his attention to the waiter instead. "Keep the change," he said.

Ingrid dropped her voice and leaned toward him. "Tom will be back any minute, so we have to hurry," she said urgently. "Very little of what your brother just told you about Mr. Pilgersen is true." She pronounced the words as if it were the most self-evident statement ever made. "And if you want to know more, you'd better make plans to see me again soon."

"What? What did you say?" asked Byrne.

"Yeah, what did she say?" echoed Tom, returning.

"I said he's invited. Doreen too."

"To what?" asked Tom.

"To my birthday party at the Germans' tomorrow night. Or have you forgotten already? I don't suppose Jacob and Ella will mind if we invite two more."

"Maybe their chef will," said Tom, turning to his brother. "Did you pay yet?"

"Yeah," said Byrne. "I've paid."

They stood together on the sidewalk in front of the restaurant. "Need a lift?" Ingrid asked him. He wondered where they might be going. Back to her place, no doubt, to dispose of the mouldering corpse of her late boss. "No, thanks," he replied. "I can walk." A yellow cab, one of the last of the city's Checkers, pulled over to the curb.

"Don't get mugged," said Tom, slapping Francis on the shoulder. "Keep me posted, buddy," he said.

"Good night, Francis," said Ingrid, over her shoulder, as the taxi door slammed shut. She looked just as fetching climbing into a cab as she did bending over a filing cabinet.

Chapter Eighteen
Moscow
Friday, October 5, 1990; 11:00 P.M.

The rooster clock in the Mezhdunarodnaya Hotel was crowing twenty-three when Zlata and Natasha arrived. The kitschy timepiece stood in the lobby of the faux Hyatt near the banks of the Moskva River, built by Armand Hammer to accommodate the business traveler to his beloved Soviet Union. There really was nowhere else to go. The glorious old National, opposite Red Square, had become Georgian Mafia Central; the unspeakable Inturist, just up Gorky Street, was a high-rise firetrap with the ugliest whores in Moscow. The Metropole was closed for renovations; ditto the Berlin. Everything else—the hideous Belgrade, for example, just across from the Soviet Foreign Ministry—was an eldritch horror.

There is an unmistakable odor about socialist countries that pervades every public place. It is a strong animal smell, composed in equal parts of sweat and unwashed clothes, Russian cigarettes, cheap perfume, piss, disinfectant, and leaded gasoline; in the heyday of Communism, every socialist country smelled the same. But in the mother church of Marxism-Leninism, the reek was stronger, sharper, more pervasive. It was the ur-stench of the Soviet system, the stink of a dying animal, and with each passing year it got stronger and more difficult for foreigners, even fellow travelers from the West, to ignore. To Zlata and Natasha, however, it was simply part of the background; they would have noticed it only by its absence. Olfactorily innocent, they alighted from a gypsy cab, which stopped about twenty yards from the hotel's front door to let them out.

Although the Mezh was technically off limits to Soviet citizens, this regulation, like all regulations in the Soviet Union, was subject to spot interpretation, which could always be aided by a small pourboire to the toughs who manned the single open entryway. Clustered around the entrance as well on this Friday evening in early October were a dozen or so hoods in black leather jackets, free-lance drivers who would take you home for dollars or a pack of cigarettes. This, of course, was also illegal, but since few authorized cabs ever pulled up in front of the Mezh, the black, or free, market had taken over to provide the service. Like the odor, the cabs were another metaphor for the declining Soviet Union. In theory, everyone could afford to take a cab, so ridiculously low were the rates. (The famous Metro was even cheaper—five kopecks a ride.) But no one in his right mind would drive a cab for such a pittance, especially when one could cop some *valuta*— real money—driving on the black market. *Valuta* was almost always defined as dollars, less often as marks or pounds, or cigarettes, with Marlboros by far the preferred brand of choice. Everybody was hustling, trying to make a buck these days—not a ruble, which was worthless, but a real American greenback. With rubles, you could buy nothing. With dollars, you could buy whatever the black market had to sell—clothes, of course, and good food and drink, but also cars and even whole apartments. The Soviet Union was now a Communist country in name only; down below the official level, the populace was furiously engaging in consensual capitalism.

The two girls strolled across the thin carpet that overlay the hard concrete floor. The bar where they were to meet with Alik was off to the right, past the Sakura Japanese restaurant, where the fish was flown in fresh daily from Tokyo and the prices reflected it. Zlata was wearing an orange chiffon blouse with a matching skirt and spike heels. Her long blonde hair was curled and fluffed, and she was wearing a little too much makeup. But it was dark inside the Bar Fortuna, and sometimes a girl needed a little help when her complexion wasn't cooperating. Natasha, by contrast, needed no enhancement. She had washed at home and donned a simple shift that clung arrestingly to her curves. Her straight hair was piled up on her head and held by an arrangement of invisible bobby pins. On her feet she wore flats. Together with Zlata, she passed through the beaded entryway and into the nearly pitch blackness of the lounge.

Most of their neighbors in their block of flats assumed they were hookers. True, neither Zlata Shevchenko nor Natasha Goldsteyn worked, but that was not necessarily proof that they were whores. In the Soviet Union, you only pretended to work, just as they only pretended to pay you. The girls kept irregular hours, but in Moscow everyone kept irregular hours. Sometimes they brought strange men home to the nineteenth-floor flat that they shared way out in Ismailova, past the end of the Metro line, and sometimes their activities could get a little exotic—but sex was home entertainment in the USSR, where abortion was the primary form of birth control. Lately, however, television was starting to compete for their attention; the fact that Soviets were now watching MTV rap videos at 9:00 A.M. didn't seem odd to either of them.

Nightly, they slept together on a pull-out couch in the living room, which, along with the TV and a small butler with a couple of bottles of cognac, was the sum total of their household furnishings; there was a bedroom, but since they had no bed they left it empty. There was a hole in the living room floor, through which you could see the cheap slab beneath. Someone had tried to break down the apartment door before they moved in, and that damage had never been fixed. The courtyard below was sadly Soviet, landscaped in weeds and mud. The flat had a small balcony, but it was piled high with junk and too dangerous to go out on. Two months ago, one of the neighboring terraces had torn away from its moorings and dropped twenty-one stories. The neighbor went with it. It was a tough break, but at least the space was now available for some married couple with two children who had been living the last five years with the wife's parents. The place was a dump, but at least it was their dump. Most unmarried Muscovites had to fuck in the graveyards.

Natasha knew she was beautiful. At nineteen, she was still girlishly slender, but her legs were long, her rear end high and firm and her breasts perfectly formed. She enjoyed looking at herself naked in the mirror before going to bed, admiring, as Zlata did as well, her smooth, flawless young skin. A few copies of *Playboy* lay around their apartment, and both women modeled themselves, in terms of personal hygiene and appearance, on the girls in the pictures, right down to the way they trimmed their pubic hair. Natasha was Jewish, but everybody said she didn't look it, and she was thankful for that. Jews were never very popular in the Soviet Union, even when people still believed in Marx.

Zlata was also nineteen but she looked older, big-breasted and bottle-blonde, with a wide face that appeared more Scandinavian than Russian. Not as pretty as her friend, she was more overtly sexy, her body an eye-catching wonder. Like her friend, Zlata didn't think of herself as homosexual, or even bisexual. Both girls loved men, but men, especially sober men with hard currency, were in short supply in Moscow these days, and when men were not available they always had each other.

Tonight they were getting together with Alik, who was neither their lover nor their pimp but a combination of both. The three-sided bar was crowded with single men, nursing weak, watery drinks at stiff prices, payable only in hard currency, and waiting for Miss Right, or at least Miss Right Now. Japanese, German, Dutch and American alike, they scanned the room, their sexual radar operating at peak efficiency, despite their otherwise impaired faculties. From time to time one of them would be joined by one of the Soviet women who gathered in clumps at the tables scattered about in the gloom. There would be a conversation; drinks would be ordered and if all went well after half an hour or so the pair would leave, destination, but not purpose, unknown.

One day in 1985, a *Newsweek* photographer who lived part-time at the hotel ventured into the underground garage to get his van. The hour was late and the lighting, as usual, was poor, and in his haste he opened the back door of what proved to be the wrong vehicle. Inside, instead of his camera equipment, he found three men hunched over a video monitor and taping equipment; on the screen a Soviet swallow was entertaining a visiting Japanese in the imagined privacy of his room upstairs. Eyewitnesses—and officially there were none—would have reported hearing shouts and oaths in Russian followed by sounds of a scuffle. The *Newsweek* photographer did not report to work the next day but went straight to the hospital instead; according to the authorities, he had broken both his arms and blackened his eyes in a drunken fall and they demanded his immediate recall since he was obviously a public nuisance.

It was a common misapprehension in the West that Soviet women were warty, fat babushkas. On the contrary, the young Russian, Ukrainian and Byelorussian women that one encountered on the streets of Moscow were the most attractive women in Europe, with fine features and luxurious hair; when a man looked into their cool gray-blue eyes he could see all the way to the steppes of central Asia. Even their names were tinged with a forbidden, oriental exoticism: Irina, Tatiana, Natasha, Nadezhda, Olga.

Among diplomats it was a cardinal rule that one didn't get involved with Soviet women. The CIA's first chief of station in Moscow had been caught in a honey trap, and every new member of the embassy staff, male and female, received the standard speech warning of the dangers of fraternization. But if a man was looking for trouble, wanted to find it, and could afford to get into it, then the Mezh was the place.

Natasha and Zlata headed for their regular table. It was the large one against the back wall in the only reasonably well lighted section of the bar, and from here they could see everything. From her vantage point, Zlata let her blue eyes scrutinize the lounge. Irina was there, deep in conversation with a German; Tatiana, whose glorious red hair was unmistakable even in this half-light, and whose English was perfect, had corralled an American at the bar. Three Japanese had joined Olga and Nadia at one of the small tables off to the side and were laughing loudly. Zlata wondered idly what language they all thought they were speaking. Mentally she ran through her own languages: Russian, English and Czech, the last a gift from her mother, who had also provided her large breasts and her unusual first name: Zlata, the Golden One. Natasha, by contrast, was basically monolingual, although she could speak and understand a little English.

Zlata produced her cigarettes, selected one, and slapped the pack down on the table. She fished a lighter out of her purse, sparked her plastic yellow Bic and exhaled a puff of smoke. As the smoke dissolved into the murky air, she spotted Alik standing at the bar and looking for them. With a rustle of chiffon, she rose and paraded slowly across the room, so all the men could get a good long look.

Natasha watched her disappear, and lit a cigarette of her own. Occasionally, she caught the glances of passing men, but her remote position would discourage any but the boldest. Even though they were both the same age, Zlata had been a prostitute for much longer; she was bigger, tougher and harder-edged. By comparison, Natasha was an amateur; despite the experience of some of the other girls, she was less interested in money than in a ticket out of the USSR in the form of a marriage proposal from one of the Western businessmen, preferably American, and she knew that on her back was the quickest way to get it.

Tatiana was already married, to an American named Gerard who worked for a computer company in Austin. She had, in fact, even lived in Texas for a time, but life as a suburban housewife was not her style, and she took advantage of one of her husband's business trips to take a plane back to Moscow, leaving a note on the refrigerator door. Natasha couldn't understand that—no matter how awful the marriage, surely one would never leave the American promised land to willingly return to the Rodina—but she supposed Tanya must have had a good reason. Whatever the case, she still used her married American surname, Stokes, which was a handy icebreaker whenever she picked up an American, as she was doing now. Make that "had done"; Tatiana and the American were gone.

Irina, on the other hand, had been promised marriage twice already; Natasha was a little fuzzy on the details. She thought that one of the suitors, an Australian tractor-parts vendor, had actually married her in a Soviet civil ceremony, but had neglected both to tell Irina he had a Mrs. Tractor Parts back in Brisbane and to take her with him when he left. Irina, the story went, divorced him and married an Italian, who knocked her up and left her with a son when he went home to his wife and kids in Perugia. Now Irina was courting an American, although so far she had not informed him of little Mikhail's existence.

Both Tatiana and Irina were magnificent, especially in the dark, but they were both over thirty and not getting any younger. Natasha knew that in freshness and sophistication of looks, she was untouchable. She was not the best in bed—her uninhibited roommate was undoubtedly the champion in that department—and unlike most Soviet girls she insisted that her lovers use a condom, which some of them found annoying. But a four-hour three-way could earn her twenty dollars. The current official exchange rate was more than one dollar per ruble, but on the street, you could get at least fifteen rubles for the dollar; three hundred rubles was a month's salary for most working people. Where else could a girl make that kind of money in Russia? Where else could she meet so many foreign men? And if she had to report on them to the KGB through Alik from time to time, it was worth it. It was not betrayal, it was simply business—besides which, she planned to betray the KGB the very first chance she got.

She patted her hair to make sure it was still in place, and then turned to look in the smoked mirror behind her table. Still desirable, although time was running out; she would be twenty soon enough. She took a long drag on her cigarette as Alik and Zlata sat down.

"Look at that one," remarked Zlata, indicating a tall, gray-haired German in a sport coat and slacks who smiled at them as he passed by. "He's got money, for sure."

"Forget it," said Alik. "An American friend of mine has just arrived."

Natasha let out a small squeal of delight. She knew that the words *American* and *money* were if not synonymous then certainly related. "Is he rich?" she asked.

"Of course he is," replied Alik. "And guess what: we're going to be making a movie."

"A movie!" exclaimed Natasha. Everyone had always told her she was lovely enough to be in the cinema, and in her opinion everyone was right.

"When will we have time to learn our lines?" asked Zlata, ever practical.

"Don't worry about that," said Alik. "You'll do just fine."

Zlata seemed disappointed, but Natasha didn't care. "And will we have beautiful costumes?" she asked.

Alik shot her a quick, appraising glance. "The most beautiful costumes in the world," he said. "Come on, let's go. They're waiting for us at the *Block*."

Chapter Nineteen
Moscow
Saturday, October 6, 1990; 1:00 A.M.

The *Alexander Block* was a small barge anchored in the Moskva River not far from the Mezh, a floating nightclub in which Muscovites and foreigners could rub shoulders and down strong drink together. Although officially there was no crime in the Soviet Union, the combination of liquor and women often proved explosive and arguments over the pretty ladies-in-waiting were frequent, and frequently fatal. The place was a favorite with members of the mafia, Georgians mostly, and they sat with their whores along the back wall of the main lounge, nursing their drinks and their grudges with equal fervor.

"Did you know that body of Lenin is really wax dummy?" Natasha was saying to Alik's American in her best English. "*Pravda!*" she exclaimed. "Is true! Is really wax dummy. Is tunnel under Red Square, and when he melt they bring new one, so he always look fresh. Big joke!" She laughed heartily. The American, who called himself Sasha, was well-dressed, handsome and had good teeth. He was drinking watered whiskeys, sold at eight dollars a pop, *valuta* only. For her part, Natasha was sipping a weak Russian beer; one or two a night would not spoil her figure, at least for a few more years.

"You might be right," said Sasha. "Today our KGB guide took me right to the front. There were a bunch of tourists already on line—Italians, I think—but she just marched me right up. I paid my two rubles, or whatever it was, and I took the tour." He took a sip of his scotch. "Sure looked like a wax dummy to me!" A couple of the Georgians glanced up, frowns on their faces, while their women just stared blankly into space and smoked their cigarettes. One of them, a big, fat man in a white shirt that was at least two sizes too small and black pants held up only by his gut, had a visible weapon peeking out from under his cavernous armpit. Involuntarily, Natasha shuddered, for the Georgians always frightened her. She hoped there wouldn't be any trouble and counted on Alik to make sure there wasn't.

Natasha patted Sasha's leg affectionately and stood up. The beer was having its effect. "I'll be right back," she said, heading for the ladies' room. Which, this being the Soviet Union, was the same as the men's room. When she emerged five minutes later, Alik and Sasha and Alik's other friend, an ugly, pockmarked German with a snorting laugh, were deep in conversation. "Millions," Alik was saying. "In the right hands, it's worth millions."

"And I've got just the hands you're looking for," said Tom Byrne. In Russia, he always went by his middle name, Alexander, which meant everyone called him Sasha. Tom had already decided he would drill both the blonde with the big knockers and her cute friend—that was the least Alik could do for him, after all he was about to do for him. "Where are the goods?"

"Somewhere safe," replied Alik. "Where I can get my hands on them quite easily. Within driving distance. But first we must drink, to comity and cooperation."

Byrne downed his whiskey, slid his hand over Natasha's and was pleased when it was not withdrawn. Instead, her fingers wrapped themselves around his and squeezed, gently. He knew now, after only three whiskeys, why some men married foreign girls, or kept one or two on the side. The problem was keeping them straight. The problem was keeping his whole life straight.

"You like to hear Russian joke?" Alik asked in mock–broken English flavored with an exaggerated Russian accent. "Is really parable: two farmers, Ivan and Mikhail. Both are miserable poor. They have nothing, shit. One day Ivan gets cow. Just one cow. But big difference! Cow can plow field, instead of wife; cow can give milk; cow produce calves. Now Ivan's life much better.

"So Mikhail, he kneel down, start to pray. 'Oh, God,' he say, 'Ivan and I always equal. When I had nothing, he had nothing. And now look at him. Rich, like boyar. So, God, please make us equal once again." And you know what? God hear Misha's prayer. He appear to Mikhail, in his miserable shit farmhouse, and he say, 'Mikhail Yuriyevich, your prayers are answered! Equal again!' Misha overjoyed at news. 'Horasho!'" he exclaim. 'You going to kill Ivan's cow!' "

Everybody laughed heartily, except Natasha, who didn't understand it. At this moment, one of the women sitting with the Georgians got up and addressed Tom. "Hallo," she said, in English.

"I'm busy," replied Byrne, glancing up at her. The whore was tall, with short-cropped red hair, large breasts encased, barely, in a purple stretch top that was stretching as far as it could, and tight black leather pants. She assayed him as if he were Ivan's cow. "Busy," she said. "Busy, busy man." She pronounced it *beezy*.

"Very busy," he repeated, but she wasn't listening.

"What size are you?" she inquired, undeterred. Alik gave him a cautionary pat on his shoulder and Natasha's hand ranged from his hand to his thigh, squeezing tighter.

"What size are you?" she repeated. Her eyes scanned him from his face to his groin, there to settle, and Tom finally understood what she meant. He felt himself standing, and cursed the three lousy whiskeys he had already had.

A hand—not Natasha's—now grasped what the nuns used to call his privates. There were catcalls, jeers and obscene commentary coming from the thugs at the back of the room. The whore's free hand slid behind the back of his neck, firmly pulling his head down and forward toward her ample chest. The pressure below his belt was growing more intense. The pain was excruciating and he thought he was going to faint. God, she was a big, strong girl.

"What size?" she said again.

"Too big for you, my love," he finally managed to say.

The girl looked at him resentfully. "I think no," she said, and let him go. At the far end of the room, the mafia howled in delight.

Alik handed Byrne another drink as he sat down. "Good thing you didn't try to fuck her," he said. "They would've shot you for sure. I know those guys. They're punks." He raised his glass to the crowd across the room; Byrne suddenly noticed that what he had taken for Alex's vodka was instead plain bottled water, and cursed himself for his own lack of abstinence. "On the other hand," continued Alik, "maybe they'll be so insulted that you didn't try that they'll kill you anyway."

No question about it, reflected Tom: Moscow was demonstrably worse than even a couple of years ago. Crime was up, police presence down. Everything was for sale: the women, of course (they had always been at least for rent); the men, who were so naive that when you bribed them they stayed bribed; what remained of the infrastructure (wanna buy a bridge?— here, you could); uniforms, sidearms and, for all Tom knew, the tactical nuclear devices of the Red Army. The average citizen had become an entrepreneur; the other day Tom had flagged a passing driver at random— not a taxi driver, just an ordinary citizen whom he enticed with a pack of Marlboros to drive him to his destination—and the man had looked him over and said, "Would you like to buy some beer? Some wine? Some champagne? It's in the trunk." And it was, too. For that was the shame of the Soviet Union. A capitalist running dog lackey of imperialism could live in Moscow like the Czar of all the Russias. Caviar? Every meal! The best Havana cigars? Dime a dozen! Just stroll into any *beriozka* shop and flash your American Express card—or, better yet, some cash. The world, such as it was, was yours. Russia, where every woman was a hooker and every man a pimp, of one kind or another—the country couldn't last, could not go on, for much longer, and the only mystery was why nobody in the West seemed to realize it. Or wanted to believe it.

"I hate those bastards," said the German. "Why don't you get rid of them? In my country, they'd be in jail."

"Ah, but Russia is a free country!" replied Alik. "Unlike in Germany, they have rights! Under the Soviet constitution, everybody has rights!"

"Let's get out of here," said Natasha. "They scare me. Besides, what about our movie?" She turned to the German. "Are you director?" she asked. "Is my part big?"

"Mr. Schiffen will act as the distributor," said Alik, and Tom, tuning back in to the conversation, realized he had no idea what they were talking about. The Moscow street dialect was too fast for the Russian he had learned as a child, augmented though it was by his training at the Defense Language Institute in Monterey. Why couldn't his mother have been from Moscow instead of a boondock like Archangel?

"The biggest," said Schiffen.

"Ooo," squealed Natasha, and hugged Zlata.

"A toast!" Alik suddenly shouted, and the Georgians across the room looked up from a card game they had begun.

Alik got up and walked across the room. From behind the bar, the bartender was sizing up the situation, evaluating it for potential trouble and possible damage. When he spotted Alik he didn't know whether to laugh or cry.

"A toast!" repeated Alik, addressing the mafia. "A toast to Soviet-American friendship. A toast to the victors of the Great Patriotic War, and to the losers"—he nodded in Schiffen's direction—"as well. A toast to the best-looking women in the *Alexander Block*"—this time a nod to Zlata and Natasha—"and to the ugliest crew of motherfuckers in Moscow." This toast, unmistakably, was directed across the room. "The scurviest, blackest-toothed, hairiest collection of whores' sons and daughters that ever it has been my misfortune to behold!"

One of the mafiosi, the big guy in the white shirt, rose unsteadily to his feet. "You speak to us, faggot?" he said.

"Hey, *metraki!*" shouted Alik, insulting the man in Georgian: "butt-fucker." The bar had become very quiet. Even the Japanese tourists sitting in a group by the stairs had finally realized that something was up. "You. The one who looks like a piece of cow shit that a tractor has just run over." The man in the white shirt stood a good head taller, and outweighed Alik by at least fifty kilos. His face was like a Moscow road, pitted and bumpy, and his pistol was visible to everyone.

"I understand," said Alik, "that your mother screws horses." The Georgian said something over his shoulder to his companions, and then started to make his way, slowly, toward the center of the room, tacking unsteadily across the dance floor, a stiff wind of booze and hostility blowing his bulk across the poorly made parquet. "I can prove it," said Alik as the man approached. "Do you know how?" This brought the man's progress to a temporary halt, and a puzzled look spread across his thick features. The Georgian was standing near the center of the room, half onto the dance floor, his mouth moving bovinely when Alik put his mouth to the man's ear and whispered into it. In the same motion, he swung his left hand between the thug's legs.

Instead of screaming, or striking back, the hood tossed his ugly mug back and laughed. This was the signal for his entire cohort to start laughing, and soon the whole room had joined in, although whether the onlookers were laughing from enjoyment or relief was not exactly clear. The Japs were laughing too, but then they always laughed.

In a flash, the laughing had stopped. The *mafioznik* was on the floor, writhing; Alik was standing over him, a knife blade having somehow sprung from his right sleeve and which was now being applied to the man's nuts. Jesus, he was fast.

"*Traksi makoce!*" he shouted in Georgian: "Kiss my ass." "If you or your whores ever annoy me or my friends again, I'll cut it off and feed it to the dogs. Like this." In one motion, he released the fat man's balls and brought the knife up to his face, where he sliced through the fleshy part of his nose and tossed it away so quickly it took a few moments before the victim had realized what happened. Bleeding profusely, the man scrabbled in vain after the missing tip of his nose, then struggled to his feet and crashed into the toilet.

Alik stood before the rest of the mobsters, his bloody knife still visible. None of them so much as thought about their weapons; they had recognized him now and were starting to skulk from the room. "*Sen dedas seveci! Yeb tvoju v dushu mat!*" He wasn't even breathing hard.

"Georgians are like jackals," shouted Alik, "cowards, who won't fight unless the odds are ten to one in their favor; scavengers, who prey on society's collapse. Look at them!" he commanded, and even the Japanese knew better than to disobey. The last of the *mafiozniki* was now disappearing up the stairs. "They are the dark mirror of our great Russian soul, and no decent land should tolerate them. But I am only one man, and what can I do? Even I cannot kill them all. *Gore, gore Rusi. Plac', plac', russkij ljud!*" His eyes flashed hard and cold.

As they stepped ashore across the narrow gangplank that separated the *Block* from the mainland, trying to avoid drowning themselves in the Moskva, Tom asked, "What was that you said to him?"

"I told him, I knew his mother fucked horses because he was hung like one. Georgians are suckers for big dicks. It's the biggest compliment you can pay them."

"No, after that. When they were leaving."

They staggered outside into the Moscow night. The streets, as usual, were nearly empty, the broad boulevards deserted save for the odd car navigating by only its parking lights. Across the river, the massive pile of the Hotel Ukraina, one of Moscow's Stalinist "wedding cakes," was garishly illuminated, as if it were some kind of architectural feat to brag about.

A black Chaika, a knockoff of a ' 57 Chevy, was waiting for them in the darkness. Alik got in the front seat next to the driver while Byrne and the German sandwiched the two women between them in the back.

"I said, 'I fuck your mother in her soul!'"

Chapter Twenty
One Police Plaza
Saturday, October 20, 1990; 11:00 A.M.

OFFICE OF THE CHIEF MEDICAL EXAMINER
OF THE CITY OF NEW YORK

Pathological Examination Report   No. EE-34652-S   Page I

Name: Edwin Paine, aka Egil Ekdahl
Race: White

Sex: Male
Autopsy date: October 19, 1990
Medical Examiner: Seymour Sheinberg, M.D.

External Examination:

External examination reveals a 5 foot, 11½ inch white male, the estimated weight is 165 pounds. Rigor is present.

Identification bands on the left wrist, the right wrist, the left great toe. The head is examined. The hair is blond and slightly wavy. Considerable amount of dried blood which has run from the hairline to the right and backward. Slight frontal balding.

Byrne read Dr. Sheinberg's spare, functional prose with a practiced, if not to say jaundiced, eye. In his career, he had read hundreds of autopsy reports, and he supposed that Sheinberg had written thousands of them. What kind of a personality did it take to be a medical examiner? It was bad enough being a cop. But at least, every once in a while, you got a cat up a tree, although not too many lately in New York. Chop-shop docs never got to save a patient. Of course, they never got sued for malpractice, either.

Microscopic:

Aorta: There is disruption with fresh hemorrhage. No inflammation or organization.

Heart: There are hemorrhages in the epicardial fat, mild interstitial edema and focal fragmentation of the muscle fibers.

Lung: Areas of atelectasis and focal alveolar hemorrhagic extravasations.

Liver: Disruption with fresh hemorrhages, otherwise noncontributory.

Bowel: There are massive disruptions of the stomach with hemorrhages adjacent.

Spleen: There is disruption along one margin, otherwise noncontributory.

Thyroid: Noncontributory.

Central Nervous System: Multiple sections are examined and they are noncontributory.

Gross Description of Brain:
Following formalin fixation the brain weighed 1434 grams. The right cerebral hemisphere was found to be markedly disrupted. There was a longitudinal laceration of the right hemisphere which is parasagittal in position approximately 1.23 cm to the right of the midline which extends from the tip of the occipital lobe posteriorly to the tip of the frontal lobe anteriorly. There is moderate loss of cortical substance above the base of the laceration, especially in the parietal lobe.

When viewed from the vertex the left cerebral hemisphere is intact. There is marked engorgement of meningeal blood vessels of the left temporal and frontal regions with considerable associated subarachnoid hemorrhage. The gyri and sulci over the left hemisphere are of essentially normal size and distribution. Those on the right are too fragmented and distorted for satisfactory description.

When viewed from the basilar aspect the disruption of the right cortex is again obvious. There is a longitudinal laceration of the midbrain through the floor of the third ventricle just behind the optic chiasm and the mammillary bodies. There is considerable laceration of the optic nerve of the right eye, which is missing.

Cause of Death:

Hemorrhage, secondary to severed carotid artery and gunshot wounds of the head and abdomen.

He was typing up his Fives—the fundamental paperwork that described each step of the detective's investigation—when the phone rang. He grabbed it on the first ring. "Byrne," he barked.

"Yo, Frankie." It was Mancuso. "Did you hear about the new hot dogs at Fenway Park?"

"No," he said.

"Yeah," said Mancuso. "They're called Barney Franks. If you don't like 'em, you can shove 'em up your ass!"

"Very funny. What else you got?"

"There's prints all over the car, of course. Aprahamian got several sets of nice ones, but without corresponding file prints from the consulate, not to mention the body, what's he supposed to match 'em up with?"

"Are we sure there's nothing?" asked Byrne.

"Felix's the best, Frankie," said Mancuso. "You know that. If he says no prints, then there's no prints."

"You're probably right."

"Of course I'm right. I'm always right. 'Member that time you questioned my judgment about that diner in Teaneck? Was that the best meat loaf you ever had or what?"

"You're right, Vin."

"Our boy's little toy, on the other hand, comes up a winner." That was just like Mancuso, to save the best for last, just like he did with dessert. "One clear set. Prob'ly his, but you never know."

"Trace 'em. And do it yesterday."

"What do you think I'm doin', pickin' my nose? It takes a while, is all."

"Yeah, well don't let it take forever," snapped Byrne.

Mancuso made a series of clucking noises, indicating he was taking Byrne's commands in. "Just for fun," he added, "I also ran our little objet d'art past Languages, and sure enough Sheinberg was right, the inscription does read something like 'Mother's small friend' or 'Mother's best companion.' Guess they don't have quite the same expression in Russian."

"What they do say is 'Fuck your mother,'" said Byrne. "I read that in a book somewhere."

"What kind of a thing is that to say, 'Fuck your mother'?" inquired Mancuso.

"I thought you greaseballs said 'motherfucker' all the time. Isn't that about the same thing?" asked Byrne.

"I guess you could say that," admitted Mancuso. "But their way sounds a lot worse. I would never want to fuck my mother."

"Yeah, well you're Italian, what can I say? You're busy trying to fuck somebody's sister instead."

"You should see some of the sisters," said Mancuso, and rang off.

Idly, Byrne looked over his notes. He had jotted down a list of the principal suspects, but he might as well have inscribed names of people who *didn't* have something to gain by Ekdahl's death, since the list would have been shorter. What was this? *Murder on the Orient Express?* For what it was worth, he lined them up, together with whatever supporting evidence he could muster.

The Mafia: all that business downtown recently. Despite White's wishes, Andretti was giving him a hand, sotto voce, and if he knew Gino, a few off-the-record beers with some of the guys from the old neighborhood and he'd have a couple of solid leads by tomorrow. Would that they had men like Andretti to work the Russian mob in Brighton Beach, about which the department still knew next to nothing. If they were behind it, it would be a cold day in hell before NYPD found out about it.

If not the Russian-Jewish mob, then maybe the real Russians. If Ekdahl was on the trail of the Oswald file, and if the file was as hot as everybody seemed to think, the KGB might well have popped him. In which case the perps were long since safely back in Moscow, or wherever they came from.

The FBI, as represented in the person of his brother? Nothing would please him more than being able to bust his sibling, but the videotape and the missing round from his pistol currently made that difficult. On the other hand, when it came to Tom he was not without his own means of coercion, which he intended to use when the time was right.

The CIA? That was out of his league; if the CIA had whacked Ekdahl, who was he to object? Mazel tov and good night. This Oswald stuff was prehistoric and had nothing to do with him.

Pilgersen? He was dead, although he certainly seemed to have a motive. Maybe someone from the Danish security services. But what had Ingrid told him last night? That almost nothing Tom said about Pilgersen had been true? What did that mean?

And Ingrid? Who was she, really? A secretary, or something more? And what game was she playing?

Not to mention his mother, and the photo. What was that all about? How did it get in Ekdahl's car? And who was that other woman?

The gay subculture? Could be. The shit that happened when testosterone collided was amazing. Maybe he was just letting his prejudice color his theories. But what about that Paine pseudonym? What did that mean?

"What a pain," Byrne muttered to himself.

"Talking about yourself again, Frankie?" It was Captain White, who had stuck his head out of his office. "I've been saying that for years. Only reason I promoted you is that I had to fill my quota of white guys, and you were the only one with an IQ higher than room temperature."

"What're you doin' here on Saturday, Matt?" asked Byrne, as if he didn't know.

"Waiting for you, is what," replied White. "So get your majority-colored posterior in here right now. I want a progress report."

He went into White's office and sat down. There was no point in complaining that the case was only two days old.

"I've been looking over Dr. Sheinberg's report." He tossed a copy of the medicolegal autopsy over to the captain. He had already decided to keep the news of the videotape he had found in Ekdahl's flat to himself, until the time was right. Not to mention Pilgersen's unexpected demise.

White grunted as he perused it. "Pretty messy," he said. "Is it a real sex crime, you think, or is somebody just trying to give us a hard-on?"

"I'm not sure. It was certainly made to resemble one. And the guy did have some bona fide kinkiness in him. This dildo thing, for example. Apparently, he had a problem with impotence."

"That doesn't explain why it was found up his heinie, instead of somebody else's," objected the captain. "Have you checked out that club yet?" asked White.

"Don't worry," said Byrne. "It's on my dance card. Even though I got a feeling the dildo business was just an afterthought, to cover up something else."

"Like what?"

"Like maybe his latent heterosexuality—I don't know yet. But what I can tell you is that Ekdahl isn't his real name either. Pilgersen—that's the Danish consul general—told me on deep background that Ekdahl was really an undercover security agent, a spy if you will, assigned to the consulate to, to, to do what? We're not sure. Keep tabs on the Russians, maybe, or even spy on other Europeans. Pilgersen said he wasn't told, that deniability was important and that's why he was kept in the dark. The Danes are taking this one very seriously."

"That explains all the fuss from Washington," said White. "But I just know there's more, so don't make me beat it out of you."

"Yeah, well," he began, editing furiously. How much could he tell, without implicating his mother, his brother and himself? And yet, he hated to lie to Matt White, even if the captain did have him by the balls. "Then, once we get a little confidence thing going and I swear on my love for pizza that I won't spill it, he tells me—now we're talking top-secret, mind you—that they just discovered Ekdahl wasn't a consular official at all, but a Russian infiltrator, an agent the commies had wheedled into the Danish diplomatic service. And that, furthermore, Ekdahl seems to have turned free-lance and was hawking the KGB's file on the guy that shot Kennedy—Jack I mean, not Bobby—and then the next thing he, Pilgersen, knows Ekdahl winds up in a field next to a '76 Duster and an old washing machine."

"Is that all?"

"Oh yeah, and that Ekdahl sometimes used the pseudonym Edwin A. Paine for security purposes, although I don't believe that. For fun and games purposes, is more like it. I'll know more after I visit the Rambone and make a couple of other stops. So I'd appreciate it if you could keep the feds as far away as possible for as long as you can. Last thing I need is a bunch of my college classmates with better grades than I had breathing down my neck. If anybody asks, it's a sex-murder investigation involving a foreign national that at Washington's request is best kept out of the public eye, and that includes your buddies over at the *Times* and Channel 5 rooting for you to make commissioner."

That got the captain's attention. The public clamor for "Moby Dick" Flanagan's head, led by the newspapers, was intensifying; a coup in the Ekdahl case might cement White's call on the job. Byrne was counting on the fact that beneath White's cool exterior burned the desire to be the black Teddy Roosevelt, police commissioner of the city of New York.

The captain shifted his massive weight in his chair. "Look, Lieutenant, I know you're busting your hump, and I want you to know that I appreciate it. We can both make each other look good on this one, and if you pull off another Coloredo for me, well, I can promise you there's going to be a whole lot of happiness around here. Hell, I may even let you sit in my chair, and wouldn't that just frost Finnegan and Malecki? So as long as you swear on your mama's head that you're giving me a hundred and ten percent and aren't just blowin' smoke up my you know what, I'll cover that big Irish backside of yours for you. But screw up and you'll be back walking a beat in Morrisania. You dig?"

Byrne said he dug. And speaking of his mama . . .

"The media will have something else to worry about besides Ekdahl in the next couple of days," White went on. "New York will see to that. You'd think that triple homicide in Flatbush last night would be plenty for them, but when black folks die it's just not news like it is when some ofay gets offed." He brought his fists down on the desk so hard that Byrne winced. "Remember, Frankie, this is a great white victim, and if there's one thing New York hates, it's a great white victim. The citizens and their rabble-rousing tribunes, the tabloids, want answers, and they look to me, as the captain of this ship, for solutions. I can't trust either of my first mates, so I have to trust you. So, in the words of my favorite New Yorker, sing out when you find him, lower away and after him, a dead whale or a stove boat when you catch up with him. Death and devils! No excuses."

Byrne missed the literary reference but decided not to let on. "Far be it from me to make excuses," he said, introducing the subject cautiously, "but I think this guy Ekdahl might have had something to do with a member of my family."

"What do you mean, your family?" Suddenly, White became very serious; for him, family was sacred. "Are we talking about your brother Tom, the FBI agent?" Byrne knew that behind the shades a light had come on in White's eyes. "Is he the reason the brass hats were comin' out of the woodwork to get me to assign Ekdahl to you? Is he the reason I got feds on the horn every six hours like Old Faithful, asking me what we got?"

Well, that explained that. "He does seem to be working the case," Byrne admitted. "But I don't think he's got anything more to do with it." A lie, of course, but at the moment what choice did he have? He couldn't mention the videotape until he had a chance to confront Tom, and last night had hardly been the right time.

"Then who?" asked the captain. "There's only one other person in your family and that's your mama. Don't tell me she all of a sudden has taken to stepping out on the town with a dildo and a .22 in her little black bag. I know your mama's tough, but she ain't that tough."

Byrne looked at the captain hard. "When we first inspected the car at
the site, I found something," he said. "Something I haven't told anybody
else about. Something that wasn't in my report."

"Don't tell me: a confession."

"Not exactly," said Byrne. "It was a photograph of two women, taken
years ago. One of the women I don't know, but the other one is . . ."

"Yo mama!" exclaimed White.

"My mama," answered Byrne, handing it over.

White studied the picture carefully. "Which one is her?" he asked softly.

"The one on the right." Byrne could hardly get the words out.

"And who's this with her? Could be her sister. She's even prettier, no offense."

"That's what I have to ask her."

White rose and went to the humidor in a cabinet across the room. He
extracted one of his prize Hoyo de Monterreys, rolled it between his fingers with the affection of the connoisseur, took a deep draught of its aroma
and stuck it between his lips. Byrne knew he had no intention of lighting
it. "You know," he mused softly, "I used to enjoy smoking, but it no longer
soothes. This thing that is meant for sereneness."

His broad back was still to Byrne. "Family secrets are the worst," he
began. "The worst because they're often the deepest and the darkest, as well
as the most unnecessary. They're one generation's revenge on the next, a revenge born of impotence and frustration and just plain spite. I mean," he
continued, "what do we really know about our parents, except what they
tell us? I know my daddy was born in Texarkana, on the black side, in
Arkansas, moved to Houston when he was a young man, may or may not
have done time for manslaughter and wound up an oil wildcatter, which
was a pretty unusual thing for a black man to do in those days. That's what
I know. At least, that's what I *think* I know."

Abruptly, White turned and faced Byrne. His words bore the force of
moral, not physical, authority.

"Let me tell you something, Frankie, that I ain't never told nobody."
Sometimes, under stress, White reverted to the speech patterns of his Texas
youth. "Families lie. They lie all the time. We know that kids lie to their
parents, but what about parents who lie to their kids? I don't just mean
about Santa Claus, either. I mean about important things. When I was
growing up in Houston—I know it was Houston 'cause it was hot and

humid and flat and ugly and there wasn't nothing to do except to make sure you didn't wander into the white parts of town—when I was growing up there my mama told me that her daddy had died when she was just a little girl, that she had grown up half an orphan. This was just after the Depression, just before the war. Grandmama Jefferson, she said the same thing when we would ask her about the grandpop we never knew. Oh, he done died, he done died. 'Cept he didn't done die; he lived into his eighties, ten blocks away from our house, with his second wife and their daughter, and I and my brothers and sisters never knew a damn thing about it. Turns out he had divorced my Grandmama Jefferson, and hard as this may be to believe these days, back then even black families just didn't break up the way they do today, especially not black Catholic families, which we were."

That took Byrne by surprise; like everyone else, he assumed that Matt White was a Southern Baptist.

"Can you believe it?" asked White. "Nobody would care today, especially not in the community. The de-Christianization of African Americans, if you ask my opinion, is the worst thing that's happened to my people since the slave ships came and brought Christianity in the first place. We got our freedom, but what is the price of that freedom when the leading cause of death among young black man is other young black men? When babies are having babies, and most of the births are illegitimate? When babies are killing babies? As the Good Book says: What does it profit a man if he gain the whole world and yet lose his soul?"

White broke out of his reverie and went back to his narrative. "Anyway, he divorced her, and in a particularly nasty way. A year or so after they broke up, he was feeling a little peckish, so he invited her to meet him for lunch, said it was all a terrible mistake, he was lonely, the usual horny male baloney, and anyway she met him for lunch and they had some wine and they had some more wine and then they found a nice cozy little hotel room not far away and the next thing you know my Auntie Emma was conceived. And you know what the sumbitch did then? He sued Grandmama Jefferson for divorce on the grounds of adultery! Said she got pregnant by another man, child couldn't have been his because after all they had been separated for months, and the court saw it his way and he got his divorce and married his girlfriend two months later. Grandmama nearly died of shame, and from that moment on, Raleigh Jefferson was anathema to her, good as dead, and no one ever spoke about him again except in the past tense. And I guess in a way he was dead. But, do you know, he died for real just two years before the old lady did, and finally, after they were both gone, my mama told me the truth. I have to admit I was miffed. Would have liked to meet him, if only to punch him in the nose for what he did to my Grandmama. But I never got the chance." He sat down, his cigar still unlit. "So you see, even your own mama can lie to you. And if your own mama's gonna lie to you, then who can you trust in this world?"

"Nobody, I guess," said Byrne, wondering if that was true.

"It's a terrible thing when a man can't trust his own mama," said White, and Byrne knew the sermon was over. "I hope, for your sake, that you can trust yours. Now get out of here."

Chapter Twenty-one
The West Village
Saturday, October 20, 1990; 2:00 P.M.

Byrne walked into the Rambone and wondered if it was an occasion of sin. This despite the fact there were no women in the place.

"Can I help you?" The question was more of an invitation. Byrne couldn't help but notice the Puerto Rican doorman was wearing mascara and false eyelashes.

"NYPD," Byrne said, flashing his shield discreetly. Gays and cops didn't mix very well, although he knew a few officers, fag-bashers in the locker room, who didn't mind copping a blow job now and then just to keep in touch with their sources on the street. It was like in India, where you weren't considered a fag as long as you were the fucker instead of the fuckee; you couldn't get AIDS as long as it was your dick that was getting sucked. Or so they believed. "I'd like to speak to the manager," he said.

"Is this business or pleasure?" asked the doorman. "If it's pleasure, I'm going to have to charge you."

This was too much for Byrne. "What do you think?" he barked.

"You don't have to get sore about it," said the man. He batted his eyes and stuck out his hip. He was wearing a tank top and tight blue jeans. Byrne wondered how he kept his waist so small, and mentally patted his own paunch. He'd start doing those crunches tomorrow, just like he'd been promising Doreen for months. "She's not available right now."

She? "Where is she?"

"She's busy."

"Doing what?" said Byrne.

"How should I know, man? Am I my sister's keeper?" He had one of those only-in-New-York accents, half ghetto, half Brooklyn. He sounded like a Hispanic Mike Tyson, lisp and all.

"Then go find her," commanded Byrne. "I haven't got all day."

"Just keep your pants on and I'll be right back," said the doorman as he huffed away. Byrne looked around, his pupils widening in the smoky gloom. He wondered how anybody breathed in here. Or heard anything, with the music pounding like that. The current tune was a rap ode to the joys of anal sex called "Tina's Got a Big Ol' Butt." You definitely could get AIDS from that, especially in this joint; in fact, you could probably get AIDS just from breathing the air.

He was in a big loft over one of the district's many warehouses. Unlike most cities built near water, New York was determined to ignore its waterfront. Except for the piers where the great passenger ships had once docked, the lower west side of Manhattan had always been spectacularly ugly, its streets riven by railroad tracks and ruled by Irish gangs like the Gophers and the Hudson Dusters; now that the piers had collapsed along with the West Side Highway the destruction was complete. This part of the West Village had been given over to the roughest of trades—slaughterhouses—and as the butcher shops faded they had been replaced by another kind of rough trade. Sometimes the transvestite prostitutes got so rowdy that they would get into fights with the family men who lived on the outwardly pleasant, tree-lined streets to the east. Then the cops would have to come and try to separate the men from the real girls, if any.

The Rambone was a vast open space with, incongruously, a toilet in the middle of the room. The room, however, was far from empty. It had been furnished to look like a cross between a circus, a torture chamber and a lumber yard. Trapezes and hammocks hung from the ceiling; there were all kinds of benches, chairs and divans scattered around the floor, even a saw horse or two. There were stocks, whips, chains and harnesses attached to the walls. Hammers, nails, power drills and screwdrivers were everywhere. It looked like a convention of perverted carpenters; some of the customers even wore workmen's belts, bristling with tools, around their otherwise bare midsections.

The all-male clientele this Saturday afternoon was just as eclectic as the decor. Some men were entirely naked. Others wore black-leather full-length pants, with the crotch and backside cut out; their only other item of apparel was a police patrolman's hat. So that's what they got in return for their blow jobs; that and another night on the streets.

There were also patients wearing hospital gowns, and hairy-legged schoolgirls in blue jumpers and no panties, and nurses, and brides and grooms; one guy was wearing a Reagan mask and nothing else; Nixon and Carter were there too, as if they were attending the sickest costume party in history. Carter was fucking Reagan in the ass, to the cheers of several onlookers. Byrne couldn't tell if Carter was wearing a condom and was disinclined to get close enough to look.

"Something to drink?" A Rambo clone had sidled up to him. The waiter was wearing a muscle shirt, a jock strap and a French maid's apron.

"No, thanks," said Byrne.

"Suit yourself." He waddled away with that peculiar gait bodybuilders call The Walk, shoulders wide and arms swinging freely, like a steroid-fueled gorilla.

"I found her." The doorman was back. "This is Shannon." Byrne turned and his eyes met those of a delicious honey blonde in a purple outfit with a white blouse whose buttons she was busy doing up.

"Yes?" she said.

"Lieutenant Francis Byrne, NYPD." He was all business. "Could I have your name, please?"

"Shannon." She waited a beat. "Just Shannon."

"Well, Miss Shannon—"

"That's just Shannon, if you don't mind."

"Ms. Shannon, I wonder if I could ask you a few questions." Establish authority: it was one of the first things they taught you at the police academy.

"I wonder if you'd mind telling me what this is in reference to, Lieutenant," she said, touching him lightly on the arm. She spoke slowly, in a low, husky voice.

"It's something I think we should discuss in private, if you don't mind."

"I don't mind doing anything in private." She gave a little laugh. "Or in public, either. Are you related to David, by any chance?"

"Ma'am?"

"David Byrne, you know, the Talking Heads? I remember when they played over at CBGB, before they got famous."

"No, ma'am, I'm not. At least I don't think so. It's a common Irish name."

"And are you a common Irish cop, Lieutenant Byrne?"

"My girlfriend doesn't think so." It was the cleverest, most defensive riposte he could make under the circumstances.

"Oh, so you have a girlfriend," Shannon said, the disappointment histrionically apparent in her voice. "Bitch. And I bet she's tried them all, hasn't she?" Byrne started to say something, but held his tongue. "I know I have. Cops, I mean. Would you light my cigarette, please?" She offered him the tip of a long filtered fag and a book of Rambone club matches. Byrne obliged. He made a mental note to check whether the city's new antismoking provisions were being violated. Not to mention the health code.

"Follow me," she said. Her derriere swayed seductively as she preceded him, but Byrne managed to control his concupiscence. In this environment, it was fairly easy.

Even though it was only midafternoon, there were already two hundred men in the club, in various states of costumed undress. Byrne wondered if he knew any of them in real life. One man was suspended, starkers, from a pulley, his hands in handcuffs, his feet about sixteen inches off the ground. On either side, men were holding his legs wide apart, while a third man was burning his penis with a lighted cigarette. A couple of other men stood idly nearby, masturbating to the sight.

In another part of the loft, two consenting adults were nailing each other's cocks to two-by-fours. The only sounds they were making were dull, ecstatic moans. Byrne winced at each hammer blow. Didn't that hurt? He supposed that was the point.

Off to one side, a naked man sat in a four-by-four metal cage, handcuffed to the bars, his feet in manacles. There was a tin dish in front of him, and from time to time he bent over and licked up whatever was in it; Byrne couldn't see what it was, and didn't really want to know.

As one man finished using the toilet, he bent over and let another lick him clean. On a rubber mattress in the corner, a man was being pissed on by three other men, all dressed as firemen. His mouth was open and he was drinking the urine as fast as he could.

In the glory hole, one man was fellating half a dozen anonymous cocks. His face was glistening with fresh semen. Men were jerking off everywhere, which seemed to be the only safe sex being practiced in the place.

If this were a heterosexual club, reflected Byrne, the city would have closed it in less than two shakes of a girl's tail. But go after a gay club and hear the screams of homophobia from all directions; it was a queer double standard in more ways than one.

"William Burroughs used to come here," said Shannon over her shoulder. "He said it was a wet dream come true."

"Yeah, I should think Tarzan would be pretty popular around here," said Byrne. He wondered if she heard him.

A door behind the bar led into a back alcove, furnished solely with a cot. "This is where I like to do my work," said Shannon, reclining. There was no place else to sit, so Byrne remained standing.

"First of all, I'm not here about the club," Byrne assured her. "Although I note that a great many unsafe sexual practices are going on."

"I got news for you," interjected Shannon. "They're not practicing. You know what they say: sex really is dirty if you're doing it right."

"Well, that's for the public health authorities to decide," said Byrne. "And I think they've decided that this kind of sex"—he indicated the room beyond—"is pretty dirty."

"What are you going to do about it?" asked Shannon, suddenly contentious. "You and the rest of the assholes in this town can preach safe sex from now until you're blue in the face, but that isn't about to stop people from doing it any way they want."

"What about AIDS?" asked Byrne. "Do they want to die?"

"Maybe they do," said Shannon. "Or maybe they just don't care. That's never occurred to you, has it? That maybe they just don't give a damn, that maybe the loss of sexual satisfaction is just not worth a few extra years of life. Why is it that everyone thinks that living to be eighty is so fucking important?"

Byrne was taken aback at her outburst. "Well, I . . ." he said.

"Fuck you," said Shannon, "and the rest of you breeders. Let me explain something to you that you're going to have a hard time understanding and that you're not going to like very much. These men live to fuck; that's what they do. That's how they define themselves as gay men. It's their identity." She spat the last word out so hard Byrne could feel the spittle on his cheek, but made no effort to remove it; they said you couldn't get AIDS from saliva, not unless maybe you licked it up.

"Their identity, Lieutenant," she repeated. "That's a concept alien to you people, who take your heterosexuality for granted. You don't wake up every morning and say to yourself, 'I'm straight,' and wonder what you're going to do about it the rest of the day. These men do. They're queer, they're here, and they're proud. And they express their pride by rubbing your straight nose in their behavior."

"That's not all they're rubbing noses in," cracked Byrne. "Anyway, I don't see what all this has to do with AIDS."

"You're missing the point," said Shannon. "When AIDS first appeared, first there was denial and disbelief. How can this be happening? Why now, when gay people have finally won the right to indulge their sexuality with the same openness that straights do? It seemed like an impossibly cruel joke. Then, when people started dying, there was panic; condomania set in. Almost overnight, gay men changed some aspects of their behavior. They still had sex, some of them with as many men a night as they possibly could, but now they used a rubber. And the infection rate began to decline. But they couldn't change their nature, and after a while they went back to the old ways. And do you know why, Lieutenant? Because safe sex just isn't any fun. When was the last time you wore a condom?"

"I don't think that's any business of yours," he replied, although he had to admit she had a point. Rubbers were no fun; it really was like taking a shower in a raincoat. "I thought gays had all become sweet loving couples these days," he said. "You know, monogamous, caring, sharing—no different from straights except for their, um, sexual orientation. At least that's what their apologists want us to believe."

"Some of them do, maybe," said Shannon. "But the point is that for other gay men, sex, even painful sex, and lots of it, is what they need to live; take that away from them, take away what makes them gay, and life is no longer worth living. These men are more masculine than you are, Lieutenant, I guarantee you; they are the male principle in action: unfettered seed-spreaders, their passion untrammeled by feminine scruples or inhibitions. There are some things worth dying for, Lieutenant Byrne, and if sex isn't one of them, then I don't know what the hell is."

"I'm not here to discuss the psychological ins and outs of homosexuality," said Byrne, changing the subject. "I was wondering, however, if you have tubs, showers, that sort of thing. That's more or less what I meant by the sex here being dirty."

"Does this look like a bathhouse to you, Lieutenant?" she asked. "We have a few showers, for the guys to clean up afterward, but no tubs. If it's water sports you want, I suggest you try the Golden Shower or Into Every Life. They're both on West Street." She looked him up and down. "But you don't look like that kind of guy to me."

" 'Into Every Life'?" he asked.

" 'A Little Rain Must Fall,' " she answered.

"I'd like to take a look at the showers just the same," he said. "Does the name Egil Ekdahl mean anything to you?"

"What in the world is an Egil Ekdahl?" asked Shannon. "It sounds delicious." She smacked her lips in emphasis. "Is it some kind of Swedish pastry? I'm Scandinavian, you know. Well, part."

Byrne was not about to ask which part. "It's not an it, it's a he," said Byrne.

"I like him already."

"Mr. Ekdahl was murdered earlier this week."

Her eyes opened wide in mock amazement. "And we never got a chance to meet!"

"We have reason to believe that he frequented this establishment."

"All of our clients frequent this establishment," she interrupted. "And I do mean frequent. 'Come early and often,' that's our motto."

"Maybe the name Edwin Paine rings a bell?" suggested Byrne. "A black BMW with gray interior? His car was registered to this address."

"I'm sure I have no idea why," she said. "Nobody lives here, except me sometimes, if it's been real busy and I sleep over." She patted the bed in emphasis and, Byrne thought, implicit invitation.

He pretended not to notice. "Then perhaps you'll recall a black dildo with a silver tip? With 'Mother's Little Helper' written on it in Russian?"

She rolled her eyes. "In my dreams," she said. "A girl doesn't forget something like that, Lieutenant," she said. "Do you have a picture? Of him, I mean."

"Yes, I do." Byrne fished in his wallet, found Ekdahl's black-and-white passport photo and showed it to her.

"Could you hand it to me, please? I can't see it from here."

Byrne reached over and gave it to her. He had no intention of coming any closer.

"Oh my, my, isn't he gorgeous?" said Shannon, contemplating the photo. "He makes me hard just looking at him." She caught the quizzical look on Byrne's face and quickly added, "You know what I mean." Her skirt was inching up her thighs. "A silver-tipped dildo, you say? Wasn't his own tool good enough?"

As Shannon studied the picture, Byrne studied her. She was, he had to admit, very attractive. Shannon looked to be about thirty. Her hair was combed up and her eyes were green. Her blouse was open two buttons and the unmistakable cleavage of real breasts jutted through. Unconsciously, Byrne edged nearer. Without half trying, he could make out her pink right nipple as he looked down her shirt.

She glanced up quickly and caught him peeking, the way any woman would have. "There is something vaguely familiar about him," she admitted, "but I'm afraid I'm shooting blanks on this one for now." Another quick lick of the lips. "You'll have to give me time to, you know, refresh my memory." With girlish enthusiasm she rolled over, holding the picture in front of her and letting Byrne admire the roundness of her ass. "I'm so rude," she said, looking back at him, "to keep you standing, erect, like that. Please sit down." She patted the bed again.

"I'd prefer to stand."

Shannon was quiet for a moment. "Lieutenant," she said, "do you find me desirable? Would you like to fuck me?" She appraised him with the practiced innocence of a professional schoolgirl. "It would be the ride of your life."

Byrne took the picture back. "I'm sorry to have bothered you, Ms.

Shannon." He opened the door and started to step out. "If you'll just point me toward the showers . . ."

"Wait," she said. "That was very naughty of me. Sometimes I just can't help myself. All these queers . . . a girl has to take it where she can get it. So to speak."

"Yeah," he said. "I bet a girl does." He looked back into the club. Somebody was doing something to someone else with one of the power drills. He thought he recognized one of the deputy mayors, but couldn't be sure.

"Ask Roberto if he knows him," came the voice from behind him.

"Who?"

"Roberto, the doorman. I have to run now, but he can be very helpful."

"I bet," said Byrne.

The shower room was at the back of the club, at the far end, and Byrne tried not to look at what was going on around him as he made his way toward it. He didn't exactly expect to find the place covered in blood, but if there had ever been any evidence there it was long since cleaned up, although he made a note to send a tech crew anyway, just in case somebody might have missed a drop. Blood spots were awfully hard to get out, as Lady Macbeth found to her sorrow.

Neither the showers nor his interview with the proprietor, though, was the real reason he had come to the Rambone. He wanted to see the place, to get a feel for what had been part of Ekdahl's environment. For the thing that puzzled him most about the man was that he seemed to be two completely different people: elegant international diplomat, lover of at least one beautiful woman on the one hand, while on the other—what? Bisexual impotent sadist with a taste for the louche?

He found Roberto watching a daisy chain. "Don't you ever get tired of this stuff?" he asked.

"Why should I?" asked Roberto. "It's the way I am. You got a problem with that?"

Byrne held up Ekdahl's photograph. *"No mas,"* he said. "Know who this is?"

Of course he did. "Everybody knows who that is. That there's Eddie."

"Eddie?" said Byrne. "Did he have a last name?"

"Eddie the momma's boy; Eddie, with his little helper. Eddie the wild man. Eddie Paine." Roberto had grabbed the picture and was studying it.

"Yeah, man, that's definitely Eddie," he said. "Eddie is a friend of the house, but we have to watch him just the same in case he gets carried away."

"Carried away?" asked Byrne.

"Yeah, with that damn 'Helper' of his. Gonna kill somebody with that thing some day. He likes to hurt, Eddie, and sometimes he likes to hurt bad." His eyes practically misted at the memory. "Of course, we got guys who like to get hurt bad, so usually it all works out okay."

In the distance, Byrne could hear the sound of hammering. Someone was finally starting to scream. "Danish guy, was he?" he hazarded.

"No, man, Eddie's an American from Brooklyn. Sheepshead Bay, Brighton Beach, somewhere like that. But sometimes, when he's really beating on a guy, really fuckin' reaming him, he shouts something in a funny language."

"What is it?"

"Hey man, give me a fuckin' break, Spanish and English are enough for me."

"Anybody hear what he says?" demanded Byrne, and something in his tone of voice commanded attention, because one of the daises broke the chain and stood up.

"That's Paul," said Roberto.

"Pavel," the man corrected. Byrne could hear his heavy Russian accent.

"What did he say, Pavel?" asked Byrne.

"Well," said Pavel, "he says, '*Yeb tvoju v dushu mat!*' Is common Russian curse."

"What does it mean?" asked Byrne.

The man blushed. In here, of all places. "Means, 'I fuck your mother in her soul.'"

"Come again?" said Byrne in disbelief.

"Or, 'I fuck your mother's soul.'" Pavel shrugged. "Is typical Russian," he said, and smiled broadly. "Like me!"

"What did you mean, 'friend of the house'?" Byrne asked Roberto.

"You know, a friend. Eddie's Shannon's boyfriend."

By the time he got back to her office, Shannon was gone.

"Come again," said Roberto as Byrne left.

Chapter Twenty-two
Sunnyside, Queens
Saturday, October 20, 1990; 6:00 P.M.

Byrne parked his unmarked 1987 Plymouth Fury down the block from his mother's house near the intersection of Forty-eighth Street and Forty-eighth Avenue, just off Queens Boulevard and close by New Calvary Cemetery. The Queens street-numbering system drove visitors crazy—there were also Places to go along with the Streets and Avenues, and if you just went by the numbers you could drive around for hours and never get where you were going—but to him it was second nature; if you didn't know where you were going, you probably didn't belong here. Down the avenue, in the far distance, he could see the spire of the Empire State Building, its lights just coming on, a symbol of the mighty city that both enticed and mocked the residents on the other side of the East River. The neighborhood was changing, and he knew from long, bitter experience that the perps could spot a cop car the way flies could spot shit. He didn't want to cause his mother any more trouble than he already had.

"Yo, fuck me if it ain't the X-man." The cry came from out of the shadows.

Reflexively, Byrne made sure his shoulder holster was open and ready as a black man emerged from between the buildings. He wore expensive, unlaced Adidas, torn baggy pants that threatened any minute to drop down to his ankles, and a White Sox cap, backward. His T-shirt had a picture of a smoking handgun on it, above the legend NEW YORK: IT AIN'T KANSAS.

"Jesus, Ruf, you scared the crap out of me," said Byrne. "I almost wasted your worthless motherfuckin' ass."

"You can talk the game," said the black man with the cornrows, "but can you *play* the game?" He dribbled an imaginary basketball in circles around Byrne. The cop took up the challenge.

"Yo, Ruf!" he cried. Impulsively, he lunged for the ball, stole it and drove it to the equally imaginary hoop. In a flash, the black man was on him.

"Rejected, mo'fo!" he shouted. "The Magic Man has just done rejected yo' white honky ass." They high-fived each other.

"White boys can't play for shit. Can't jump, can't dribble, sure as hell can't phi slamma jamma. 'Bout all you can do is pass the motherfuckin' ball, and that don't score no points on my playground."

"Yeah, well, maybe if you spent more time playin' good 'stead of just lookin' good you might make the NBA." They high-fived again and shook hands. "What's goin' down, Rufus?" said Byrne. "Got that rent money yet?"

Rufus smiled. His real name was George Johnson, Jr., but for some reason he preferred to be known as Rufus Rastus Johnson Brown, like in the old coon song. It seemed to be his secret joke on the world.

"Nothin', so far as I kin see, X-man," said Brown.

"Everything quiet?"

"Quiet as my grandma in her grave."

"Your grandma ain't dead, Ruf."

"Well, as quiet as she would be if she wa' dead, which in fact she may be any day now, 'specially the way her 'hood is gettin'."

"Ain't nothin' wrong with her 'hood that a few less homeboys wouldn't cure."

"You talkin' trash again, X-man. Ain't the niggers done fucked up my 'hood, it the damn spics. Sometimes I thinks to myself, shit, we oughts to get along better wit' da white folks and like, you know, team the fuck up together against them Nuyoricans who can't even fuckin' speak the King's English, and send 'em all back to San Juan."

"First, get a big boat . . ." said Byrne. "That's what we used to say about you guys."

"Let bygones be bygones, my man, dat's what ol' Rufus Rastus Johnson Brown always say. Besides, ain't that what them English done to you?"

Indeed they had. Byrne slapped Rufus on the back. "How's my mom?"

"She be fine. She fine as wine on Sunday evenin' at nine."

"Thanks for looking out for her, Ruf. You know I worry."

"Shit, you white boys always worryin'. My mama, I don't worry about her nohow."

"She's dead, Rufus."

"Like I said . . ."

Byrne walked up the steps to the small brick apartment building. "Yo, Ruf," he called out. "Thanks, man. Keep up the good work, and lemme know if you see anything. I don't want that guy comin' back."

"No problem, short-dick. I see anybody, he be one sorry motherfucker."

"I hope he already is, Ruf," said Byrne, watching the man disappear into the darkness again, where he would remain for as long as Byrne told him to.

Byrne turned his key in the apartment door and went inside. It was true: he did worry about his mother. Woodside wasn't what it used to be and Queens sure as hell wasn't what it used to be, either. Neighborhoods seemed to turn over weekly now; "minorities" fleeing the carnage in the Bronx were arriving every day, bringing with them the same mess they were trying to leave behind: drugs, guns, the works. Byrne caught himself: mustn't be racist, mustn't stereotype; at least that's what the department's sensitivity training preached. But dammit, it wasn't the Irish or the Italians who were killing New York; not anymore, anyway. There was a crack house two blocks away, where the Dolans used to live. And where were the Dolans today? Old man Eddie was dead—thank God he didn't live to see this, he would have had another heart attack—and young Patrick, the last he heard, had moved out to Denver. Moira was working in the city as a secretary on Wall Street and the old missus Dolan was living in a retirement home up-state. You worked like a dog all your life and what, in the end, did you have? The modern-day equivalent of twenty-four dollars' worth of beads and trinkets; the spirit of Peter Minuit, embodied in his descendants, the city's merchant princes, was still screwing the natives.

And when he'd actually confronted the prowler in her home a few days ago—thank God he'd come by, it was just by chance—a man threatening her, from the sound of his voice, his temper got the better of him, the temper he always was struggling to keep in check but this was different, this was his mother, and he hadn't waited to listen, hadn't waited to find out what was happening, hadn't waited for anything because in a situation like that to wait now was often to mourn later, but had come around the corner of the living room, gun drawn, catching a glimpse of the man, just a quick look, no ID possible but sensing by the cop's honed reflex of self-preservation the aura of menace, the implied threat, the presence of a weapon and, just as instinctively, crying out "Police! Don't move!" or maybe he didn't actually say anything, it was hard to remember it all happened so fast, just like it always does, except in the movies, where it happens slow, but in any case the man hadn't responded quickly enough to suit him, just like Joey Hanrahan hadn't, except that this guy was a million times more dangerous than Joey Hanrahan, God rest his poor Irish soul, and instead turned toward him with a snarl of fear and anger and disbelief, like a particularly dangerous jungle beast, turned and dropped his hands, dropped them toward the weapon that Byrne sensed, rather than knew, but still was certain was there, and so he squeezed off a single one shot, not set, not in firing position, not aiming but squeezing nonetheless, just like they taught you at the academy, no warning, nothing, which they did not teach at the academy, firing not at a man but at a shape, a target, a blur, for the man was moving now, quick as a cat, springing through the window with a shatter and a crash, a white man, that much Byrne could tell, but there were still millions of white men in New York City, not to mention America, not to mention the world, and so he couldn't be sure, he might have just been assuming, he didn't get a good look, maybe he just thought the guy was white, or even that it was a guy at all but what else could it have been, disappearing into the night with a single groan, and Byrne not knowing whether he had hit him square or just winged him but rushing to his mother as the shape molted and the shadow vanished and the pieces of the broken window sailed through the air, rushing to Irene who sat in her chair, frozen, immobile, transfixed, unable to move, but her eyes, the look on her face something he'd never forget, something that already was haunting his dreams and her voice soft, resigned, quiet, a whisper, a murmur, as of the heart and not the lips, upon which rested a word that he could not quite make out, a single word that sounded like, but was not quite, Lubin or Lublin or some such Jewish name, it was then that he'd put Rufus on the case, either that or put Rufus in jail for small-time dealing and running a string of teenage hookers who gave ten-buck blow jobs back behind the New Calvary tombstones, half the proceeds of which he collected from Rufus in order to give to the Catholic charities, starting with his mother, because charity begins at home. Lublin, Luboy, something like that; he could still hear it in his mind's ear, and in his heart.

"Is the shvartzer still outside?" asked Irene Byrne from the living room, where she was watching *Wheel of Fortune* on the television. It was one of her favorite shows. "Why don't you let that poor man go home? People will think we're dating."

"It's me, Ma," called out Byrne, as if she didn't know.

"Surprise, surprise," she said. "At least it isn't Tom." It never was. "Better a burglar than him. A burglar would be friendlier." She had not turned around. "What's the occasion?"

Byrne walked over to the TV and turned it down. "Jeez, Ma, how can you hear yourself think with that thing on all the time?" he asked her. "What are you, deaf?"

"It keeps me company, Francis."

"The guy could come back and you wouldn't hear a thing. Plus Vanna never says anything anyway." Byrne bent over her chair and kissed her. Though the weather was still warm, her cheek was cold.

He looked around the living room. It hadn't changed a bit since he left home. His mother sat in her usual wing chair, an uncomfortable overstuffed relic of the late forties that had belonged to his father's parents. A small end table separated Mrs. Byrne's chair from its twin, which had been his dad's favorite. By custom, it was empty. No one had sat in it since his father died.

In 1968, detective first-grade Robert Byrne had been working a case on the Lower East Side with his partner, detective second-grade Alfonso Rodriguez, when they were both shot from behind at close range by an unknown assailant. Rodriguez dropped first, dead on the spot on Elizabeth Street, but Byrne, with a bullet in the back of his neck, had managed to draw his gun as he fell. When the squad car got to him, the safety catch was off but he had not fired; there had been too many people on the street, and even dying, Robert Byrne had not thought it safe to return fire. The killer was never apprehended.

The television set was a nineteen-inch Sony that Byrne had bought for his mother several years ago. It sat atop an old sideboard that, family tradition had it, had come over from Ireland with the Byrnes when they left from Queenstown in 1892. Framed photographs adorned the tabletop on either side of the television. There were pictures of Francis's paternal grandparents, Leo and Marion Lykes Byrne, taken in New York in 1922 after they had returned from what proved to be their only visit to Ireland, which they had cut short because of the Civil War. Leo was a passionate supporter of Michael Collins, and when the Big Mick was ambushed and killed on his way from Skibbereen to Cork, Leo, who had been born a couple of years after the family had made the passage, abruptly quit his father's homeland, never to return. He hated De Valera the rest of his life, and

Byrne remembered his grandfather in the late sixties, regarding Dev as the real architect of the Troubles and cursing his memory. "I blame the English," Grandpa Byrne would rage, "but I blame Dev even more! The limey bastards should have been gone long ago!" Even worse, as far as he was concerned, De Valera had been born in Manhattan, and no good could come out of the city.

There were no pictures of his mother's family. There never had been.

Irene Byrne kept two portraits of her sons, photographs taken when the boys were in grade school. Francis was eternally embarrassed by his: it showed him in eighth grade, wearing a bow tie and a doofus smile, his hair hanging lank and stringy. *I can't believe she let me go out in public like that,* he thought, as he looked at the picture for the thousandth time. By contrast, his brother Tom, nearly eight years older, was sharp and spiffy. Did fashion change so much so soon? Or did standards go to hell so quickly?

There used to be a lovely photograph of his mother and father on the beach at Fire Island, but after Robert Byrne's murder it had disappeared. Byrne never asked his mother what she had done with it.

"So tell me what you're up to," Irene said. Byrne settled on the couch across the room and looked at her. His mother's attention was divided between him and the puzzle. It said: "_o_ _ _r's _i_ _ _ _ _ _ _p_r." For some reason, Vanna seemed to find this amusing, but then she probably found the quick brown fox jumping over the lazy red dog amusing too.

"Nothin', Ma," he replied. "Just thought I'd stop by and see how you are. Doreen and I are going to a party tonight, so I can't stay long."

"Such a nice girl," she snorted derisively. "I'm sure you'll have a wonderful time."

Byrne watched his mother as she delivered the ritual lines. Irene was still a handsome woman—not beautiful, exactly, but attractive, although the idea of considering his own mother attractive struck him as somehow perverted—with fine, firm posture and clear, bright, cold eyes.

"You know what your problem is, Francis?" she asked.

"What, Ma?"

"Number one, you live alone, which is making you crazy."

"Ma . . ." he protested.

"Shut up and listen. And don't give me that Doreen baloney, either. She's a tramp and you know it. Number two, you're a stubborn Irishman, just like your father."

"You're right, Ma, I shoulda been more like you."

"I don't know what possessed me to marry that man, Francis. My friends warned me, they said don't do it, but I did it anyway and I've regretted it to my dying day."

"You're not dying, Ma. Not even close. And you don't have any friends."

"Well, I will. And I used to."

"And you haven't regretted it. You loved Dad."

"That's what you think!" she exclaimed. "I hate all men! You're all no damn good." She folded her arms across her breast, just like a nun. Robert Byrne's death was still an open wound, and the way she dealt with the awful, inexplicable loss, Byrne understood, was to deny the happiness they had had together. But he wanted to believe there wasn't a day gone by that his mother hadn't mourned his dad. Not that she would ever show it; at the funeral, surrounded by hundreds of New York City policemen and a half dozen or so strange, quiet men in business suits, Irene Byrne had sat stoically, almost dispassionately, as if the terrible day was happening to someone else. She would not give them the satisfaction of seeing her suffer.

"Ma, your sons are men," protested Byrne.

"And you're no good. Shooting off guns and chasing criminals and running around with fast women and God only knows what else."

"That's not what we usually do, Ma."

"That's what you say, but don't you try to tell me different." There the argument rested. "I know. I watch television." She took a short, silent victory lap.

"Any more problems, Ma?" he asked. "Seen anything funny?"

"There's no funny shows on anymore, that's my problem. When you were little I used to enjoy *Bewitched*, but now, it's a crime what they put on television. You should do something about it." Throughout the conversation she continued to stare straight ahead at the set, as she habitually did when he visited.

"That's not what I mean, Ma," protested Byrne, but it was clear she had nothing further to say on the subject. "I saw Tom."

She snorted.

"He's fine," said Byrne. "He looks good. He sends his love."

"Bullshit!" his mother said. "That one's a devil."

"Ma!" protested Byrne. "He's still your son."

When they were younger, Byrne had always wanted to get some leverage on his big brother, but it had been so difficult. They looked very much alike, each favoring his father, but Tom was a little taller, a little stronger, a little faster, the best student, the most talented, the guy who got all the girls. He never broke a sweat, and following in his wake Francis could only seem like an imitation Byrne, a pretender. When Frankie was little, Tom used to steal his toys, and break them if he felt like it. As grown-ups not much had changed. Take Mary Claire, for example: he had stolen her but not broken her; Byrne had done that all by himself.

"He's no son of mine, but he's still your brother. So what did Mr. Personality have to say?"

"Not much. We talked business, mostly."

"I thought you two weren't speaking after that business with your girl-friend."

"Well, sometimes things change."

"Must be a pretty big case, to have the two genius Byrne boys working on it together. Where did you bury the hatchets? In each other, I'll bet."

"We didn't. We just put 'em in their cases for a while."

The old lady grunted. Byrne was trying to decide which, in her opinion, was worse: that he had seen his brother, or that he had told her about it.

"You've got Irish Alzheimer's, Ma," he said at last.

"I do not," said Irene with conviction. "I don't have Irish anything!"

"Yes, you do, Ma. You've got Irish Alzheimer's."

Finally, she took the bait. "And what's that?" For the first time, she turned to look at him.

"You only remember the grudges."

"Very funny," she said, and resumed her contemplation of the television set. "As if you don't."

"I gotta ask you something, Ma," Byrne ventured, but she had turned her attention back to Vanna. The puzzle read: "_o_h_r's _i_ _ _ _ h_ _ p_r."

"We spent all that money on parochial school, not to mention Fordham, and you probably can't even figure this one out." Byrne wasn't sure if she was referring to the puzzle or his latest case.

One of the contestants, an unemployed aerospace engineer from Pomona, California, spun the wheel and hazarded a guess. "Is there a *t*?" he said.

"Of course there is, you idiot," exclaimed Irene. "Really, some people are so dense. So what do you want to ask me?"

This time it was Byrne's turn not to have listened. The bell rang, the board lit up and Vanna turned over two *t*'s. The puzzle now read: "_oth_r's _itt_ _ h_ _p_r."

"Ask for an *l*, you moron," shouted Irene at the screen. "An *l*!" She shook her head, appalled by the man's stupidity. "No wonder he's out of a job."

Byrne still couldn't see it. "Does the name Ekdahl mean anything to you, Ma?" he asked.

"Uh, is there an *l*?" asked the Pomonan. Vanna was pleased to show him that there were three.

"Ekdahl?" she replied. "What kind of a name is that?"

"It's some kind of Scandinavian name, Ma," Byrne told her. "It's Danish, or somethin' like that. Do we know any Danes? Swedes? Norwegians?"

"Norwegians in New York, that's a good one," said his mother. "There haven't been any Norwegians here since the last one died out in Bay Ridge because she couldn't get smoked herring anymore, unless maybe it was kosher, or on a pizza."

"It might not be his real name."

"Then how do you expect me to know? I used to know a Mrs. Eckert, but I don't think she was Norwegian. She lived in Flatbush. And when you were little there was a family named Dahlheimer living down the street, but they moved away in the late sixties, which is when I should have moved too." She barked at the TV: "It's so obvious."

"Are you talking to me, Ma, or to the television?"

"Buy an *e*, for crying out loud!" said Irene.

"Ma, I want you to look at this picture and tell me who this lady is." He fished in his pocket for the photograph he had found in Ekdahl's car. "Can you identify her?"

"Is there a *g*?" asked the housewife from Elyria, Ohio, in the polyester pantsuit.

"What a moron," said his mother. "And will you look at those clothes."

"The picture, Ma," insisted Byrne. "Do you know who this woman is?"

She glanced away from the television long enough to take in the photograph. "Of course I do, dummkopf," she said. "It's me."

"I know it's you, Ma," said Byrne. "It's the other lady I'm trying to identify."

"What's it to you?" said Irene, both eyes on Vanna.

"I need to know, is all."

"Why?" She wasn't looking at either him or the picture.

"Because I need to know." This was getting ridiculous. More than once he had wished he could stand up to his mother, would have the courage to actually ask her the question that was on his mind, but he never had. It was just like with Tom; he could be tough with everybody in his life except his family. No time like the present, though, for growing up. Byrne made a move toward the TV.

"Touch that set and I'll kill you," she said, and Byrne half believed her. She was still staring straight ahead, at Vanna, who was pointing at the board.

"Could I buy an *e*?" said the computer salesman from Covington, Kentucky.

"That's the first question you should have asked, schmuck. *L-e* . . . Let's see if this jerk finally gets it," said Irene.

"Who is she, Ma?" he insisted.

"Shut up and let me watch this, will you?"

"It's important," Byrne insisted.

"It's important," scoffed his mother. "If it's so all-fired important now it will still be important at the next commercial." He gave up and turned his eyes away from the photograph to the television set, just as Vanna turned over the missing letters.

"Mother's little helper!" shouted Irene and the computer salesman simultaneously. "No wonder you didn't get it," she said.

Maybe now. "Her name?" prompted Byrne.

"That's what our mother used to call us, when we were little girls," his mother said.

"Who?" asked Byrne. "Used to call who?"

"My sister and I," said Irene. She pronounced the word *sistra*.

The family resemblance was clear, clearer even than between him and Tom. Irene on the right, with her long, straight nose and widely spaced eyes, looking a little like a young Kate Hepburn, her eyes turned in the direction of the even prettier girl with her, whose nose was a little straighter and whose eyes were a little closer; a millimeter of difference, but all the difference. Her sister! And to think until today he didn't even know she had a sister.

"She's been dead for years," said Irene dispassionately. "Thank God."

"Her name, Ma?" asked Byrne again, but she was no longer listening to him. A fresh new puzzle had appeared.

Chapter Twenty-three
The Upper East Side
Saturday, October 20, 1990; 8:00 P.M.

There was no doorbell for apartment 8-B. After being heralded by the doorman—ALL VISITORS MUST BE ANNOUNCED, proclaimed the sign in the lobby—you took an automatic, remote-controlled elevator straight up to the eighth floor and there you were, walking right into the foyer of Dr. and Mrs. Jacob B. German of 168 East Sixty-fourth Street, New York, New York, no front door or anything. Byrne was greeted by a smiling, stately, expensively dressed woman of, he guessed, fifty-five or so years, maybe a little older, who shook his hand and ushered him into the domicile proper. She wore her dark hair short, although not severely, and framed her deep brown eyes with a modicum of eye shadow. Her skin was still fine, white and almost translucent, without liver spots. She looked exactly like what she was: a rich Upper East Side Jewish matron, who probably subscribed both to the Philharmonic and the lecture series at the Ninety-second Street Y. "You must be Tom Byrne," she said. "I'm so glad you're able to be here with us."

"Hello, Mrs. German," Byrne replied. "Actually, I'm Francis. He's my older brother, but people often confuse us."

"A mistake I won't make again, you can be sure of that." Mrs. German laughed, recovering quickly and taking him by the hand. Byrne wondered if she even knew he was coming. He felt like a four-year-old, being led to the school bus by his mother, but he offered no resistance. Her flesh was warm and soft.

" . . . hasn't arrived yet," Mrs. German was saying, as she steered him toward the clump of guests gathered in the middle of what Byrne assumed must be the living room. By New York City standards, it was as big as Giants Stadium.

"Pardon me, Mrs. German?" he asked.

"I said, Ingrid hasn't arrived yet," she replied. "It's hardly a surprise, but that's what my husband wants to pretend"—Byrne was so busy gawking at the splendor of the place that he temporarily lost track of what she was saying—"and here he is now," she concluded, handing him off to a thick-set, balding man of medium height and above average weight, who was at least twenty years her senior. He wore a scholarly countenance and had tufts of hair growing out of the tops of his ears. It was the famous psychoanalyst and author Jacob German. "This is Francis Byrne, Jacob," she said coolly. "He's a friend of your Ingrid."

"It's an honor to meet you, sir," said Byrne, shaking hands. His mind was still registering Mrs. German's use of the second-person possessive pronoun when he noticed with a start that there was a heavy bandage where the little finger of the psychiatrist's right hand should have been. The surprises were already starting.

"The pleasure is mutual, Lieutenant Byrne," Dr. German replied. "I've heard a lot about you."

Byrne wondered exactly how much he had heard, and why. "You probably mean my brother, Tom," said Byrne. "He's Ingrid's boyfriend—you know, the FBI agent?"

"Yes, I do know," said the doctor, with a barking laugh that startled Byrne with its violent intensity. "I also know the difference between a celebrated New York City homicide detective and an FBI agent, and believe me I am pleased and proud to have the honor of addressing the former and not, thank God, the latter."

"Why 'thank God,' Dr. German?" asked Byrne, but his host was already steering him into the party with the gentlest of pressure on his arm, a man used to being obeyed.

"Francis, if I may presume to call you that, please say hello to Mr. and Mrs. O'Donahue, Ellen and Fred. They're both in publishing." Byrne shook hands with a tall, middle-aged woman whose youthful beauty might be fading but whose penetrating and intelligent visage dared him to say it to her face. Byrne had time only to register a firm shake from her husband when his attention was redirected. "And this distinguished gentleman taking up more than his fair share of space on our planet is Bernie Weissman, the trial attorney—perhaps you've met in court?—and his better half, Lisa."

"As a matter of fact," began Byrne, but that was as far as he got.

"The lieutenant and I have crossed swords on several occasions," boomed Weissman. "But never in anger; it was always strictly business. Isn't that right?" He looked around, playing to the jury, as ever. "I have always had the greatest respect for the men and women of the New York Police Department."

"Yes, sir," said Byrne, deciding this was not the time to remind the lawyer about the last courtroom date they had shared. After Weissman had gotten finished cross-examining him in the Finley murder, Byrne had never wanted to kill an attorney so much in his life. As if he had deliberately forgotten to include in the application for a search warrant the pair of muddy running shoes with traces of Mrs. Finley's blood on them that he had found stuck in the garbage chute: how was he supposed to know they were there? And so Jay Finley, one of the city's sleaziest arbitrageurs, beat the rap while Audrey lay pushing up daisies at the Westchester County cemetery of Valhalla. "You really taught me the true meaning of *schadenfreude* on that one."

"*Schadenfreude*: the enjoyment of the discomfiture of others. Literally, damage-joy. You speak the language of my homeland, Lieutenant?" asked Dr. German.

"Afraid not," Byrne replied. "My mother speaks a little German, and she tried to teach me a few words here and there when I was growing up, but they didn't stick."

"Was she born in Germany?" asked the psychiatrist, but at that moment the elevator door opened once again, disgorging a couple of new guests, and he excused himself, leaving Byrne standing alone uncomfortably.

He knew he was out of his league. For all his boho vulgarity, Tom could wear sharp suits, get around in French and his other languages and move with a fast Washington crowd, but Francis was still just a Queens mick, trying to keep the peace on the streets of Manhattan—the city, as he still thought of it. That's the way the folks in Queens referred to the borough of Manhattan. And even though, unlike most cops, he actually lived in Manhattan, he still called it the city too.

One of the new arrivals, he noticed with relief, was Doreen. "Hello, darling," he greeted her, and kissed her.

He had to admit she looked fabulous. With her petite but enticing figure and exotic appearance, Doreen Grace Watanabe could wear a burlap sack and deelieboppers and still look like a million, but for this occasion she was sporting a Hanae Mori black pantsuit and a string of pearls—real

Mikimotos that Byrne had gotten for her birthday privately from a whole-sale jeweler on West Forty-sixth Street who owed him a favor; Byrne had put the QT on a robbery when the perp turned out to be the guy's son, stealing from his immigrant dad to support a coke habit. She wore her thick, glossy, jet-black hair, which was the envy of every woman they knew, bobbed in a modified Prince Valiant, and her fingernails had been lacquered Chinese red for the occasion. When she dressed like this, only her light brown eyes, more oval than almond, gave her paternal parentage away. Byrne was very proud to be seen with her. He was glad the faint bruise over her left temple didn't show.

"Sorry I'm a little late, Francis," she said, kissing him back. "Mrs. Smith—can you believe anybody is still named Smith in New York these days? Wait till the Patels start buying art—couldn't get a cab and I had to wait for her."

"I didn't know you two knew each other," said Mrs. German, who had somehow materialized behind them.

"We're together, Mrs. German," explained Doreen. "I'm Dori Grace. The art dealer?"

"Of course you are, dear," said Mrs. German. "I keep thinking this is Tom. They do look a bit alike, don't they?"

"This is Francis, his younger, smarter and much better looking brother," said Doreen, "and, for better or worse, I'm stuck with him. Isn't that right, love?" she said, giving him a confirmational squeeze.

"You bet," said Byrne, just as Ingrid came into the room, with Tom right behind her. In an off-white, off-the-shoulder evening dress, worn with silk stockings and, no doubt, a garter belt, she was devastating. She had curled her hair, and the curls bounced prettily on her bare shoulders.

"Surprise!" yelled everyone.

Ingrid, he thought, did a remarkable job of feigning astonishment, al-though Byrne knew that in her heart she believed, with the arrogance of all beautiful women, that she fully deserved whatever homage and accolades came her way. Her eyes opened wide, and as they inspected the room he could feel their blue-laser heat. She tossed her blonde hair back and thrust her breasts forward—Byrne's hands tingled briefly with the muscle mem-ory—and gave out a pleasingly feminine little laugh that tore briefly at his heart. Then he looked back at Doreen and mentally bit his tongue, or what-ever it was that ought to be mentally bitten. Despite the fact that her novelty had worn off, Doreen was as beautiful as Ingrid by any rational standard, even his. Not that, at this moment, rational standards meant much.

"That's Ingrid," he said, and immediately felt like an idiot.

"No shit," whispered Doreen. "And may I introduce you to your awful brother who, you'll notice, has his hand on her ass. Really, Francis, you got all the class in the family."

Ingrid flashed by in a blaze of Opium, throwing her arms around him and kissing him on both cheeks. "Hello, Lieutenant," she said.

During the clinch, Byrne couldn't resist a question. "How do you rate all this?" he hissed, and gestured with his head.

"Politics makes strange bedfellows, Francis, as you say in English." She took a step back but continued talking softly. "Dr. German's name was given to me when I came over. Both he and Ella are very active in Jewish affairs, and they've given a great deal of money to fund a memorial to the saving of Denmark's Jews during the war, a cause he's passionate about. If you're from Denmark, then you're okay in his book."

"But you're not from Denmark," he pointed out.

"He doesn't have to know that," she said, raising her voice. "And you must be Doreen. I've heard so much about you."

"How about that?" said Doreen. "Francis has never even mentioned you." She turned to his brother. "Hello, Tom," she said without the slightest trace of affection. "Catch any enemies of the people lately?"

"I'm workin' on it, babe," said Tom, moving away from her swiftly. "Mrs. German, how are you?"

Byrne turned to say something to Doreen, but just then a voice spoke softly in his ear. "Lieutenant Byrne," it said. "Could I have a word with you, please? Just the two of us? It will only take a moment."

It was his host, standing near the entrance to his impressive library, which could easily have housed a family of six. "You're working on the Ekdahl case, I understand," he practically whispered. The question caught Byrne by surprise, for Ekdahl's name had not yet surfaced, either on television or in the newspapers.

"Who?" he asked ingenuously, but his eyes betrayed his annoyance.

Dr. German noted the flash of anger. "Don't be alarmed, Lieutenant," he soothed. "I'm something of a crime buff, and I do have my sources within the department." Byrne should have remembered that, for the doctor had been an expert witness in several high-profile trials over the past decade. The psychiatrist piloted him into the room, away from the others. "What have you found out so far? About Ekdahl? If you don't mind my asking."

Instinctively, Byrne bristled. Why was it that while doctors and lawyers invariably refused to answer professional questions in a social setting—they called them kitchen consultations—they treated everybody else's business as a hobby? "More than I did yesterday," replied Byrne vaguely, "and not as much as I will tomorrow."

"I see," said Dr. German, with what might have been a smile of satisfaction. "In other words, very little." He rubbed his hands together. "I fear I have you at a disadvantage, then."

"I thought this was a social occasion, Doctor," said Byrne, smiling, but with some irritation in his voice. In his experience, self-described crime buffs were the worst kind of civilians; they saw police work as a Hercule Poirot mystery, in which the lone detective brilliantly deduces the murderer's identity from the comfort of his armchair, instead of what it really was: a long, hard slog around the neighborhoods, asking questions until somebody squealed on the bad guy or, more often than you would think, he simply turned himself in. Unless Dr. German was ready to confess to something, preferably one of the department's uncleared homicides, Byrne wasn't interested in discussing his work.

The psychiatrist stood flat-footed opposite Byrne, his back to the groaning bookshelves, looking at the cop as if he were a prospective patient, or a student at one of his Columbia University psych lectures, and worrying his bandaged hand. Social situation or no, Byrne's congenitally suspicious brain couldn't help but kick in: library, Ekdahl, hand; in the doctor's mind, the three must be somehow related. With "his" Ingrid in there as a wild card. Byrne broke the conversational Mexican standoff. "What do you mean, a disadvantage?"

Dr. German, however, seemed no longer interested in pursuing this line of conversation. He dropped his damaged hand and began gesticulating in the direction of his bookshelves.

"A man's athenaeum says a lot about his character, wouldn't you agree, Lieutenant?" he observed. "Just like his choice of friends." From what Byrne could observe the collection was mostly professional. He had to twist his head this way and that, for many of the books had the titles on their spines reversed, indicating a European publisher, most often German or

Austrian. There were volumes on psychiatric theory and practice, including some by Jung, Masson and even Szasz; at least Dr. German was not a Freudian dogmatist. There was a handsome collection of Judaica, which featured many tomes in Hebrew and the collected works of Singer in Yiddish. It seemed odd when, over in a corner, he spied a number of books on the Kennedy assassination: Marrs, Garrison, Epstein, Lane.

"My little hobby," said a voice over his left shoulder. "Here we are, nearly three decades later, and still so many unanswered questions. To go along with our unanswered prayers, I suppose."

Byrne turned back to look at the psychiatrist.

"I was not in your—our—country on that unhappy day, Lieutenant," said Dr. German. "I was living in Vienna. You look surprised. Not all of us either fled the Nazis just in time or never made it out of the camps. Or went to Israel. Some of us, believe it or not, felt that central Europe was our home, and that nobody was going to take it away from us, certainly not Herr Schickelgruber. I was one of those people. Or used to be." He indicated one of the wing chairs for Byrne to sit down, but the detective shook his head and remained standing; in any interview, he always made sure the physical dynamic was either equal or in his favor.

"When I first came to this country—that would have been in 1965— I still didn't speak English very well," he said. "Nor did I read it very adeptly, either. Indeed, for many years I continued to prefer reading for recreation in my own language—I still thought of it as 'my own,' no matter what Herr Hitler thought. Which accounts, I suppose, for the preponderance of books in German."

"Mmmm," said Byrne. He had no idea Dr. German was a Holocaust survivor; maybe the man wasn't hinky after all, just justifiably weird.

"However, as you can see, I do have many English-language volumes as well." As Byrne drew near, he could see that the particular section the doctor's large frame was partially obscuring contained books on the destruction of the European Jews. "It's a sad commentary that some of these works have never found a publisher in my own homeland, Lieutenant, or indeed in Israel."

"Looks interesting," lied Byrne. The Holocaust had never particularly interested him; wasn't an Irish fight.

The psychiatrist sensed his indifference. "Begging your indulgence, Lieutenant," he said, "but I would like to endorse several in particular. Of course *Eichmann in Jerusalem*, by Hannah Arendt, a basic text. Nora Levin's *The Holocaust*, an exhaustive and objective study. Arno Mayer's *Why Did the Heavens Not Darken?*, a brilliant meditation on how God can turn a deaf ear and a blind eye to the cries of the innocent. All well worth your time, especially the sections on Theresienstadt, which I can recommend to you in particular."

"I'm sure they are," said Byrne. "But in my line of work I don't get a chance to do a lot of recreational rea—" He broke off abruptly; there was something about Theresienstadt that rang a bell.

"You should," retorted the shrink sharply. You can take the boy out of Germany, reflected Byrne, but you couldn't take Germany out of the boy, even the Jewish boy. His mother had always told him Germans were rude and insistent, and understood and respected only brute force, and after meeting Gunther and Dr. German in the past twenty-four hours he was beginning to believe her stereotype might be true. After all, she was from Poland, and who had had more experience, mostly negative, with krauts than the Poles?

Byrne, however, was less interested in the books than in the photographs the doctor kept framed on one of the shelves. He moved closer. Old pictures, grainy and black and white, snapshots from some primitive Kodak. Closer: World War II vintage; closer still: concentration-camp era. Men in American uniforms, inmates wan but not completely emaciated, a few civilians, probably Germans.

"What are these?" he inquired, moving as close as possible. He was beginning to wonder whether it was time for glasses.

"Little souvenirs of the bad times," replied the doctor. "Memento mori of the worst days of my life. Luckily for me, they came early and I survived them. Very few of my colleagues from those days can say the same."

"Which one is you?" asked Byrne, pointing to one of the pictures. They were grouped in a single black-metal frame, and all appeared to have been taken about the same time. The background in each was the same: a large, ugly building that looked like an army barracks.

One of Dr. German's good fingers stabbed forward, missing Byrne's nose by an inch. "Here I am," he said, and there he was. There was no belly, of course, and plenty of hair, but there was the same haughty, even arrogant mien and consummate self-confidence.

And there, too, nearly half a century younger, was Sy Sheinberg. There was no mistaking the pathologist's height and build, even if he was forty-five years younger and thirty pounds lighter. Although Dr. German was looking straight at the camera, Sy's eyes were downcast and diffident, and he was standing apart from the group, which included an American army officer—Counter-Intelligence Corps, guessed Byrne—and a couple of other men who might have been German civilians, although one of them looked vaguely familiar. But that was a problem with being a cop: everybody looked vaguely familiar.

"Are you gentlemen going to join us, or are you going to stay in here talking all night?" said Ella German, who had appeared in the doorway. "Dinner is served."

"Lieutenant Byrne is surprisingly sanguine about Germany's chances in the World Cup this year," said the doctor as he and Byrne turned to follow her. "And here I thought Americans lacked sophistication in international sporting matters."

"I'm so glad he finally found somebody to talk about soccer with," whispered Mrs. German to Byrne as she led the way to the dining room.

Their hostess had placed name cards next to each of the settings at the large dining table. "I hope you don't mind," said Doreen to him privately before they sat down, "but I switched places with that gorgeous black girl there, so I can schmooze Ella. I figured you wouldn't mind." She shrugged prettily and smiled. "Like you boys always say, so much opportunity, so little time." Ella German was one of the city's most prominent private art collectors, and Doreen was not about to pass up an opportunity like this to plug, discreetly, the virtues of her professional services.

After a brief hunt, Byrne found himself sitting between Ellen O'Donahue and the striking black woman to whom Doreen had referred. Ingrid occupied the place of honor beside their host, to whom she was chattering in German. There was an empty seat next to her.

"Hi," he introduced himself, "I'm Francis Byrne."

"That's funny," the black woman said. "My name is Frances too." If her hair were longer, she would have looked like Grace Jones. If her nose were less pert, she would have looked like Nanette Fabray.

"Bet your last name isn't Byrne," he said, hoping she would think that was funny as well.

"How do you know?" she asked him. "I might be black Irish."

"Champagne, sir?" asked the waiter, who happened to be black.

"Frances Binghamton," she said, extending her hand.

"Her husband is Lord Binghamton, the life peer," whispered Mrs. O'Donahue in his right ear. "Frankie used to be a fashion model. She met her husband after he sent her a mash note on the runway at the fall collections in Paris. It was wrapped around a thousand-pound note. He's one of the few Brits who's not all hat and no cattle, as we say back home in Texas. Her accent's acquired, of course, but the diamonds are real."

"Lady Binghamton, I presume," he said.

"Ladies and gentlemen," said Dr. German, rising and clearing his throat loudly. "We are gathered together here this evening to honor a special friend on her twenty-eighth birthday: Ingrid Bensten, without whom—and I think this is safe to say—without whom the Danish consulate would simply not be able to function. I know I speak for my good friend Nils Pilgersen, who unfortunately could not be here with us tonight due to a sudden indisposition, when I say that Ingrid has been one of the finest advertisements for Denmark—a country that holds a special place of honor in Jewish hearts all over the world—and for Danish culture, and that we are all the better for having her living among us here in New York. To Ingrid. Happy birthday, darling."

"Happy birthday," echoed the guests, raising their wine glasses. Ella German, Byrne noticed, was not smiling, especially not at that "darling." One more thing to ask the doctor about.

"Who is that adorable Asian girl?" whispered Lady Binghamton. "Or is she Amer-Asian?"

"She is beautiful, isn't she?" said Bernie Weissman admiringly. "When that combination works, boy . . ."

"Friend of Ella's?" wondered Mrs. O'Donahue.

"More likely a friend of Tom's," said Mrs. Weissman, smiling conspiratorially. "I hear he—"

Byrne decided it was time to intervene. "Actually, she's my girlfriend," he found himself saying. Weissman reached over to shake his hand.

"Glad I didn't say anything rude." He laughed. "And I'm certainly glad you managed to cut Lisa off in mid-cry. It just goes to show you that you never know who you're talking to." The spellbinding attorney now took over. "Funniest story I ever heard in this regard was told to me by my friend Bobby Feldstein, the comic, who was once married to a very attractive opera singer. It seems that Feldstein was standing in the wings watching his wife, the soprano Maria Bandolini, perform in something by Verdi, I forget exactly which opera it was, it might have been *Falstaff*, but anyway there he is in the wings when the tenor, who was temporarily offstage, comes up behind him. '*Que bella bambina!*' he exclaims. 'Will you look at the figure on that girl!' he says, although his language was a bit more spicily Italian, of course. 'What a divine mouth! Those breasts! That bottom! Couldn't you just . . . Wouldn't you just . . .' and so on and so forth. After the performance, Bobby goes backstage to congratulate his wife and along comes the tenor. 'Pino,' says Maria, unaware they had both been admiring her, 'I'd like you to meet my husband.' The Italian didn't blink an eye or miss a beat. '*Complimenti!*' he said, and shook Bobby's hand. Now that's what I call a splendid recovery." He sipped his wine. "So, on behalf of the entire table, Lieutenant, may I say, *Complimenti!*"

Everybody laughed and Byrne felt himself reddening.

"Is she real Japanese?" asked Ellen. "You know what I mean."

"Doreen was born in Tokyo, but her mother moved back to Nagasaki right after she had the baby," replied Byrne. "Doreen was born out of wedlock—her father was an American serviceman who she never met—and the shame was so great that her mother had to leave her job and return to Kyushu, where her parents told the neighbors that their daughter's new husband had died in a railway accident. They just hoped like hell that Doreen would resemble her mother more than she did her dad, and they got lucky. A few people suspected, but at least her father was not black—in Japan, I'm sorry to say, that's a cardinal sin—and so they didn't ask too many questions. Mostly, they just left them alone, and when Doreen was old enough, she came to America to go to school. Because her father was American, she was eligible for a passport, and so she stayed."

He hadn't wanted to say so much, to give so many personal details, but he couldn't help himself. He hoped Doreen wouldn't mind. Luckily, there was no shame attached to being a bastard these days.

"I understand Jacob and Ella met in the Soviet Union," interjected Lisa Weissman. "Ella's Russian."

Byrne wondered briefly if it would be appropriate to ask his hostess whether "I fuck your mother in her soul!" was really a common Russian oath, but decided it was not dinner-party conversation.

"He met her in the early sixties, sixty-three, sixty-four I think it was," continued Lisa. "Something like that. Anyway, they met in Moscow when she served as his translator, and, can you believe this, in those days she was something of an expert in thermodynamics! That's what I'm told, anyway."

"How is everything here?" asked Dr. German after dessert had been cleared. "Everyone having a good time?"

"What a marvelous dinner, Jacob," said Frankie Binghamton, pushing away from the table. "Did you kidnap the chef?"

"I'm afraid we spirited him away for the evening from La Caravelle," said Dr. German. "He selected the wines as well."

"Well, the whole thing was simply delicious," said Frances. "And the conversation—well, you would have thought Dorothy Parker and the Round Table had never left us."

Dr. German laughed. "When I was a boy growing up in Weimar, you don't know how I longed to be a part of that scene, how I fantasized about New York, about sophistication and fancy cigarette lighters and top hats and tails and the Stork Club and championship fights at Madison Square Garden." He shrugged a considered, eloquent shrug. "And now look at our poor city. I suppose the road to hell really is paved with good intentions. Let's go into the sitting room, shall we?"

Everyone rose and began to migrate. As Byrne stood up, Ingrid came over and touched him on the shoulder. "Lovely party, isn't it?" she said, theatrically. "What a surprise!"

"Fabulous," agreed Byrne. "And so many nice people. All friends of yours?"

"Oh, yes," replied Ingrid. "The O'Donahues I met right after I came over from Scandinavia, terrific people. Bernie Weissman helps us out at the consulate with legal matters from time to time, and of course he is a good friend of Mr. Pilgersen . . ."

Who's dead, thought Byrne, lying God knows where stiff as a board, as you well know, you heartless . . .

" . . . as is Dr. German. And then there's Frankie Binghamton; we like to party together when her husband's out of town, which thank God is most of the time."

"Where's your friend Egil tonight?" asked Doreen.

It took a moment for the question to register in Byrne's consciousness. When it did, he felt like someone had just slugged him in the chest; even the anesthetic of the wine couldn't dull the sudden, urgent pain. Egil? The name had never passed his lips at home. He felt Ingrid's eyes on him, but when he looked up she was smiling at Doreen.

"Oh, he couldn't make it," she said blithely. "Something came up. I'm sure he would have loved to see you again."

"I thought you two . . ." began Byrne, but he suddenly felt a hand at his elbow, gently but forcefully pulling him away from the two women. It was Dr. German, to his rescue.

"Can I be of assistance, Lieutenant?" he asked.

"Gee, thanks, Dr. German," he said, glancing over at Ingrid and Doreen. Byrne's respect for Dr. German's psychological acumen had suddenly increased. "I was afraid I was going to be caught between those two when the fur started to fly."

"They don't like each other very much, do they?" asked the doctor.

"No, but give them time. They just met. Once they really get to know each other better, it will get even worse."

"You have a sense of humor, Lieutenant," said Dr. German. "That's rare in your line of work."

"It's what keeps us sane," replied Byrne. "Relatively."

"It must work," said Dr. German, "because so few of your people ever come to see me."

Byrne couldn't decide if the shrink meant Irish or cops or Queens natives. "I'll tell you why in four little words," he said. "We can't afford it. Not on thirty or forty thousand a year."

"I suppose you can't," said the doctor. "However valuable or necessary, analysis is something only the fortunate few can manage."

"Think of it as God's way of telling rich people they have too much money."

Dr. German laughed. "I thought that was cocaine," he said.

"Name your poison," said Byrne. "Either way, in my opinion it's a waste, no offense."

"Perhaps you ought to come and see me, and find out." The other guests were busy enjoying the hospitality of the doctor's liquor cabinet, well out of earshot. "Ingrid told me a little bit about the Ekdahl murder. I expect that's why Nils Pilgersen wasn't able to be here with us tonight."

"I expect so." At least now he knew where the leak had come from.

"For some reason," said Dr. German, "it always strikes me as particularly poignant when someone dies far from home. It seems like Fate plays a hand here, leading the person across the seas just to meet his death. One wonders why."

"Me, I also wonder who, where, when and how," said Byrne. Now it was his turn to take the doctor's arm and lead his host back into the library. "That's what they pay me for. And not a couple hundred bucks an hour, either."

Dr. German looked at him quizzically. "You don't have much respect for my profession, do you, Lieutenant?"

"I guess I've seen a little too much of your handiwork back out on the streets to call myself an aficionado," said Byrne. "Because when you guys are wrong, guys like me have to deal with the consequences. What did La Guardia say? 'When I make a mistake, it's a beaut'?" Professionally, he shifted course. "Would you mind if I borrow one of these photos?" he asked.

"May I ask why?" The voice was flat and controlled.

"Well"—Byrne smiled—"I know it sounds ridiculous, but I thought I recognized someone in this picture, and I'd like to show it to him if I could. I'll bring it back in a couple of days, and we can have another little chat."

"Whom do you mean?" asked the doctor, his voice low and suddenly uneasy.

"Are you boys at it again?" interrupted Ella German. She was standing in the doorway, with Ingrid right behind her. "Jacob, you really must come and attend to your other guests. I'm sure Ingrid knows as much about soccer as Lieutenant Byrne here. Don't you, my dear?"

Ingrid clapped her hands delightedly; if the sarcasm bothered her she wasn't about to let it show. "Is it time for presents yet?" she asked.

"Coming right up," said Dr. German, turning away.

"Mine first," said Byrne to himself, discreetly removing one of the pictures from the frame.

Ingrid pulled the wrapping paper off his gift to her: over Doreen's objection, a box of Godiva chocolates. "Thank you, Francis," said Ingrid, kissing him more affectionately than the gift warranted. He heard Dr. German suck in his breath. Lustily, she ripped open the package containing a beige and green Hermès scarf that Dr. German had bought her, but the biggest explosion of all was when a diamond engagement ring came tumbling out of a small wrapped Tiffany's box.

"Luckiest guy in the world," his brother was saying as the guests applauded. Dr. German looked as if he was about to throw up on his expensive Sarouk.

"To Ingrid and Tom!" shouted Mrs. German, the happiest she had been all evening.

"All the best!" shouted Bernard Weissman, in a voice that could be heard across the park on Central Park West.

"Have you set a date yet?" someone else cried.

"Shall we say Tuesday morning, Doctor?" said Byrne. "Your office?"

"Mazel tov," said Dr. German, raising his glass to no one in particular and staring down at his shoes.

"I just love surprise parties," said Byrne.

Chapter Twenty-four
Greenwich Village
Saturday, October 20, 1990; 11:00 P.M.

W hat's the matter with you tonight, Francis?" asked Doreen when they got back to her apartment in the Village. Doreen lived in a second-floor walk-up near the intersection of West Fourth and West Tenth Streets in the West Village, the apparent contradiction appealing to her sense of humor. "It's the next best thing to living at the corner of Waverly and Waverly!" she would explain to baffled out-of-towners, who were then even more mystified at this recondite New York City geography. From the outside the apartment didn't look like much, but on the inside it had been transformed into a faux-retro Biedermeier/Georgian living module. That, at least, is how Doreen explained it to anyone who asked. To Byrne, it just looked like an old-fashioned flat with plaster on the walls and furniture that would break if you sat on it.

"Nothing," he said.

"Don't give me nothing. You're in a funk. What's the deal?" She was undressing; in fact, she was already down to her bikini panties. They had been lovers long enough that Doreen no longer bothered to strip for him, and on this evening her casual attitude toward her body was annoying.

"Nothing," he said as he unbuttoned his shirt, but Doreen was in the bathroom, brushing her teeth.

"What?" she shouted over the running water.

"Nothing," he muttered to himself. He got into bed and turned on the television to see the sports report.

"I bet I know," she said, emerging from the bathroom. She slipped under the covers beside him and tousled his hair playfully. "The lovebirds."

The sportscaster was cracking wise about some golf match, so Byrne switched off the set. Doreen knew perfectly well he had no interest in golf and couldn't fake it. "Which lovebirds?" he asked. "The Germans?"

"Get off it," she said. "I mean your brother and Ilse, she-wolf of the SS."

"I thought I got a whiff of some kraut chatter over your way," said Byrne, fooling with the reading lamp on his night table while he tried to figure out what to say next.

"That was her, talking to Dr. German. And I must say it kind of pissed me off," said Doreen. "You didn't hear me making smart remarks in Japanese, did you?" She tossed off the covers, leaned over Byrne, whose head was still propped up on his pillow, and brushed his face lightly with her breasts.

"Come on," he said. "Not right now."

She flopped back onto her back. "Really, Francis, I think you're turning into a old lady. Whatever happened to my hot Irish stud?"

"He's still here," he said, raising the covers and glancing down. "He's just resting."

That was all the encouragement Doreen needed. "I think I know how to get his attention," she said. The next thing Byrne knew, she had disappeared headfirst beneath the sheet and for the next half hour or so, he completely forgot whatever it was he was going to ask her about Ingrid and Egil Ekdahl.

When she had finished, Doreen swung out of bed to get a drink of water. As much as her body, Byrne found her oral techniques extremely exciting—Irish Catholic girls like Mary Claire just couldn't achieve the same level of sixth-degree black belt mastery—and whenever she gave him the pleasure of her undivided attention, it boosted his affection for her and bolstered his resolve to try and remain faithful. He loved the way her bottom looked as she swayed from the half-light of the bedroom into the full light of the bath. The light winked out as she shut the door and Byrne knew he had only a few minutes to contemplate how he was going to conduct this interrogation. He hoped it wouldn't turn hostile; he'd had enough hostility for one evening.

While Doreen was attending to her ablutions, Byrne's mind turned to thoughts of his ex-wife. He supposed some of his guilty equanimity regarding Doreen could be traced to the breakup of his marriage. The anonymous phone call, telling Mary Claire about Byrne and Doreen; the helpful brother-in-law, ever ready to console; the ensuing affair and her passionate involvement in it; and the hideous way the whole thing ended, with everybody a loser except Tom. It surprised him how fresh and deep the hurt still was.

"That party must've really turned you on," Byrne said as Doreen returned. "I mean, we get home and the next thing I know you're playing six choruses of 'Yankee Doodle Dandy' on Mr. Happy. I think it must have been Bernie Weissman who got you so hot."

Doreen laughed. "I'd rather fuck a mongoose," she said, kissing him. He could still taste himself on her lips.

Byrne saw his opening. "Or Egil Ekdahl?" he inquired.

"He's not bad," she replied, unself-consciously.

"You know this guy?" asked Byrne. "I mean," he was starting to stammer, "I didn't know you knew Ingrid, uh, what's her name . . ."

"Bentsen," Doreen filled in the blank.

"Bentsen, either," finished Byrne. "Yeah."

"Why don't you ever talk about your work with me?" she asked him abruptly. "Don't you trust me? You could have told me you'd met the Danish Mata Hari in the line of duty and saved us both some embarrassment."

"And then what?" asked Byrne.

"And then I could have told you to watch out for the little bitch," said

Doreen. "And for Ekdahl, too. I overheard you talking about him with Dr. G."

"Oh, you know him, do you?" said Byrne.

"Of course I do," replied Doreen. "He works at the consulate with her."

"Not anymore he doesn't," said Byrne, "on account of he's dead."

"Jesus Christ!" exclaimed Doreen. She sat bolt upright. "He can't be! I mean, I saw him just the other day."

"Yeah, well, somebody else has seen him since, because the job he, she or it did on him was something to behold. His own mother wouldn't have recognized him. Throat cut from ear to ear, several bullets in his head, the works," said Byrne. He decided to leave out the part about the missing dick, especially since his was still sensitive from her ministrations. "Minus his name, the story was on the news and in all the papers." The front page of yesterday's *Daily News* had shouted: "The Unkindest Cut: Victim Found Unmanned," while the *Post* played it even bigger: "OUCH!!!" Typically, the *Times* had buried a two-graf story on page B-4 under the headline "Unidentified Body in Upstate Field."

"You know I hate television and never have time to read the papers," replied Doreen. "Ekdahl dead. I can't believe it. And that's why you met Ingrid at the Hunt Club last night," said Doreen. "It was about Ekdahl."

"How did you know I met with her?" asked Byrne.

"She told me."

"When?"

"Tonight, you idiot, at the party. Why didn't you tell me?"

"How was I supposed to know you two were friends?"

"We're far from friends, Francis."

"Acquaintances, then."

"Well," said Doreen, "you weren't supposed to know. You know our deal."

"All too well," said Byrne, deciding that this conversation should go no further. He pulled the covers over his shoulders and closed his eyes.

Doreen, however, was far from sleepy. "Look, Francis," she said, "I'm sorry."

"You don't have to be sorry. That's our deal, too."

"Yeah, but I'm sorry anyway. I always hope we won't overlap, and this time it looks like we did."

"You might say that," said Byrne, feigning drowsiness. "But it's not the first time."

A slap across the face woke him up in a hurry. "What was that for?" he yelled, rising. One minute a blow job, the next minute assault and battery of a police officer.

"God damn it, Francis!" shouted Doreen. "I'm sick of this shit!"

"Of what shit?" said Byrne, trying to remain calm for both their sakes.

"Sick of this I-don't-care shit, is what I'm sick of," said Doreen.

"I thought that's the way you wanted it," said Byrne.

"Maybe it was." She was crying now. "Maybe that's the way it used to be. But maybe I want it to be different now."

"You make the rules, love," he said. It was hard to fake indifference, but he was giving it his best shot.

"I'd like to change them," she said.

"Fine by me," he said. He started to turn away but another slap got his attention, delivered so hard he almost struck back.

"Don't you dare roll over and go to sleep!" she cried. "I'm trying to talk to you."

"You're the one who just gave me some head, remember?" he said sarcastically. "And now I suppose you want to talk about our 'relationship.' What a fucking joke." With a violence that surprised even him, Byrne suddenly flung the nightstand lamp across the room, which expired in a crash and a flicker. That made him even angrier, and he leaped out of bed, picked up the lamp and smashed it against the floor until it had shattered into a thousand pieces. He turned back to her, looking to hurt her as she was hurting him.

"Don't," she said, suddenly afraid. "Don't hit me."

He stopped, breathing heavily.

"Don't," she repeated. "Remember what happened the last time."

His heart was pounding, but he let himself crawl back into bed; except for his breathing, he was very still. The last time she wound up in the emergency room at St. Vincent's, being treated for a variety of bruises contracted in what they both told the doctor was a fall down the stairs.

"You and your damn temper," she said, looking at him reproachfully; there was only sorrow, and no malice, in her tone. "One of these days, you're going to kill someone."

"Why is this day different from all other days?" he asked, remembering Joey Hanrahan.

"Because it is," said Doreen. "Because tonight, when I saw the way you were looking at her, and looking at your brother looking at her, I realized I could lose you, and I don't want to. Because tonight I remembered again why I love you."

When Francis Byrne met Dori Grace, it had hardly been the stuff of romance. She rear-ended his unmarked car on Queens Boulevard as he was returning to Manhattan one night after visiting his mother. The damage was minimal, and Byrne wasn't about to cite a girl as pretty as Doreen for following too closely, so instead he did something completely unethical: he told her he would forget about the accident if she would have lunch with him the next day.

"You are a cop, aren't you?" she had asked almost immediately, forcing Byrne to wonder, not for the first time, if he were carrying some sort of sign across his ass that said PROPERTY OF NYPD. Map of Ireland on your face, great seal of the city of New York on your butt. "I hear there's a certain kind of girl that practically collects policemen, the way others do rock stars."

"Not as often as you think," said Byrne. "And certainly not as often as some guys on the force would like. Or would like to have the world believe." They made love that evening at Doreen's place, at the intersection of Fourth and Tenth, the next best thing to Waverly and Waverly. Afterward, she told him she was bisexual. He told her he was married.

He took her naked body in his arms, tearing away the protective sheet that she had been holding in front of her breast, and drawing her close to him.

"Did you have sex with Ekdahl?" he murmured.

"I got into bed with him, yes," said Doreen, "but I didn't fuck him. I swear to God, Francis, I didn't fuck him. That's our agreement, and I've stuck to it."

"Just like you stuck to it, so to speak, with my brother?"

He thought he might be in for another assault, but Doreen stayed peaceful. "That was different," she said. "That was only because I'd had a little too much—"

"Cocaine." Byrne finished the sentence for her. "You'd had a little too much coke, and there was my good-looking brother, Tom, a guy who's never met a girl he didn't think he could fuck, and what do you know? He's right!"

"I love you, Francis," she said, in that tone that always got to him, no matter how angry he was. "Why don't you just forget about what happened between me and Tom? Are you going to keep reminding me about it for the rest of my life?"

"I hope not," said Byrne. The fight was out of both of them now. "Tell me about Egil and Ingrid."

And so Doreen told him. How she and a couple of her friends had sashayed right into the city's premiere Eurotrash night spot—no club in New York City could turn away a woman who looked like Dori Grace—where she immediately attracted the attention of two handsome, blond Scandinavians, how she did one or two or six lines of coke with the girl in the bathroom, not to mention the XTC, the ecstasy without the agony, and how the guy, a little strange but suave as all get out, chatted her up at the bar, how after a while he ran his hand, brushed it really, down the front of her dress, while the girl's hand just happened to stray against her bottom, how the whispered invitation to continue the party came in both ears, almost at once, and how somehow her girlfriends had both disappeared, well, not exactly disappeared, had been picked up, Monica by an Italian shipping company executive, the other by some Iranian involved in God knows what—what a tramp that Courtney was—and how she stumbled out of the club and how some ugly, pockmarked foreigner propositioned her as they were going out the door—said he was a movie producer, or some such bullshit—but how Egil had told him to get lost in a weird language and how they jumped in a taxi—there were always taxis waiting outside the doors of the Hunt Club at all hours—and the next thing she knew she was in somebody's apartment—from the description, Byrne was sure it was Ingrid's—and then she was in bed naked, both of them under the covers with her, although she was interested only in the woman.

"Anyway, Ekdahl's impotent," concluded Doreen.

"You mean he's queer, don't you?" asked Byrne, as dispassionately as he could. He was, after all, still conducting an investigation, even sitting here, stark naked, in bed, and now finding himself getting a semi.

"I doubt that," said Doreen. "From the way he touched me it was obvious that he was used to caressing a woman because he knew all the buttons to push. But we never got it on."

"Meaning you didn't feel like it?"

She gave him a funny look. "Meaning he couldn't, even if he wanted to."

Byrne failed to catch her drift. "Do you think there was anything between her and Ekdahl?"

Doreen looked at him as if he were insane. "I told you," she said, "Ekdahl is impotent. And Ingrid is gay."

Now that was a switch. "You mean bisexual, don't you?" he asked. "Goes both ways?"

"Goes only one way, my dear, right straight between a girl's legs. She really knows her way around the female anatomy. Anything else she might say or do is pure disinformation."

"I don't understand what you gals see in each other," said Byrne, doggedly pursuing the wrong line of questioning.

"Has it ever occurred to you, Francis," said Doreen, "that sometimes a woman doesn't want to be smothered by a big hairy crypto-rapist? That maybe she's looking for some sisterly affection? That since we all start out at our mother's breast, that perhaps some of us see nothing wrong with returning to it from time to time? And some of us never leave it? That maybe, just maybe, some of us find it sexy to know that guys are turned on by us women making love to each other?"

"But Ingrid told me she and Ekdahl had been lovers." Byrne realized his protestations were sounding lamer by the minute. And what did she mean by hairy crypto-rapist, anyway? He was beginning to take this conversation personally.

Doreen laughed. "She and Mother's Little Helper, maybe. But her and him? Forget it! Maybe it takes one to know one, but in my opinion our little Miss Denmark is strictly a girl's girl. And he's a mama's boy if I ever saw one." She cupped his chin in her hand. "What's the matter?" she said. "You look disappointed. Don't tell me you have the hots for—"

"No," said Byrne. "I won't tell you. I want to show you." He pulled her roughly, fiercely, to his breast.

But Doreen still had something to say. "Besides, Ekdahl couldn't be a woman's lover even if he wanted to."

Byrne tore his mouth away from her neck long enough to ask why.

"He doesn't have a dick, silly," she said.

Part Two
REVELATION

Prologue
Camp Peary, Virginia
Winter, 1965

Nosenko suspected he had been on the Farm for months, maybe even years, but he had lost track of time ever since they found and confiscated his makeshift calendar. He had constructed it from the lint in his clothing and had been painstakingly trying to date his period of incarceration, but one of the sharper-eyed guards had eventually found it and taken it away from him. They had also found and removed a little chess set he had fashioned from threads, and when hiding beneath a blanket one day he had tried to read the writing on a toothpaste box, they had taken that away as well. Then there was no more toothpaste.

Technically, Yuri Nosenko's new home in the Virginia countryside went by the name of the Armed Forces Experimental Training Activity, Department of Defense, Camp Peary. During the war, it had been a POW camp for captured Germans, but all ten thousand acres of it along the York River had since been converted into a CIA facility where aspiring agents went for their indoctrination and basic training.

Nosenko's cell, built especially for him, was made out of windowless concrete. It was about twelve feet square. The only opening was at the top half of the door, which was covered with steel bars; when he looked out, all he could see was the guard. A closed-circuit television camera watched him night and day. As in the safe house, the room's only furnishings were a bed bolted to the floor in the middle of the cell; there was also a privy. The bed had a mattress, but no sheets or pillows; on cold nights they sometimes brought him a blanket, but since the toothpaste incident they often forgot. Most of the time he slept in his clothes, a pair of government-issue gray pajamas worn with a light windbreaker to ward off the chill. Someday, they had promised, he would be permitted to exercise in the yard, but that day had not yet come. They told him he would be staying for ten years.

One afternoon the door opened and in walked the tall, balding doctor whom he had seen on the first day, carrying a folder. Nosenko was surprised when the man spoke to him in fluent, slightly accented Russian. "Hello, Yuri Ivanovich," he said. "How are we feeling today?" The doctor held out his hand. "I'm Dr. Schlussel. Remember me?"

Nosenko still retained a painful memory of that particular examination. "Why am I still a prisoner?" he shouted as his anger welled up inside him.

"You know I can't answer questions like that, Yurka," replied the doctor. "In fact, I'm not supposed to answer any questions at all. I'm just here to see how you are feeling. Take off your shirt, please, and let me have a look at you."

Nosenko complied sullenly, pulling the rough shirt over his head. He had lost weight, which was hardly surprising, but otherwise he was fit enough. Dr. Schlussel seemed pleased.

"Not too bad, Yuri Ivanovich, not too bad at all." They were sitting next to each other on the bed. The doctor patted his leg; instinctively, Nosenko shrank from the touch. "I know this has been very difficult for you, my friend," Dr. Schlussel said. "And I sure wouldn't want to be in your slippers. But you can make all this much easier on yourself."

Nosenko was immediately suspicious. He had seen plenty of KGB doctors in action, and knew they could be even nastier than regular interrogators. Doctors were normally committed to saving lives, but once restraints were removed they could be the most vicious of human beings. Free to experiment at will, they could delude themselves into thinking they were serving humanity, when in reality they were only indulging their own darkest desires. And all in the name of "research."

" . . . easier on yourself," the doctor was saying. "And I can make it easier on you. We just need a little cooperation."

"Then why won't they let me testify to the Warren Commission?" complained Nosenko.

"I'm afraid it's too late for that, Yuri Ivanovich," said Dr. Schlussel. "The report was issued last month and it has already been accepted by President Johnson. The commission found that Lee Harvey Oswald, acting alone, and just for the hell of it, shot and killed President Kennedy from the sixth floor of the Texas School Book Depository on November 22, 1963. He brought his rifle to work one day, looked out the window, saw his chance and took it. The end."

"What did they say about my information?" asked Nosenko.

"I'll tell you exactly what they said. They said nothing. Dick Helms met with Chief Justice Warren on June 24, 1964, and told him that CIA was unwilling to vouch for your bona fides. Both Justice Warren and Congressman Gerry Ford recommended against using your stuff and so, although some other members of the Commission were in your corner, in the end they decided to deep-six you and your story."

"Did they say anything about Soviet involvement?" asked Nosenko.

"Not a word. That doesn't mean they still don't suspect it. But Oswald's time in your country, his commitment to Marxism-Leninism, his marriage to Marina—all these things were officially found in the end to have no bearing on his actions. There will be no war between the United States and the Soviet Union. Not over this incident, anyway."

"Now what happens?"

"That's a good question, Yurochka. Hoover thinks you're okay, but CIA . . . well, CIA thinks you're full of shit. Still, they're going to give you another chance. The Soviet Russia Division would like you to spend some time composing your autobiography. They'd like you to write down a complete account of your professional life, leaving nothing germane out. They want the name of every person you ever met in the course of your KGB duties, no matter how insignificant he or she may seem to you."

Nosenko snorted. "They want to analyze my handwriting," he said.

"Of course they do. But even more important, they want to check your story against the known facts."

"But I've told them the truth!" Nosenko jumped to his feet and paced around the small cell. "I've told them the truth from the beginning. And this is my reward!" He gestured wildly, his voice rising. Schlussel cut him off in midcry.

"I'd lower my voice if I were you, Yuri Ivanovich. You don't want the guards to get alarmed and put a stop to this pleasant little chat of ours, do you? I'm not supposed to be talking to you at all, so if you'll please come back here and sit down I can continue with your medical examination."

Nosenko sat. "Why are you doing this?" he said.

"Let's just say I'm interested. In you. In your case. In what you're doing to CIA. In the assassination. There are still a million questions left unanswered, and I'm starting to believe you may be able to answer some of them—even if you don't really know the truth yourself. Say aaahhhh." Schlussel busied himself by looking down his patient's throat. "Because it almost doesn't matter whether you believe you're telling the truth or not. Just as it didn't matter to that poor boy Oswald whether what he thought he was doing was right or not. Agents are useful even when they're in the dark. Perhaps especially when they're in the dark. Stand up and drop 'em." Obediently, Nosenko unbuttoned the flap on his pajama bottoms and let his pants fall to the ground; his undershorts followed. Dr. Schlussel had his testicles in his hand and began to squeeze them, ever so slightly. "Cough," he commanded.

"You've got a few friends here, but one very big enemy's got you by the balls, so to speak," said Schlussel quietly as he released him. "You look fine to me," the doctor said loudly, for the guard's benefit. Nosenko could smell the liquor on his breath, which repulsed him; enforced sobriety was making him lose his appetite for booze.

"Or maybe I should say two enemies: James Jesus Angleton and his prize pupil, Golitsin. Anatoly is doing a number on you, my friend, telling Angleton that you're a complete phony. Golitsin's a real stone in your shoe. *Livarsi na pietra di la scarpa!* as Carlos Marcello once said of President Kennedy." The doctor looked Nosenko in the eye. "A real stone," he repeated slowly, for emphasis. "That's his code name in the Agency, Stone. And you know what yours is? Foxtrot. Isn't that wonderful? Although you look to me like your dancing days are over."

"I know this name, Golitsin," said Nosenko. "From Moscow. KGB defector."

Dr. Schlussel raised an eyebrow. "You may know his name, Yuri

Ivanovich, but he certainly doesn't know yours. In fact, he says he doesn't know anything about you at all—never saw you, never met you, and tells us categorically that you never worked for the KGB a day in your life. Which has led folks around here to believe that maybe you're a fiendishly clever and inhumanly well prepared dangle; I would characterize this as the Soviet Superman theory, Mr. Angleton's view. A corollary possibility is that you're not even Yuri Nosenko at all, that the real Nosenko is dead and you're special agent John Doe or Ivan Schwartz or Boris Kovetsky, and that you've taken Nosenko's place because KGB caught on to Nosenko while he was an agent-in-place and executed him, and now you've come over here to tie CIA up in knots. Meanwhile others think that you're some little pissant opportunist who decided to hitch a ride out of the USSR on the back of the Kennedy assassination, that you're winging it, making the whole thing up, using a little knowledge in a dangerous way. This school of thought, my dear Yurochka, says you're just a glorified secretary the KGB might have leaned on once in a while, and when they let you out of your cage in Geneva and you got a load of the lush life on the outside you figured it was time for Boris Kovetsky to fade into history and for Colonel Yuri Nosenko to be born. In any case, you've got the place so confused nobody knows what to do. They're talking about sending you back to Mother Russia, but Helms is against it." He began to read from a document. "Listen to this," he ordered. "This is Dave Murphy, chief of the Soviet Russia division, talking here, my friend:

Nosenko is a KGB plant and may be publicly exposed as such some time after the appearance of the Commission's report. Once Nosenko is exposed as a KGB plant, there will arise the danger that his information will be mirror-read by the press and public, leading to conclusions that the USSR did direct the assassination.

The Agency's greatest contribution to the resolution of the questions at hand would be to break Nosenko and get the full story of how and why he was told to tell the story he did about Oswald. While we have no certainty that we can ever do this, if we are to succeed we need time and must in the meantime avoid creating pressures which might force us to release Nosenko to the public domain. (There, articulate and plausible, he would unquestionably be able to establish himself beyond hope of dislodging, since his story cannot easily be pierced even by trained specialists, much less by private citizens however intelligent.) The release of the fact that Nosenko knew specifically about the Oswald case would, of course, create such pressure, and no hedging on source description could protect his identity.

"So you see, you're in big trouble," said Dr. Schlussel. "I want to be-lieve you, Yuri Ivanovich. I think what you have to say may be important. I'm not running things around here, but if you help me I can make your existence here marginally better. I might even be able to sneak you in a visitor now and then, and if you're a really good boy, I may even get you a lady for an evening. A nice Russian-speaking girl. You'd like that, wouldn't you?"

Nosenko nodded. It had been a very long time since he'd had a woman.

"And if you don't play ball, I sure as shootin' can make your life a hell of a lot worse. You know they want me to use sodium pentothal on you? That's truth serum." Schlussel smiled and rapped loudly on the door to get the guard's attention. "It's a thought," he said as the door opened. "Keep it in mind. I surely will."

That night was the first time Nosenko could remember that they had turned the lights all the way off. He guessed he had been asleep for two or three hours when he heard his cell door open softly. There was a rus-tle, as of silk brushing against skin, and a sweet, feminine smell in the air. Suddenly, her hands were upon him. Soft, smooth, pliable, elastic, welcoming, erotic. In the daylight she might be the ugliest woman in the world, but at this moment she was the loveliest.

Even before she opened her mouth, he knew the sound of her voice. It was soft and melodic and it sang to him in the musical accents of home.

> *Who is going to the field so early?*
> *Who is welcoming dawns in the field?*
> *It is a collective-farm girl,*
> *A kind that would make a fellow lose his sleep.*
> *Her hair is long*

And her eyes are languid.
Old and young alike, all the people in the street,
Look at the girl with admiration.

Oh, there must be a reason
Why Russian beauties are famous!

Is it not she who comes down to the river?
Looking intently at the water
With her eyes so bright
She bends over the water;
She looks down and wonders:
"Could this be me?
"Perhaps this is only a red dawn
"That is flaming in the sky
"Which is reflected in the river?"

Oh, there must be a reason
Why Russian beauties are famous!

She caressed him gently, the way she might stroke a child. And yet there was passion in her touch, and fire in her kisses. He had forgotten how sweet a woman's mouth could be, sweet like wine, sweet and rich and dark and musky. He put his arms around her, and she embraced him in return. *"Kto ti?"* she whispered. *"Moi angel li khranitel, ili kovarni iskusitel?"* Before the lust overwhelmed his senses he recognized the words of Pushkin: Who are you? My guardian angel? Or a wily tempter?

And then he took her, with a passion that he had never felt for any of his wives, and loving her all the more in her anonymity and his desperation. The next morning when he awoke she was gone.

Chapter Twenty-five
Hell's Kitchen
Sunday, October 21, 1990; 9:00 A.M.

On Sunday morning, Byrne rose early from Doreen's bed, showered, dressed and went to the deli around the corner to get a couple of bagels with a shmeer and the *Times*. Unlike most readers, he skipped the magazine, the book review, Arts and Leisure, the front-page thumbsuckers about whither Israel and all the other quotidian claptrap that seemed to occupy its attention and turned right to the Metro section, just to see if anything was going on locally.

Not much, but then, in the *Times*'s view of New York, nothing much ever happened unless it had something to do with doctors, lawyers, politicians, the Hasidim and, lately, homosexuals. There was nothing about the Ekdahl case; aside from a brief folo yesterday, the paper of record was silent concerning the late Mr. Ekdahl.

Here, however, was an item about an incident so unextraordinary in the life of his community that it was dispensed with in a few short paragraphs and buried at the bottom of a page deep within the section.

3 Charred Bodies Are Found Inside 2 Dumpsters

In what appeared to be a bizarre coincidence, firefighters late last night discovered three charred bodies while putting out two separate fires inside Dumpsters in Brooklyn and Queens, authorities said.

Investigators were comparing notes and did not rule out the possibility that the incidents—discovered within little more than an hour of each other—were connected.

The police would not speculate on a motive behind the deaths, and it was not clear how or when they took place. The police have not yet identified any of the bodies.

Well, that's what he got for going to dinner parties. The first Dumpster, in the East New York section of Brooklyn, contained the flaming remains of a man and a woman. Byrne immediately put that one down to drugs: the bodies, he knew, would belong to a black or Hispanic couple in their late teens or early twenties; more than likely, they had each been shot several times in the head at close range. It was that kind of neighborhood.

It was the third body that interested him.

In the second incident about an hour and a half later, a worker at an ironworks company reported a Dumpster on fire in an industrial section of Elmhurst, Queens, the authorities said.

Searching through the Dumpster's contents after putting out the fire, firefighters found the badly burned body of a man. Police could not say how or when the man died, and the medical examiner planned to conduct an autopsy today.

He supposed Sy would know something about that one. Luckily, they were having a drink together that evening. Byrne was already brimming with questions, not just about burning bodies in trash bins, but about what he had seen at Dr. German's last night. About the second peculiar photo that had come into his possession lately.

Doreen was still asleep, lying on her back with the sheets just barely covering her navel. She looked delicious. She also looked to be asleep for the duration—she'd been hitting the wine last night even harder than he had—and so, impulsively, he decided to do something he hadn't done in a very long time: he decided to go to Mass. He needed all the help he could get.

It was not that he considered himself a lapsed Catholic, officially. He made his Easter duty, dutifully if not religiously, at least one Easter out of three, although he generally left out the confession part. He hardly ever read the Bible, but then what Catholic did? The letters of Saint Paul to the various Ephesians and other forgotten races were a blur, and, as for most Irish Catholics, the Four Horsemen of the Apocalypse were Notre Dame football players of long ago. Genesis was a fairy tale, Revelation a horror story.

The pope in Rome, in his opinion, was a reactionary Polack whose blind dogmatism was ameliorated by his gumption, which made him an improvement over his colorless predecessor, Pope What's His Name Who Went to Shea Stadium, Even Without His Best Fastball.

But on this Sunday, he found himself stepping into his neighborhood parish church of Saint Malachy's on West Forty-ninth Street. It was not the grandeur of the liturgy that brought him there—that had been abandoned long ago, with the Second Vatican Council the defining event of his father's religious faith. "What the hell's happening to this goddamn church?" he remembered Dad exclaiming one Sunday morning; his mother, as usual, never answered rhetorical questions, preferring to let them hang in the air as they deserved. Robert Byrne had been an altar boy, had learned the Latin responses perfectly—even as an adult, he could whip through the *Suscipiat* like nobody's business—and to the day he died he loved and missed the old Mass, in all its majesty and mystery. His father was not alone: fifty, even thirty years ago, reflected Byrne, this church would have been full on Sunday, but Vatican II had done its work too well, and today the church was nearly empty.

It was not the ceremony itself that drew Byrne but rather the preaching of Father Michael Dignan. The priest was a second-generation Irish American, and Byrne found in his homilies a sense of kinship, a sense of cultural connectedness that he could not quite describe but which he felt strongly nonetheless. It being no special feast day, the celebrant was attired in basic black, which suited Byrne's mood just fine; with vague disapproval, he noted that one of the altar boys was an altar girl. Nor did he care for the priest's spoken greeting to the congregation, which was echoed back by the forty or so souls scattered around the cavernous interior. He felt himself resentful during the Introit, and actively hostile well into the Gloria. Then the worshipers and the altar persons sat, and Father Dignan took up his position at the lectern and cleared his throat.

"A few weeks ago, as you know, I had a chance to visit the Holy Land," he began. Byrne didn't know, but to everyone around him this was apparently old news. "It was the first time I had ever been to Jerusalem." Did Father Mike have a trace of an Irish accent? Byrne decided that he did, possibly affected but appropriate nonetheless. It was a gratifying link with the old clerical Irish mafia of New York, which, like Irish power throughout the city, was withering and dying, cut off from its impoverished roots, abandoned by its affluent, uncaring suburban children.

The Holy Land, not Israel; in the Catholic scheme of things, Israel was for Jews. "And my greatest ambition was to make the Stations of Cross. Not these beautiful painted Stations that we see here at Saint Malachy's, but the actual Via Dolorosa." He drew out the syllables, Do-lo-ro-sa, reveling in their implied misery. "I wanted to walk where Christ had walked, to see what Jesus had seen as He carried the Cross to Golgotha, the Place of the Skulls. To put myself in His sandals, to witness what He had witnessed, to experience, in my own humble way, what He had experienced.

"And so I went to Jerusalem, and to the Via Dolorosa. And do you know what? It was a bummer!" Byrne winced at the neologism. "It was noisy and dirty and smelly and crowded and there were thousands of people, Jews and Moslems and Christians, pushing and shoving and sweating, and there was the sound of ugly rock music playing and the smell of greasy food frying, and there were advertisements for Kodak and Mitsubishi everywhere. And I wanted to stop and shout, I wanted to get up on my soapbox and yell at them. 'Don't you people know what this is?' I wanted to say. 'Don't you know that this is the Via Dolorosa? That this is the road Jesus took on the last walk of His life? That this is a sacred path, a way of righteousness and glory? How dare you defile it with your dirt and your greasy food and your bad manners and your cheap commerce?

"But of course no one would have listened to me. They would have been too busy going about their business, too busy sweating and shouting and swearing and looking at the ads for camera film and listening to their music and cooking their food, and they would have ignored me completely. So I said nothing. But I was so offended that I broke off my Stations—with a muttered oath, I might add—and returned to my hotel. It was nothing like I had imagined, and the disparity between what I thought it would or should be and what it actually was was so great that I could not reconcile the two. And so I left.

"On my way back to New York, I chanced to meet a fellow priest in the airport transit lounge. We greeted each other in collegial fashion, and while we waited for our flight back to the United States, we talked about what we had seen and done. And I told him about my trip to the Via Dolorosa, and how terribly disappointed I had been by what I had found there, by the noise and the dirt and the crowds and the awful music and the smelly food.

"He just laughed, and then he cut me down to size. 'But Father,' he said, 'you don't understand: that was the way it was. That was what Jesus saw. The streets were dirty—they were made of dirt—and they were crowded, and there was garbage on them, and the smell of food being prepared in the surrounding houses was wafting through the air, and popular music was being played and sung, and people were cursing and jostling each other and engaging in commerce and somewhere there were people making love, and somewhere else someone was cheating someone, and someplace else one person was hurting or killing another. All this is what Jesus saw, Father, so why should it be any different for you?'

"And I must say, he really made me think. For what does Jesus tell us in the Gospels? That we must render unto Caesar. That we, His followers, must be in the world, not above it. For as Christians we believe that Christ was both man and God. Was He not tempted by the Devil, by wealth and riches and power unlimited? Did He not have feelings of the flesh? Was He not hungry, was He never thirsty? At Cana, did He not change water into wine; are we to think He did not drink some, if only to see that it was good?"

A delightful vintage, thought Byrne impiously. I think you'll be amused by its pretensions. Especially considering it came out of that camel well ten minutes ago. You're looking lovely today, Miss Magdalene. . . .

" . . . made flesh and dwelt among us. And for us who are flesh, and who hope for salvation in our Lord Jesus Christ, there is no greater good than to be of the world in all its filth and brutality and, through the power of our love for our Lord Jesus Christ, to change it. For God does not expect us to live like hermits in a mountaintop cave. Instead, He has put us here, on this earth, to dwell among our fellow men, as He did, and through the power of our example as Christians, to make it a better place.

"What does He therefore expect of us? He expects that we will transform and transfigure society as we walk along our own Via Dolorosa, carrying our own crosses, on our way to our own Place of the Skulls. He expects our love and our hope, our best efforts on His behalf, that we may show the world, in all its dirt and disease and cruelty, that we can rise above it, that we can demonstrate to a sorrowful, sorrowing planet that we Christians, who believe in the redeeming love of Christ, have the power within ourselves, within each of us, to make it a better place. Not Heaven on earth, perhaps; that condition is reserved for Heaven alone. But a piece of Heaven.

Even here. Even in New York. Even here, in the New Jerusalem. And not just today, but tomorrow and every day, for the rest of our lives. Until we reach that hilltop upon which we, too, shall be judged. Will it be the hilltop of the shining city? Or will it be the Place of Skulls? The choice is ours. Let us pray. We believe in one God, the Father, the Almighty . . ."

As one, the communicants rose to recite the Creed. It took Byrne a few seconds to catch up with them because his mind was on other things: a charred body in a Dumpster. A dead body in a field. Both faceless, both beckoning. What had the priest said? Something about putting oneself in His sandals. All his life he had been trying to reach the City on the Hill, but here he was, forced to dwell in the Place of the Skulls. How long, O Lord, how long?

Chapter Twenty-Six
Midtown Manhattan
Sunday, October 21, 1990; 8:00 P.M.

Byrne had arranged to meet Dr. Sheinberg at O'Reilly's Tavern, an Irish bar that sat on a little triangle of land where Thirty-first Street meets Broadway. Unlike, say, the Water Front Bar across the river in Williamsburg, cops never went there, which meant that the place was reasonably free of groupies. Byrne liked it for other reasons as well: the barmaids had fetching County Galway accents, the Guinness was cold and frothy and Doreen would never think to look for him here. Or Ingrid, for that matter.

Dressed in jeans, a work shirt, a sport coat and a pair of cheap sneakers, he wondered whether, on a detective's pay, he would ever be able to afford decent clothes. He envied his brother his flashy Barneys wardrobe; heck, Tom's shoes alone must cost three hundred dollars a pair. Byrne couldn't imagine spending that much money on shoes. Or even a suit.

He stood at the bar, waiting for the doctor, and surveyed the premises. As usual, Sy was running behind schedule; talk about a guy who would be late to his own funeral because he was performing his own autopsy. This was not the kind of place you read about in the *New York Post*, the sort of joint where off-duty cops were forever being shot by other off-duty cops— transit cops usually, he realized with some satisfaction, or, worse, Housing Authority flatfoots. To read the papers, it seemed that far more cops got killed off-duty than ever died in the line of fire. This kind of thinking always took him back to his father's death, and he decided to change the subject.

The guys at the bar were mostly working stiffs like him, killing their late-Sunday sorrows. So many football bets, so few winners. Did their dads want them to grow up to be something different, something better than they were, as his father had? Francis X. Byrne was going to be a lawyer, that's what Robert Byrne had always boasted. "Frankie's going to go to college and get a law degree," his father told all and sundry, and the other cops would laugh and ruffle his hair, which always embarrassed him. "And then he's going to be a big-shot attorney who'll be only too happy to defend you miserable sods when you get hauled up on charges for stealing apples from the greengrocer or shooting an unarmed little old lady trying to cross the street." One of the few things he could remember about his father was his laugh, loud and musical, like the clanging of the time bell.

There were a couple of stag girls down at the end of the bar, talking to each other and studiously rebuffing the efforts of a few men to pick them up. Reflexively, he gave them the once-over; just as reflexively, they picked up his incoming and returned it with assessments of their own. Christ, thought Byrne to himself, you just went to Mass and here you are thinking impure thoughts already.

Even so, the ladies weren't getting much action. A few pro forma pickup lines from a couple of stray dogs, instantly rebuffed (by the large blonde with the big tits) or coldly ignored (by her smaller, prettier, but flatter, brunette companion). Byrne noted that the blonde was the target of most of the attention, which figured in a place like this. Himself, he generally preferred brunettes, but his taste was in the distinct minority. No, that wasn't quite true. There was one blonde who interested him, but she was so transparently trouble that he wondered why he was even considering responding to her flirtatious provocations. Curiously, though, ever since Ingrid had come into his life, Doreen had loomed larger in his thoughts. Maybe a little competition was good for everybody. Or maybe it just confused matters even more.

"What'll it be, Frankie?" asked Teddy the bartender. Teddy was black, a Rastafarian with ferocious dreadlocks, which also figured. This was New York City, A.D. 1990. The exhausted Irish couldn't even muster a barman anymore. He ordered a Guinness. "Make sure it's cold, for Chrissakes, Teddy. And don't rush it, either. A good Guinness is like a good woman: hard to find, but you can't be in a hurry with her." The barman started drawing the dark wine of Ireland slowly and carefully.

"Got that right," said one of the unescorted women. The dark-haired one, with the intellectual's bustline.

He tried to think of something clever to say, but just then he caught sight of Sheinberg's gaunt frame tacking through the front door and so was spared the embarrassment. "Over here, Sy," he called, and waved. The ladies looked them both over, briefly debated their merits in low voices and went back to their girl talk. Sheinberg gave them a wink as he passed by.

"Hey, Teddy, a glass of milk for my uncle here," requested Byrne.

"Skim or regular?" asked the bartender.

"Regular, of course," replied Sheinberg.

"One glass of reg'lar coming right up." Expertly, and with a flourish, Teddy poured a double Glenfiddich into a shot glass and sailed it down the bar. Sheinberg caught it without taking his eyes off Byrne. "Slainte," he said.

"L'chaim," replied Byrne.

"You sure they let hebes in here?" Sheinberg inquired as he drained his glass. "I wouldn't want it to get around."

"Only if they can drink like micks," said Byrne, and ordered another round.

"No problem with that, thank God," said Sheinberg. Around the office he was known as the drinking man's Jew, and even the Irish cops who prided themselves on their ability to belt back a few with the boys had to admit that Seymour Sheinberg, M.D., could hold his booze with the best of them.

Whoever said Jews don't drink obviously never worked in the Medical Examiner's Office. "How's the family? Mom okay?"

"Fine," said Byrne. "Had a little problem the other day. I caught some guy in her house."

"Jesus, Frankie, she's old enough to date without your approval."

"Wasn't that kind of fella, Sy," said Byrne.

"Is she all right?" There was genuine concern in his voice. Sheinberg had known Irene Byrne for years.

"Yeah," said Byrne. "Everything happened kind of fast, but the bottom line is I guess I just lost it." He took a long, reflective draught of the Guinness. "Don't know if I hit him, but I must have scared the snot out of him because he cleared out in a hurry."

Sheinberg shook his head in awe at his friend's extravagantly Hibernian temperament. "You fired your weapon in your own mother's house? You're getting to be a real Irish cowboy. Which is why I suppose you insist on meeting in this, er, charmingly ethnic establishment. Too bad the Sunbrite's out of business, but the entertainment there was always a little too exotic even for my degenerate tastes."

"Better a Dumpster than a milk carton, huh?" suggested Byrne.

"Curious about that, huh?" asked Sheinberg. "Names were Jose Luis Rivera and Maria Delgado, both fairly recent arrivals from San Juan. Drugs, of course. The paper didn't mention they found the wallet and the purse nearby, which makes me look like a genius in the eyes of my adoring public."

Byrne smiled. "It's the other body I was interested in, Doc," he said.

"You mean the heavyset white guy who somehow burst into spontaneous combustion while conducting business in an Elmhurst trash can?"

"That's the one."

"Well, slap some mustard on him because he's done—overcooked, in fact."

"Who is he?"

"Hard to tell. Big guy, about fifty. European, probably; his teeth certainly were. Jesus, don't they have dentists over there?"

"They got rid of their Jews, remember?"

Sheinberg smacked himself dramatically on the forehead. "You mean we're not in Lvov anymore?"

"Sorry to be the one to have to break it to you," said Byrne. "How did he die?"

"Gunshot wound. Single shot, .38-caliber, right in the heart. Friend of yours? Maybe your mom's new boyfriend?"

"Hope not," said Byrne, and mulled his beer. A typical Tom touch, leaving the body within NYPD's jurisdiction, just to keep his kid brother's concentration focused. "A .38, you say? I wouldn't mind having a closer look at both those shells. Wouldn't it be a pisser if turns out to be a mate for the one we took out of Ekdahl?" Since he already knew the provenance of the bullet that killed Pilgersen there was no chance of that, but it never hurt to deflect suspicion in case anybody actually started to care about a derelict John Doe who got mugged, shot, tossed in a Queens Dumpster and set aflame; these days, that kind of thing happened all the time. But what if he could somehow match the .38 slug taken from Ekdahl's body with his brother's gun? . . . Well, nothing would give him more pleasure.

"They're at my office," said Sheinberg, patting him on the shoulder. "Stop by at anytime. Now tell the doctor where else it hurts."

"Right here," said Byrne, indicating his left shoulder. "And here," pointing to his groin.

"If it's a tattoo you're interested in, Santa can supply a little something in the 'Born to Die' line for a reasonable price. As for your other problem, you'll have to speak to your mother about that, but I bet the warranty's expired." He looked across his drink at Byrne.

"Seriously, I was thinking more like a leopard," said Byrne. "I hear it drives the ladies wild. But then, how you gonna satisfy them when your John Thomas ain't working, and never did?"

Sheinberg put down his empty scotch glass. "Gimme another one of these babies, would you, Frankie? And then maybe we should sit down over there."

Working on his third double Glenfiddich, Dr. Sheinberg took a seat in the lounge area. Byrne followed him, carrying his Guinness as carefully as the priest carries the chalice at Mass.

"You're referring of course to the schwanzless wonder we took apart on Friday."

"The one and only."

"Not exactly the only. I've seen this particular variation before—several times, in fact. Had a stiff a few years back, one of Genna's boys I think, a floater who bobbed up in the East River when his broken ankles couldn't support his cement overshoes anymore and his feet came off. What the hell was his name—Chirico, something Chirico—well, he came popping up near the South Street Seaport and scared the shit out of some tourists who were gazing at the glory that is Brooklyn. Seems he was drilling some made guy's daughter or wife or girlfriend, and that's a mob no-no, so the big guy gave the order to have him whacked. And just to make sure everybody got the message that this particular piece of ass was not to be messed with, whoever she was, they made him eat his weenie before they chucked his guinea ass in the drink. Found it in his stomach when we opened him up."

"I musta missed that one," said Byrne.

"You can't get all the good cases, Frankie," observed Sheinberg. "Anyway, it's not that unusual." He took a drink. "Now you tell me something: what about that Mafia hit in the Village on Wednesday?"

"The Carmine Street mess?" asked Byrne. "Jesus, Genna must be getting pretty shaky if they'd try to cap him right there in his own safe house."

"That's not my point," said Sheinberg. "Did you know that one of the bodies had its throat cut, just like our boy Ekdahl? And it looks to me that it was done with the same kind of weapon."

"Same knife?" asked Byrne, who did know, thanks to Tom.

"Not a knife," said Sheinberg. "A razor. The same thing that removed Ekdahl's peter."

The Mob had just moved up a notch on the suspects list. Even so, Byrne wanted to pursue Doreen's revelation. "You say it was cut off, Doc. But what if Ekdahl never had a dick? Is that possible?"

Sheinberg turned to look at him. "You sure you're over twenty-one, sonny?" he asked. "I think you've already exceeded your limit. Of course he had one. Everybody has one. Or the other. What are you talking about?"

Byrne didn't care to reveal the source of his information, but pressed on. "You're a doctor, Sy," he said. "Is it possible that he could have been some kind of freak? Like the Elephant Man or something? I mean, these things happen, don't they?"

"Never say never," said Sheinberg. "You know the old Yiddish saying, *Az mein bubbe vot gehat baytzim, vot zie geven mein zayde*: 'If my grandmother had balls she'd be my grandfather.' But as my report stated, there were traces of male genital tissue and mutilated flesh that clearly indicated something had been cut away. So I doubt if Ekdahl was anybody's granny."

"Well, what if he was deformed or something?"

Sy took a sip of his scotch. "Frankie, my practice these days concerns dead people, as you well know. I've seen a lot of weird stuff in my day, but I've never seen that. Which doesn't mean it can't happen. But most likely people who might suffer from such a, uh, deformity would be in the care of a doctor, and probably a shrink as well; they're not the kind who end up on my slab as murder victims, generally speaking."

Was he evading the question, or did he really not know? Byrne couldn't decide, but he could forge ahead. It pained him to have to sweat one of his best friends, but he supposed O'Reilly's was a more congenial place than doing it downtown. "Speaking of shrinks," he segued, "I met the famous Jacob German at a party last night."

"My, aren't we moving in fancy circles."

"I was just taggin' along," said Byrne. "You know, following Doreen on her never-ending quest for another sucker to buy that stuff she calls art. Quite a place he's got."

"Dr. German does very well for an asshole," said Sheinberg, finishing his drink. "Excuse me—I mean, for himself."

"You know him?"

"We go back."

"This far back?" asked Byrne, producing the camp photo he had taken from the doctor's house the night before.

Sheinberg drained his glass and set it down carefully on the table. He wiped his hand on his pants leg to dry it and picked up the picture. There was no emotion in his face at all. He stared at it for a long time and then put it down and passed it back to Byrne. "Gimme another drink, will ya?" he said. "This is thirsty work."

Byrne signaled Teddy for another round and sat back, waiting to see what Sy would do or say next. The bartender brought the drinks over himself, and Byrne slipped him a fiver for his trouble.

"Jack German and his Motley Crew," said Sheinberg after a sip. He seemed to be recovering. "You know I'm not one to wallow in the past, especially a past like this. But it's just like German to hang on to something like this. Where'd you find it?"

"Framed, on his bookshelf."

"Figures. This way he can remind himself every day of the eternal perfidy of the goyim, or maybe just eternal perfidy, period. Probably makes him feel better about himself; I understand shrinks are big on improving self-esteem." He took another drink. "Let's change the subject to something more pleasant, okay?"

Byrne saw his opening. "How about pretty girls?" he said, and took out his other problematic photo.

Sy Sheinberg was smooth but he wasn't that smooth. Byrne hated himself for acting like a cop when he was with his buddy, but an interrogation was still an interrogation, even over a couple of drinks. Although the doctor recovered well, Byrne couldn't help but notice the widening of the eyes, the burning glance and the short, involuntary intake of breath that accompanied Sheinberg's perusal of the picture.

"How come I never meet women who look like this?" Sy finally said.

"I don't think there's too many of them living north of the park anymore," said Frankie. "Maybe you ought to visit Queens more often."

"I hate paying tolls." Sheinberg took an evasive sip of scotch. "Although all God's chilluns gotta pay sooner or later."

Two photos, two hits. Byrne was wondering how hard and how far to press his friend. Maybe it was the stouts, but however fishy Dr. German's behavior at the party might have been, it seemed to Byrne that ancient personal history had nothing to do with a fresh murder. Now, though, the hit on his mother's photo raised a whole new set of questions. "Let's start with the tattoo," he said, changing the subject.

"Yeah, the tattoo," echoed Sheinberg, brightening. "I suspect we're going to see a lot of them in the coming years. Attached to members of the Russian mafia—Georgians, Armenians and, I'm ashamed to say, Jews, tough little motherfuckers all."

Sy put down his glass and faced Byrne squarely. "Frankie, did you ever hear of a place called Vidnoya? It's just outside Moscow, about twenty-five miles from Red Square, and it's where the central Russian police and forensic detective unit has its headquarters. It's pretty primitive by our standards—although I sometimes wonder if anyone could call our environment sophisticated—but they do good work there, amazing work, really, given the conditions. I was there on an exchange visit last year and believe me I came away with a great deal of admiration for those poor bastards."

Byrne laughed. "I always did suspect you of pinko commie faggot leanings."

"Screw you, Frankie," said Sheinberg. "I'm not talking about communism—that's finished anyway, it's just a matter of time, and it's about time, too—I'm talking about good men doing an impossible job that nobody gives a damn about with no money, no facilities and no hope of clearing even ten percent of their cases."

"Sounds familiar," said Byrne.

"And yet they continue, day after day, fighting the good fight. It's a lesson some of our guys could profitably learn. Anyway, I met with one of my opposite numbers, a guy named Kolesnekov, and he said something I've never forgotten. He said, and I quote, 'The crime here is not only too difficult for us to solve, it's too fantastic for outsiders to accept as real.'"

"I guess he's never been to the Big Apple," said Byrne.

"Believe me, he doesn't need to; our crooks are amateurs here compared with some of those boys. The Russian mafia—they're called *mafiozniki*, or *tyazhki*—play for keeps and then some, my friend." Sheinberg gave a low whistle of appreciation. "Luckily, at this stage, they're still mostly just whacking each other."

"Gimme a for instance," said Byrne, suddenly interested.

"When we were there, there were a dozen or so bodies in the morgue. One of the stiffs had been found naked, tied to a tree with a razor wire in the woods outside Moscow, his eyes gouged out. Couple of other guys were found along a road in the boondocks. Both were shot through the head, and their fingertips had been sliced off. Remember that book *Gorky Park*, where the people got their mugs erased? Wasn't so far wrong.

"But what's really interesting are the tattoos," continued Sheinberg. "Most of the bodies at Vidnoya have them. They make them out of a mixture of urine, ballpoint ink and the burned ash of shoe heels, pricked into the skin with hypodermic needles. They're a kind of homemade rap sheet; the *mafiozniki* have a whole system that tells them who's who in the zoo. Say what you will about communism, and I've said plenty"—Byrne suddenly remembered that the handful of Sheinberg relatives who managed to survive the Nazis during the war wound up on the wrong side of the border, in Wroclaw, after it—"but it kept the lid on. 'Use a gun, go to jail.' That's bullshit here and we both know it. But over there, use a gun—or a knife, or your bare hands—get caught and go to the worst fucking jail this side of Turkey or Paraguay. Talk about hard time."

"So how does this relate to Ekdahl?" asked Byrne.

"Well, Ekdahl's fingertips were missing, remember?"

"And he had a leopard tattoo," added Byrne. "Which means . . . ?"

Sheinberg paused to think. "Which means, according to Kolesnekov—well, let me tell you about some of the other tattoos first. A skeleton on the right shoulder indicates the guy was a professional assassin. A frog on the back of the head means that any violence directed against the tattooed will be paid back with interest by the guy's buddies. I think it's a boyfriend-girlfriend thing, except that they're both boys, of course. Stars on the knees mean that the guy was a trustie screw who ran a prison population, while military-style epaulets tattooed down the shoulders are marks of prison camp enforcers. Prisons—the Andovers and Exeters of the convict world, my friend." Sheinberg finished his drink and set his shot glass down heavily.

Byrne knew he'd have to hurry. "What about the leopard?"

"What's that barman's name, Francis me boy?" inquired Sheinberg.

"Teddy," answered Byrne, but Sheinberg had caught the bartender's eye and was signaling for another round. "Gee, I don't know, Doc," demurred Byrne, but the drinks were already on their way over, even though Byrne still had half his Guinness left.

"The leopard," said Sheinberg, "with its teeth bared, means that the bearer of this particular tattoo is a professional assassin who spent time in a Sakhalin Island prison camp."

"What's that?"

"The Soviet prison camp on Sakhalin Island," explained Sheinberg, "is the next worst thing to Siberia—it makes Siberia look like Hawaii—and it breeds the meanest killers in the world, guys with ice water in their veins. Guys that would kill you sooner than spend the energy to rotate their eyeballs in your direction." Sheinberg downed his fifth scotch in one gulp. Byrne marveled that the pathologist could eat and drink the way he did and never gain any weight. A classic ectomorph, he reflected. "Who'd make you fuck your own mother and then do the both of you while you were still hard."

The cute brunette at the bar, whose looks were improving by the minute, overheard the doctor and started to giggle. She raised her beer glass and gave them a salute.

Sheinberg noticed the exchange. "Looks like you might get lucky tonight, Frankie," he said, and began wobbling to his feet. "I'd better go."

"Wait a second, Sy," said Byrne. "You didn't finish."

"Oh yeah," said Sheinberg, sitting back down. "Who'd carve out your eyes and blow you a new asshole, free of charge." His voice was getting louder and both women were looking at them now, all of a sudden the two most interesting men in the place. "Who showed no mercy whatso-fuckingever. A hitman so cold-blooded he even terrified the *mafiozniki*."

"You know Ekdahl, don't you?" Byrne asked.

"Maybe I did," said Sheinberg, slurring slightly. "Once upon a long time ago."

They had staggered out onto the street and Sheinberg was searching for a passing taxi when he tripped on the curb and fell. As much as he wanted to, Byrne knew he'd get no more out of his friend tonight. "Fucking cabs are just like cops," Sheinberg said. "Never around when you need them."

"I'm right here, Sy," said Byrne, taking his arm and brushing him off, "and so's the taxi." Out of nowhere, careening down Broadway, a yellow cab had appeared. Byrne noticed the driver was a Sikh, with full beard and turban.

Sheinberg leaned in. "Eighty-ninth and West End," he commanded. "Yes I know it's the wrong way, but you can't go uptown on Broadway or haven't you noticed?" Then he turned and gripped Byrne by the shoulder. "They say confession is good for the soul, Frankie," he said. "But don't forget one thing. I'm not Catholic. Not even one of the *anusim*, Jews who converted to save their skins, if not their souls. I'm just one of the Chosen People, still waiting to find out what he's been chosen for."

"Tell me what you know, Sy," pleaded Byrne. "White's got me by the balls, and he's starting to squeeze. Promise me this: that you didn't kill him, and that you don't know who did. But give me something to go on and I'll do the best I can to protect you."

Sheinberg nodded. "I've heard that song before," he said. "But I'll answer your questions right now: no, and I'm not sure." He ducked his head and settled into the taxi's back seat. "And I'll tell you this, too," he said through the open rear window on the right passenger's side. "Did you ever notice that the Russians have only a few names for people? They're all called Sasha and Sergei and Natasha and Tatiana. And Ivan, of course, the name of the Russkie Everyman. Ivan the Terrible. Ivan the Schmuck. Or, in our case, Ivan the Schmuckless. Frankie, meet Ivan." With a screech of tires, the Sikh driver took off.

"Ivan," said Byrne to himself as he watched the cab disappear. Unconsciously, he imitated his friend's pronunciation. "I-*van*."

"That's a nice name," said the brunette. "Mine's Donna. I thought I'd get some fresh air. It's awful smoky in there," she explained, almost apologetically. "You a cop?"

Byrne looked at her. At this hour, in his condition, she was the most beautiful woman in the world. "Where's your friend?" he asked.

"Cheri? She's inside," Donna replied. "She asked me to come out here and call 911."

"911?" asked Byrne.

"You know," said Donna. "Make a cop come: dial 911."

"I'm on my way," said Byrne. Thank God he hadn't gone to Communion.

Chapter Twenty-seven
The Upper West Side
Monday, October 22, 1990; 12:15 A.M.

Seymour Sheinberg got back to his co-op on the Upper West Side a little after midnight. There was nobody home to greet him. There never was. He had lived alone for a long time.

"Zelda!" he called out. There was no answer. Yes, the cat was out on the town. He didn't worry very much about her, for his neighborhood was a warren of tiny backyards and big brownstones; there was plenty of room for a kitty to roam. Sometimes Zelda would stay out all night. Once she had been away for almost three days and he had just started to worry when she came mewling in through the bathroom window, her favorite point of entry and of exit (even off duty, Dr. Sheinberg continued to think in pathological terms), a dead rat held tightly between her jaws. He had tried to take it from her, but she guarded her trophy jealously. He had managed to put up with the rat in the kitchen for nearly a week until the smell was too much even for his jaded nostrils to ignore and, when Zelda went out, he threw the corpse down the garbage chute and into the incinerator. She didn't speak to him for days after that.

Although he had already had at least two too many, he walked over to the liquor cabinet and poured himself another double scotch.

People—hell, women—often asked him how he could stand working in the morgue. He usually made a few polite noises about its being a dirty job, et cetera, but the truth was he didn't mind. It wasn't exactly pleasant, but neither was it disgusting. The patients he received were past all help; stripped of their dignity, they were nothing but empty vessels who came to him with but one request: Tell the world how I died. Remember me.

Of course he forgot. Everybody forgot. Maybe it was just as well, for sometimes remembrance could be a curse, not a blessing. Pace Santayana, what was so great about remembering the past, anyway? Take his own people. The history of the Jews was a series of catastrophes, one piled atop the next like a pyre, a blazing holocaust, a human burnt offering to a deaf and dumb God, and any sane person would try to put this gloomy past behind him as quickly as possible. And yet remembrance was a central tenet of Judaism, part of the glue that had held the people together from the time of the pharaohs to the time of the storm troopers. Never forget, never again. Half right, anyway.

He settled back into his favorite chair and took off his glasses, his drink in one hand and, he noticed, a bottle of Glenlivet in the other. *Deus lo vult!* he decided. *Inshallah.* He toasted himself and poured another drink.

Never forget. Well, he'd been trying to forget for nearly half a century and still hadn't quite managed. He had been young, just fourteen in November of 1938, but he remembered the sound of the boots on the pavement outside the window, the harsh, barking German voices, the chanting—the unholy chanting, like a sick tribal ritual—of their neighbors: *"Juden Raus! Juden Raus! Deutsche! Wehrt Euch! Kauft nicht bei Juden!"*

"Jews out!" Did it matter where they went? From Babylon to Brooklyn, yea, they sat down and wept. Jews always ended up weeping. For if they didn't weep for themselves, who would weep for them? Certainly not his fellow Breslauers, who on Kristallnacht had stormed his father's temple, Ohel Jakob, and burned it to the ground. His neighbors! The mothers and fathers of the kids he had played with in school since he was in kindergarten! And then came the rocks through the windows, the spittle on the streets, the yellow stars on the clothes. Stars for Leon and Rachel and Sarah and little Siegfried Ishmael—that was his name in those days, because there was no Wagner lover like his dad. He took a sip: *And I only am escaped alone to tell thee.* Where was his Rachel, the devious-cruising Rachel, searching for her missing children? Would she ever find him, an orphan of the twentieth century's storm? No: she was dead, like the rest of them.

He found that someone had drunk his scotch while he was remembering, and poured himself another drink. Just one more, he promised, and then I'll watch the repeat of the late news and go to bed. Where the hell was that damn cat, anyway? "Zelda!" he called from his chair. It was too much trouble, he decided, to get up and go to the window and look for her; she'd be back.

Shit! He was supposed to see Rhonda tonight, and had totally forgotten. Rhonda had a husband somewhere up in Harlem, but she hadn't heard from him in nearly a year; supposed he was dead of a drug overdose or in jail. Every time they were together, Sheinberg assured her that Darryl hadn't turned up on the slab yet, but that he would be sure to let her know the minute her husband came through the door, feet first. He wondered why she hadn't called to complain, but there were no messages on the answering machine.

Rhonda Mourning was black, like most of his girlfriends these days, and even in New York, where tolerance supposedly reigned, people sometimes looked at them funny when they walked down the street together. He: tall, thin, losing his hair (well, actually, he had already lost most of it). She: short, a little heavy, buxom, with beautiful skin. In bed: he, enthusiastic and, with the passing of time, passably skilled; she, alive and adept, with a velvet mouth and a satin sheath that was ever ready no matter how brief the foreplay. "Don't you know that black girls are always wet?" she had told him the first time they had made love, and proceeded to illustrate the proposition throughout the night. He would have said this was a typically racist notion, if he had not experienced it for himself. Sliding around on top of and under him like an eel, the bed beneath grown slippery from their liquid passion. "Let me open myself up for you," she would say, and, even while he was in her, she would reach down and spread herself even wider—how did she do that?—and he would sink deeper into her, losing himself willingly in her femaleness.

So fuck anybody who looked at them askance. Didn't they know about the historic relationship of blacks and Jews? He was struggling to remember the precise nature of that relationship that the *Times* was always carrying on about—were the Jews instigators of the African slave trade or were they the heroic boon companions, Goodman and Schwerner and Chaney?—but he lost his train of thought when Egil Ekdahl suddenly appeared to him.

Ekdahl was kneeling, naked, his hands bound in front of him, his head bowed; Sheinberg couldn't quite see his face because Ekdahl's body was turned slightly away, but he knew it was him because he could see the leopard on his shoulder. Nor could he quite make out the figure behind Ekdahl, who was his executioner. Ekdahl did not appear to be frightened, nor was he resisting in any way. He was kneeling passively, motionless, and the executioner had him by the hair, a razor in one hand.

There was blood on the floor. There was blood everywhere. There was blood dripping from the gash in Ekdahl's throat, blood dripping from his loins and down his backside, blood spilling from his face. His heart had stopped pumping, but the blood was still flowing, splashing on the floor of the bathroom and whirling down the open floor drain. Sheinberg had never seen so much blood in his life.

The razor flashed, and there was a loud thump in the bathroom and the squeal of a cat.

"Zelda!" Sheinberg called out, and this time Zelda answered. She spoke in the deep, resonant tones of an adult male.

"How ya doin', Doc?" Zelda said. He turned to look at her.

No, it was not Zelda after all. He couldn't tell who it was. "Where's Zelda?" he asked, and started to rise, but the man put a hand on his chest and shoved him back into the chair. "Sit down," he ordered. "Relax. Take a load off. Don't mind if I do."

His visitor took the whiskey bottle away from him and poured himself a drink. Where did he find a clean glass? Sheinberg wondered, but the man was speaking again.

" . . . just a little chat," he was saying, and Sheinberg tried to focus on his words while he pondered who it might be. "Rhonda's over at the Black Hand, waiting for you. And is she ever pissed off. I even thought about doing her myself while I was waiting for you, but I prefer white meat."

"*Bitte?*" he said.

"Don't give me that kraut shit, Doc," said the man. "And no Russkie, either. Speak English, *por favor.*" The man was settled comfortably in the opposite chair, smiling at him and, he now noticed, pointing a .38 Smith and Wesson at his chest.

"You're not Zelda," was all he could say.

"And I'm not the Tooth Fairy, either," the man replied. "But don't worry your pretty little head about who I am. Just gimme some info and I'm outta here. Bullshit me and you're toast."

"Like Ekdahl," Sheinberg said, concentrating on his train of thought. "I saw him die."

His guest seemed pleased. "Now you're talking my language, Doc." The man tapped one foot on the floor, as if listening to an inaudible melody. Or maybe he was just impatient. "The late Mr. Egil Ekdahl."

"He's dead."

"Oh, yeah, he dead all right," mocked his guest.

"They're all dead," replied Sheinberg. "*And behold, there came a great wind from the wilderness, and smote the four corners of the house, and it fell upon the young men, and they are dead.* That's the way I see them. Leon and Rachel and Sarah and all the others. That's the way they come to me now. Michael and Enrique and Tyrell and old lady McArthur on Fifth Avenue. She wandered too far north for her evening constitutional one night—maybe you remember that murder, it was in all the papers." He held out his glass, hoping the stranger's mood was hospitable. He was disappointed. "But one did survive the wreck. Did you know that Ishmael means 'God hears'? Except that must be a joke, because God doesn't."

"Cut the scripture, Doc, I don't have all night." At least the intruder seemed to be enjoying his whiskey. "What I want to know now, and once I know this for a fact I'll leave, I promise, is this: who killed him?"

Why, the Nazis of course, thought Sheinberg. I saw them kill my father on the thirty-first of October 1944 when a butcher-turned-Sturmbahnführer named Himmelheber drew a pistol and shot my father in the workyard at Theresienstadt because he hadn't responded to a command quickly enough. Putzi Himmelheber, the Raiser of Heaven, who raised hell on earth for the Jews. "That was the model camp, you know," he explained. "That was the one the Red Cross was allowed to visit." His voice dropped. "All in all, it wasn't so bad, until the end."

"You're going to need the Red Cross in a minute if you don't start making some sense," said his visitor. Sheinberg felt a stinging slap across his face. "Wake up, you goddamn lush! Who killed him? And what happened to the file?"

What file? All the files were destroyed, as many of them as they could get their hands on anyway, just before the Allies liberated the camp. And as for who killed him . . . "I thought you did," said Sheinberg.

Another slap, this one much harder; almost a punch. "He looked just like his dear old dad, didn't he? The dad he wanted to find so very badly."

Sheinberg made a supreme effort to stay focused.

"Didn't he? *Didn't he*, Dr. Schlussel?"

Sheinberg blinked. "What?" he said. "Who?"

"And you would recognize the son, wouldn't you, Doctor?" Slap! "Wouldn't you recognize the boy you helped conceive and brought into this world and watched grow up for the first eight years of his life? How could you forget him? You, who never forgets anything."

"Remembering is easy," said Sheinberg through the fog. "Forgetting is hard."

"Then remember this: Where is the file? You were there! You must know! I must know!"

Sheinberg hesitated, flinching. "I don't know." Another slap. "Stop it!" he protested, sobering now. "He was already dying when I got there." Sheinberg fought desperately to collect his thoughts. "Just stop hitting me, please." He held out his hands in a gesture of surrender. "I've been trying to figure it out. Trying to figure out who shot him. That's my job."

"Yeah, well, I don't think the answer is in this bottle, Doc," said the man, pouring the last of the whiskey onto the floor and then smashing the flask. "It's a good thing you're not a real doctor anymore. You'd probably kill more patients than you'd cure. Just like little Amy Stevens."

"That was a long time ago!" Sheinberg cried. "And it wasn't my fault."

"Wasn't your fault, my ass. You're one lucky sheeny son of a bitch that your Company connections found you this plush job cutting up stiffs or you'd probably still be in the can. You sure as hell couldn't get any malpractice insurance."

"I'm going to need more time," he pleaded.

"Time is the one thing neither of us has," said his visitor. "Although I bet I have more than you do." He chuckled. "Shame about the cat. What was its name?"

"Zelda," replied Sheinberg.

The man snorted. "I never liked Fitzgerald anyway." The first blow caught him just below his left eye, but the best part of being drunk was that it didn't hurt much, and you passed out so quickly.

Chapter Twenty-eight
The Bronx
Monday, October 22, 1990; noon

How's your day going?" she asked.

They were having lunch in a little home-style Italian place called Cangelosi's near the corner of 187th Street and Arthur Avenue in the Bronx. Byrne had spent an hour trying to figure out where to meet her: not in the Village, surely, where he could be spotted by one of Doreen's innumerable friends or even more innumerable acquaintances; not in any of the chic midtown places he sometimes frequented in her company, for the same reason. So here they were, not far from where he had gone to college.

"Fine, so far," he said. "How's yours?"

"The usual." She sighed, and tossed her head. It made her hair fly, sail like a cheerleader's skirt, and Byrne had to admit it was very effective in communicating something: confidence, ease, femininity, sex. She was dressed simply and casually, in a gray Ralph Lauren suit, silk blouse and pumps. When she looked across the table at him with her shining eyes and smiled, he knew for sure that he was falling in love with her and had been since the day they met in spite of himself.

"I don't think it's possible for a woman to be more beautiful than you are right now," he blurted out.

Ingrid appraised him with a smile on her lips. Then she leaned across the table and kissed him, slipping her tongue in his mouth so expertly he felt his heart stop. "Thank you," she said, raising her napkin and patting her lips. "Hope the food is half as good. What are we going to have to eat?"

On cue, the waiter arrived. Byrne knew his name was Natale; he had been born on Christmas Day and was the best present his mother could have wished for. "Something to drink?" he asked.

"Perrier," she said.

"I'll have a beer," said Byrne. "Moretti."

"*Bene*," said Natale, and disappeared.

"It's Italian," he explained. "The beer, I mean."

"Thanks for the language lesson," she said.

They were not the only diners in the restaurant. Cangelosi's was not a fancy establishment, but the service was good, the wine list excellent and the food both inexpensive and tasty; New York still had places like this, thank God. Mention Rao's, the tiny little eatery up in what used to be Italian Harlem, and a few of the cognoscenti could tell you that it was the chic place to dine if you wanted a little frisson with your Valdostana. Manhattanites who didn't know any better always blanched when you told them you knew a couple of good places in the Bronx—all they knew about the Bronx was what they read in the *Times*'s Metro section—but anyone who had actually lived there knew that parts of the Bronx weren't bad at all, even when they were, as Cangelosi's neighborhood was, surrounded by bad sections. But this was Belmont, a cohesive Italian district where the neighbors still watched out for one another. He had felt a little guilty about asking Ingrid to venture this far from her East Side turf, but here she was. She'd probably taken a limo. Then again, knowing her, she might have walked.

Natale set their drinks down. "*Vino bianco per la bella donna!*" he exclaimed with a theatrical flourish. "*E una birra per l'uomo bello!* You like to order now? We have a few aspecials."

Byrne was going to tell him to come back in a few minutes, but Ingrid seemed fascinated with Natale's recitation—a savory litany of chicken breast, red snapper and various veal dishes, not to mention the daily pasta specials, which on this evening included a pappardelle con coniglio—and so he let him rattle on.

"Sounds delicious," she said, and something in her accent caught the waiter's ear.

"Where you from?" he asked.

"Norway," she answered, truthfully so far as Byrne knew.

"How come you speak so good English?" asked Natale. "I been this country twenty years, and I no speak so good English as you."

"Thank you." She blushed and smiled; for her, apparently, every man was fair game.

"We need a few minutes," said Byrne.

"I come back," said Natale, getting the message.

"Well," said Byrne. "How come you do?"

"It's nothing, really," she said modestly. "In Norway we start studying English in the second grade. Plus all the movies and television shows we get from the States are always broadcast in English, so we get to hear the language every day. Anyway, what choice do we have? All the Scandinavian countries are small and if we want to communicate with the outside world we had better learn how to talk with it. We don't mind."

They studied the menus. After a decent interval Natale reappeared, and so they ordered, capping the list with a Gaja Barolo that was one of Byrne's favorite Italian red wines.

"Very good choice," said Ingrid. "Are you sure you can afford it?"

Was that merely as an observation, or was she putting him in his place? Byrne took a sip of wine and pronounced it acceptable.

"Aren't you starting to mix business with pleasure, Lieutenant?" she inquired. "I thought that sort of thing was frowned on. You know the old saying, 'Never mix, never worry.'"

"I thought that had something to do with booze," he observed.

"It works in many social circumstances," she said.

"Don't look now," said Byrne, "but I think you started the whole mixing business back on your couch."

Was that a blush? "I'm a secretary, Lieutenant," she said. "I follow orders."

Natale poured the wine and slipped the appetizers under their chins so dexterously that Byrne hardly noticed their arrival.

"Speaking of which," he began. "How's Mr. Pilgersen?"

She didn't bat an eye. "Mr. Pilgersen has been recalled by the Danish government," she said, and Byrne once again had an opportunity to admire her acting skills. "The new consul general will be on board in a couple of weeks, and in the meantime, we're managing."

"Eat," he said, tucking into his linguine with clam sauce.

"So what's going on?" she asked. "Why the urgent invitation?"

Byrne took a long draught of wine; he had so many things to say, and not the slightest idea how to begin saying them. "You really are beautiful" was all he could manage for the moment.

"More beautiful than Doreen?" she asked, bringing him up short. "Did she tell you about us?"

What was it with women? Were looks a zero-sum game to them? Was it impossible for any woman to accept the fact that she could be found attractive without a correspondent reduction in some other woman's allure? A man could not profess love or admiration without his being subjected to incessant interrogation, the questioning based on the premise of I Bet You Say That to All the Girls, which maybe they did. But what a woman never seemed capable of understanding was that men could actually mean their compliments, at least at the moment they were delivering them. Life was not a closed system for a man: you could find one woman beautiful without implicitly denigrating the rest of her sex; you could tell a woman you loved her, and mean it—and then tell another one on the same day that you loved her and mean that as well. Maybe that's why women were always doubtful where men's bona fides were concerned, always probing, because they knew that men were just two-legged dogs. And yet, in the end, they usually fell for it. Maybe they were supposed to; perhaps their susceptibility to flattery was the equalizer in the war between the sexes. Or maybe they just made you think it was.

"You might have mentioned it the other day," said Byrne.

"How was I to know? I didn't see any 'Frankie forever' tattoos on her."

"I bet you looked for them, too."

"No, really," she said, smiling once more and tousling his hair. "I didn't put you two together until the party. You make a handsome couple."

"Just like you and Tom," he said.

"Jealous of our older brother, are we?"

"More than you know," he admitted. He took another drink of wine; she, he noticed, had hardly touched hers. "Unfortunately, this deplorable sibling rivalry has been made more complicated by my feelings for you."

"And just what are those feelings?" she asked.

"Lust," he replied. "Love. I don't know."

"It's a little early for love, isn't it?" she asked.

"Better than too late," he said, thinking of Mary Claire and maybe Doreen as well. He was damned if it was going to happen again. Impulsively, he grabbed her hand. "Look, Ingrid, I may live to regret everything I'm about to say to you, but here goes."

"Live dangerously, I always say." She raised her wine glass to him in a toast and Byrne took it as a signal to proceed.

"First of all," he began, "you have to understand that I'm happy with Doreen."

"No you're not," she corrected him, setting her wine glass down brusquely. "You're not or you wouldn't be here with me right now. Don't lie to me, Francis Byrne, and don't lie to yourself either. I hate it when people lie, and if you want to have any chance with me I'm advising you here and now to always tell me the truth."

"Okay, strike that," he said, knocked off stride by her mood swings. This wasn't the way he had wanted to begin this particular quiz show, so he changed gears. "Let's not talk about us for a while. Let's talk instead about Ekdahl, who was the real missing guest of honor the other night. I know that he was a pervert named Eddie Paine. I know that he was involved in some way with a woman named Shannon over at the Rambone, where he had a rep for violence and speaking in tongues. And I know that whatever this bedtime story Tom is feeding me about the Kennedy assassination has little or nothing to do with why Ekdahl was murdered. But what I don't know is who Ekdahl really was or the nature of your relationship with him. And that's what I'm here to find out, without my big brother looking over my shoulder."

It was amazing how her expression never changed, no matter what the subject. "You're right about all those things," she said matter of factly. "But isn't it also possible that Egil had many good qualities too? Don't we all have our hidden sides, the sides we don't go around exhibiting for public consumption? I've heard about yours."

He wondered how much she had heard, and from whom. "Of course," he agreed. "But this Ekdahl character seems to have a lot more sides than most of us. Let me count them: night crawler, bisexual Danish diplomat, Soviet illegal . . ."

"You know that stuff about illegals is bullshit," she interjected.

"Do I?" he asked. "Are you saying that was just Pilgersen's story? And that you and Tom played along, until Tommy decided Pilgersen wasn't worth playing along with anymore? Whose side are you on, anyway?"

"He was a very dangerous man," she said. "Tom told you why."

"And then you told me everything Tom said was a lie," said Byrne. "So who am I supposed to believe?"

"You really hate Tom, don't you?" she said.

"Even more than I have to," he replied.

"I heard all about him and Doreen. That hurt you, didn't it?" Did she not know about Mary Claire too, or was she maybe human after all? "More than finding out about Doreen and Egil and me?"

"A lot more," he admitted.

"Why?" she inquired. "Sex is sex."

"Not to me," he answered.

She shrugged, and he felt his temper rising. What was it with this woman? Why did he want to make love to her and throttle her at the same time? Why did he have such intense emotions about her, and in such a short time? Was it him? Or was it her? Or was it them?

"What else?" she prompted. "What else was Egil?"

"I dunno. A spy. A contract killer for the Mafia. A former inmate of a Soviet prison camp. A homicidal sex maniac who couldn't get it up."

"Did Doreen tell you why?" The food was growing cold in front of them, but he didn't care.

"She said"—he let his voice drop—"that he didn't have a dick."

Ingrid gave him a frank return gaze. "He didn't."

"What the hell is that supposed to mean?" he asked in exasperation. "Every guy has a dick."

"But not every guy can use it," she said. "Egil had a handicap."

"So what was that song and dance you gave me about you two being lovers?"

"I didn't say that," she replied. "I know I am speaking a foreign language, but I try to choose my words carefully, so please listen to what I say and stop jumping to conclusions. I told you about Mother's Little Helper. There are plenty of ways to make love to a woman without having intercourse with her. Read the Kama Sutra. Or ask a doctor."

"I intend to," he told her. "I'm going to see Jacob German again tomorrow morning."

"Watch yourself," she said. "He's a formidable and dangerous man. You'd better go in there prepared to be challenged because otherwise he'll cut you up and have you for lunch. Frankly, I'm not sure you're up to it."

"Thanks a lot," he said. "You know him that well, do you?"

"Like I said, politics makes strange bedfellows."

Byrne suddenly recalled Ella German's frosty demeanor at the party: bedfellows indeed. "Why's a secretary concerned with politics?" he asked.

"Where I come from," she retorted, "secretaries are just as entitled to political opinions as anyone else."

Natale gave them some breathing room, setting the main courses down in front of them with aplomb, pouring some more wine, and then vanishing.

"I'm a patriot," she went on. "A Norwegian patriot, and that means more to me than being an American patriot means to you."

"And why is that?"

"Because your country isn't under attack right now," she replied. "Your country's way of life isn't threatened by outside forces."

No, thought Byrne to himself, only by internal forces, such as the ones he had to deal with every day. He kept his mouth shut. "And yours is? By what, may I ask?"

"The EC," she said. "And you probably have no idea what that is, do you?"

"Listen, lady," he said angrily, "don't you sit there dining on my nickel and make fun of my American ignorance. This is a big place, in case you haven't noticed. We could fit every extant Norwegian into New York City and still have plenty of room left over. Let me guess: the EC is probably something like that stupid soccer sport of yours, the political equivalent of bouncing a ball off your fucking head. Am I right?"

"No, you're wrong," she said. "I suppose there's no reason for you to follow the ins and outs of the European Community, but in Norway it's a big issue. Do we join Europe, and benefit from the common market and all of that? And if we do, do we also leave ourselves open to intra-

European laws regarding not only farming, which is important because our farmers are so politically powerful, but immigration and social policies that may not be exactly to our liking?"

"I don't understand," said Byrne.

"Meaning that we have a nice country, Frankie. Not just Norway, but Denmark and Sweden, too. And even Finland, except that the Finns are pretty weird. Meaning that I'm worried about what might happen when and if we do join the EC." She took a small sip of the wine. "We are very naive in Scandinavia," she said, "and easily taken advantage of."

Somehow he doubted she was speaking personally. "That's what those French and Italian boys on the Riviera are counting on," he said.

"I mean socially," she corrected. "Do you have any idea what immigrants from the Third World get when they settle in Norway?"

"All the moose meat they can eat?"

"Even better," she said. "Free housing, free medical care, a monthly living stipend. And what do we get in return? More theft, more violence, rising crime."

"Yeah, I hear in Oslo and Copenhagen you can't hardly go out at night anymore."

"No, really," she complained.

"Really this," said Byrne. "Get a grip, Ingrid. Here we are in the middle of the Bronx, in a neighborhood that would scare the crap out of any of your poor Pakis or Nigerians. Don't give me you've got it bad in white man's heaven because no matter how bad it gets it can't get any worse than this. And yet life goes on, and most of the people, no matter where they come from, manage to get along."

"I hardly think 'managing to get along' is the highest condition to which mankind can aspire," she said. "I mean, look around you."

He knew she didn't mean just Cangelosi's. "I repeat," he said, "if you hate it so much here, why do you stay?"

"Two reasons," she said. "One, what choice do I have? I have a job and until I find another one that amuses me more, I'll continue to do it. And two, I've met you."

When she smiled that smile, with that wide, inviting mouth of hers, there was nothing he could say. Did women know what weapons they have at their disposal? Or were their smiles, their eyes, their skin tone and their figures simply instinctual attributes they employed without ever quite appreciating their formidable power? Who knew? About her, however, he was pretty sure; nothing was left to chance. And now that she had him in her tractor-beam gaze, even full reverse thrust wasn't going to spring him free.

"What about Tom?" he asked.

"Tom!" she exclaimed. "I'd rather kiss a caribou. Can't you tell?"

"Then what was that little charade I witnessed on Saturday?"

"Oh that," she said. "It was, how to say it, a marriage of convenience."

"Meaning?"

"Meaning that I had to do something to get Jack German off my back." This caught him by surprise. "Dr. German was hustling you?"

"And how," she said, as if relieved to finally get the subject out in the open. "Is there anything more embarrassing than a dirty old man like him throwing himself at a girl like me?"

Byrne decided she had answered her own question by the way she phrased it. "Was he bothering you?"

"Oh, big time," she said. "I don't think he would have done anything really stupid, but you never know, and so Tom agreed to help me out by announcing our 'engagement' at the party. Of course, I let him off the hook right afterward. No breach-of-promise suit in his future."

"But what about earlier?" asked Byrne. "What about, you know, Friday night, right after, you know, when we were eating in the Chinese place?"

"We had to practice," she explained. "And I figured if we could convince you, then we could convince everybody else the next day."

"I don't know," said Byrne. "Your relationship seemed so, well, real. You know, the loathing, the disgust, the hostility . . . you sure had me fooled."

"That was the whole idea."

"But it was all an act."

"One hundred percent. Except for the loathing part."

"You're not in love with Tom?" He wanted to be sure.

"Give me a break," she exclaimed. "He dragged me into that whole dreadful business with Mr. Pilgersen—'national security,' he said." All of a sudden, there was a look of alarm in her eyes. "He made me do it, Frankie, and now he's blackmailing me. I'm scared. I need you to help me." She took his hand and squeezed it.

"How?" asked Byrne. "What has he got on you?"

She lowered her eyes and stared at her plate. "He was following us the night Egil and I met Doreen at the club, and he saw everything," she said.

"He threatened to tell Pilgersen about the drugs or, worse, have me arrested and expelled. But I swear I didn't know what Tom was going to do that night. And now I'm a part of it." She was starting to cry.

"Everything okay?" asked Natale, ignoring all evidence to the contrary, as a good waiter should. "Some dessert?"

Byrne looked at Ingrid, trying to pretend everything was normal. "What do you think?"

"I think I'd like you to take me home, Lieutenant." She sniffled, and Byrne made a mental note to up Natale's tip for his discretion.

"You heard the lady," said Byrne. "We'll take a check, please."

"Very good, sir," said Natale, setting the bill down in front of him and handing Byrne the corked, half-empty bottle of wine. "Don't forget this," he said. "It's too good to waste."

Byrne paid and together they walked to his car, which was parked across the street in a fire zone. As he drove back into the city, he reached out with his free right hand and patted her gently on the left thigh. Instead of brushing his hand away, she covered it with her own and pressed it down firmly onto her leg, where it remained for the rest of the trip.

"Are you coming up?" she asked. With her red eyes and her smudged makeup, she was irresistible.

"If I do, you know I'm going to make a pass at you," he warned her. "And this time I know Pilgersen's not going to interrupt us."

"That's for sure," she said.

"And this is okay with you?"

"Did I say it wasn't?" she asked. She stopped and turned to him, just as she was putting the key in her lock. "Just one thing," she said.

He could feel his heart beating faster. "Anything."

"Don't rush me." This time, he felt, she wasn't playing with him. A woman's mouth could lie, but could her body? He was going to find out. "Let me come to you. I may give you my body now, but my heart takes longer. Don't expect me to fall in love with you as fast as you are falling in love with me. Give me time, and give me space, and maybe I'll get there. I think we have possibilities. There are no guarantees in this world, Francis, but I'm giving you your chance. Don't blow it."

"I'll try not to," he said, as they swept through her doorway and into each other's arms.

Chapter Twenty-nine
Bensonhurst, Brooklyn
Monday, October 22, 1990; 3:00 P.M.

Lieutenant Byrne, would you come in here, please?"

Captain William J. Finnegan was behind his desk, as usual, when Byrne got back downtown. Finnegan was a man of average height but wider than average girth, whose manner was more pastoral than authoritative; the word around the department was that he had studied for the priesthood before joining the force. Sheinberg found it amusing that three Roman Catholics were in charge of protecting the citizenry; he called the top brass the *shabbas goys*. "Catholics protecting Jews from their special relationship with blacks. And who better than the Three Putzim?" Speaking of Sheinberg, where the hell was he? Byrne had put in a call to him, but the doctor hadn't shown up at work yet. Must be still sleeping it off.

From the desktop's pristine condition, one would never know there had already been three murders in New York City that day. Finnegan believed that a good executive should handle each piece of incoming only once, and accordingly had neatly organized in and out baskets on his desk. Byrne did too, the only difference being he simply threw everything away.

"Hey, Bill," said Byrne.

"Where have you been, Lieutenant?" inquired Finnegan, who always addressed the men by rank. Byrne wasn't sure he even knew their names. "I certainly hope you're not getting into the habit of taking long lunches at the taxpayers' expense."

Byrne had little use for Finnegan. The captain had been passed over as department head by Matt White and bitterly resented what he saw as reverse discrimination. His natural inclination toward racism had been exacerbated by White's promotion, as had his natural tendency toward alcoholism. Byrne wondered which would kill him first: White or his liver. Forty years of assiduous butt-kissing had won him powerful protectors, although with Moby Dick on the ropes Finnegan's days might well be numbered.

Finnegan was also from Boston, which was another reason Byrne didn't like him. The Boston Irish were different from their New York cousins; more clannish, more cocksure, more Byzantine. The Irish in New York had adapted quickly to the realities of the Tweed machine; their easy tolerance of corruption in the name of civic virtue made them a model minority. But the Boston Irish stayed close to the Church and to each other, and often evinced a distressing tendency to moral scruples.

"I know you're a busy man these days," said Finnegan, "but I've got a job for you and Sergeant Andretti." He could see from the look on Byrne's face that the lieutenant was not pleased.

"Where's everybody else?" complained Byrne. "Where's Davidowicz and Riley? You know I'm working the Ekdahl case."

"They have their hands full," said Finnegan. "They're seeing action up in Apache country. Must be pay day in Santo Domingo or something." He shuffled a report. "Don't worry, it's right up your alley: a no-brainer about a guy who clobbered his girlfriend."

Byrne sat down.

"Modern crime, so relentless and so predictable in its banality," began Finnegan, whose penchant for sermonizing exceeded that of a priest. "It makes one long for the good old days of Murder Inc. and the Mad Bomber. And yet things have not really changed all that much. When I was a young cop on the beat—we still had beats in those days—people were just as capable of the same kinds of crimes. We had them all: lovers killing lovers, parents killing children, sons killing fathers and daughters murdering mothers, all for the most trivial of reasons, or for no reason at all. The behavior of our very own beloved Irish was no better than that of today's Negroes—excuse me, African Americans. It's just that we had less firepower and our drug of choice was booze. We like to think of ourselves as civilized, Lieutenant, but believe me, we're just one step out of the asphalt jungle ourselves.

"And so here," he continued, referring to the lone file on his desk, "we have a white guy, a Brooklyn hood named Russell Hines, who strangled his girlfriend Saturday night while they were making love." Finnegan seemed curiously satisfied at this development, as if it broke the monotonous parade of people of color before the majesty of the Law. "Of course, he claims a black guy did it, but according to the lab, which by the way I understand also has some reports for you regarding your Mr. Ekdahl, the semen in the girl's vagina matches Hines's blood type and his prints are all over her neck. Apparently we've been over to his domicile a couple of times in the past on family trouble complaints, and the late Ms. DiCiccio was treated at the hospital several times for falling down the stairs, banging her head on the cabinets and various other household accidents. There are many things in this life that I'm fated never to understand, Lieutenant, and why anybody would want to get beat up or hurt while having sex is one of them."

Byrne had the feeling that Finnegan's approach to foreplay was the usual Irish "brace yourself, Bridget" approach. "Some of them like it," he observed. "They like it right up to the moment that they don't, and then it's usually too late." He took down the address. "You say the lab has something for me?"

"Here it is," said Finnegan, handing him the material. "But deal with Mr. Hines first, please. Gently, Lieutenant, gently. I'd like a live defendant this time."

He flipped through the reports as he walked back to his desk. Good old Felix had come through, as usual: he'd gotten a match on the set of prints found on the dildo. They belonged to a woman named Natalia Medved of Brighton Beach, Brooklyn, whose name meant nothing to Byrne.

"Who is she, Felix?" he asked when he got Aprahamian on the phone.

"It took a while," said the latent-print specialist, "but we finally got a hit with INS. Natalia Medved is a recent Russian immigrant who was admitted under the quota for Soviet Jews; her prints were on her visa application." Probably a Hunt Club denizen, thought Byrne, or a hooker: more and more of them were showing up from Russia these days. He'd check her out as soon as possible.

He and Andretti were in Brooklyn within the hour. "Mr. Hines, I'm Lieutenant Francis Byrne." Byrne flashed his badge at a crack in the front door of 1647 Avenue J, Apartment 3C, Bensonhurst. "And this is Detective Sergeant Andretti."

The door widened a bit and he could make out one eye, part of a nose, half a mustache. "Whaddaya want?"

"Coupla questions, if you don't mind," said Byrne amiably.

"You got a warrant?" said the voice. There were two eyes now, one complete nose and a bristly black 'stache that framed a mean mouth and a weak chin.

"I'm hoping we won't need one," said Byrne. "Can we please come in?" The door closed briefly while the chain lock came off, and then swung open.

The interior was drab and meanly furnished. A television was the principal object in the room, around which were arranged a sofa and a couple of chairs: a secular shrine to *Monday Night Football*. Byrne looked in vain for any trace of feminine amelioration; the apartment smelled like dirty ashtrays and stale beer.

"Mr. Hines," began Byrne, "I can appreciate that this has been a very trying ordeal for you, and I want you to know that we're here to help you."

"Right," snarled the man belligerently. He was not tall but heavyset, about forty years old. His forearms were thick and muscular, his shoulders broad but sloping. His waistline, Byrne noted with some satisfaction, was not what it probably once had been.

"There's still a couple of details we need to go over with you, so we can find the man who did this as quickly as possible. As I'm sure you can appreciate, it's a jungle out there."

"You're tellin' me," said Hines. "Fuckin' jungle bunnies multiply faster each week. And one of 'em killed my Donna."

Byrne took a chair opposite the couch where Hines was sitting. Andretti continued to stand, on his right. Unapologetically, Hines lit up a cigarette.

"Would you mind not smoking?" requested Byrne. "Detective Andretti is very allergic to cigarettes and we'd both be very grateful if you'd just put it out. It would make our time here so much more pleasant, and the more pleasant it is the sooner you'll be rid of us." Establish authority early on, no matter how petty the issue.

"Hey, it's my own fuckin' house," complained Hines, but he complied.

"Thanks," said Byrne. "Now, let's see what we can add to your statement here."

Hines's story was fairly straightforward. After an evening on the town, Russell Hines and Donna DiCiccio had been having consensual sexual intercourse in the back of a limo hired for the evening from ABC Transportation Services of Queens, which was parked near the abandoned docks off the remains of the West Side Highway in Manhattan, when, according to Hines, they had been interrupted by the sound of gunfire coming through the driver's-side window. The driver of the limo, Yehuda Golden, had been killed instantly, and as Hines struggled back into his pants, the back door of the car was wrenched open and he was struck on the head by what he supposed was the butt of a pistol. When he came to, some time later, he wasn't sure how long, Miss DiCiccio was sprawled across the back seat, naked from the waist down, her throat a mass of livid bruises.

"What is it, may I ask, that you do for a living, Mr. Hines?" said Byrne.

"I'm a crane operator," he replied sullenly. "For DeMarco Construction."

"You're a soldier in the Genna family, you mean," barked Andretti. "Everybody knows who owns DeMarco."

"Yeah, well, you're so fuckin' smart," said Hines.

"In any case," interrupted Byrne, "I do see here on your record one or two arrests. Here's a vehicular manslaughter rap. You ran over a Mr. Slobodan Vasevic."

"Don't I know you?" said Hines, who had been staring at Byrne since he came in.

"I'll ask the questions, if you don't mind," said Byrne testily. "Apparently Mr. Vasevic had accidentally dented a vehicle newly registered to one J. Aiello in a parking lot."

"Genna's main man," supplied Andretti.

"So it must have been a terrible coincidence that you just happened to accidentally kill him with your car a week later."

Hines shrugged. "Shit happens," he said.

"Right," said Byrne. "Shit does happen. Luckily for you, the charges were dropped after Mrs. Vasevic refused to testify. Funny about that. Well, getting back to Miss DiCiccio . . . as I understand it, you and she were out on the town. Were you celebrating something?"

"Yeah," said Hines, "we was celebratin'. Hey, I do know you."

"Would you mind telling us what, exactly?" said Byrne, ignoring him.

"Our engagement. We was gonna get married."

"Congratulations," said Andretti sarcastically. "First she does, then 'I do.'"

"And then?" asked Byrne before Hines could respond.

"And then how the fuck should I know?" replied Hines angrily. "There was this loud noise and then I don't remember nothin' until some cop woke me up. My head still hurts."

"Let me take a look," said Byrne solicitously. Hines leaned forward and Byrne briefly examined the wound. "Hmmmm," he said. The injury was to the right rear of the head, near where the parietal bone meets the occipital, the kind of blow a right-handed man might inflict on himself, should he so choose. And Hines, Byrne had observed while he was smoking, was right-handed.

"Let's reconstruct your positions in the car, if we can," said Byrne. "Where were you in relation to Miss DiCiccio? She was behind the driver?"

"I think so," replied the man. "The doctors say I've got some memory loss."

"And the attack came from your side," said Byrne. "It was your door that opened, when you were struck."

"That's the way I remember it," said Hines.

"Now, I know this part is not only painful, but maybe a little embarrassing as well," began Byrne, "but we need to go over this very carefully. You say the two of you were making love in the back seat at the time?"

"Yeah."

"Don't you think you could have found a better place than the West Side Highway for that sort of activity?"

"Donna just liked doin' it outdoors sometimes. But she weren't no pervert, if that's what you're thinking. Anyway, it was dark, and the limo had tinted windows."

"Were there any other aspects of your relationship that might be considered unusual?" asked Byrne. "We've had reports from your neighbors that they often heard shouts and screams when the two of you were here. Did you fight often?"

"Don't everybody fight sometimes?" said Hines.

"Sure they do," admitted Byrne. "I'm just trying to understand what the level of combat was for you two. I understand you've had a couple of visits in the past from our colleagues in Brooklyn. Family trouble complaints, disturbing the peace, that sort of thing."

"So we got a little rowdy sometimes, so what?"

"I'm trying to ask you, in a nice way," deflected Byrne, "whether maybe you two might have been having what some people call rough sex that night. Did Miss DiCiccio like it rough? Did you?"

"Can I have a cigarette?" asked Hines. "Helps me think."

"I suppose so, if you really need one," said Byrne. "It is your house, after all. Detective Andretti, I think you'd better step outside while Mr. Hines has a smoke. I can finish up by myself." Byrne looked at Andretti, to make sure he got the message.

"Okay, Frankie," said Andretti. "I'll be down in the car if you need me."

"Get me a turkey on rye at that deli we saw, will ya?" Byrne called after him. Hines lit his cigarette and sat back farther on the couch, relaxing a little. Byrne watched the flame dance at its tip as he sucked on it.

"Let's get back to your personal relationship with the deceased. Tell me what was happening in the back seat when Mr. Golden was killed."

"Well, we was doin' it."

"I know that already. How exactly were you doing it?"

"Okay," said Hines, who stubbed out his cigarette and stood up; Byrne remained in his chair, his notebook on his lap, his pen in his right hand. "Okay, sometimes, just before she would come, I would put my hands around her neck. She liked that a lot."

"And then what?"

"And then I would give her a little squeeze, you know, a love squeeze."

"Why?" asked Byrne. "To heighten her orgasm?"

"Donna always had a difficult time coming," explained Hines. "She said it helped her."

"It helps a lot of people," said Byrne. "But you would be amazed at how many people die each year from it."

Hines looked at him warily. "Yeah?" he said.

"Yeah," said Byrne. "Mostly teenage boys. They tie a rope around their necks and hang themselves while they're jerking off, only sometimes they don't get out of the noose in time and sayonara, sonny."

"Is that a fact?" said Hines.

"Yes, it is," said Byrne. "In the old days, when they used to hang people, a man would cream his pants and shit himself silly when he hit the bottom of the drop. It's just one of those funny physiological facts. Go figure. Did you know Donna was pregnant?"

This seemed to catch Hines by surprise and his brown eyes narrowed. "Whaddaya talkin' about?" he said.

"I'm talkin' about she was pregnant, Mr. Hines," said Byrne. "As in, with child. As in, knocked up. I was wondering if you knew that."

"No," said Hines crabbily, "I didn't."

"I understand from Detective Andretti that Miss DiCiccio came from a good Catholic family," Byrne said affably. "I'm Irish myself, and I'm sure that if I had had a sister, and if she'd have gotten knocked up, first my dad would have beat the shit out of her and then he would have beat the shit out of the guy, and then he would have insisted that she have the kid. I'm guessing that Miss DiCiccio's family was probably about the same."

"I guess so," admitted Hines.

"But you, Mr. Hines," said Byrne. "I doubt you wanted her to have the child. A child would have been a little, shall we say, inconvenient, given your other girlfriends and all?" Byrne looked the man up and down. "I don't know about you, Mr. Hines," he said, "but if someone was to ask me whether or not you're father or even husband material, I'd probably have to answer in the negative. I mean, you were not exactly Old Faithful to Miss DiCiccio, were you? I gather that you've got quite a reputation as a stud around here. A regular Italian stallion. I bet your little infidelities didn't exactly please the lady when she found out about them."

"I get my share. You prob'ly don't."

Byrne decided to stop pushing him for a while. "About this black guy—can you describe him?"

"Hey, I told you it was dark," said Hines, edging away. "You know how them spooks all look alike at night."

"Maybe," said Byrne. "But what I can't figure out is why he hit you on the right side of your head. I mean, I'm trying to visualize this now, no offense: you're on top of Miss DiCiccio and the door opens on your side. And why would the guy go all the way around the vehicle when it would have been so much easier—"

Hines had disappeared around the corner. Byrne moved quickly, but not quickly enough; he heard the cock of the pistol just before he saw the gun, the gun that undoubtedly had killed Yehuda Golden and was now pointed at his head, which was just before he could tell Hines that he was under arrest and which was just before he felt the force of a powerful left hand that knocked him backward and nearly down. He caught a wall with both hands and steadied himself.

"You little fuck," Hines was saying, "you're that cop that's workin' with the faggot selling the Kennedy stuff. I seen you guys together in the restaurant last week, before the shit went down on Carmine Street. So plant your ass back on that chair over there and lemme walk out of here and we'll forget the whole thing, okay?"

"What restaurant?" asked Byrne, complying, but Hines wasn't listening.

"Jesus she was pissin' me off with all her fuckin' whining about when are we gonna get married, when are we gonna get a better place than this dump, she wasn't gonna move in wit' me here, when are we gonna tell her parents she was pregnant, I swear to God she did that on purpose, the bitch told me she was on the Pill, yattata, yattata, what'm I going to do with a wife and kid, for Chrissakes. And that nosy Jew driver, as if what we was doing was any of his fuckin' business. Gimme your piece."

"You know I can't do that, Mr. Hines," replied Byrne. "I'll get in a lot of trouble with my boss if I surrender my sidearm, and if he's pissed off at me then I'm going to be pissed off at you, and we wouldn't want that, would we? If you've got a lawyer, I suggest you call him right now."

"Gimme the fucking gun," demanded Hines, and Byrne was drawing it from his holster just as Andretti came flying through the door and in one sickening moment everybody froze.

"Drop it," commanded his partner, falling to one knee and training his weapon on Hines, who was already a dead man and didn't know it. Andretti was the best shot in the department.

In response, Hines spun Byrne around, held him in a hammerlock and pressed the gun to the side of his head. Byrne could hear the man's breath coming in short bursts, as if he were trying to suck in courage along with air. Hines was strong; now Byrne knew how Miss DiCiccio must have felt, just before she had the life choked out of her.

"Shut up!" shouted Hines. Byrne could smell the garlic on his breath, mixed with beer and cigarettes. There was fear in Byrne, fear of Hines, fear of the gun against his temple. This was the kind of fear that came upon you in a rush, the unwelcome visitor who shows up at the door just as you're about to leave, and you have nothing to offer him, no food, no beer nuts, no drink, not even a place to sit. The kind of fear that arrived so fast that at first you didn't even recognize him, he could have been in drag, or wearing a Groucho mask, so briskly did he come stepping across the threshold, the threshold of fear that everyone harbors, that everyone must respect, no matter how stupid or foolhardy you were. This was the kind of

fear that made you weak in the knees, the way love or infatuation sometimes did, that made your stomach drop and your sweat glands stink, the
kind of fear that shot adrenaline through your body like crack, that transformed you in an instant from a thinking, sentient being into an animal,
fighting or fleeing, and here was Byrne, unable to do either.

But mostly there was that other kind of fear, the fear of being a coward or, worse, being thought a coward. And it was this fear, the greatest of
all fears, that had driven Francis Xavier Byrne since he was a child. For
there was, there could be, no fear like fear of your father, of his wrath, of
his ridicule, of the loss of his love. Mothers you loved, passionately and
unequivocally, mothers you looked to for refuge and protection; but fathers you feared. Byrne feared this fear more than anything, even today, so
many years later, so long after the hand he had so feared had been stilled.
The other fears he could, in the privacy of his soul, give in to; in his imagination, he allowed himself the luxury of whimpering like a dog, of plead-
ing with his captor, of begging for his life. But that other fear, the big fear,
was the one to which he could never capitulate, the one that he had to conquer anew every time, lest it finally conquer him.

"Jesus, you smell like shit," he told Hines as casually as he could. "I'm
gonna have to take a shower when I get home. Especially if Sergeant Andretti has to blow your brains all over my suit."

In response, Hines tightened his grip around Byrne's neck; his fear was
making him even stronger. He forced Byrne's head toward him, so he could
look him in the eye, but the motion caused him to relax his grip just a bit,
and to move the pistol back from Byrne's head for an instant.

An instant, however, was all Byrne needed. His right elbow shot into
Hines's solar plexus, and the man's gun hand flew back as he started to
double over; Byrne was already coming up with his own gun, which he
whipped across Hines's face like a racquetball backhand. Blood spurted
from above the man's right eye where the sight caught him, ripping away
part of his eyebrow, and he had already started to fall when Andretti put
him down with two quick shots. Pop, pop, like the firecrackers everybody
always said they heard before they realized it was gunfire. Pop, pop, like a
car backfiring; pop, pop, and a man falls, not staggering like in the movies,
or talking, or singing, like in the opera, not even moaning, but falling
down, dropped, dead. Pop, pop; that's how quick it was. Death didn't need
much time when it was in a hurry.

Byrne looked down at the remains of Mr. Russell Hines, already beginning their irreversible slide into carrion, with only a brief stopover on Dr. Sheinberg's slab before their consignment to the conqueror worm.

"Fuckin' scumbag," said Andretti, who was already starting to think about the paperwork.

Chapter Thirty
The Upper East Side
Wednesday, October 17, 1990; 6:00 A.M.

Sometimes, not often, Ivan dreams.

Tonight, he is in a ballroom, dancing. His partner is Mother.

They dance through a swirling crowd, but he cannot make out the other faces. The music is the delirious polonaise from Tchaikovsky's *Yevgeny Onegin,* and all around them couples dressed in the finery of imperial Russia are moving to it. The place is Saint Petersburg, in a time that never was. How splendid he looks in his magnificent officer's uniform! And how beautiful Mother looks in her white silk gown, her bosom heaving, her shoulders bare in the light of a thousand candles, glistening, glittering, reflecting her majestic radiance in a way that would make the moon weep. Her right hand in his left, his right arm wrapped around her slender waist, his nostrils filled with her exquisite scent, her breath the very breath of life itself.

The room is big; indeed, endless. No matter how far he and Mother glide across the floor, the walls never get any nearer, nor do the other couples ever come into focus. But it does not matter, for there is no one else of any importance in the room. "You look beautiful tonight, my son," Mother says in her soft, musical voice that puts the orchestra to shame. Gazing into her Kirghiz eyes, he can see all the way to the steppes of central Asia, to Siberia, and beyond, to the Island.

They are approaching the source of the music. It is a small band, with only six or seven musicians. How can they play Tchaikovsky? Several of the performers have guitars and some kazoos and jew's harps; the conductor is holding a small doll whose arms have been cut off, and he is waving the mutilated doll as if it were a baton. The doll's eyes open and close with each downbeat. Suddenly, he finds himself dancing with the doll, now grown to human proportions, although still missing its arms. The doll's skin is cold, but her breath is hot in his ear. He cannot see Mother. He has lost her.

Ivan tries to disengage himself, but the doll holds him close. How can she do this with no arms? Her eyes are still blinking, up and down, up and down. They are dancing now to the mad little waltz from the last act of *Wozzeck*. Her breath hotter now, on the back of his neck, and the hairs rise in response. He is sweating. It may be that he is afraid, but fear is an emotion he can feel only in dreams. Now he understands how she is holding on to him. She is clutching him with her teeth, which are sunk into the side of his face.

"*Immer zu, immer zu!*" the doll says, "*Ihre Augen glänzen ja!*" Your eyes are gleaming. He sees she has no eyes. Now the band is playing Mozart: *Eine Kleine Nachtmusik*. No wonder the doll is speaking German. No, not speaking. Barking.

Like a dog. The doll is gone, replaced by a huge black cur, whose fangs are biting him harder and harder, tearing the flesh. Mother, he says, it hurts. Make the pain go away. He rushes from the ballroom, the dog still gripping the side of his head. Of course there is no door, so he goes out the window, splintering it as he and the black hound crash through and all at once the animal is gone, and the doll is gone and he is outside. He can still hear the music, but only faintly.

As he rises he observes that the ballroom has vanished and he is alone in a dead and blasted world. The poisoned ground is gray, and no grass grows upon it. Thick, acrid black smoke pours forth from the spires of a hundred churches, as the worshipers within sing their oblivious hymns to an obscenely indifferent God.

The oldest man in the world stands before him. "You do me wrong to take me out o' th' grave," the man says. "Thou art a soul in bliss; but I am bound upon a wheel of fire." What Ivan at first has taken for a walking staff he now sees is a fiery Catherine Wheel, whose flames singe the old man's hair. "That mine own tears do scald like molten lead."

Ivan tries to speak, but he cannot. With profound sadness, he realizes that all his languages have deserted him, and although he knows he is dreaming, he can no longer tell what language he is dreaming in.

But the dream is in color. And the Wheel of Fire burns.

It has set the old man's clothes aflame; scorched them off in fact. "Thou art a soul in bliss," he repeats as the wheel starts to turn and, crucified upon it, he begins to roll away. His figure is retreating into the distance, toward the steeples, but his voice remains loud. "But I am bound upon a wheel of fire." It is, he knows, the voice of the father.

And now he, Ivan, is on the wheel. His wheel is rushing, and his tears do scald his face like the molten lead that is raining from the skies. It burns his flesh, and the odor stings his nostrils with its corrosive redolence. He knows that his body is melting away, but he cannot see any longer, because his eyes are gone.

The dancers have stopped dancing, the worshipers have ceased worshiping. They are all outside, in the burning rain, and they are watching him die.

You do me wrong, thinks Ivan, *to take me out of the grave*; and no one will gainsay him. Not even Mother, who with his last moment of vision he has seen standing silently on the side of the road, Veronica without a veil, Martha without a sister, the Magdalene without a savior.

Weeping.

Chapter Thirty-one
Greenwich Village
Wednesday, October 17, 1990; 2:00 P.M.

Angelo Genna is pacing uneasily around the small apartment on Carmine Street, just south of Bleecker and across from one of his favorite restaurants, Cent'anni. *Cent'anni* is an Italian toast; it means "May you live a hundred years." That would be nice, but unlike his predecessor he wasn't counting on it. "Where the hell is he?" he says.

"He'll be here, boss," responds Joey Aiello, invisible as usual, standing to one side of the window that looks down, three floors high, onto Carmine Street in what used to be the Italian part of the Village.

"You believe a guy who is not a made man," observes Genna, "then you are one fucking humanitarian, Joey."

"You always say you want guys that done more than killing," answers Aiello.

The don takes a bite of a canole and considers his words. They have picked up the pastries at Cafe Roma, on their way uptown from Brooklyn. Genna doesn't trust many other bakeries in Manhattan, the erstwhile City of the Irish, Italians and Jews and, latterly, the City of the Chinese, Colombians and Russians.

"You know, Joey, I don't like you," he says, and a chill passes over the consigliere. "No, I don't like you," Genna goes on. "I love you. As far as this life, no one knows it better than me. If a guy offends me, I'll break him— that's the fuckin' end of it. But it's not just for me that I do such a thing. It's for this 'thing of ours,' this thing we got together." Another crunch. Easier to find a good canole than a tuna sandwich.

"And this 'thing of ours' means more to me than anything else in the whole wide world, and that's the fucking truth. Anybody threatens this thing of ours, well, he's a dead man." He finishes off the canole and reaches for another, even though it was true that his suits were getting tighter with each passing day, not that anybody would have the nerve to point it out. "Anyway," he continues, "I didn't say you done anything underhanded, I'm just askin' is all."

"You know I would never do anything like that!" protests Aiello.

"I know that, Joey," Genna assures him. "But this business in the Village got me worried. You know I got guys beefin' at me every fuckin' hour of the day. Yesterday one of them fuckin' capodecinas sent for me for a glory fuckin' meeting. And people think that this is my fuckin' green eyes. They think I'm fuckin' in this for the money. They got no fuckin' *honore*, is what they don't got, and what they don't got they don't understand. 'Cause at the end, at the fuckin' bitter end, whatta we got if we don't got our honor?"

The doorbell hisses, and Aiello nods to one of the two other men in the room. "Tell Hines to send him up," he orders, and the man nearest the door speaks softly into the intercom. Distantly, they can hear the buzzer unlocking the downstairs entrance.

The don's question is still hanging in the air when Sacco raps softly on the door. "I hope we don't have no more trouble like the other day," says Genna by way of greeting.

"No, sir," says Sacco, "we won't." He hopes he doesn't sound as nervous as he feels. "Besides, I think you ought to hear what he's got to say. About this Foxtrot."

"Yeah, but what we don't know yet," objects Genna impatiently, "is what's in it for us?"

"What's in it for us," replies Sacco, "is some serious protection. And protection money."

"May I inquire," asks Aiello, "from whence comes this protection?"

"From the U.S. government, is where," says Sacco.

This gets Genna's attention. He is not so sanguine as to think that his lawyers can keep him out of the can forever. Alone among New Yorkers, Angelo Genna does not believe everything the press writes about him, especially the part about the Teflon Don. Nobody was perfect; with him, that was an article of faith.

Genna puts his fingertips together, just like he had seen Al Pacino do in *The Godfather, Part II.* "I've been givin' this whole thing some thought," he says. "And what I think is, I want you to waste the fucker."

"Pardon me?" asks Sacco, incredulous. "Waste him? Why?"

"You want he should draw you a picture?" says Aiello.

"Because I don't trust him," replies Genna. "Because I don't trust you, either, nothin' personal. I don't trust any of this. This whole thing is too good to be true, and if I'm wrong, well sue me."

"But—" objects Sacco.

"Hey!" shouts Genna, and Sacco feels his blood run cold. "Yours is not to fucking reason why."

Aiello laughs. "Just do it," he says.

"I thought we were going to make a deal," sputters Sacco.

"You are," says Genna, "and here it is: Listen to what he's got to say, get whatever he's got to give—take it from him if you have to—and then waste him. And if he doesn't have it with him, kill him sooner. That's my kind of deal." A final munch and another canole had disappeared. The last one, as it happened.

Times like this wearing a wire is a real bitch, thinks Sacco. A guy can get electrocuted just from the sweat.

Buzz.

"Yeah?" says one of the bodyguards, La Russa, into the intercom.

"It's Dutz," comes the reply from Hines below.

"Frisk him and send him up," says La Russa. It will take about three minutes for Dutz to make his way up the stairs.

"Ten minutes and we're outta here," says Genna. Aiello nods. "I don't want he should be nervous. The guy's a fuckin' wacko, you ask me."

Ekdahl has come prepared. The silenced Cobra lies in his briefcase, in the false compartment at the bottom, where he knows the goons downstairs will miss it. The Walther he has stuffed into his underpants upside down, the grip nestled between his cheeks, the barrel just barely protruding between his legs. The throwing knife is taped down tight and flat between his shoulder blades, while his razor is attached to the underside of his forearm, beneath his shirt sleeve. It would take a strip search to find his weapons.

He shakes hands with Rawlston at the door. "Good to see you again, John," he booms in hearty American tones.

"Have a seat," says Genna. Funny, the guy doesn't look like a *fegelah*. "John here tells me you've got something we might be interested in. Maybe you'd like to walk me through it."

"I'd be happy to," says Ekdahl, punching his hands together to see who jumps and who therefore is likeliest to be quickest on the draw. Aiello twitches and La Russa starts. "Let me suggest some of the possibilities we have here. Number one, what I'm offering is the missing piece of a puzzle that has obsessed folks for nearly thirty years. Number two, it's a highly classified set of documents that the Soviets would pay dearly to have back, so you can always sell them at three times the price. Number three, ditto, for which the CIA or the FBI would also cough up big bucks to get their mitts on. Number four, it's something you could put away for a rainy day, for that little extra bit of leverage that might come in handy if, you know, the feds start to lean on you."

"This here thing you're talkin' about's got something to do with Russia, ain't it?" asks Genna. "I don't like Russians. I got troubles enough without I got to get one of them psychos in Brighton Beach to translate this fucking thing for me."

"We can get it translated for you," offers Ekdahl. "Although what do you care what's in it as long as you have it? Besides, you can trust me." Instantly, he realizes it is the wrong thing to say.

Genna leaps to his feet. "Look, you fucking little punk cocksucker motherfucking faggot bastard. I don't trust nobody, not even Joey one hundred percent, no offense Joey, not even my own flesh and blood. You know why? Because I can't afford to. As in, I do and one day I wake up in the shithouse. It's nothing personal, Mr. Dutz, but the way it looks to me is that you've caused me a lot of trouble with your little stunt the other day, you and your buddy Mr. Rawlston over there, and if there's one thing that really pisses me off it's somebody, some asshole I don't even know, causin' me trouble."

"I'm sorry for your trouble," interjects Ekdahl, but the don is not mollified.

"Lookit what I got to deal with," he shouts, counting on his size and bulk to intimidate his opponent. "I got niggers getting uppity, and spics comin' into Queens like they owned the fuckin' joint, and now I got these Russkies who think they're the fuckin' bees knees and don't nobody say a word about them on account of it's anti-Semitic. And they all want a part of me, of what we got here. But I tell you this is gonna be a Cosa Nostra till I die. Be it an hour from now or be it tonight or a hundred years from now . . ."

"*Cent'anni,*" says Aiello.

" . . . when I'm dead. It's gonna be the way I say it's gonna be. A Cosa Nostra! Just because a guy brings you basket, a file, some kind of fuckin' gift, whatever, don't make him a good guy. It makes him a motherfucker to me. Don't make him a good guy. I don't need a guy who come, tell, tell me, 'I feel sorry you got trouble.' I don't need that. I'm gonna be all right. They got the fuckin' trouble. And I don't mean the cops. I mean the people, the people who can make this a joke. I mean assholes like you, come in here and bring me trouble and call it a fuckin' present."

Ekdahl shifts his weight. He is prepared for the trouble Genna is promising him. He is sorry his offer is being rejected, but he can always take his business elsewhere.

Genna is still ranting. "You know I know whose fuckin' stomach is rotten. I can smell it." The don edges closer to Dutz; he wants to smell the man's rotten stomach; he wants to smell his fear. "And as for you, Mr. Rawlston," he says, addressing Sacco, "well, you got trouble too. And that trouble is spelled D-U-T-Z or putz or futz or whatever this fuck's real name is. This asshole is nothin' but trouble for the Family and we can't have trouble for the Family, can we, Joey?"

"No, boss, we sure can't," replies Aiello.

"So, Mr. Dutz, you have brought me trouble and now my trouble is your trouble. And when my trouble is your trouble, then you got some big fuckin' trouble."

Ekdahl is already mentally calculating the dimensions of the room, charting the position of each man and planning exactly how to dispatch him when the time comes. He does his best to look distressed.

"Mr. Dutz," says Genna, "would you mind me and Mr. Rawlston havin' a little privacy here?"

"That's okay," says Ekdahl, "I've got to take a leak anyway. All this talk about trouble has scared the piss out of me. But maybe you should ask him why he was followed to that coffee shop the other day. You got some security problems around here, you ask me."

"Over here," commands Aiello, and Ekdahl rises and walks across the room. The consigliere takes him by the arm—a quick feel under the armpit, just to be on the safe side—and guides him toward the bathroom.

"Don't worry none," Aiello reassures him. "The boss likes you. He's interested in what you got. But sometimes the don he likes to squeeze a guy's balls a little, just to make sure he's got some. Okay, maybe he don't entirely understand, like who the fuck does, probably not even you yourself, but he's interested otherwise you wouldn't still be here, and I would guess he's givin'

Mr. Rawlston his marching orders, so to speak. You know, work out some
kinda deal with you, everything hunky-dory, one big happy family, end of
story."

"Can I ask you a question?" says Ekdahl.

"Fire away." Aiello is only half paying attention; with his other ear he is
straining to hear the conversation in the parlor. You never knew with the
don; he was changeable.

"Do you think Mr. Genna really understands the importance of what
I'm offering him, or what I've gone through to get it? I mean, if you play
your cards right, it's the feds you'll have by the balls, not just me. We're talking a free pass here, for years."

"Maybe, if those files are what you say they are. I always did wonder myself about that Ruby asshole—"

"No," interrupts Ekdahl, "that's just the point."

"What's the point, kid?"

"It doesn't matter whether they are what I say they are. It doesn't matter
what's in them. It doesn't even matter if they are real or not."

"What are you sayin'? That you're tryin' to peddle bullshit?" Aiello is an
empiricist.

"What I'm saying is that, in the intelligence business, it doesn't matter
whether a document is real. What matters is what your opponent thinks.
What matters is who can look down the hall of mirrors and count to the
very last one."

Ekdahl ducks into the john, does what he has to, and follows Aiello back
into the living room. The don and Rawlston are all smiles.

"He says it don't matter what's in the files, boss," Aiello is saying. "They
can be bullshit or whatever. He says it's what the other asshole thinks what
counts."

"Yeah, well I guess great minds think alike because me and Mr. Rawlston been discussin' the very selfsame thing. Which is why I am authorizin'
Mr. Rawlston to make a deal with Mr. Dutz here."

"An offer he can't refuse?" said Aiello, laughing.

Genna turns to Dutz, nostrils flared. No fear; he cannot smell it, he
cannot see it in his eyes. He does not like this man's unearthly self-
confidence. "Before I leave for another meetin'—Jeez, that's all I do these
days is go to glory fuckin' meetings—before I leave I want to ask one last
question."

"Shoot," says Ekdahl.

"Where is this famous file? I mean, how fast can we get our hands on it?" Dutz's dead eyes, Genna realizes, make his own icy stare look like a puppy dog's adoring gaze.

"To show my good faith," says Ekdahl, "I'm going to answer that question directly. The file, or files, are still in the Soviet Union. Oh, they're safe; in fact, the KGB in Minsk doesn't even know they're missing yet and when they do find out they'll never know where to look for them."

"What's this, whattyacallit, KGB stuff, anyway?" interjects Aiello.

"It's a Russian acronym," replies Ekdahl.

"Russian acrobat?" says Aiello.

"Acronym," corrects Ekdahl. "Three letters that stand for Komitet Gosudarstvennoy Bezopastonsti: KGB. 'The Committee for State Security.' But in Russia, we say the initials really stand for Kontora Grubykh Banditov." He lets out a small chuckle, to show he has made a joke. "That stands for 'Office of Crude Bandits.'" Nobody else seems to find this funny. "So supposing that Mr. Rawlston and I can get the unpleasant details out of the way quickly and painlessly, you will be their proud possessor in a week, maybe less. I personally guarantee it." Ekdahl reaches into his coat pocket. "And here's why."

"Whoa there," says Aiello, but Ekdahl already has his wallet out, and is putting his identification on the table. The Italians stare at the documents, which are in Russian.

"As you probably suspect," Ekdahl says, "my real name is not Dutz. Just as Mr. Rawlston here's name is not really Rawlston. My real name is, well, it doesn't matter what my real name is, but you can call me Alik, and the long and the short of it is that I am a captain in the KGB."

"That's the second time you used that word," says Aiello, scratching his head. "But I still don't know what the hell that is."

"It's the commie CIA," explains Sacco, trying to figure out what is going on.

"So how come you speak so good English?" asks Genna.

"Our language schools are the best," responds Alik. "Plus, I spent some time in the States as a kid. The way I can personally guarantee the safety of the files is that I stole them and hid them myself. They are as safe as the Bank of England." This metaphor, he notices, falls flat, so he tries another. "Or as the gold in Fort Knox."

Genna hauls his bulk skyward, nodding to La Russa at the door. "Tell me again what's in it for us."

"It's very simple," says Alik. "The KGB files on Lee Harvey Oswald hold the key to the unresolved mystery of the Kennedy assassination. What's in them is worth a fortune to you."

Genna ponders this for a moment. "Not just to us," he notes shrewdly.

Alik has a sudden appreciation for Genna's intellect. "Precisely. Not just to you."

"So I'm assumin' you've been peddlin' this stuff all over town," says Genna.

"The thought did occur to me that perhaps the FBI or the CIA would welcome a chance to examine the materials," says Alik. "But they don't have any money. You do. And if there's one thing we both understand, it's money. Besides," he continues, "I think you want the files more than they do. I think you need them more. As an insurance policy."

"*Attendi*," says Genna to his henchmen. "Just like we discussed. Take care of it. *Hai ben compreso?*"

"*Ho ben compreso*," says La Russa.

"See?" says Sacco, with obvious relief. "I told you there would be no problem."

"Guess you were right," says Alik. He tries to shake hands with Genna, but the don ignores him. He does not shake with dead men.

"*Come faccemo del Vittorio Palmieri*," says Genna, and departs with Aiello.

The two goons, notes Alik, have shifted position. One is blocking the door, while the other has wandered over to the couch and is now standing directly behind him. "Hey *tovarish*," says Alik, "would you mind moving? You're blocking the light." He rummages in his briefcase.

Sacco nods to La Russa, who retreats a few steps. "Where I can see you, please," says Alik. "That's better."

"We want the files," begins Sacco. "But we don't want to pay for them."

Alik allows a look of puzzlement to cross his face. "What do you mean you don't want to pay for them?"

"I mean," says Sacco, "the Family wants the files but we don't want to pay the kind of money you're asking for them. The don figures that maybe you will see his point that it doesn't really matter whether we have them or not. Which is the same point, come to think of it, that you have been making yourself. As you said, what matters is what the other guy thinks. You see this here"—Sacco shows him the wire he was wearing; La Russa would be too stupid to know it wasn't the Family's—"we got you on tape, we got the agreement recorded, so what do we need the files for? Don't worry, it's off now. Having the real files would just cost us a lot of money. And with you gone, nobody else is going to get them. If I understand you correctly, nobody else even knows where they are."

"You don't know that for a fact, John," says Alik, shifting one hand behind his back.

"It doesn't matter. If you've already double-crossed us and sold them to the CIA or the FBI then you're just trying to rip us off. If you've left them with someone else for safekeeping, well, we have the tape, and whoever that person tries to hawk them to will always wonder whether he has the genuine article. And if nobody gets them then we're no worse off than we were before. I think you see my point." Sacco rises. He wants out before the shooting starts, out and away. That little crack about his being followed put him in serious hot water; Dutz, or Alik, or whatever his name really is, may have thought he was being clever, but he has just ordered his own execution. It is, however, the perfect ending. With Dutz gone, he has avenged the death of Pavone and proved to both Genna and the FBI he wasn't setting either of them up. And without Dutz, the files disappear, too, which will make everybody happy. Because the truth hurts. Even when you don't know what it is. "It's been a pleasure doing business with you."

The thug at the door is still immobile but La Russa is moving toward Alik as Sacco gets to his feet. Both of La Russa's hands, he knows, will be occupied with the garrote, which gives him plenty of time to drive the knife deep into Sacco's side—plunge, twist, pull—and with his left hand to come up firing with the Colt. Down goes the man at the door, whatever his name was, and Alik's ears take in the sweet music of his life escaping through his pursed lips. La Russa has dropped the garrote and is fumbling for his piece, which is under his arm, but it takes him far too long, his movements are too awkward and his lack of planning—no plan B for this greaseball!—is now going to cost him. That was the trouble with the Italians, they had lost their edge, lost their killer instinct, in Russia he wouldn't have been able to leave the room in less than three pieces. The Cobra spurts again and La Russa falls, his brains spattering the wallpaper behind him, interesting what kind of pattern this shot always made, really a subject for a Rorschach test or perhaps a chicken-entrail-reading contest, but one shot is all it took, all it should ever take if you were any good at your job, and suddenly Alik is the only one still standing because he is very good at his job, but he is not the only one still alive because Sacco is groaning on the floor, crawling, scratching, trying to get a foothold or a toehold on the blood-stained carpet and moaning like a sonofabitch.

"*Aiuto*," the man is saying. Help me.

"*Au contraire*, Giovanni," says Ekdahl as he levels the Cobra's muzzle against the man's temple.

"Please!" begs Sacco, but that's what they all say, the plea bargain is always the same and always has the same effect on him, which is none. "Listen. I'm FBI. I can help you."

"You should have thought of that before," says Ekdahl helpfully. "Besides, I already have the FBI on my side." He rubs the muzzle of the Colt lasciviously against the man's ear. "Just be thankful I don't cut off your legs and stuff you in an oil drum, like they did to your daddy. So save your breath. You're going to need it for your last few moments. Shall we count them together? Repeat after me. *Uno, due . . .*"

"*Soccorso!*" gasps Sacco. His breathing is short, hard and labored. "Save me!"

Ekdahl brings his face close to the dying man's lips, which are beginning to froth. "It's not up to me, John," he says affably. "The best I can do is promise to kill you quickly, as opposed to letting you bleed to death on the rug. If it's any consolation, they weren't going to let either one of us out of here alive. They were on to you, John; somebody burned you. Somebody in the Bureau. Tom Byrne, who's watching from across the street. He left you to hang out to dry, John. He fucked you big time, buddy. And now I'm going to fuck him."

Ekdahl puts the Cobra back in his briefcase. "Gotta hurry," he says. "The clowns downstairs will be starting to wonder what's going on." He looks at his watch. "*L'ora! Mi fai ribrezzo!*"

"For the love of God," entreats Sacco.

"I'm going to let you in on a little secret, John," says Ekdahl tenderly. "God doesn't care."

He draws the sharp edge of the razor expertly across the man's throat, bleeding him onto the floor, and listens to his death gurgle with the appreciation of the connoisseur.

"I ought to know," he says.

Chapter Thirty-two
Moscow
Saturday, October 6, 1990; 3:00 A.M.

They bumped down the potholed roads of central Moscow, the Chaika rattling everyone's bones as it sped northeast along the inner ring. The sullen black-leather-jacketed driver chain-smoked acrid Russian cigarettes and drove like a maniac; Tom Byrne reflected that there must be some cause-and-effect relationship at work, since all Russians seemed to smoke and drive with the same intensity. At the intersection of Gorky Street, the car turned right and he caught a glimpse of the Hotel Minsk looming off to the left as they headed toward Red Square and the Kremlin. "Beautiful, no?" said Alik, which caused the girls to giggle and the big German to squirm in his seat. In Russian, the words for *red* and *beautiful* are same.

Beyond the windows of the Chaika everything was black; Tom knew that were it daylight, everything would be gray: gray apartment blocks, gray overcoats, gray faces, gray people. There was no joy in the Soviet public; it was only when they got inside, away from the pervasive grayness that colored every aspect of their lives, that some color returned to their cheeks, and to their conversation.

Just past the Hotel Inturist—Byrne was hard pressed to think of a less appealing name, although it suited its subject admirably—the driver managed to maneuver the car for a left turn. Maneuver was the word; in Moscow, it was almost impossible to turn left. Instead you had to drive past the street you wanted until you came to one of the rare places where traffic was permitted to cross over. Then you swung around and headed back the way you came until you could make the turn to the right. Hoover would have loved this place, thought Byrne to himself. It was true: after a minor traffic accident, the late FBI director had forbidden his driver to make left turns, instead insisting on a three-corner sequence of rights to get him where he was going. Imagine: a lefty country where you can't turn left. The USSR was full of little ironies like this.

For example: there stood the Bolshoi Theater, and just past it, Desky Mir, the huge children's toy store located directly across the street from Dzerzhinsky Square and the Lubyanka prison. That was Moscow in microcosm: high culture, a sentimental love of children and a KGB torture chamber all within a couple of blocks of one another. In the distance, the huge red stars of communism sat serenely atop the Kremlin's churches like giant Christmas ornaments, atheistic stars of Bethlehem enlightening the heart of darkness.

At the Transportation Ministry, another wedding cake memorial to the shotgun marriage between the Russians and Marxism-Leninism, the car turned left again, past Komsomolskaya Square, across the Jauza River and finally onto Scolkovskoje Sosse, a wide boulevard that was in even worse shape than most Moscow streets. Byrne still wasn't sure exactly where they were heading, but with Natasha's head in his lap, it didn't much matter.

Women, he knew, were his great vice. He envied his brother Francis for his stoic ability to pass on the free nookie his occupation afforded him, even if it often was professional pussy or quim of questionable provenance. And while Tom liked liquor as much as the next guy, booze made him do stupid things, made him romantic when he prided himself on being cool, rational, on top of things. Nowadays, he supposed his satyriasis would be called a disease, but the only people who would call it that were geeky little creeps in glasses and beards who weren't getting any.

Besides, how could it be a sickness? The real sickness, Tom thought, was *not* liking women, not believing that women were the only things worth living for, or dying for. Who could not love them, despite all their stupidity and vanity and selfishness and treachery? In the heat of passion, did you care the woman lying beneath you was not a good person? Did you care that some time in the past she might have committed a crime? That she was perhaps a whore or a dyke, and was just putting out for you to get something she wanted? Of course you didn't. Because at that moment, the woman you were making love to was the female principle come to life, the goddess it was your duty to fertilize. And if that was a disease, or a crime, so be it.

Natasha came up for air, and kissed him hard. The German looked politely away.

The car hit another pothole, sending Tom's head bouncing off the roof. Could anyone doubt that the country was on its last legs? Conventional wisdom about the Union of Soviet Socialist Republics held that it was the Only Other Superpower, a First World country with a nuclear arsenal that could blow up the world fifty times over, et cetera, et cetera. But considering the country's low level of sobriety and its technical ineptitude, if the Sovs ever did decide to fire off their missiles, say, in the unlikely celebration of the successful completion of a five-year plan, half of the rockets would blow up in their silos and the other half would come straight down on the Russkies' heads. Try telling that to the State Department bigdomes, the Ivy League jerks who had been reading Pushkin since they were twelve but couldn't find their way from Ismailova to Red Square without a tank and an armed guard; they were convinced that inside the Raskolnikovian exterior of your average Russian beat the soul of Prince Myshkin. Much of the CIA, most of the FBI and all of the journalistic lickspittles in Washington had made their careers and reputations assuring the American people that the Soviets were Just Like Us, except for the color of their flag and the vileness of their intentions.

They were wrong, and no one knew it better than the Russian people themselves. Two and three generations lived crammed together in cheesy flats that even a Jap would turn up his nose at; young couples waited—they fondly wished for—relatives to die so that they would have a shot at a place of their own. How were you supposed to have sex while Grandma sat calmly across from you on the sofa? Byrne supposed people did; in fact, there was a Russian protocol which dictated that family members retire discreetly on the few occasions a year when a single son or daughter brought home a date. Even married couples got to have sex privately once in a while. Mostly, though, Moscow kids fucked in the back seats of cars, like American teens in the fifties, or in back-alley doorways, or in cemeteries. Or they didn't fuck at all, since the men were usually so drunk it was impossible for them to get it, or keep it, up. And didn't the Moscow girls know it. The politics of scarcity, made human.

Indeed, if he had to use one word to describe the Soviet Union, it would be *crumbling*. The newer Moscow apartments were tiny little gimcrack things, made out of spit, shit and baling wire. No Westerner in his right mind would ride in a Soviet elevator, or take a spin on one of the amusements in Gorky Park. The rides were manufactured by German or Austrian companies, but it wasn't the origin of the thrills that worried him, it was the deferred maintenance. In their own recreational way they were a symbol of the Soviet military arsenal as well. Tanks that couldn't run because they had long since been cannibalized for parts. Shortages of combat rifles, ammunition and other ordnance, half of which was siphoned off by the black market before it ever reached the supply depot. Dilapidated roads and bridges, railroad ties in a state of terminal disrepair; if Hitler attacked now, right now, thought Tom, he'd win in a walkover. Some superpower: "peasants with guns" was more like it.

Not that he didn't like Russians; after all, his mother had been one. But in Tom Byrne's experience, if a Russian didn't wake up every morning facedown in the gutter with a hangover the size of Siberia, he thought something was wrong. How did you drag a country like this into the twentieth century? Peter the Great hadn't even been able to carry it into the eighteenth.

His mother. He rarely thought about her, except when he was in the Soviet Union, where she had been born. He had never visited her home town of Archangel, and he probably never would, but that was all right because if by some miracle she would appear to him, alive and whole again, not sick, not eaten up or wasted away, when what should have been within her breast was life and not death, he would very likely not recognize her.

It was only after his father's death that Tom learned his natural mother had died of cancer in 1952, when he was three years old; he had come across the death certificate and her other papers when he was going through Robert Byrne's things. Vera Byrne, born Verina Nikolaevna Medvedeva, admitted to the United States of America in 1948, country of origin, Union of Soviet Socialist Republics. Place of birth: Archangel. Date of birth: April 22, 1926. Frankie had been only fourteen when their dad was killed and, of course, hadn't even been born when Vera died. Robert Byrne had seen no need to explain to Tom that Irene was not his birth mother, nor did the second Mrs. Byrne ever volunteer this information to her son. In any case, the brothers looked enough alike to pass.

The car stopped in front of a high-rise apartment building. They were far from Red Square now, on the outskirts of the city in one of the satellite suburbs that consisted of Cabrini Green–style housing projects for white people. There was mud everywhere, although it was starting to harden as the Russian winter approached. Against his better judgment Tom got into the rickety elevator, Natasha pressing closely against him in the cramped quarters.

The place, as he expected, was a dump. In fact, it was a nearly empty dump; there was hardly any furniture. The closets were hung with a minimal amount of clothes, especially for two women and, curiously, there was no bed in the bedroom. The only places to sit were the couch in the living room and a small wooden chair near a sideboard, and Alik motioned for Tom to take the more comfortable place. He said something to the girls, who disappeared around the corner and, Tom supposed, into the kitchen. The German had vanished.

"Now to our little business," said Alik in English, as they sat down.

"Do they know about this?" asked Tom, indicating the women with a nod of his head toward the kitchen.

"Do you think I would be so stupid?" asked Alik in return. "They are silly creatures, beautiful but frivolous, and like all women they are only interested in one thing."

"And that is . . . ?" inquired Tom.

"Money, of course," said Alik. He walked over to the hole in the floor and pulled up one of the floorboards. "Typical Russian apartment," he said. "With typical hole in the floor. If you want to hide something, you never hide it here. But naked is the best disguise, I always say. If there was a bed, I would have hidden it in the mattress!"

Byrne was about to get down on his knees and have a look, but just then he caught sight of Natasha out of the corner of his eye, walking from the kitchen to the bathroom and shutting the door. She turned and smiled at him. "It's in here," Alik was saying, pointing to the hole. "The Nalim. Initial KGB report of contact, signed by Rima Shirokova; Oswald's application for Soviet residency, his hospitalization report after his suicide attempt; his transfer to a mental hospital . . ."

"*Chai,*" said Zlata, setting the steaming tea in front of them. Russian-style, the tea came in glasses perched in silver-frame holders; the glass was much too hot to touch, but by holding the silver grip, you could manage to drink it once it cooled. If you were American, that was; Alik, he noticed, practically drained his glass in one swallow.

"But there's more," continued Alik. "When Yuri Ivanovich Nosenko defected to the United States in 1964, he told CIA that KGB had no interest whatsoever in Oswald. Naturally, the Americans found this difficult to believe. After all, Oswald was a marine radar operator, who had been stationed at the secret U-2 base in Atsugi, and later at Iwakuni, in Japan. How was it possible for KGB to have no interest in a man like this, especially one who publicly threatened to spill all the secrets he knew? Nosenko told part of the truth, that part of the truth he knew. KGB was frightened of this Oswald, this little nobody, this nothing who was making two governments dance to his tune. Either he was crazy or the best operative the Principal Enemy—that's you, of course—ever sent over, and we had to find out what the truth was. He cut his wrist in his hotel room, and why? So he could stay in the Soviet Union! Anybody who wants to stay in the Soviet Union must be crazy! That's why they sent him to the mental hospital."

"I've always found CIA's explanation of Oswald's Soviet period unbelievable," said Tom.

"Two sides to every story," said Alik, "one believable and one unbelievable, but both, as it happens in this case, incontrovertibly true. Isn't that always the way? Don't things happen every day that nobody would ever believe? The extraordinary, the coincidental and the unbelievable cannot be predicted, but they do happen. Aren't your sports announcers always screaming 'Unbelievable!' over something that is, in fact, believable, because it has just occurred? So it is here. Unbelievable, and perhaps, therefore, entirely believable. Sometimes bullshit is the truth, and sometimes the truth is bullshit."

"What are you talking about?" asked Tom. He didn't have time to indulge himself in the Russian love of hair-splitting philosophical conversation.

"I simply mean that everything about this Oswald was unbelievable, but it happened. And what you will soon be holding in your hands is the means to understanding why. The Nalim, the Oswald file, the file that KGB wants nobody to see. And why? Because it implicates the Soviet Union in the murder of your president?" Alik was up on his feet now, pacing around the room, waving his empty glass of tea. "That would be the easy reason to withhold it, the obvious reason; we are guilty, and this file contains evidence of our guilt; therefore this file must be buried."

"Why not just destroy it?" asked Tom.

"Exactly," exclaimed Alik, "why not just destroy it? For it hasn't been destroyed, has it? And why hasn't it been destroyed? Because either it does not contain evidence of Soviet complicity in the assassination, in which case why not release at least part of it, or—and this is important, so pay attention—or . . ." He paused.

"Where is my tea?" he snapped at Zlata, who promptly ducked back into the kitchen.

"Or?" prompted Tom.

"Or, it contains something entirely different, something unexpected, something embarrassing to someone, and therefore in our black-is-white world can be used as a weapon."

"I'm not sure I follow you."

"Follow me, then," said Alik. "Open your mind and your ears and trail me into the wilderness of mirrors. Think, Tom. Why have I brought you all the way out here?"

"To get the file?" ventured Byrne, knowing immediately that was not the correct answer.

"Now I know why I hate America," said Alik with some asperity. "The intellectual climate." He tried again. "Why?"

"I give up," said Tom.

"That's the problem with you Americans, you give up too easily. Do you think we Russians would still be here if we gave up as easily as you do? If we had given up against Napoleon? Against Hitler? We are chess players, Tom, and we can look at the board and see how the forces are marshalled. We don't fall for bluffs. A chess player resigns when it is impossible for him to win. We don't believe in miracles. We believe in facts."

"That's terrific," said Tom, "but you're forgetting one thing. We Americans may be lousy chess players, but we're damn good at poker. Ever play?"

"As a matter of fact," said Alik, "I do. The question is whether you can." Tom suddenly realized that he feared this man, with his Siberian veins and volcanic heart. "Here I am, trying to explain to you not only how valuable this particular piece of merchandise is to you, but exactly *why* it is so valuable." Alik's voice rose menacingly. "And you won't listen. I know you have no respect for this country, Tom, because you know what so many of your countrymen don't, that it's just an overgrown Potemkin village that has your side convinced we can play with the big boys."

"I thought you said Russians don't bluff," said Tom.

"That's just the point: we don't," replied Alik. "But we can't help it if you bluff yourselves. Anyone who sets foot in this country knows in one minute that the Soviet Union is a joke—a lethal joke at times, perhaps, but a joke nonetheless. And there are so many willing stooges, 'useful idiots' in the words of the sainted Lenin, who are willing to look the other way, to claim that here the normal laws of human behavior have been suspended. Don't blame us, Tom; blame yourselves."

There was no sound from the kitchen, where Zlata was hiding out, but from the bathroom Tom could hear water running. Natasha must be taking a shower.

"Look at it from our point of view," said Alik. "You've spent enough time in our poor, sad country to know we are not a race of supermen. We are just people like you, with big hearts and not quite big enough brains; we try, and we fail. But is that a crime? In the eyes of you Americans, apparently it is. And yet you fail all the time: you fail at supplying food and clothing for your people; you fail at providing them jobs and homes; you fail at healing them when they are sick; you beggar them and cheat them; you let your cities fall apart; you isolate your blacks and despise them and kill them when they commit their inevitable crimes. You think all the planet's people want to be just like you. But have you ever stopped to consider that you might be wrong? And we, the poor stupid Soviets, might actually be right about some things: that not everyone sees material wealth as life's goal; that not everyone despises politics so much that they run their country with two interchangeable parties; that not everyone believes that peace is always to be preferred to war. Do you think I learned nothing from the time I spent in your country? I learned plenty, and what I learned mostly was to despise it and everyone in it. Have you ever stopped to consider that? Or are you like the rest of your ignorant countrymen, whose purview stops at the American border, who see the tips of their noses and who think they behold the world?"

"What's your point?" asked Byrne.

"My point," said Alik, his voice rising again, "my point is that nobody believed Nosenko. They threw him in jail, they tortured him, all because what he said didn't jibe with what they had already decided was the truth. And what did he say? That KGB had no interest in Oswald. That Oswald was not working for KGB when he shot Kennedy. That Oswald was unstable, anarchic, insane? All statements true—from our perspective.

"But what about Oswald's? Didn't every one of his actions have a purpose? Can't you view his activities leading up to the assassination as the brilliant program of a master operative? Didn't he get us to admit him, to take care of him, to nurse him back to health? Didn't he fuck our women, and marry one of them? Didn't he have a good job, a nice apartment? Didn't he get all these things for free, by playing KGB against CIA? Didn't he use the very principle of uncertainty to attain his goals? Who knows what he really was, or what he really wanted? Maybe not even he himself. But if he did, if all his actions were consciously directed toward the achieving of his goals, then who can deny that this was the work of a genius? And if it was all accidental, if Oswald simply lurched from victory to victory, each small triumph leading him ever farther down the past to his final destiny, if this was all a cosmic joke"—Alik's voice had risen to a shout now—"*what difference does it make?* Was Lee Harvey Oswald the greatest secret agent in intelligence history? Or was he a misguided idiot who stumbled through life as a perfect fool, a Parsifal who found his Grail in a sixth-floor window? Was Nosenko telling the truth, or was he a fiendish Soviet plot to destroy the CIA? No matter what your answer is, the truth is it doesn't make a damn bit of difference. Kennedy is just as dead, the CIA is just as paralyzed. Even if Oswald wasn't working for us, he may as well have been; even if Nosenko was for real, he may as well not have been. We win either way. And that is the mark of a good intelligence operation. Whether you are the world's biggest liar or its most honest man, it's two sides of the same coin. People will treat you not as you are, but as they think you are. Appearances are everything, and the truth is nowhere."

Alik was calming now. "And yet, we are going to lose this struggle. Unbelievable! Haven't you tried to tell the truth to your superiors, only to have them laugh at you and ignore you? They don't believe you when you tell them that this place is theirs for the asking, that a pittance—less than half of what you give every year to Israel and Egypt—would help ensure that when the chips fall, as they surely will, they will fall on your side of the iron curtain. The For Sale sign has been hung out, but you don't see it. Take these two girls; you can fuck them both for practically nothing. Just be nice to them, don't beat them, and buy them each a new dress. That's how far we have fallen. Everybody wants out, and everybody has something to sell. It might be weapons, it might be secrets, or simply our bedraggled asses.

"What if I went with you to Washington and offered to tell the truth about Russia? Who would care? Nobody. Because I, a lone defector, am worthless. They would bury me like they did Nosenko, with a smile on their lips and a laugh in their heart, and my treachery would have gained me nothing. Why? Because I am telling them something *they do not want to hear.* I am giving them the truth when they would rather have a lie. But if I have something to sell or trade, if I have something you want . . . that is a different story. Then you take my treachery, my pure, honest treachery as it were, and you transform it into something of value. My bona fides are suddenly very important to you because *you want to believe.*

"At Moscow Central, we like to say that there are three kinds of collaborators. The first is the committed man, fools like the Rosenbergs, Burgess and Maclean, people who for absurd reasons of guilt or self-loathing or naivete actually believe in the rightness of their cause. They come to us, hat in hand, asking, How can we help you? What can we steal for you? The second type is the mercenary, who is only in it for the money. And the third is the compromised dupe, whom we can blackmail. And of these three types the only one we really trust is, of course, the third. Ideologues are dangerous, because they can turn on you. Mercenaries are better, but once the transaction is complete, you never know where your subject's loyalties are going to lie. So you see it is the third category, the blackmail victim, that is the preferred agent. Because money comes and goes, but blackmail, if you do it right, is forever."

He cleared his throat loudly. "Where's Natasha?" asked Alik.

"I'm right here," said Natasha, stepping out of the bathroom and disappearing around the corner. She was completely, angelically naked.

"Get ready," commanded Alik. "Come here, Tom," he said, inviting him down to the floor. "Prove to yourself that I speak the truth." Tom reached into the hole, prepared to retrieve whatever was in there.

It was empty.

"So that's what this is all about," said Tom.

"Just because a man doesn't tell the whole truth," said Alik, "doesn't mean he is lying about everything." Alik was beside him now, very close. "That's what this has always been about."

"There's no file, is there?" asked Tom. "There never was."

"Of course there's a file," replied Alik. "There's always a file. But not here, and not right now. Perhaps it's already in America."

Zlata came into the room. She wore a black leather jacket with matching cummerbund around her midriff, and black leather riding boots over black silk stockings. The jacket flapped open as she walked, and Tom saw that underneath it she was sporting a black leather half-bra, which supported her breasts without covering them.

"Do you like it?" she asked, twirling around like a runway model.

Now Natasha entered, naked no longer, but hardly dressed. Like Zlata, she was wearing a harness bra, although her perfect breasts hardly required one, and there was a red sash draped around her belly.

"*Krasny*," was all he could say. In Russian, the words for *red* and for *beautiful* are the same.

Chapter Thirty-three
Sakhalin Island, USSR; 1984

They never turned the light off. That was the rule.

There were many rules in prison. The way you had to sleep, for example. Only one position allowed, facing the light. The light, which was always in your eyes. How did they expect a man to sleep this way? They didn't. That was part of the punishment. That was part of the treatment. That's how you made the New Soviet Man: by shining the light in his eyes until he finally saw it.

No matter how you tried, you couldn't avoid the light. You couldn't roll over during the few hours they allowed you to sleep. You had to lie on your back, facing the light; if you fell asleep on your side or on your stomach, the guards came in and woke you up, flipped you over, and made you observe the light, ponder it. There was no escaping the light, although it did give you, the prisoner, adequate radiance to illuminate your crime.

After a while, however, you got accustomed to it, used to the position, used to the lack of sleep, used to the light. The light was like the Almighty, drawing you nearer. Into the light, as if you were dead, shooting along the dark tunnel that was this earthly life into the eternal light of the next.

The light. Always on, unblinking, indifferent in its magnificence, secure in its omnipotence. It knew your crime, it penetrated to the farthest recesses of your brain, bore into you, right down to the secret depths of your being. There was no hiding from the light, or hiding anything from it. It could tip your soul and peer within, could pierce and puncture your flabby, feeble defenses, strip you naked of your pretenses and leave only your guilt-ridden essence. There was no use pretending that you were not culpable. You must be at fault. Otherwise you would not be here. Everybody is guilty of something, and all must be punished. By the light. By immersion in the light, which was at once your tormentor and your savior.

For after a while you began to love the light, no matter how brightly it shone, no matter how hot it burned, no matter how deeply it pervaded. When they first put you in here, you thought you were alone, without friend or hope, but eventually you realized that when all else had failed you—and, in here, all else had—you always had the light. It was like God.

It was certainly multifaceted, the way God, the mythical God of the Hebrews, was supposed to be. Omnipresent and infinite in its variety. If you stared at the light long enough, you could fracture and fragment it into a thousand component shafts and strands, each one in a different color, your eye a spectrograph analyzing each degree of the color spectrum, breaking it down from infrared to ultraviolet. The ultraviolent light. Each one a different face of God, or maybe even a different God, your own private, personal collection of lares and penates.

How long had he been here? There was no way to tell. Better to ask the light, but the light never spoke. It was magisterially silent, as God was. Besides, the calendar was irrelevant when it came to judging his separation from Mother, which seemed infinite. Because she had taken care of him, had promised that she always would, that she would always be at his side, omnipresent, just like God, but better than God, because she was Mother.

The room was small, about ten feet long by six feet wide. There was a slop jar and a rude bed made of packed straw, but no other furnishings. There was a window, but it was so high up on the wall, and so small, that he could see nothing out of it, and had long since given up trying. The only other thing in the room was the light, burning bright. Neither prisoner nor jailer, it was simply the light, immutable and immortal, dispassionate and fair.

He seemed to remember that once there was another man in the cell. Mother, however, had warned him about other men; how they were never to be trusted, how they were all traitors, informers, spies; defilers, corrupters, seducers. Men were all alike.

This man had tried to speak with him, to draw him out, to inquire after his crimes, but he had ignored him for as long as he could, concentrating on the light, learning to love its arid luminescence, the light that never gave off warmth no matter how close to you got it, because in the end you could never get close enough, never close enough to be warmed by it, but only to be bathed in its cold, uncaring, relentless brilliance.

One day, while the man was sleeping, he pulled out his tongue. That man was the last human being he had seen. Even the guards no longer came in, no longer peered through the peephole in the door at him; they sent his food in on a tray, and most of the time he had simply put the swill directly into the slop jar, for he was rarely hungry anymore. After a while, they stopped bringing the food and then, because it was no longer necessary, they took away the slop jar too. This they did when he was asleep, like children afraid of the dark. Even though the light was on, as always.

During the day, whenever that was, he was not allowed to recline; at night, just as arbitrary in its diurnal rhythm, he had to lie on his back with his hands outside the covers at all times. This was meant to annoy him, but he had transcended annoyance. The light had given him something to aspire to: grand dispassion, supreme apathy, a godlike indifference to the human condition. By becoming one with the light, he would become like God.

The solitude was designed to break him, to sap his will, to make him beg, or crawl, or plead. But he laughed at it: he had been alone so much of his life, alone except for the times he was with Mother, and now even she had been taken away from him, although he knew she must be near, watching him and watching over him, as she promised.

Other men, he knew, fought the light. They were mystified by their sudden isolation, bewildered, confused. They fought, they made demands and shouted questions: On whose authority do you hold me? On whose commission have you arrested me? They screamed that they were victims and protested their innocence, as if that mattered. But here, there were no innocents. Here, there were no victims.

After a while, even the most resolute protest subsided. The punishment was too severe, the hopelessness too overwhelming. Nothing a man said availed him anything, for no one was listening, including God. No man had the strength to protest all his life; acceptance of what you could not change was part of growing up, and thus even the most dedicated resisters either died or conformed. In the end all men were collaborators, either with the enemy or with Death. Every man might be a hero to his dog, but no man is a hero to his jailer. No man, caught in the pitiless glare of the light, could harbor heroism in his breast. He could only scrabble for his soul.

And so they gave up, surrendering to the inevitable. They became resigned, contemplative, peaceful and peaceable. They stopped protesting, stopped expecting, stopped awaiting, and they let themselves go, ignoring their surroundings, where once they took such a passionate interest in them;

ignoring their fellows; ignoring their captors; ignoring the ever more infrequent swellings of hope that were gradually abandoning them. They ate, rudely shoveling in the foodstuffs, not caring whether they got everything in their mouths because they could no longer taste. They took an inordinate interest in the products of their bowels; the food and the slop jar had become two aspects of the same reality. Neither disgusted them any longer. The two inanimate vessels were all that was left to remind them of their distance from the animals, and after a time even that distinction disappeared.

Normally it took four to six weeks to reduce a man to the condition of a beast. He, however, was nearly the same man he was when he came in; nearly the same, but better. His mind harbored some of the same thoughts and desires that it always had, but these feelings had become more intense, more refined, more sophisticated. With nothing to do but contemplate the light, he had studied it and learned from it. It had become his beacon, his compass, a lamp unto his feet; it was his leader and teacher; it had become his friend. It even spoke to him.

"*Tovarish*," it said. Comrade. "Of course you know why you are here?"

The voice had come out of the light, and at first he had a hard time locating it. He had been staring at the light forever, appraising its majesty, and so the voice had sounded like an angel's, disembodied, hortatory, Gabrielian.

But he was no longer in his cell. He was in an office. The man sitting across from him, on the other side of a gunmetal gray desk, was thickset and muscular, bald on the top with a monk's ring of hair hovering above his ears. He was wearing a dark brown business suit and a pair of cheap black Soviet shoes, the kind made out of cowhide and plastic, the kind that lasted a couple of months if you were lucky and took very good care of them, which mostly involved not wearing them. He could see the tips of the man's shoes peeking out from underneath the desk.

"*Tovarish*," the man said. "The State is kind. The State is just. The State is merciful."

There were, he noticed, guards on either side of the man, wearing big boots, their weapons trained on him. But he was no danger to anyone right now. He felt no anger, no enmity. This is where he belonged. This was where his long journey had been leading all along.

Paris had come and gone in an instant, and then there was the trip across

Germany and Denmark, to Sweden and the Finland station, until finally there was the Rodina, just as Mother had promised, a journey from imprisonment to freedom, from strangers to friends, from foreign lands to home, from hate to love. In Russian, the word *Rodina* means Motherland.

Moscow was golden. Gold-painted were the walls; though they may be crumbling, they yet retained their honeyed gleam, as if to negate the tawdriness that surrounded them, a passive protest against what Marx and Lenin had wrought, yet fruitless because behind and beyond these walls was dirt and mud and filth and decay. But if you closed your eyes, squinted, the way you looked at the light, and saw the city through a haze of moisture and eyelids and lashes, you could forget the grime and see only the gold.

Mother and he shared the flat with two other families, a crude thing in a district that the authorities ignored as surely as the residents ignored the vermin. In memory it was golden, warm in the winter as all Moscow flats were warm in the long hard winter, fresh and cool in the short hot summer. *"Ya podvig sily besprimernoi gotov skryvatsya vam v ugodu,"* was what he always told Mother before leaving the flat: "A feat of unexampled strength I am now ready to perform for you." A quick thrust of the knife and the drunk in the gutter, the man on the sidewalk, the woman in her kitchen, even the miliman directing traffic on the lonely street, had given up their fortunes. He knew the Moscow Metro better than its architects; knew how to disappear down the rabbit hole of its many entrances; knew how to make himself invisible in the motley Soviet crowd. During the long summer days and endless winter nights he would ride the Metro to the end of each line until he could name each of the stations by sound and by smell.

Then they took Mother away from him and the gold disappeared. The next day, they came for him too. There had been one last journey, a very long train ride until he had reached the Island.

"Tovarish," said the man with the plastic shoes. "You will take off your trousers and lie down on the floor. On your back, *pazhah'lsta.*"

He had seen this before. The prisoner was held down while the man with the boots stepped on his testicles, gently at first and then ever harder, until either the man confessed or his manhood was crushed to powder.

They forced him down, his legs wide apart. The man placed the toe of his plastic shoe on his scrotum and pressed down. "Are you ready to confess your crimes?"

"I am ready," he said. But he showed no pain, he did not cry or cry out, and after a few minutes even the stupidest man in plastic shoes could tell something was not right.

Then they looked at him more carefully, examined him lying there, spread-eagled on the ground, poking and prodding him and summoning the doctor, who squeezed his empty sack and investigated his rectum with thick, probing fingers, and after that they allowed him to dress. He could hear them talking animatedly in the next room.

"The results of your medical examination are most interesting," the man said.

"I hope I am well," he said. "I hope there is nothing wrong with me."

"Nothing wrong, no, comrade," said the man. "You are, however, an unusual man. A man, and yet not a man. Man, and yet not man. Man, and yet more than man. It is a mystery, which perhaps your mother can answer."

"My mother," he said, and tensed. He always tensed when someone spoke of his mother. "When will I see her?"

The man put down the piece of paper and looked away from him. This man is going to tell me a lie, he thought, and it will be a lie about Mother.

"Soon," the man said. "Very soon."

"I am happy to hear this, comrade," he said. "I am sometimes lonely in my room, without my mother." In response, the man tossed back his head and laughed.

In a flash he had crossed over the desk and buried his teeth in the man's neck. The guards were too slow to stop him, as he knew they would be, and before they could react he had torn out the man's throat and popped out his eyeballs with his thumbs. They beat him then, of course, beat him into unconsciousness, struck him with their rifle butts and kicked him with their heavy boots, but the blows were like drops of rain, painless, and the oblivion was welcome because, through the haze, he could see Mother, surrounded by the light and smiling at him.

He was awakened by something being shoved down his throat. It was a rubber tube, the narrow end of a kind of baster whose bulbous body was made of rubber. Two of the guards were holding him by the arms while a third was forcing the tube into his mouth. He tried not to swallow the salty liquid, but his stomach filled quickly with warm salt water. Then they put him in the solitary box, a small chamber hacked out of the side of one of the prison's walls, just barely big enough for a man. It was like being buried alive, and there he stayed for the next twenty-four hours, his stomach burning, his bladder bursting with nowhere to relieve himself but on himself, and when he pissed the salt burned his urethra and almost made him cry out in pain.

Back in the light, it did not occur to him to ask why he was still alive. There was no longer any barrier or border between life and death, no meaningful distinction; he had no love of the former and no fear of the latter. Life brought him closer to Mother, and so he loved his life; death would only take him away from her, and so he loathed it. He would triumph over death, slay the slayer, trample it underfoot. Because death could not kill what had never really lived.

And so he amused himself in his cell, immune to the pangs of loneliness and isolation that corrupted other men. Mother, he knew, was still alive, and as long as she lived he lived too. His life was devoted to her, to the warmth of her body and the radiance of her voice and the gentle stroke of her hand. Were he blind, deaf and dumb, he would yet know Mother. His world had always lay in being close to her, to hearing the soft sounds she made, feeling the warm puff of her breath on his face as she bent over him, to touch him, to minister to him, to heal him. For there was no truth but the truth of her flesh; the word was not made flesh; the word was flesh, and he was the word.

Which is why it amused him as well to open his eyes and stare into the light, to see the face of God, which was not so very different, he knew, from the face of Mother. Was God a female? And did it matter? Male and female, He did make them—and some He made both. Which was right, and just. For did not both sexes breathe and defecate and make love? And was not part of every man a woman, and part of every woman a man? Was not the baby in the womb, for a time, a hermaphrodite? Were there not creatures who combined both sexes in one body? And did God not love them equally well? Did God not love him, and Mother? Was he not, as all men were, the son of God?

Still, he knew that women were the supreme beings. And whereas each man was only a man, only one man, each woman was more than a single individual. Each woman was also a part of the great Eternal Feminine, a lone aspect of that sacred Femaleness toward which all men aspired and for which all men longed unto death. There was, in the end, only one Woman, and all women were facets of Her—sacred unto themselves but how much more sanctified by virtue of belonging to the life force that was larger and

stronger than any one mortal. Woman was holy, and the font of all holi-
ness. To approach Godhood, one must approach Womanhood. Only God
could create; only Woman could give birth. It took a woman to be Mother.
Was this not proof that God is Woman?

During his solitary confinement he was no longer permitted any time in
the yard, which disappointed him because many amusing things occurred
there. Sometimes the men would be mustered to stand, naked and barefoot,
in twenty-two-degrees-below-zero-Celsius weather. Floggings with a rubber truncheon were then administered to the most emaciated of prisoners,
the weak. The blow would fall across where the buttocks should have been,
but that part of the body had long since fallen or rotted away from starva-
tion and pellagra, and so the blow landed on the sciatic nerve, which trans-
mitted the torment directly to the brain. The victims of these beatings
would go mad with pain; their fingernails, if they had any left, would snap
off at the cuticles as they struggled to clutch the floor, scuttled futilely to
escape the blows that were raining down inside of their brains. Then the
man would be dragged away, and for the next few days he would shit himself silly, shit himself so hard that the skin of his backside would rip open
from the effort, and he would die. After a prisoner was dead they conducted an open-air autopsy, not to discover the cause of death, but to make
sure no one was faking. A bayonet through the torso was as effective as a
scalpel in determining the presence or absence of life, and if a bayonet was
not at hand, then the skull could always be crushed with a hammer or a
rock.

It was while he was looking into the light, imagining the life of the world
outside, that the door opened and another man appeared. This man's name,
he said, was Herman, and his shoes were no better than the other's. It must
not be a good thing to be an official on the Island; far better to be in the
world, even though there the sores of present-day society were especially
evident.

"*Tovarish*," said Herman. "We have much to discuss. Do you know why
you are here?"

"Yes, comrade," he replied. "Because of my crimes."

"No," corrected Herman. "For your crimes we should have killed you
and then you would not be here. No, *tovarish*, you are here because of your
father."

"My father," he said, "is a very great man. Mother tells me so."

"A very great man—and a very great criminal," replied the man called Herman. "A very great criminal who comes from a very great family. A weak man, who found strength; a fatuous man who found wisdom; a commonplace man whose cleverness could not be surpassed. A brilliant blackguard, a holy fool—this is your father."

"My father," he repeated.

"Your father betrayed us, and by rights we should have liquidated you to atone for his sins. That we did not speaks well of us."

"Very well of you, *tovarish*," he agreed.

"But your father's family—now that is a different story," Herman told him. "It is a very great family. All the greater, then, the shame he has brought on them—and upon your mother."

"My mother," he said.

"This is why we did not kill you," explained the man. "Because of your father. And his family. And because of your mother. A feat of unexampled strength you will now perform for us."

He took instruction well. Pistols, previously a mystery, became his friends, although no mere pistol could ever take the place of his razor or his knife, because with a pistol, although you were close, you were never close enough to really enjoy your work. They made him shoot, sometimes six hours a day, at targets shaped like humans, popping up here and there, this way and that. He learned quickly, and after a month or so he could put down all the figures with one shot apiece, never more. If you could not put down your man with one shot then you were shooting in the wrong place. Some men went for the body because it was bigger and easier to hit, but that did not guarantee a one-shot kill; even if you hit your man directly in the heart, he sometimes could get off a round in return, and that round, the one you did not hear and could not see, might be the one with your name on it. So you shot him in the head, because no one could survive a bullet in the brain, a bullet that blew out the side or back of your head, a bullet whose explosive force was so great that when the shell penetrated the skull the head was thrown violently in the other direction, the result of the jet effect of exploding brain matter; it was almost as though your man was coming back toward you, coming back for more, long after he had had more than enough.

He already knew the American and Russian and French languages, but they drilled still more tongues into his head, which was not very difficult because he apprehended speech the same way he apprehended the light, and God, and Mother. There were long hours of lectures about the Party and the Committee, which were boring because it was clear that the men delivering the homilies did not really believe what they were telling him. But they did believe in weapons, and in languages, in the skills he must learn in order to become more perfect, more Godlike, more worthy of his Mother, and so he did, too.

And when he was finished, he was brought before the man named Herman once more. "Honor thy mother," commanded Herman. "Because of her, you live."

"Because of her, I was given life," he corrected. "Without her, there is no life."

"Then you shall have life once more," said the man. "To me has been given the power of life and death over you. I am the creator, and you are my creature. I am, to you, like God."

"There is no God," he reproved. "So you have told me."

"And you believe us?"

"No," he said. "But for you to say you are like God makes me want to kill you. No one should have God's power over me, except my mother."

"*Horasho!*" exclaimed the man. Both hands came down hard on his desk, and the guards flinched. "You are strong, not weak; brave, not fearful; deft, not dull. How unlike him you are!"

"*Ya podvig sily besprimernoi gotov skryvatsya vam v ugodu,*" he said.

"You are the executioner of God's judgments," said Herman. "The instrument of the State. That is what the tattoo we have given you signifies. By this sign shall you be known: and let all men who see know that this is what you are, and let them fear you. Vengeance, retribution, justice—the revenge of the People against the traitor. Henceforth so shall you be known."

"'God hears.' This shall be my name. For I am the son of God. With every death, I partake of God, I become like God. With this death, I shall become God, one with the Mother."

"*Horasho!* This death . . ." said Herman.

"The death of my father," he said.

Herman said: "They will try to stop you. Every man's hand shall be against you, and yours against every man's. Ishmael: 'God hears.' So shalt thou be."

"I will find him, and kill him. For the *Rodina*. For the Motherland. For my Mother."

"*Horasho*," said Herman, for the third time. "There is much anger inside you."

"And much love."

"Always remember," said Herman. "One must never kill in anger, but only in love, as God does."

"And who better than I," said Vanya, "knows what love is."

Chapter Thirty-four
Midtown Manhattan
Tuesday, October 23, 1990; 10:00 A.M.

D r. German will see you now."

Where had he heard that locution before? It seemed that he had been working on the Ekdahl case for years, but Byrne realized with a start that it had been less than a week since he first viewed the corpse in the woods near the Brandmelders' house. Yes, at the Danish consulate, from the lips of Ingrid Bentsen.

The receptionist, thank God, was middle-aged and not very attractive.

Dr. Jacob German's office, at 243 East Fifty-second Street, however, was. Freud's Berggasse, he reflected, was probably never like this. Expensive and, as far as he could tell, real art was hanging on the walls, even in the antechamber—he thought that big green thing might be an Ellsworth Kelly—while the inner sanctum was done up in teak paneling, leather furniture, hand-carved bookshelves, Persian rugs and a marble fireplace with a pricey set of pokers and andirons nearby. Even though it was still warm outside, a fire roared merrily in the hearth.

The wooden door—ash? oak?—was at least two inches thick. "Thank you, Miss Neumann," said Dr. German, closing the door behind him; it shut with the satisfying whoosh of a soundproof room. He showed the lieutenant to a chair and sat facing Byrne behind his desk.

"Is that a Kelly I saw in the waiting room?" Byrne inquired noncommittally.

"Very good," exclaimed the doctor. "You have an eye for detail, I see. I expect that serves you well in your profession, as indeed it does in mine."

Byrne deflected the compliment. "Well," he said, "my girlfriend, Doreen—you met her the other night at your party—is an art dealer, and I guess I picked up something along the way."

"A quick study, then?" asked the doctor.

"I try to be," said Byrne. "Like you, I mostly study people."

"I trust my photograph was of some assistance," said Dr. German, the pleasantries out of the way. A degree of anxiety had crept into his voice, just as it had the other night. "Although how it could possibly relate to your current investigation is quite beyond me. Have you shown it to whomever it was you thought you recognized?"

Byrne waited a beat and studied the doctor carefully before answering. Byrne had noticed that whenever he was nervous or ill at ease, the doctor's damaged right hand stole to his receding hairline, where his fingers worried at his remaining hair, twisting the locks into ever-tighter curls as if he would pull them out by the roots, and so cheat the prolonged humiliation of going bald. His scalp was under serious attack now. "It brought back some pretty bad memories for Sy," Byrne said.

"Sy Sheinberg!" the doctor exploded, his relief palpable. Byrne thought for a moment that the man was about to spring from his seat, but Dr. German stopped and calmed himself. "Yes, I would suppose so," he said. "It was a terrible time for all of us."

"I can imagine," said Byrne, although he couldn't. "What happened to your hand, Doctor, if you don't mind my asking."

"Can I offer you something?" asked Dr. German. "A cup of coffee, perhaps?"

"Coffee'd be great, thanks," replied Byrne.

Enter Miss Neumann, bearing coffee. Ekdahl hates the stuff, but accepts the cup because it is easier than explaining that he doesn't like it, and then having to listen to its adherents rhapsodize about its virtues as a heart-starter in the morning; he has other ways of starting his heart. "Do I sit or lie down?" he asks the doctor.

"Oh this," said Dr. German, acknowledging his missing finger. "An accident with a power tool. I wish I could say it's an old war wound. Makes a better story than what really happened. Which was that I was trying to be handy around the house on the Island. I should have listened to Jackie Mason and hired a gentile instead." He glanced at his watch. "We have forty-five minutes," said Dr. German, settling back in his leather chair. "So why don't we get started?"

"I'm waiting for you, Doc," said Byrne. "I mean, I'm here for you to talk to me, not vice versa."

Another laugh. "Excuse me, Lieutenant," said Dr. German. "I'm used to sitting in this chair and listening."

"At how many dollars an hour?"

"Two hundred and twenty."

"Two hundred and twenty dollars an hour." Byrne marveled at what a man could make just for sitting in a chair. "Dr. German," he said, "no offense, but did it ever occur to you that that's about what a good hooker in this town makes as well?"

German gave him a look. "No, Lieutenant, it has not," he said.

"Well, it is," said Byrne, warming to his subject. "Now, a hooker is what a guy rents when he's feeling horny and has the money to pay for it. Whereas a shrink is what a guy rents when he's feeling crazy and has the money to pay for it. Although you have to wonder whether anybody who thinks he's crazy and is sane enough to go to a shrink is really crazy in the first place. Catch-22, huh? Although, on the other hand, anybody rich enough to spend two hundred and twenty dollars an hour for someone to talk to really must be crazy, I guess. I mean, what kind of self-indulgent . . ." He felt his class resentment carrying him away. "So I guess what I'm trying to say is, aren't you and your colleagues just, you know, intellectual prostitutes? No offense."

His answer, however, did not satisfy the psychiatrist. "There were three great modern millenarian movements with roots in the nineteenth century, Lieutenant Byrne," said Dr. German formally, as if he were addressing one of his classes at New York University. "Communism, which promised to free the proletariat from the oppression of the property-owning class. Do-

decaphonicism, which promised to free music from the tyranny of arbitrary tonality. And psychiatry, which promised to liberate people from the
prisons of their minds. And what did they all have in common?"

"They were all bullshit?" asked Byrne, starting to enjoy himself. Maybe
Dr. German wasn't so smart after all.

"That they were profoundly Jewish in origin!" replied Dr. German, his
voice rising. "Marx! Schoenberg! Freud! Founding fathers all! Not to mention Trotsky, Zinoviev and the many other Jewish Bolsheviks. Not to mention the hundreds of other Jewish psychoanalysts and composers of our
time; why, even Aaron Copland wrote twelve-tone music toward the end
of his life." For some reason, he seemed to find this particularly exciting,
and threw his hands up in the air for emphasis. "Men with a dream, a belief in the possibility of improving the human condition, materially, mu-
sically and mentally! Men who respected one of the most fundamental
tenets of Judaism, to help your fellow man, men imbued with an intellectual restlessness and a burning moral fervor, men who asked why not when
everyone else was asking why."

"And a grateful world is still trying to find the proper way to thank
them," answered Byrne. "I suppose they probably all seemed like good
ideas at the time." He looked at his fingernails, suddenly grateful that he
still had ten of them. He was trying to think of a household implement
someone like Jacob German was likely to have that could remove a finger
accidentally. On the street, a missing digit usually signified a low-level drug
dealer who'd been caught dipping into the merchandise.

Dr. German looked at Byrne as if he were a patient, not a policeman.
"Hookers, you say. People have been calling us names for years, Lieutenant
Byrne."

"And it doesn't bother you?" asked Byrne. "It pisses me off when people call me a pig."

"Not a bit. Sticks and stones . . ."

"May break my bones," finished Byrne. "And sometimes rocks follow
words. As a Jew, you should know that."

"No one knows that better than I," said Dr. German.

"And Sy," added Byrne.

*"It's a very complicated situation," says Ekdahl, leaning back in the chair, "and I'm afraid
I'm not very good at discussing my feelings." He feigns embarrassment—"I'm only doing
this because Sy asked me to, you understand"—and looks sideways across the short distance*

that separates him from Dr. German. For the occasion, he has adopted an accent just clipped enough to be continental, but not so extreme as to be faux-British; it's the way, he feels, the real Egil Ekdahl might speak English, if there were a real Egil Ekdahl. "Besides, I've always felt that those who hide behind the so-called 'traumas' of their childhood are really just cowards and weaklings, and I have nothing but contempt for them." He wonders how long it would take him to kill the analyst, and how quietly he could do it.

"Which brings us, I suppose, to the real purpose of your visit," said Dr. German. "As you are no doubt aware, any conversation I might have with a patient is privileged communication. But when Ingrid told me that you were working on the Ekdahl case, I thought I should come forward—privately and off the record, of course. The ethics of my calling—"

"You mean Ekdahl was a patient of yours?'" asked Byrne in astonishment.

"In fact, Mr. Ekdahl was referred to me by our mutual friend, Dr. Seymour Sheinberg, M.D.," said the doctor. "Sy. Ziggy, we used to call him. Short for Siegfried. You must know your Wagner, Lieutenant."

"Didn't he used to be mayor?" asked Byrne.

"Not Robert Wagner," said Dr. German. "I'm referring to Richard Wagner, the composer."

"Wasn't he anti-Semitic?" asked Byrne. It was one of the few things he could remember from Mr. Jurkowitz's music education class. "Or was he Jewish? I can't recall."

Dr. German looked at him with something approaching respect. "Jewish, probably not, although like Hitler and Heydrich he feared he might be; anti-Semitic, in some of his writings, certainly," he answered. "*Judentum in Musik*—'Jewry in Music,' for example. Wagner is considered to have been a great influence on the Nazis, philosophically speaking, right up there with Father Jahn, Gobineau and Houston Stewart Chamberlain. Chamberlain married Wagner's daughter, Eva, and wrote *The Foundations of the Nineteenth Century*, which posited that the introduction of the assimilationist Jew into a western European culture inevitably debased and destroyed that culture, the way a parasite destroys its host organism. Hitler attended the Wagner Festival each summer in Bayreuth, and for a time there was widespread speculation that he was going to marry Winifred Wagner, the Englishwoman who was Siegfried Wagner's widow."

"Englishwoman, did you say?" asked Byrne. "That figures."

"She was English, yes," replied Dr. German. "The English are at least as anti-Semitic as the Germans; after all, they are Saxon brothers under the skin."

"Please don't get me started on the English," said Byrne rancorously. "Any place that hasn't discovered the virtues of dentistry and central heating really doesn't have much to recommend it, in my opinion. Not to mention the souls of a million dead Irish men and women on its conscience."

"Pardon me, Lieutenant?" asked Dr. German, taken aback by his outburst.

"Forget it," said Byrne. "Just letting my ethnic grudges show, I guess."

"You really shouldn't let history influence how you view the present, Lieutenant," said Dr. German. "An unhealthy attachment to past wrongs is the sign of an unbalanced mind."

"That's funny," said Byrne. "A lot of my Jewish friends have not been, and will never go, to Germany because of the Holocaust. It's a way to remember and honor the past."

"Six million died," said Dr. German. "It's understandable."

"To you, maybe," said Byrne. "To me it looks like many more than six million died. Ukrainians, Poles, Hungarians, Russians, Germans, Gypsies, clerics, Christians. What about them? Should they avoid Germany too?"

"Everybody knows about them, and of course it was a tragedy," said Dr. German angrily. "But don't forget, many of them were anti-Semitic."

"Does that make them any less dead, Doctor?" asked the homicide detective.

"On the other hand," said Dr. German, once again ignoring the conversational turn, "Wagner did entrust the premiere of *Parsifal* to Hermann Levi, a Jewish conductor."

Byrne, however, was both bored and conscious that the clock was ticking. "Let's cut the music lesson, Doc," he interrupted. "I'd rather talk about Ekdahl."

"Interesting name, that," said Dr. German. "Of course, you're familiar with the name Ekdahl in Kennedy assassination lore."

"Can't say that I am," said Byrne.

"Ekdahl was the name of Marguerite Claverie Oswald's third husband, with whom she lived in Texas for a time," said Dr. German, roaming over to his bookshelf. "After Pic and Oswald. Mr. Oswald died a few months before Lee was born. Edwin A. Ekdahl was the only father Lee ever knew. The marriage, alas, didn't last. Marguerite caught Ekdahl with another woman, in semiflagrante—she had long suspected her husband of infidelity—and they divorced in 1948. After a few years in Fort Worth, Marguerite and Lee moved to New York—he went to school in the Bronx, played hooky a lot and even underwent some psychiatric evaluation—and then returned to New Orleans. Back to French Street and the Murrets, to Saint Mary's Street, on the edge of the Garden District, lovely place, that, and thence to Exchange Alley. Are you familiar with Exchange Alley?"

"Sure," said Byrne. "It's near Wall Street."

"Not our Exchange Alley," corrected the psychiatrist. "The one in the French Quarter. It's not much today, but apparently it was quite the sinful little *Gasse* back then. The quintessential back alley, as it were, where the most iniquitous transactions could safely be made under the cover of darkness and the unwatchful eye of the New Orleans Police Department. A street on which anything could transpire, as long as the general populace didn't have to know about it. You really don't know New Orleans?"

"I've heard about the Mardi Gras."

"You should," said Dr. German, who wasn't listening. "Most decadent city in America, hands down. Oh, we New Yorkers like to think we live in the most wicked place on the planet, Baghdad on the Hudson, but what we don't know about real sin would fill the *Malleus Maleficarum*. Our degeneracy is of the most base, brutal variety. But New Orleans—perhaps it's something in the lazy, languid air, I don't know. There, they have a positive genius for inventive crime; the Mafia got its start there, not in New York. And crime-fighting. Consider the Garrison investigation. The mother of all modern conspiracy theories."

"Conspiracy theories?" asked Byrne, who had no patience for such nonsense.

"When you're Jewish," said Dr. German, "conspiracy theories loom large in your life. Did you ever notice how many Jewish names pop up in the Kennedy assassination investigation: not only Jack Ruby, but Bernard Weissman—no, not our Bernie Weissman—the man who signed that inflammatory newspaper ad welcoming the president to Dallas that day; Seymour Weitzmann, the Dallas cop—a Jewish cop in Dallas, can you believe it?—who found Oswald's rifle and said it was a Mauser; Fred Kaufman, the Associated Press photographer who took the first picture of Oswald, right after he was arrested at the Texas Theater for the murder of Officer Tippit; Mark Lane, who appointed himself Marguerite Oswald's attorney; Evelyn Strickman and Irving Sokolow, who examined Oswald as a thirteen-year-old here in New York; as well as Dr. Renatus Hartogs, the psychiatrist; even a little guy named Rubin Goldstein, the owner of Honest Joe's Pawnshop on Elm Street, who was spotted the day of the assassination driving around the School Book Depository in a car plastered with signs advertising his business; Ruby had been a customer once. Not to mention Abraham Zapruder, who serendipitously captured the assassination on film. Or Norman Redlich and Alfred Goldberg, who essentially wrote the Warren Report.

"Do you know how Jack Ruby explained his murder of Oswald? 'I wanted to show the world that Jews have guts.' That's what he said." Dr. German shuffled the few papers on his desk in embarrassment and checked his watch. "At the end of his life, when he was dying from cancer, Sparky Rubenstein, who never took an anti-Semitic slight lying down, was convinced that a second Holocaust was taking place in America, that Jews were being put to death right there in the same Dallas jailhouse. All it takes is one hater to cobble together a the-Jews-did-it theory, and frankly I'm amazed it didn't—or hasn't yet—happened."

Byrne didn't follow, but tried not to let on. Inside his head, a mantra was repeating: library, Ekdahl, hand, Ingrid, Sy, Theresienstadt. And now the JFK assassination. Find the connection, he told himself; seek the thread.

"In fact," continued Dr. German, "there was one such theory. A lady named Flora Filko Hyatt, of Houston, called Marguerite Oswald in April 1964 and invited her to come down to Houston to hear her theory of the assassination. And do you know what it was? That the assassination was the work of a conspiracy between top officials of Nieman-Marcus in Dallas and the Sakowitz store in Houston! Communicating with each other through their ads in the newspapers! Yes! Mrs. Hyatt, this crackpot anti-Semite, told a gullible Marguerite Oswald that the two families were members of an organization called the Black Ax, which dated back to medieval Germany. Nothing is too crazy for some people."

"You should see some of the letters we get," responded Byrne. "Every time there's a prominent murder, dozens of folks write in with their theories and, often, confessions. Nut cases don't surprise or bother me in the least, Doctor."

"I can see you're not Jewish then, Lieutenant Byrne," said Dr. German, and laughed his barking laugh. Byrne was beginning to find it grating. "If you were, you might understand what I mean."

"You don't have to be Jewish . . ." said Byrne.

"To love Levy's," finished Dr. German, returning to his chair. "Wasn't that a great ad campaign? Remember the one with the Indian, chowing down on a pastrami on rye? And now what do we have? 'Be like Mike'? It's just not the same."

The doctor rose from his chair and walked to the north windows, gazing out onto his tiny backyard. "There's an old Jewish saying," he told Byrne. "*Do not judge your comrade until you stand in his place.* Did you know that JFK had a premonition of death the night before he was killed? 'Suppose someone had a pistol in a briefcase,' he said to the Secret Service men. A gun in your pocket, a pistol in a briefcase, a rifle in a sixth-floor window. He quoted Scripture that evening as well. *Your old men shall dream dreams, your young men shall see visions . . . and where there is no vision, the people shall perish.*"

"Spoken like a true Irishman," said Byrne. "Especially that part about dreams and visions."

"Ecclesiastes was always one of his favorites. 'There is a time to be born, and a time to die.'" Slowly, the psychiatrist was coming out of his reverie. "You know," said Dr. German, snapping back. "I like you Irish. You're a race of dreamers. And yet you're tough as nails."

"No," said Byrne. "We're not tough. We're dumb. And that makes us tough. We drink too much and don't fuck enough, and that makes us romantic, but it also means we beat our wives as well. We'd probably also be some of your best patients, if only we made two hundred and twenty dollars an hour. So maybe I don't make as much money as you do," he continued. "But whereas tomorrow you may wake up crazy, Dr. German, I shall most assuredly wake up sane. And alive."

"To paraphrase Churchill," said Dr. German.

"I always thought that was Groucho Marx," said Byrne. "But what's in a name?"

"More than you obviously suspect," said Dr. German.

Ekdahl hates the way Dr. German sits there, his fingertips lightly pressed together, as if he were praying. To which God? To whom does a Jewish atheist pray? And for what? For mercy, perhaps. If so, he was in for a disappointment.

"It has to do with my mother," he begins. "My mother was very religious. She was taken from me when I was still a boy, but I remember her very well."

"Yes," says Dr. German. "Tell me about her."

"My mother was a devout Christian—I hope this doesn't offend you, Doctor?" Ekdahl feigns concern.

"Not at all, Mr. Ekdahl. Please continue."

"She prayed every day. We had a statue of Mary in our garden and there were pictures of the Sacred Heart of Jesus and of the Blessed Virgin on the walls of our house."

"This is not unusual in a Catholic home, Mr. Ekdahl," observes Dr. German. "But it is a little out of the ordinary in a Scandinavian Protestant house. How do you account for this?"

"Good, Doctor, very good!" exclaims Ekdahl delightedly. "So you too can see that appearances sometimes can be deceiving. You do not immediately assume that because I have a Danish name that I must be Protestant." He smiles. "You see, my mother's somewhat exaggerated Christianity was in response to her fear that she was . . ."

"Take my name, for instance."

"'German'?" said Byrne. "What's to know?"

"Does it seem particularly 'Jewish' to you?" asked the doctor.

"Now that you mention it, no," ventured Byrne. "I suppose it means someone who comes from Germany. I hadn't thought about it."

"Of course you hadn't," said Dr. German. "Why should you, until this moment? But if you knew anything about languages, if you were a good linguistic detective so to speak, you would know at once—by knowing where my family comes from—what my name really is. Don't be fooled by what seems obvious. *German* has nothing to do with Germany. In Russian, the letter *G* is the same as the letter *H*—Horowitz was Gorowitz in Russian—so my name can really be seen as Herman. Now, doesn't that sound Jewish? Just the difference of one little letter—and your misconception of the sound that letter represents. Cultural chauvinism at its finest."

"So?" asked Byrne, ever the stubborn empiricist.

"So confusion reigns where ignorance holds sway. Not knowing something as simple as the way Europeans write dates—the day first, the month second—can send whole teams of investigators down the wrong path, hopelessly lost in a maze of their own device. When worlds collide, the opportunities for mis- and disinformation multiply exponentially. And in just the same way can two disparate anythings—ideas, facts, theories, what have you—be related, once one understands the crucial missing step, the missing link. In this way, our jobs are not so very dissimilar after all."

"Born a Jew. Now, doesn't that surprise you?" says Ekdahl. "Me, a Scandinavian, raised

a Catholic by a mother who feared she might be part Jewish. How do you regard me now, Doctor? Does that change your feelings about me? Are you experiencing any emotions in the light of this knowledge?"

If Dr. German is perplexed, his face does not betray him. "I can assure you, your mother's religious origins are totally irrelevant to this discussion. Please go on. What about your father?"

"I never knew him. Mother never remarried, although she had a series of unsatisfactory relationships with men. In fact, she eventually came to despise men—me excepted, of course. But my father, well, my father was a saint, at least in my mother's eyes, although I gather he betrayed her badly in the end. I guess you could say finding out more about him has become something of an obsession with me."

"I'm sorry, I didn't know," says Dr. German. "Please go on."

Ekdahl enjoys challenging the pompous charlatan sitting across from him. "Even though you're married, Doctor, don't you sometimes fool around?" he inquires. There is a disturbing gleam in his eye. "Don't you sometimes have appetites and desires that, given the removal of all social and cultural restraints, you would like to act on, even if they aren't very pretty? Sex with boys, for example, or grossly overweight women, or amputees, or sheep? Wouldn't you, for example, like to sample some of the charms of our mutual friend Miss Bentsen? Or perhaps you already have."

"I don't think that my appetites are at issue, Mr. Ekdahl," says Dr. German. His manner has turned curt, even chilly. "Please remember that we try not to make value judgments here."

"And that, Doctor," says Ekdahl, "is exactly what is wrong with you."

Byrne decided it was time to play one of his trump cards. Ever since he had discovered the video in Ekdahl's apartment, he had carried it with him. "Speaking of my job," said Byrne, "I found this the other day. Do you have a VCR? I should warn you, it gets ugly."

"However ugly it may get, Lieutenant, I can assure you I've seen far worse." Dr. German took the cassette and hit the play button. The second time around, Byrne found he could watch the tape a bit more dispassionately. The video quality was poor but the images were, alas, clear.

A lusty blonde is sitting astride a naked man, riding him as she would a small horse or a large dog. The man is turned away from the camera, and is wearing a kind of half-mask made out of leather. There is what appears to be a silk curtain on the floor.

The dominatrix is dressed in black leather: a black leather halter around her neck, black leather jacket, black leather cummerbund, thigh-high black leather riding boots. The only nonleather item of apparel is her black silk stockings, whose tops peek out of her boots. Her large breasts are supported, but not concealed, by a black leather demi-bra. On her left hand she is wearing two rings, with a studded bracelet around her wrist. Her right hand is holding a black leather bridle, with which she is controlling the man. He does not appear to be objecting.

The willing slave is down on his hands and knees, naked except for his face mask, through which the bridle passes, and his black leather handcuffs, which are joined by two black leather straps. Another, svelter blonde enters the picture. She is very beautiful and she, too, is wearing a black leather harness bra, but she is naked below the waist except for a red Lycra sash across her midsection. Attached to her labia is a slave ring, complete with chain. The zaftig blonde begins having sex with her. She has offered one of her big tits to the smaller woman and the girl is sucking it eagerly.

There is another man in the room, his face partially obscured by a leather mask. But nothing conceals the leopard on his shoulder. It is Ekdahl, sitting with the big blonde on a sofa. He sports a black leather shirt, as well as a black leather belt around his waist. The golden blonde, her breasts swaying, is bent over him.

The camera moves back to the first man. The smaller blonde is sucking the man's stiff cock. She is still wearing her red sash, only now she has put on white leather boots as well. Simultaneously, she is fucking her bigger companion from behind with a large black dildo. The instrument's silver tip gleams in the light. The big blonde has a look of transfiguration on her face that would do justice to a Titian saint.

Ekdahl is lying on his back now, the smaller blonde straddling him. A cock appears at the right of the frame. Ekdahl guides it into the girl's mouth and slips out from underneath her, just as the other woman tugs her head gently back, holding her by the hair.

Ekdahl reappears, a straight razor in his right hand. The girl's throat is exposed to him, but she doesn't notice until it is too late, if indeed she ever does, because with one swift motion Ekdahl has drawn the razor across her neck and she collapses in a bloody froth, her friend still kissing her passionately.

Byrne looked over at the psychiatrist, but the man's face betrayed no emotion, neither pity nor horror. "I'm sorry for the disturbing nature of this, Doctor," said Byrne. Not since he was a kid had he seen his brother naked.

Dr. German shrugged. *"Homo sum; humani nil a me alienus puto,* as Terence said. Nothing human is foreign to me. I can tell you one thing. That video was shot in Russia or in a Russian environment. Consider the teacups. Which means that the first man we saw was either Jewish or an American."

Byrne asked how he could be so sure.

"He was circumcised. Except for Jews, European men generally are not."

"And the other guy's Ekdahl for sure."

The doctor nodded. "I can't say that I'm surprised. When Mr. Ekdahl visited me, it was immediately clear that he was suffering a great deal of emotional distress stemming from a physical condition and from, er, a certain kind of sexual fixation."

"May I ask what this fixation was?" said Byrne.

"We had only one session," replied the doctor, ignoring the question.

"Why?" asked Byrne, his notebook at hand.

"I ended it before any real therapy could begin," replied Dr. German, "because I could see that he was not serious about getting help."

"I wonder if you could be more specific."

"Mr. Ekdahl came to me for help in confronting his anger over his psychological and physiological impotence," said the doctor. "His plight was first brought to my attention by our mutual friend, Miss Bentsen, with whom he apparently had an ongoing relationship that predated their arrivals in America. She informed me, privately of course, that he was anorgasmic, and that this condition was causing him considerable psychological turmoil."

Byrne couldn't help himself: he let out a loud laugh.

"I don't find sexual dysfunction amusing, Lieutenant," said the psychiatrist in reproach.

"I'm sorry, Dr. German," said Byrne. "It's just that I've heard this song about Ekdahl's alleged impotence before, and yet I'm having trouble reconciling that with the fact that he appears to have been in bed with everybody in Manhattan at one time or another, present company excepted."

"You saw the video," answered the doctor. "Did you see him achieve orgasm? In fact, did you see his penis?"

Byrne had to admit he had not.

"Well, don't bother viewing it again—unless, of course, this sort of thing appeals to you. He didn't have one. Not a fully functioning organ, anyway," said Dr. German. "Mr. Ekdahl was a pseudo-teratological hermaphrodite."

"Pseudo-what?" asked Byrne.

"There are no real human hermaphrodites, of course," said Dr. German, lecturing again, and Byrne thought of the photographs of the she-males he had seen in Ekdahl's apartment. "True hermaphroditism is found only in the lower orders—mollusks, stone flies, certain toads. Gynomonoecism is far more common than andromonoecism—that is, a female producing sperm happens more frequently than male ovulation—which I suppose makes sense. We all start our existences as females until the Y chromosome kicks in. Which feminist writer was it who said, 'Think of maleness as a kind of birth defect'? No, what we have in humans is malformation of the sexual organs, which in infancy can produce the appearance of bisexual organic development or incomplete anatomic development, resulting in an error in determining the true sex of the newborn."

"Meaning what?" asked Byrne.

"Meaning that at his birth there apparently was some confusion about Mr. Ekdahl's true gender." A cough from the doctor punctuated the revelation. "As I understand it, he suffered from cryptorchidism, which means that his testicles were undescended. When this condition goes uncorrected either by surgery or the administration of gonadotrophic hormones, as it apparently did in his case, it eventually causes injury to the seminiferous tubules with the result that, physiologically, he became sterile."

"Are you saying he was some kind of eunuch?"

"Not exactly," said Dr. German. "Perhaps a better analogy would be like a prepubescent child of either sex. A boy on the verge of his first orgasm, delayed for a decade. Just think how explosive that would be in a man of twenty-four."

"What would the psychological effect of this, er, condition be on a child and young adult?" asked Byrne.

Dr. German replied: "This is not my area of expertise, you understand, but I would suppose it must have been extremely embarrassing and frustrating for him, resulting in the marked antisocial tendencies he later displayed. Of course, I didn't get this from Mr. Ekdahl himself, but only later, upon making inquiries."

"Do you mean they thought he was a girl?" asked Byrne.

"They might have, yes," said Dr. German. "Obviously, the confusion was cleared up somewhere along the line."

"What sort of inquiries did you make?" asked Byrne, writing as fast as he could. "And where?"

"At the consulate, among other places," said Dr. German, "regarding his past medical history. I also spoke with Sy Sheinberg about him."

"Why didn't Sy mention that at the autopsy?" asked Byrne.

"Am I my brother's keeper, Lieutenant?" asked Dr. German. "Sy Sheinberg has had a long, if not always distinguished, career in this city, and I imagine he has come into contact with a great many different people over the years."

"Yes," agreed Byrne, "but most of them are dead."

"Now, Lieutenant," said Dr. German. "But don't forget that Sy had a flourishing private practice until, until that unfortunate incident with the Stevens girl. He may have met Ekdahl somewhere along the way."

"But Ekdahl had only been in New York about a year," reminded Byrne. "Long after Sy's private practice was over."

The doctor seemed annoyed by this intelligence. "What does it matter?" he barked. "In any case, Dr. Sheinberg confirmed Mr. Ekdahl's psycho-physical handicap."

"What do you mean, psycho-physical?" asked Byrne. "You've got me thoroughly confused."

"I mean," said Dr. German, "that the fear was its own fulfillment. That the child, so to speak, was father to the man."

"Pardon me?" The psychiatrist's Delphic utterances were beginning to get on his nerves.

"I simply mean that Mr. Ekdahl's sexual problems were as much psychological as physical, and that the original misdiagnosis, coupled with his mother's expressed wish to have a girl instead of a boy—apparently, she mentioned that to one of the analysts in his youth—meant that sexual activity could not take place except under, er, unusual circumstances."

"All right, let me get this straight: are you telling me that Ekdahl was some kind of freak?"

"We frown on the use of such terms," objected the shrink.

"Some kind of penistically challenged person, then, almost feminine. And yet what I can't quite reconcile in my mind is that apparently he was also a hardened killer, a professional assassin who did time in one of the toughest prison camps in the world. I just can't figure out how these two things go together."

Dr. German laughed, and Byrne noted his assessment of Ekdahl's career did not seem to have surprised him. "Well, Lieutenant, it's really very simple. Either they do or they don't. If they don't, then we're talking about two different people. But if they do—well, there's no reason why they can't, is there? Just because Mr. Ekdahl had a physical disability does not make him incapable of homicide. What did I just tell you about appearances? Remember my Cyrillic parable. I cannot speak directly to the issue of whether he was extraordinarily violent, but whenever you eliminate the impossible . . ."

"Whatever remains, however improbable, must be the truth," said Byrne, completing the sentence for him.

"Excellent!" exclaimed Dr. German, clapping his hands. "You know your Canon."

"I guess there's a little Sherlock Holmes in all of us," said Byrne. He glanced down at his notes. "You mentioned something about 'unusual circumstances' relating to Mr. Ekdahl's impotence. Can you tell me what those circumstances were?"

Dr. German looked at him, square in the eye. "Yes, I think I can," he replied. "It's only a guess, but I'd be very surprised if it were not also the truth. Despite his disability, Mr. Ekdahl, as you have obviously learned already, was a creature of extensive, if not to say excessive, sexual appetites. There's no motivational factor like wanting something one can't have."

"Meaning he was a pervert?" prompted Byrne.

Dr. German seemed disappointed. "Nothing that simple, Lieutenant," he said, shaking his head. "Really, I expected better of you. I mean that Mr. Ekdahl saw the world in almost exclusively sexual terms. Sex was his ruling metaphor, the way he rationalized and explained the universe to himself. You're familiar with Dr. Sacks's book, *The Man Who Mistook His Wife for a Hat*? I'm told somebody even made an opera out of it. The man in question suffered from a neurological condition called agnosia that caused him progressively to lose his ability to synthesize visual images into a coherent whole. That is, he could make out shapes, but could not assemble them into a single object. He had eyes to see, but he could not see. So he used his ears—the music of Robert Schumann was his favorite—and grasped the world through musical sounds. Mr. Ekdahl used the central, creative impulse of sex in order to determine his place and function in the cosmos. He desired the fulfillment of his sex drive, even as his life was devoted to its exact opposite, the yin to its yang, the Thanatos to the Eros he could not experience. I remember him saying to me . . ."

"My mother used to sing a little song to me, when I was young," says Ekdahl. "Would you like to hear it?" He makes a show of clearing his throat. "Please excuse my voice."

> Because the world is beautiful
> Because you are handsome
> And in sacrifice (there is no limit)
> Because I love you
> Do not implore
> For all the dreams and torments
> I thank you.

"I love my mother more than anyone else in the world. She is all I have. Is there anything wrong with that?"

"Of course not," says Dr. German. "But such affection must not be carried to unhealthy extremes."

". . . that he had only ever had an orgasm once," said Dr. German. "Just after he had reached puberty. I didn't really get the full story, but I think it had something to do with his mother."

"His mother?"

Instead of replying directly, the doctor indulged himself in another seeming non sequitur. "Allow me to read you something," said the doctor, reaching in his desk for a file. "When Ekdahl was thirteen, he was asked to make a series of drawings as part of an overall intelligence test, on which he scored 118, by the way, which is in the normal-to-bright range. The psychiatric evaluations were done in the United States; apparently he spent part of his childhood here."

"What?" cried Byrne. "Are you saying Ekdahl was an American?"

Dr. German seemed surprised by the interruption. "I don't believe so," he replied. "But from the way he spoke English, I could only assume that a significant portion of his childhood must have been spent here, and further research revealed that to have been the case." He turned back to the report. "These were the results:

"'The Human Figure Drawings are empty, poor characterizations of persons approximately the same age as the subject. They reflect a considerable amount of impoverishment in the social and emotional areas. He appears to be a somewhat insecure youngster exhibiting little inclination for warm and satisfying relationships to others. He appears slightly withdrawn and in view of the lack of detail within the drawings this may assume a more significant characteristic. He exhibits some difficulty in relationship to the maternal figure, suggesting more anxiety in this area than in any other. Under conditions of emotional stress and strain he appears increasingly defensive, suggesting some concern orally, and in general incapable of constructing an effective ego-defense.' Not very elegantly written, I fear, but you get the idea. I quote once more:

"'This well-built, well-nourished boy is tense, withdrawn and evasive. He dislikes intensely talking about himself and his feelings. He likes to give the impression that he doesn't care about others and rather likes to keep to himself so that he is not bothered and does not have to make the effort of communicating. It was difficult to penetrate the emotional wall behind which this boy hides, and he provided us with sufficient clues, feelings of awkwardness and insecurity as the main reasons for his withdrawal tendencies and solitary habits. [He] told us, "I don't want a friend and I don't like to talk to people." [He] describes himself as stubborn and, according to his own saying, likes to say "no." Strong resistive and negativistic features were thus noticed, but psychotic mental content was denied and no indication of psychotic mental changes was arrived at. He has fantasies of omnipotence and power, through which he tries to compensate for his present shortcomings and frustrations. He does not enjoy being together with other children and when we asked him whether he prefers the company of boys to the one'—please excuse the infelicities—'of girls, he answered, "I dislike everybody."'"

The doctor put the report down. "There was no follow-up treatment because, shortly thereafter, he and his mother left the country."

"Dr. German?" came Miss Neumann's voice across the intercom. "Your time is almost up."

"Wait," said Dr. German, more softly. He punched a button on his phone. "We'll be running a little late today, Miss Neumann," he said.

"But Doctor, Mrs. Cooperman is already on her way over," protested the secretary. "And that man has been calling again."

"We'll be running a little late," repeated the doctor, with some petulance, and rang off.

"According to the reports, the young Ekdahl had fantasies about, and I quote here, 'sometimes hurting or killing people.' In this respect, I suppose, he was as American as apple pie. And still more: 'There are indications that he has suffered serious personality damage, but if he can receive help quickly this might be repaired to some extent.' Alas, it seems he did not. His mother was uneasy about certain aspects of his physiognomy and, according to the psychologist, 'had not been satisfied with a recent examination, particularly with the genitalia.' "

"With an evaluation like that, it's a wonder he ever got into the consular corps," observed Byrne.

"I gather the Danes did not have access to this information," said Dr. German. "That, at least, is what Sy told me. You should ask him yourself."

"I will," Byrne assured him. "I've been trying to reach him for the past couple of days, but so far no luck. I don't understand why Sy would be holding out on me, though. Why wouldn't he have told me that he knew Ekdahl when he had him on the slab during the autopsy?"

"For the best reason in the world," said Dr. German. "Because he has a personal interest in the case, and wants to discover what you know before he tells you anything."

"And here you are, betraying his secret," said Byrne.

"Violence may be American," said Dr. German, "but betrayal—that is quintessentially a European attribute. Perhaps it has something to do with the European penchant for kings. One is always trying to ingratiate oneself with the ruler, even when the ruler is a monster. Thirsty for revenge, the vanquished nonetheless wishes to emulate the victor. And if he cannot win, then the next best thing is to cleave to the side of winners."

"If you can't beat 'em, join 'em," said Byrne. "Surely you're familiar with Irish history, Dr. German."

"It's not one of my specialities," said Dr. German, at a rare loss.

"I mean the constant betrayal," said Byrne. "The endemic informers—read O'Flaherty—the relentless deceit, the constant sense of impending doom. The Irish are the most paranoid people in the world, Doctor, and that includes the Israelis. But, as the man said, just because you're paranoid doesn't mean someone's not out to get you."

"Precisely," rejoined Dr. German. "And therein lies our problem. Or should I say, Sy's problem."

"Hey, Doc," interrupted Byrne, "did you ever hear the one about the mick at the racetrack?"

Dr. German sighed. "No, I haven't," he said, fearing a joke.

"Indulge me," said Byrne. "It goes like this. A harp is at the racetrack, he's broke and this is his last shot. He puts all his money, his life savings, on the longshot who's going off at thirty to one and takes his place near the finish line. 'Oh, God,' he prays, 'please let my horse win. If he does, my firstborn son will become a priest, I'll give ten percent of my earnings to the Church,' et cetera, et cetera. And God hears his prayers; the paddy's nag is, miraculously, the front-runner coming down the stretch. The son of a bitch has a ten-length lead over the nearest horse, and is increasing the margin with each stride. Finally, the damn horse is only five yards from the finish line, a sure winner. 'Thanks, God, very much,' says Paddy, 'I'll take it from here now.'" Byrne waited for a reaction.

"So?" said Dr. German. "Did his horse win the race?"

"That's just the point," said Byrne, wondering if Dr. German was as smart as he had supposed. "God heard his prayers and delivered, but the guy welshed on the deal. In real life, though, an anvil or something would have come flying out of the air and conked the colt on the head. Because in Irish culture if anything can go wrong, it will go wrong. Why do you think they call it Murphy's Law? Look at Parnell and his girlfriend. Look at the death of Michael Collins. Or JFK. You want to know the secret of life? I'll give it to you, and it won't even cost you anything. Here it is: shit happens. But I suppose if your patients knew that, you'd be out of business."

Instead of replying, the psychiatrist hit the intercom and buzzed his receptionist. "Cancel Mrs. Cooperman, please," he ordered. "I don't care what her problems are today. In fact, please clear my schedule for the rest of the day." Miss Neumann's complaints could be heard, faintly, from outside the door.

For a long time, Dr. German said nothing. Finally, he spoke.

"'Shit happens,'" he said. "What a wonderfully common articulation of Occam's Razor: *Entia non sunt multiplicanda praeter necessitatem.* 'Beings ought not to be multiplied, except out of necessity.' Or, to put it another way, the simplest explanation for any given phenomenon or set of phenomena is most likely the correct one. *Shit happens*; it doesn't get much simpler than that." Abruptly, he changed the subject once again. "Do you know what a trusty is?" His voice was low and, Byrne thought, sad.

"Yes, Doctor, I do," replied Byrne, in what he hoped was a suitably respectful tone; the mood suddenly seemed to call for it. "It's a prisoner who is given a certain amount of freedom and responsibility in exchange for good behavior. In exchange for ratting on his fellow inmates."

"Precisely, Lieutenant. 'From among Pharaoh's slaves several children of Israel were assigned to supervise the others.'"

Byrne looked bewildered.

"Exodus 5:14. The original trusties. Children of Israel who guarded and beat and sometimes even killed other children of Israel."

"Traitors," summarized Byrne.

"Some called them that, of course," said Dr. German. "But in their own minds, who could say with certainty that they did not consider themselves patriots? That's what I meant when I told you not to judge your comrade until you have stood in his place, seen with his eyes, felt with his soul. Have you read Hannah Arendt's *Eichmann in Jerusalem*, as I suggested? No?" Furiously, he began worrying his scalp again. "It is a book about a very great crime—to Jews, the greatest of all crimes. But it is also a book about complicity in that crime, Jewish complicity, and that is something that everyone has done his best to try and forget. In Israel—although some tried to make the people remember—and everywhere else. Certainly here, in New York, where the nuances of the Holocaust have been subsumed into the dogma of victimization."

Dr. German reached for a pitcher of water that he kept on a side table and poured himself a glass. He did not offer one to Byrne, whose coffee was lying ice cold before him. In Dr. German's deep reverie, Byrne no longer existed; he was now talking to himself.

"But for a time in Israel it was different, especially just after the war. The trusties—the *kapos*, they were called—were notorious for their cruelty. All but a handful of them, even lowly deputy *kapos*, killed fellow Jews, murdered them, sometimes for sport, sometimes at the behest of their Nazi masters. Some even drove their own mothers in the trucks that took the people to the gas chambers. In her book—not translated into Hebrew when it came out, by the way—Arendt makes the terrible statement that most Jews who died in the Holocaust never even saw a German. Rounded up by the Jewish councils in each city and town and delivered to the camps, guarded by Jews, executed by Jewish hangmen, their corpses stripped and burned by Jewish workers. If an anti-Semite ever made a statement like that there would be hell to pay." He took another long drink of water and refilled his glass. "Other Jewish scholars have contested this assertion, of course, but the fact of the *kapos* is irrefutable. It is our dirty little secret, the one thing about the Holocaust it behooves us to forget."

"What choice did they have?" said Byrne.

"Not that it did them much good, of course," continued the psychiatrist, unresponsive, "since in the end most of the *kapos* were themselves killed. But some survived. They tried to mix in with the other Jews in the DP camps, and when they were recognized, the vengeance of the prisoners was a terrible thing to behold. Some of them were prominent people, or their sons; the son of Yitzhak Gruenbaum, who became minister of the interior in the Ben-Gurion government—that boy had been a *kapo*.

"In 1949, the government of Israel passed a Nazi Collaborators Law, to allow the prosecution of the *kapos*. But no one was terribly interested in bringing Jews to trial while Nazis were being given their *Persilschein*—that's colloquial German for denazification; basically, it means being laundered. The few trials that were brought were largely attended by camp survivors, and the newspapers did their best to ignore them. And why? Because, as one of the judges noted, 'It is hard for us, the judges of Israel, to free ourselves of the feeling that in punishing a worm of this sort we are diminishing, even if by only a trace, the abysmal guilt of the Nazis themselves.'"

Byrne interrupted. "Excuse me for saying this, Doctor, but don't you think all this wallowing in the Holocaust is unhealthy? Not to mention a little bit selfish? Didn't you just say that yourself a few minutes ago? The Jews aren't the only people who've suffered at the hands of their fellow man."

Dr. German's eyes flashed as he cut in. "I cannot believe you have the gall to sit there in front of me, a death-camp survivor, and to compare the unique experience of the Jews under the Nazis with anything else. As Elie Wiesel has so eloquently written, the uniqueness of the Holocaust functions as a moral touchstone. Did you know, my dear Lieutenant Byrne, that since 1981 it is a criminal offense in the State of Israel to deny the existence of the Holocaust? The maximum penalty is five years in prison. In light of the Institute for Historical Review and its noxious ilk, I sometimes find myself wishing we had such a law in this country."

"And is there a penalty in Israel for denying the existence of God?" wondered Byrne.

"There is a statute forbidding 'gross violation of religious sentiment,' yes," replied Dr. German.

"And how much time does one do for that particular crime?" asked Byrne.

"One year," said the psychiatrist. "I know what you're thinking. But please understand that no one has ever been tried or convicted under either law. The uniqueness of the Holocaust, its terrible singularity, is that one people, the Germans, tried to exterminate—exterminate!—another people, the Jews, from the face of the earth. And very nearly succeeded."

"Dr. German," said Byrne, "I witness a holocaust every day on the streets of this town. And don't give me any philosophical bullshit about the intention of the murderer being the crucial moral distinction while we're rating disasters on a scale of one to ten. A corpse is a corpse, whether it's been starved, gassed, shot, beaten, hanged or drowned, whether it's a so-called 'hate crime' or not. When you're dead, you're dead. And if someone kills you, it's a capital crime. And as far as I'm concerned, that's that."

Dr. German sat back in his seat, but Byrne could still feel the tension. He waited for an angry comeback, but instead, the doctor changed the subject. There was a little smile—of condescension?—on his face. "I admire and envy your moral certainty, Lieutenant," said the psychiatrist. "Are you familiar with the Kastner trial?"

The look on Byrne's face plainly said no.

"Don't worry; few here are. It was a very complicated affair that tore the young Israeli nation apart in 1954. Actually, it should more properly be called the Malchiel Gruenwald trial, since it was Gruenwald who was in the dock for libel, not Kastner. Gruenwald was an old man, a Hungarian Jew who survived the Holocaust but lost fifty members of his family to the Nazis. Well, perhaps not just to the Nazis: that was the point of the trial."

The doctor paused to pour yet another glass of water. Byrne noticed he was sweating profusely, and thought for a moment that the shrink might pour the water over his head instead of drinking it.

"I'm sorry, I'm rambling. The short version is that in a pamphlet, Gruenwald accused another survivor, the leader of the Hungarian Jewish community in Israel, a man named Israel Rudolf Kastner, of collaboration. Kastner had cut a deal with Eichmann to save a million Hungarian Jews from certain destruction in exchange for ten thousand trucks, which the Nazis desperately needed for the war effort. That deal fell through, but Kastner later successfully negotiated the release of other Jews."

"He doesn't sound like such a bad guy to me," said Byrne.

"It gets trickier. In 1946, according to Gruenwald, Kastner secretly testified as a defense witness at the Nuremberg Trial of SS Obersturmbahnführer Kurt Becher. And the reason, Gruenwald alleged, was to conceal Kastner's own complicity in the theft of millions of dollars of gold taken from the Jews. It wasn't the first complaint against Kastner, who was the press spokesman for the Ministry of Commerce and Industry and who had his eye on a seat in the Knesset, but it took on a life of its own and, anyway, Kastner, or rather the government on Kastner's behalf, sued.

"Kastner, who was the first prosecution witness, turned out to be his own worst enemy. He never pretended he hadn't talked with Eichmann. He admitted that he had been allowed by the Nazis to fill a so-called VIP train that transported sixteen hundred Jews to safety, including several hundred people from his hometown of Cluj, many of them members of his own family, including his mother and his wife; Becher was the SS officer who had set up the train. Becher and Kastner, it developed, had kept in contact throughout the war—Becher even sent Kastner to Berlin to meet Himmler, if you can believe that. Himmler!"

"Surely you know the old song," interrupted Byrne.

"What song?" asked Dr. German, annoyed.

"The one they sang during the war." He started singing to the tune of the *Colonel Bogey March*:

> Hitler
> has only got one ball.
> Goebbels
> has two but very small.
> Himmler
> is very sim'lar
> and Goering
> has no balls at all.

"Sorry," said Byrne, "but apropos of Mr. Ekdahl's disability, it just popped into my head."

Dr. German rolled his eyes. "Thank you, Lieutenant, for that bit of enlightening entertainment. Now, where was I? Oh, yes—and that after the war Kastner had submitted a brief on Becher's behalf. Do you know what it said? It's a classic of moral ambiguity. He wrote of Becher, this Nazi scum, that 'I never for a minute doubted his good intentions, even if the form and basis for our negotiations were of an objectionable character.' Think about that for a moment." The doctor paused to let his words sink in.

"In other words . . . ?" prompted Byrne.

"In other words, a Faustian bargain, a pact with the Devil. Becher was freed by the court, a man who had been involved in the murders of half a million Jews. He walked, thanks in part to the testimony of a Jew. Later he became a grain merchant; some said he made a fortune doing business with Israel as part of the reparations agreement. Perhaps the worst part is what else Kastner wrote: 'I make this statement not only in my name but also on behalf of the Jewish Agency and the World Jewish Congress.' Could it look any worse?"

"I don't see how," admitted Byrne. "What happened to the gold?"

"No one really knows. Some of it turned up after the war, a little bit of it. There were stories, allegations. Gruenwald's attorney cleverly implied that some of it lined the coffers of the Mapai party. Nobody knows. But the trial was ruinous for Kastner." Dr. German let out a sigh. "You must be bored with all this irrelevant, squabbling Jewish history," he said. "You know the old saying, two Jews, three opinions."

"And three Irishmen, one opinion—that of Holy Mother Church," said Byrne. "Actually, I find it fascinating. But I still don't quite see what all this has to do with—"

"Mr. Ekdahl? Dr. Sheinberg?" said the psychiatrist. He looked exasperatedly at the literal-minded cop in front of him. "Can't you see?"

"What I can see," said Byrne, deciding it was time to force the issue, "is a man with a great deal on his conscience and therefore probably something to hide. And I'm about to find out just what it is." He took a guess. "What really happened to your hand, Doctor?"

"I'd like to pursue our discussion about your relationship with your mother and your unresolved feelings for your father," says Dr. German. "But I see our time is up, so we'll

have to stop now. Please tell Dr. Sheinberg that I'm very grateful for his having sent you to me. I find your case fascinating. Miss Neumann can make another appointment for next week, if you'd like."

"I'm not sure where I'll be next week," says Ekdahl. "My official duties are keeping me quite busy these days, and there are some personal matters that I must attend to as well." The Walther is holstered in the back of his pants, the throwing knife taped to the inside of his right calf; the razor he keeps in a sheath under his left armpit. He has not been distracted from his purpose, but he enjoys talking about Mother. As if to scratch himself, he reaches for the razor; it is, after all, his favorite.

"Let me finish," insisted Dr. German. "The trial dragged on, and after a while it was not just Kastner who was on trial—for so he was, symbolically—but the entire government of Israel. Questions were raised not only about Kastner, but about the behavior of the Jewish councils in the ghettos, about the Jewish Agency, even about Weizmann's motives. It shook the faith of the Jewish people in their own country. And then the judge issued his decision. It was devastating. Let me read part of it to you."

The doctor rummaged around his bookshelves for a while, found the volume he was searching for and returned to his chair.

"'Even in a case where his life is in danger, a Jewish person is forbidden to save himself by spilling the blood of an innocent man; likewise it is forbidden to save one man by spilling the blood of another innocent man. It is also forbidden to save one man or even many by turning another innocent man over to a murderer. Even to save the majority of the community it is forbidden to hand over an innocent minority, or even "one soul from Israel," to murderers. Even more so, then, the opposite case, of turning over an innocent majority to murderers to save a few individuals. The violator of this principle deserves to die.' That's what Judge Halevy wrote, in acquitting Gruenwald of the libel."

With a movement so fast that Dr. German can scarcely credit his eyes, Ekdahl crosses the narrow space between them, his razor pressed against the psychiatrist's throat. Ekdahl's breath is warm in the doctor's ear. The psychiatrist is struggling, but Ekdahl has him firmly in his grasp; as he chooses, he can cut the man's throat or break his neck. "Such as you, my dear doctor. You are the one who needs help, and I have come to help you, as you will help me."

Ekdahl stands over his prey, his left hand wrapped around Dr. German's windpipe, his right hand pressing the razor ever more tightly against the psychiatrist's throat. "I am speak-

ing to you now in your capacity as a nonreligious member of a religious group, Doctor," he tells him. "Do you know what my favorite quotation from the Bible is?"

Dr. German shakes his head.

"'For your hands are defiled with blood, and your fingers with iniquity; your lips have spoken lies, your tongue hath muttered perverseness.'"

"Isaiah 59:3," whispers Dr. German.

"Seems appropriate to the situation, doesn't it?" asks Ekdahl. "Since you are the one who has blasphemed and lied and compromised and betrayed, you are the one who has caused helpless people to be born, suffer and die, you the one who has handed over innocents to murderers. You are the pervert, Doctor, not me."

Dr. German has not known such fear for many years.

"Isaiah," continues Ekdahl. "A belief in the supremacy of the spiritual over the earthly; faith in potency of high ideas and ideals over brute force and power. A harbinger of the Savior to come." He rubs the razor back and forth against the doctor's neck. "Although, alas, Jews don't believe in the Redeemer, do you? And yet here he stands, before you."

His face is close to the psychiatrist's, so close he could kiss him. "Do you recognize me?" he asks.

The terrified man shakes his head once more. In the back of his mind, an unthinkable notion has formed, moving forward with great speed. "No," he croaks.

"Who is it that men say I am?" asks Ekdahl. "Look closer."

Dr. German tries to avert his gaze, but he cannot, even though Ekdahl has released his grip on the man's neck and slowly, deliberately, unzipped his fly. He is not wearing any undershorts. The pressure of the razor guides Dr. German's gaze down and to the left, until his eyes fall upon what Ekdahl wants him to see. Now Dr. German nods, the light of remembrance agleam across his frightened face.

"But you died," he stammers.

"Johnny died, Ivan died," replies Ekdahl. "Murray died, and Alik died. Someday soon Egil will die. I, however, live."

He leans forward and puts his mouth to the doctor's hairy ear. "In a just universe I ought to cut off your lips and make you eat them." The edge of the blade is caressing the bare skin of the doctor's neck. "I should carve out your eyeballs and feed them to the dogs. I should slice off both your ears and chop off both your hands. You would be bleeding and in great pain, begging me to put you out of a misery that Hitler began fifty years ago. But I won't. Because I need to hear you say it."

"What?" gasps Dr. German.

Ekdahl grips the doctor's right forearm, pressing it down on the desk. The man's hirsute hand splays from the pressure, his fingers arranging themselves in a neat semicircle, which appeals to Ekdahl's sense of order and harmony. He addresses him as if with an invocation.

"My Mother gave me life, but I am Death. No one comes to the father, except through me. I am Who am, the word made flesh. Look upon me, and weep, O Israel!"

The heavy razor slashes down, catching the little finger of the psychiatrist's right hand, half an inch below the nail. It digs deeply into the flesh, but not yet through the bone; Ekdahl must lean forward, applying his weight to both sides of the instrument until the joint snaps off and the blood spurts across the desk. The heavy wooden office door muffles the man's screams. "This is nothing, compared to what you deserve, which is . . ."

"To die!" The forefinger of Dr. German's mutilated right hand pointed upward for emphasis.

"To die," says Ekdahl, and once more the razor slices down, neatly severing the second joint. There is not as much blood this time.

"To die," the doctor repeated, and paused, awaiting a response from Byrne. When none was forthcoming, he started up again. "The culture of betrayal, Lieutenant." He took a deep breath. "Sy Sheinberg was a *kapo*."

"That's impossible!" exclaimed Byrne, starting from his chair. "I know Sy's story: He and his parents were in the camps. They died; he survived, and the Americans employed him as a doctor and translator. He's told me all about it."

"I know, I know," said Dr. German quietly. "That's what he told you. And that's true, as far as it goes. But there's something else you must know. Sy Sheinberg is insane."

Byrne was starting to feel sick.

"I don't mean hopelessly mad, or even that his delusions do not permit him to function normally. I know him to be an excellent forensic pathologist. But over the years, he has convinced himself of a cover story of his own device. He is living a lie. It helps him get through the day without killing himself, this and his liquor. But his account of his past is still a lie. Take if from one who knows . . ." His voice trailed away.

"Sy," prompted Byrne. "Tell me about Sy."

"I mentioned we used to call him Ziggy," said the doctor from the depths of his trance. "In the old days, his name was Siegfried Ishmael Schlüssel. It's almost Dickensian, if Dickens had written in German. Siegfried for Wagner's *Übermensch*, Ishmael for the scorned son of Abraham. And Schlüssel. Which means in German, when you pronounce the umlaut, 'key.' Ziggy Schlüssel. He changed it to Sheinberg after he married his first wife, Roz; he took her name. To try and evade the sight of God, I suppose." His tone was growing edgy.

It was time for Byrne to play his final card. He gestured at the prison-camp photograph, which was still lying on the doctor's desk. "Remember when I said that someone in this picture looked familiar? You never asked me if it was Sy. You said, 'Who?' Now it's my turn to ask you: Who else is familiar to both of us in this picture? It's this guy, isn't it?"

A good detective always knew it was better to be lucky than smart. The instant his finger came down on the face of one of the men he had taken for a German civilian, the doctor jumped from his chair and let out a long, agonized howl of grief. Byrne was suddenly very glad that the office door was soundproof, for the doctor was wailing a single word over and over. Byrne couldn't quite make it out. It sounded like *"D'brantmeldeh."*

"What?" he asked.

"D'brantmeldeh," said Dr. German through his sobs. "It rings and rings until finally you have to shut it off. *Der Brandmelder."*

And then all at once he remembered the snaggle-toothed visage of Jean . . . Brandmelder. And her husband, Bob. He lifted his finger from the picture and stared Bob's younger self in the face.

Ekdahl reaches into the psychiatrist's breast pocket and removes his handkerchief, upon which he wipes his razor clean; the bleeding man he ignores. His ablutions complete, he folds the handkerchief carefully back into squares and reinserts it into the doctor's pocket. "Now I think you're ready to answer my questions," he says. He has withdrawn the Walther and is pointing it at the center of the psychiatrist's forehead. "Such as, when did you start using your wife's name instead of your own? The name of that 'silky, black-haired Jewish beauty with fine dark eyes, skin as white as snow, a beautiful smile and a good but unpredictable na-ture,' as the lovestruck swain wrote so many years ago. 'Her only fault was that at twenty-four she was still a virgin, due entirely to her own desire.' I don't suppose that's still true, but it is a fact that you have no children. Maybe it's you who can't get it up."

Ekdahl finds the doctor's now-undivided attention quite flattering. "Another question: do you sometimes, in your nightmares, still go by that prisoner's number tattooed on your fore-arm? Why don't you admit what really happened? In Theresienstadt and on the Farm? Why don't you tell me what I want to know?"

His voice has risen, but he is not shouting. "You think I don't know about you? You think I haven't seen the documents, the proof? You think I cannot ruin you, now, with tele-phone calls to the Justice Department, B'nai B'rith and the New York Times? What an embarrassment you would be for all of them. Tell me what I want to know, what my mother has never been able to tell me, and I'll leave. Tell me, you fucking coward. Tell me the name I have never heard." Furious, he slaps Dr. German across the face with the back of his free hand.

"Tell me," orders Ekdahl, his face flushing.

He places the muzzle of the Walther against the side of the doctor's head. "I don't suppose the police would have to think very long about the death of a kapo who couldn't live with the shame and the guilt anymore," he says. "So, my dear doctor, for the last time, I would like you now to please tell me . . ."

Miss Neumann looked at Byrne reproachfully as he emerged, leaving the door afar. It was all very well for Dr. German to dissemble, but she was the one who had to cover for him. Mrs. Cooperman was going to be furious. And when Mrs. Cooperman got angry, she sometimes got abusive as well; it was one of the problems she was working on. And that awful man with the faint German accent had telephoned again, demanding to speak with the doctor. She knew from German accents, since her mother had been born in Germany.

"The name of my father. My real father."

"Don't forget your appointment slip for next time, Lieutenant," said the secretary, handing him a small piece of paper. "I hope that will be satisfactory," said Miss Neumann.

"Pardon me?" said Byrne. For the first time in his life, he was in a hurry to get upstate.

"I said, I hope that date will be satisfactory," repeated Miss Neumann. "It's the next available appointment. On the reverse of the card."

Byrne turned the card over and looked down at it. It gave today's date and a time, 8:00 P.M. The address, written on the back, was that of the Hunt Club. The handwriting was Ingrid's.

Ekdahl licks his lips and winks at her, once, lasciviously, as he leaves. Despite herself, Miss Neumann feels a little thrill, and blushes. She wonders if she should tell her shrink about it.

"That will be fine, Miss Neumann," Byrne said. He was about to say something more when the sound of shattering glass sent them both rushing into the consulting room.

Chapter Thirty-five
Ramapo, New York
Tuesday, October 23, 1990; 1:00 P.M.

Jean Brandmelder was watching *General Hospital* on the TV when the doorbell rang. The dogs were barking like crazy and she was a little annoyed at having one of her programs interrupted, but the lieutenant was a nice young man, certainly better than the kind that was growing up around here these days, and she didn't mind letting him in. As she got up, she hit the record button on the VCR. Jean couldn't understand how some folks seemed to take pride in not being able to operate their machines; she could practically make hers cook dinner. There was no sense missing a good show just because a policeman was at the door.

"What can I do you for, Lieutenant?" she asked. She was a little upset that she hadn't had time to primp properly. "If I'd a knowed you was comin', I'd a baked a cake."

"I wouldn't want you to go any trouble, Mrs. Brandmelder," Byrne replied, patting his gut. "Beside, I'm on a diet. And I won't take up much of your time. Just a couple more questions for you and your husband, if you don't mind. Is he around?" The bugs were still biting, even in October.

"Bob, he'll be back soon," she replied. "They ever find out who killed that poor fella?" The memory of it sometimes gave her the willies, especially when she thought about her own son, Jimmy. The things that could happen to a boy when he went to the city.

"Not yet, ma'am," Byrne replied, "but we're working on it." He waved his notebook in the air a couple of times, to shoo away the gnats, not that it did much good. One of the nice things about New York City was that it didn't have any bugs, if you didn't count flies and, of course, roaches.

"Any good leads?" Jean knew the lingo; God knew, she had watched enough television. She smacked her lips and pushed her hair back out of her eyes. They were blue eyes, and she was still proud of them, even if the rest of her had gone to rack and ruin, as in her most honest moments she was well aware. "Excitin' being a cop, ain't it?" Cops on TV were always getting into fistfights and kissing pretty girls.

"Sometimes, Mrs. Brandmelder," Byrne told her. "But mostly it's just boring." He was still waiting to be invited in.

"Jean, if you please," she told him. "Why don't you come on inside? Them bugs is fierce. No sense gettin' et alive."

The Brandmelder manse was furnished in contemporary American fashion. Dominating the living room was a new Sony Trinitron with a twenty-nine-inch screen, measured diagonally. Which was about all in the room that was new because everything else was slowly disintegrating, dust to dust, pasteboard to pasteboard. An ancient sofa, upon which Byrne was invited to park his carcass, was thrusting its springs through the threadbare cushions, and its arms were scarred by innumerable cat scratches. A pair of equally well sprung wing chairs flanked the viewing area, beyond which Byrne could see a cheap dining room table. Conveniently, the television sat atop a lazy Susan, so it could be rotated to face the back room when the family took its meals. The faint but unmistakable odor of cat piss permeated the house, mingling with the smell of roasting meat wafting from the kitchen.

Impulsively, he asked his first question. "Jean, have you ever seen me before? Before the other day I mean? Seen anybody that looks like me around here, maybe a friend or acquaintance of your husband's?"

Jean gave him a look-over and shook her head. "Damn, Lieutenant, pardon my French, but I'd a thunk I'd remember a handsome fella like you."

"Okay, Jean," he said, "I'd like you to think back on what happened the night before the body was found. You're usually at home, aren't you?" She didn't exactly look like she spent her evenings at the Metropolitan Opera.

"Wouldn't miss my programs. Always sit right there, where you are now."

Byrne rotated his head, and discovered that the sofa commanded quite a good view of the front yard and the road beyond. "Much traffic around here, Jean?" he inquired.

"None to speak of," said Mrs. Brandmelder. "Once in a while we get them kids hot-roddin' and I complain to the police but nothing much ever seems to get done about it. Gonna have to have someone killed I guess before anyone pays any attention. That's what happened a few years back with that stop sign—you seen that stop sign down the road a ways? Well, that there stop sign was put up after little Kelly Miller was run over by one of them semis what comes through here as a shortcut. Big truck it was, and the driver said he never saw her and I expect he didn't because them cabs is high, but anyway he squashed little Kelly like a bug and folks around here raised holy hell until a fella from the highway department come over and promised a stop sign and sure enough, couple of workers, colored fellas they was, come along couple of days later and put it up and that's how we got our stop sign. Now the trucks mostly go some other way."

"So I guess you would notice a strange vehicle if you saw one," said Byrne. "I imagine you don't get many BMWs around here."

"Don't get many corpses, either," replied Jean.

"When did you first notice the car?" Byrne prompted.

"It was there when we got up. I remember 'cause Jimmy said somethin' about it."

"What did he say?"

"Lieutenant, I'm not goin' to tell you exactly what he said, 'cause that boy has got a foul mouth on him somethin' awful. I don't know where he gets it, but kids today, they pick up all kinds of things outside the home."

"Just go ahead and paraphrase, then," interrupted Byrne.

"What?"

"Just tell me in your own words, Jean."

"Okay. Well, lemme see. Bob and me was havin' breakfast when Jimmy come down and says 'Lookit that neat car out there,' or words to that effect, and Bob and me we look out the front window—that one right over there—and we see the car parked out on the street, but not parked right, like somebody got out of it in a big hurry. Jimmy run out and took a look inside, and when he seen all that blood he come right back in the house. The car was open, you know, unlocked, with the keys still in it, and we thought that was kinda strange 'cause usually you lock up a car like that even out here in the country, even when it's a mess—I mean, Earl Suydam could tear out them seats and fix that car up good as new in no time— 'cause folks today they just ain't honest like they was when we was kids, right, Lieutenant?"

"No, ma'am, they sure aren't."

"I mean, wouldn't you worry about your car if you left the keys in it?"

"Yes, ma'am, I would. But maybe if I had just killed the owner, I wouldn't mind as much. Which says to me that somebody else brought him

here, at least one somebody else and probably two since I doubt they hitch-
hiked home in the middle of the night. You're sure you didn't hear anything?
Voices, telephones, another car engine, something that wasn't quite right?"

"Nope. Like I said, it all happened before we woke up."

Byrne listened to the silence. Here it was a weekday workday and there
was not a sound that wasn't natural. The buzz of the flies flitting around
the house and feasting on crumbs of Fritos. The distant rush of a brook.
Jean's labored, tobacco-hindered breathing. He had never noticed how loud
these sounds were before. He shuddered involuntarily: the countryside always gave him the creeps.

"Think back: maybe you got up to go to the bathroom and something

"Bob surely did. That man can't hold it no more. Doctor said something
about his prostrate gland, but Bob usually don't pay no never mind to docs.
But Bob he forgets a lot. I tell him he's got that Allzimers thing, but he don't
think it's funny. Say," she exclaimed, "who was that guy anyway? Foreign

"We think he might have been from Denmark, yes," said Byrne.

"Myself, I'm Irish. Before I got married my name was Jean Costello.
Folks 'roun' here, they think that's Italian, but it ain't. It just looks Italian,
on account of the *o* at the end, but that just goes to show you that you can't
judge a book by its cover. I'm Irish through and through, and damn proud
of it. Byrne," she said, as if suddenly remembering the lieutenant's name.
"That's Irish too, ain't it?"

"Well then that makes two of us."

"Yes, Mrs. Brandmelder, it does." And there but for the grace of God,

"I feel better talkin' with one of my own kind. Own kind ought t'stick
together, don't you think?" Byrne wondered if that was a reflection on Bob.

"No, ma'am, not anymore."

"That's a shame. Jimmy, he was married for five minutes, but it just
didn't work out. We told him he didn't have to marry that trampy Bennett
girl, even if she was expectin', her bein' prob'ly part nigger and all, pardon
my French, but kids today they don't listen to a damn thing you say, they

just go ahead and do whatever it is they want to do and if you look sideways at 'em, well . . . You got kids, Officer?"

"No, ma'am, my former wife and I were not blessed with children."

"Just as well, really. All they do is break your damn heart." Mrs. Brandmelder choked back a sob; for the first time, Byrne could see that she had been once, against all present evidence, attractive. If that's what country living did to a person, he decided, he'd stay in the city for the rest of his life.

"We're getting off the subject, Mrs. Brandmelder," he said. "Let's go back again to that night, before you went to bed. What were you doing that evening?"

"Not much. The usual. We watched some TV, then we went to bed about eleven-thirty, just before Johnny come on. We got another TV in the bedroom."

"Bob was with you? All night? Excuse me for asking."

Jean nodded. "Bob and me, there ain't hardly been a night since we was married that we ain't gone to bed together and got up together in the morning. That's the way you keep a marriage together nowadays and we been married twenty-eight years. Course not all of 'em was good, but that's another story. And Bob he's up and down all the time on account of the trouble with his prostrate makes him have to get up to make water in the middle of the night but I don't even wake up. Once my head hits that pillow, that's it for me for the night."

"You don't wake up whenever Bob gets up and comes back to bed."

"No, sir, I don't let nothin' interfere with my beauty sleep."

"So," he summarized, "if Bob were gone for a while, even a few hours, you wouldn't necessarily notice. What about Jimmy? Where was he?"

"He was out. He's always out late. Him and Billy Walters—you remember Billy from the last time you was here—them two is always foolin' around together. Sometimes I wonder what they're up to, but Jimmy's free, white and twenty-one, so I guess he can do what he damn well pleases, whether his ma likes it or not."

"Where were they? What time did he come in?"

"I don't know, 'cause I don't ask. I think he said they was out drivin' around—that's about all they do is just drive around, I think they're drinkin' and I know they're lookin' for girls, boys will be boys—and he come back about two in the morning, I know, 'cause I looked over at the clock up on Bob's dresser, the electric one we got at K-mart with the tape player inside.

I heard him come in, just like I always do because I'm still his ma and as long as he's livin' under my roof, well then I'm goin' t'worry about him until I know he's in safe and sound."

"So you do wake up sometimes?" said Byrne. That's what he'd been hoping.

That thought hadn't seemed to occur to her. "Well, I guess I do, sometimes," she admitted, and seemed surprised. "To make sure my boy's home."

"Think, Jean," said Byrne. "Why did you wake up? Were the dogs barking?"

"No, the dogs was quiet," she said. "I guess I might've heard voices."

"How many voices? Whose? Try to remember."

"Well, there was Bob's. And Jimmy's. And somebody's else's, but I jes' figgered it was Billy, drunk again. I was half asleep, don't forget, and who else could it be?"

Now they were making progress. "But it wasn't Billy, was it?"

"Now that you mention it . . ." A look of panic came across her homely face. "My Jimmy'd never do anything like what happened to that foreign fella," she protested. "He does stupid things sometimes, but he's basically a good boy and don't cause no trouble."

"I'm not implying he would, Jean," Byrne assured her. "I'm just wondering what he and Bob were talking about, and with whom."

"He ought to be home soon," Jean said. She was agitated now. "Bob's around somewhere, too. Can I offer you something? Cup of coffee?"

"Love some."

"I'm with ya there," said Jean as she headed for the kitchen. "Myself, I can't seem to get through the day without five, six cups of the stuff."

While Jean bustled around the kitchen, Byrne took a longer look around the house. It was a small, single-story ranch, built in the fifties. The living room he had already inventoried, and the dining room beyond appeared bare except for the table and an old sideboard that had somehow survived a century or so. Through the doorway he could see Jean Brandmelder doing something over the sink. He knew there would be dirty dishes in it, and didn't want to think about where his coffee cup might have been. A short hallway led to what Byrne presumed were the bedrooms; one bath, he guessed, unless Bob had built another biffy in the basement.

He turned again and looked through the front picture window. Although he and Mancuso had scoured the area, they had found nothing that had not belonged. There was no way to tell whether there had been a second vehicle, although there must have been. Across the road were only trees; to the right and left of the house, trees. How many trees did a human being need, anyway? Central Park had plenty as far as he was concerned.

He had to have missed something. Whenever you have eliminated the impossible . . .

"Here you go," Jean said, setting a brimming cup directly on the tabletop. Its ringed, stained surface gave witness to years of yeoman's service. "And speakin' of the devil . . ."

There was a screech of tires as Jimmy pulled into the driveway. Jesus God, cars were loud out here. Everything was loud. He wondered how anybody ever got any sleep with all the racket. Then the front screen door banged shut and Jimmy was in the room. "Hey," he said.

"How ya doin'?" Byrne said. He was glad the interruption gave him an excuse not to have to put the cup to his lips. "Got a minute?"

Jimmy eyed him suspiciously. "What for?" he asked.

"Jimmy, you mind your manners, boy, and say sir when you talk to a police officer," his mother said sharply.

Jimmy shot a look at his mother, then turned his attention back to Byrne, who had risen to his feet. "Yes, sir, I sure do," he said.

"Terrific," said Byrne, rising. "Why don't we step outside and go for a little stroll?"

They walked out the front door and headed into the yard. At once, the dogs came running, barking furiously at Byrne, the stranger. "Get down!" shouted Jimmy in the harsh tones of a true dog lover. "Daisy!" He swatted away a particularly pesky golden retriever, who was jumping all over Byrne. "Don't worry, she don't bite." She didn't bark that night, either; none of them did, thought Byrne. The curious incident of the dogs in the nighttime.

"That's what they all say," said Byrne. He hated dogs, cats and all manner of domestic animals. He also hated parakeets, tropical fish, hamsters, bunny rabbits and gerbils—especially gerbils. Thank God Doreen didn't have any pets. "Show me again where you found the body."

They walked for a time in silence, through the woods and into the clearing where Byrne had first seen Egil Ekdahl. "It was right over here," said Jimmy. "Makes me sick just thinking about it."

Byrne estimated that it was about a hundred yards from this spot to the driveway where Jimmy's Camaro was parked. "Well, I need you to think about it for a minute, Jimmy," said Byrne. "Start with the night before, when you were out with Billy Walters. What were you guys doing?"

"We weren't doin' nothin'," Jimmy replied. "We was just out cruising, you know, like drivin' around 'n' shit."

"Drinking?"

The young man scuffed the ground with his Converse All-Stars. "Maybe a little bit."

"Who was driving?"

"I was. I usually drive, on account of Billy's license got suspended last month for DWI."

Byrne doubted a kid like Billy would let a little thing like that stop him. "Have you ever been arrested, Jimmy?" he asked.

"No, sir, I sure have not. Been stopped by the cops a couple of times, but for little stuff like havin' a taillight out and shit like that."

Byrne looked at him. "That's not what I hear," he said sternly. In fact, he hadn't run a check on Jimmy Brandmelder, but he had to assume the boy had some criminal record. It fit the stereotype. And stereotypes, in a cop's experience, were almost always true.

"Well, you got me there," admitted Jimmy, firing a look that said *lucky guess, asshole.* "You know what they say: shot at and missed; shit at and hit. I s'pose you mean the coke thing? Fuckin' narc set me up."

"Still on probation, huh?" said Byrne.

"Yes, sir."

"Well, Jimmy, I don't want you to bullshit me anymore, 'cause if you do I'll get on the horn and have the state cops over with a probable cause search warrant for your car so fast you won't know what hit you. Are we clear on this?"

"Yes, sir, we surely are."

"How much did you have to drink that night?" asked Byrne.

"I dunno. Some, I guess. Couple of beers is all."

"And what else?"

"Well, Billy and me was over Jeanette's house for a while—Jeanette, she's kind of Billy's girlfriend—and we all got a little wrecked."

"On just beer?"

"Maybe a little grass."

Byrne waited. Jimmy sniffed.

"Little coke, too, I guess. I don't really recollect."

"Who had the cocaine? You?"

"No, sir, I don't know where it come from. Jeanette made me have some, said I weren't gonna get none if I didn't." He pronounced the girl's name *Jean-ette*, as if she were a diminutive of his mother.

"I'm sure she had to twist your arm," said Byrne. "Jeanette and Billy do a line too?"

"Yeah, we all did."

"And then you had sex with her?"

Jimmy seemed taken aback at the question. "Yeah, I guess we did," he said.

"We?"

"Me and Billy."

"You both had sex with this girl? You do that often?"

"Nah, just now and then, mostly when we're all kind of fucked up." Jimmy's voice dropped to a conspiratorial whisper. "Tell you the truth, Lieutenant, anybody can fuck Jeanette if you bring her some blow."

It was déjà vu all over again, again. "So then what happened?" Byrne wasn't interested in the details of Jimmy Brandmelder's sex life, as piquant as they might be.

"I forget. We watched a little TV at Jeanette's place and then I come home. Billy stayed behind. He was asleep when I left."

"So you got home and then what?"

Jimmy had to think. "Well, like I said I was pretty wrecked. But as I re-call it was as quiet as a fish's fart around here." He paused. "And then I heard my dad, talkin' to somebody."

"Did you see this somebody?"

"No, sir, I surely did not."

"Why not?"

"'Cause I didn't want to get no whuppin' from my dad. Sometimes he whups me when I come home blasted, 'specially if he's had a couple hisself. That beer he drinks keep him up all night pissin' so I kinda gotta sneak in, except for my ma she always wakes up no matter how quiet I am." He looked uneasy. "Can I go now? I have to use the facilities kinda urgent."

"Sure," said Byrne. "I might need to talk to you again after your dad gets home."

They headed back toward the house. "That your dad's car?" asked Byrne. A Ford pickup was pulling into the driveway.

"Yup," said Jimmy.

Bob saw them coming and stepped outside to greet them. "Howdy, pardner," he said, as if he were a character in a Western. Maybe he really was Andy Devine.

"Hello, Mr. Brandmelder," said Byrne.

"I was down the auto body shop in town," said Bob, although Byrne hadn't asked. "Some son of a bitch done put a dent in the side of my new Bronco the other day, and it's practically brand-new. But me and Earl we hammered it out and painted it over and now damn if it ain't good as new. Take a look."

"Nice job," said Byrne. He was a city kid; he could care less about cars, and didn't have the slightest idea what an overhead cam was, or a transaxle overdrive or rack-and-pinion steering or whatever they were always shouting about on the car commercials. To Byrne, autos were a necessary evil, a nuisance that tied up the city in traffic when he was in a hurry to get somewhere. But he expected Bob didn't feel that way. "I wonder if I could have a few moments of your time."

Bob opened the screen door and ushered Byrne and his son inside. "Ever find out who killed that fella?" he asked. Jean was absorbed in her programs. Byrne was having trouble hearing what Brandmelder was saying over the din, but nobody else seemed to mind.

"Not yet, but we will," shouted Byrne. "Now Jimmy here was just telling me something interesting. Weren't you, Jimmy?" Jimmy was looking down at his toes.

"Jean!" yelled Bob suddenly. "Turn that damn thing down!"

Jean reached for the remote and turned the sound lower. She was watching an Audi ad, and on the screen a sporty red sedan was zipping down the narrow cobblestoned streets of some medieval German town and up a hillside toward that famous castle, the one that looked like Sleeping Beauty might live there. A world away and apart from Ramapo. But so very near.

"Look," said Byrne. "There's whatchamacallit castle."

"Neuschwanstein," supplied Bob instinctively. His pronunciation was perfect; not New-schwan-steen, as an American might say, but Noi-schvan-schtine.

"I thought it was called Theresienstadt," said Byrne affably.

"Why don't we have a chat in the rec room, Lieutenant?" suggested Bob.

"Guy could go crazy tryin' to talk in here." He took Byrne firmly by the arm and led him out onto a screened porch at the rear of the house. His grip was still powerful.

Byrne took a seat on a damp, overstuffed divan and Bob sat down beside him. When Byrne produced Dr. German's photograph, the man let out a low whistle. "Never saw this one before. Who gave it to you? German or Sheinberg?" he asked.

Byrne remained silent.

"I should have told you this the first day," said Brandmelder, "but a promise is a promise, and sometimes loyalty has to outweigh all other considerations. Maybe it shouldn't, but it seems to me that loyalty's one thing in pretty short supply nowadays, wouldn't you agree?" He sighed. "Even so, I found in the end I couldn't ignore my conscience."

Byrne remained noncommittal, although he noted the sudden improvement in the man's grammar. "Theresienstadt," he said. "Did you know Sy Sheinberg there?"

"I might as well be honest with you, Lieutenant," said Brandmelder. "Yes I did, right after the war. At the time, I was a prisoner in a DP camp and Sy was with the American army. There was a switch for you: a Jew lording it over a German. He speaks fluent German—it's his *Muttersprache*, his mother tongue—and he was involved in the interrogations. The CIC was trying to separate out the SS officers and war criminals from the general run of prisoners, because many of those men were hiding among us. Sy would listen in, trying to pick up discrepancies in the stories, listening for SS argot."

"And that's how you met? During an interrogation?"

"Yes, exactly. One of the Amis—that's what we Germans call the Americans, 'Amis,' not very nasty, but we're not a nasty people—got it into his head that I had something to do with the camp, and he was going to make life difficult for me. But Sy was able to vouch for me. Said I had nothing to do with it, that I was just the local butcher in town. In fact, he was one of my sponsors when I came here. Said maybe I could return the favor someday."

"And did you?" asked Byrne.

"Well, yes. I hadn't seen Sy for some years—we'd stayed in touch at first, but you know how life is—so you can imagine my surprise when I got a phone call from him last week, in the middle of the night. Didn't wake up the wife 'cause, in case you hadn't noticed, she's getting to be deaf as a post, and besides which she could sleep through an earthquake; only time she ever wakes up is when that damn kid comes home. Said he had a big problem and could I help. What kind of problem? says I; a really big problem, says he, as in life and death. Well, sure, says I—after all the man saved my ass—and an hour or so later Sy shows up driving that BMW"—it came out *Bay-Em-Vay* now, German-style—"with a corpse in the trunk. You can bet I didn't ask any questions, 'cause I owed him a big one. Sy said we'd just dump the body, make it look like one of them fairy killings, and that he'd call the cops in a day or so. But I couldn't just let the poor son of a bitch rot out there. I mean, everybody expects a German to be heartless but I got human feelings, too, and that's why I called the cops the next morning. Then you showed up and the rest you know. I suppose I'm in trouble now, huh? For aiding and abetting?"

Now he knew why the dogs didn't bark. "At the very least, I would say," said Byrne. "There's also the little matter of your attempted blackmail of Dr. Jacob German. I understand you've been making threatening telephone calls to the psychiatrist." It was a guess, but he knew he was right.

Brandmelder hung his head. "You're right," he said. "I have. But not for the reason you think. That bastard's one of those Jews who can never forget. Oh, today he's mister high and mighty, but back then he was a *kapo* at Theresienstadt. He was the one who tried to frame me, who tried to blame Sy and me, tried to tell the Americans that I was SS and that Sy Sheinberg was a collaborator. And now it starts again. You're right about the blackmail, but it's Dr. German who's been blackmailing *us*. I was trying to scare him off, to help Sy, by reminding him of his past."

"I think you've helped just about enough," said Byrne.

"Wait!" said Brandmelder, putting his meaty hand on Byrne's shoulder. "I can see it in your eyes. You find it unimaginable that a Jew and a German could be friends. You're probably one of those Americans who thinks every German kept an autographed portrait of Hitler over his bed, but believe me when I tell you that the war was terrible for everybody, even us Germans."

"Let's not forget who started it," reminded Byrne.

"Look, I've done nothing wrong!" exclaimed Bob. "I've been a good citizen of this country, I've made an honest living and I've married and raised a son. So what if I left out a few details on my immigration application?

Everybody did! Whatever happened in the past happened, but it's over now, forgotten and gone." He looked at Byrne. "We were all victims. Ask Dr. German."

Byrne thought he would barf. "Dr. German is dead," he said. "He killed himself this morning." He stood up and over Brandmelder, and it was all he could do to keep himself from pistol-whipping the man. "Good-bye, Mrs. Brandmelder," he called out as he left.

"I'll watch for you on the TV!" she said, and then her voice rose. "You forgot to drink your coffee, Lieutenant!" she shouted, although she didn't turn around because *The Young and the Restless* was coming on. By the time she noticed that Bob had gone with him, they'd be halfway to the INS office in Manhattan.

Chapter Thirty-six
Midtown Manhattan
Tuesday, October 23, 1990; 8:00 P.M.

B yrne wasn't in the mood to take any shit from the doorman, especially a balding one with a ponytail and an earring. "Police," he said brusquely, revealing his shield. The man stood well over six feet and probably went two hundred and fifty pounds, a pound for each tattoo, but it never ceased to amaze Byrne how people, most of them anyway, went all respectful and got out of the way when you flashed that badge. "Nice hairdo," Byrne remarked as he blew past him. "You might try to get some hair on top to go with it." He was sure the man was mouthing the word *asshole* behind his back, but he didn't care.

"Over here." It was Ingrid.

She was standing off to one side, near the entrance. Byrne probably wouldn't have heard her over the thumpathumpathumpa of the alleged music, except that she had taken advantage of the break between "songs"— Bitch! *Mutha*-**FUCKA!**—to get his attention.

"Don't you look handsome tonight?" she said, and this time he wanted to believe that she meant it. At least his shoes matched his sport coat. Ingrid was appraising him with her customary frank stare that in American culture would be considered either forward or rude. She kissed him lightly but dispassionately, the way she would a stranger. From her demeanor, yesterday might never have happened.

She took him by the hand, and led him through what appeared to be a tableau vivant of post-plague sexual posturing. Near the dance floor, a number of persons of indeterminate gender were simulating various sex acts, including anal intercourse and fellatio. One of them, Byrne finally figured out, was a real woman, although she was dressed like a man; the women, on the other hand, were really males, attired in bustiers and lace panties. The illusion worked for a while, until you got a load of their flat asses and lousy legs.

"Fun, huh?" shouted Ingrid, and the scary thing was that Byrne was sure she meant it.

She led him deeper into the room, past the dancers and toward the bar. Instead of ordering a drink, though, she swerved off to the right, through a doorway Byrne had missed before and down some stairs. "You have to go down to get the real action," she explained.

It didn't take Byrne long to figure out that he was the only man in the place, a sublevel beneath the street that was nearly a carbon copy of the floor above. Everywhere he looked, there were women, some pretty, some pretty ugly, some dressed in tuxedos and some in evening gowns, some with their hair cropped and some that looked like Rapunzel. Women, women everywhere, and not one of them was the slightest bit interested in him. Now he knew how Orpheus felt among the Thracian women, just before they tore him apart for not joining in the Dionysian fun. And hadn't Orpheus's head floated down the Hebrus until it washed ashore on . . . Lesbos? It seemed an appropriate metaphor.

"We call this part," said Ingrid with a laugh, "the Cunt Club. It's kind of our girl joke. There she is!" He recognized Shannon right away.

"Good evening, Lieutenant," said the Rambone's mistress, exploring her upper lip with her tongue as if there might be something good to eat there, sooner or later. "How nice of you to come." Byrne started to shake hands but Shannon insisted on kissing him on the cheek. "The lieutenant and I are old friends," she explained.

"You I want to talk to," he said. "Why didn't you tell me you knew Ekdahl? Why didn't you tell me he was your lover?"

"My, my, aren't we the clever dick," said Shannon.

"We're still missing one person," said Ingrid.

"You mean Natalia?" he ventured, recalling the name on the print report.

"I don't know any Natalia," said Shannon.

"What do you want to drink?" interjected Ingrid.

"I'll get it," said Byrne.

"You can forget that chivalry bullshit down here," said Shannon. "You might not make it back from the bar alive."

"Scotch, then," he said, fishing for some money.

"Ten-year-old or twelve-year-old?" asked Shannon. "Personally, I prefer the ones a little closer to puberty." She headed for the bar.

THUMPATHUMPATHUMPA. How the hell could anyone have a conversation in a place like this? He must be getting old, because all around him couples seemed to be enjoying themselves, communicating with as little difficulty as if they were in the reading room of the New York Public Library. Was their hearing that much better? If so, it wouldn't be for long.

"Here's your scotch," said Shannon, returning with a warm snifter with something liquid in it. "It's twelve. That's the age Ingrid started menstruating."

Ingrid laughed loudly and Byrne wondered once again whether her knack for gaucherie was congenital or cultural.

"She's not your type, Lieutenant," said Shannon, sliding up to him in an exaggeratedly sexy way. She arched her back and rubbed the front of her body against his chest.

"I'm on!" exclaimed Ingrid, and vanished.

Shannon escorted Byrne nearer to the dance floor, which had cleared. The strobe lights started to flash—Byrne had thought those went out in the seventies, but obviously not—and the music rose. At least it was a recognizable song. It was "My Girl."

Ingrid slinked on. Byrne had not paid much attention to what she had been wearing, but now he saw that it was a one-piece green shift that clung to her curves in a way that even the most liberal Supreme Court justice would have to admit appealed unabashedly to the prurient interest. A crowd had gathered, all female, swaying and clapping in time to the music and occasionally shouting encouragement.

She moved like an angel. Well, that much he had already experienced firsthand. Ingrid was the kind of dancer that made everybody on the floor look at her, even in a crowded room, and now here she was, alone, the center of attention. How she moved her head one way, her arms another, her hands a third and her hips a fourth, Byrne supposed, was an inborn trick not given to men to understand. Ingrid glided across the floor, her feet never leaving the ground, but even so it was as if she was propelled along by tiny puffs of air emerging from her heels. She was like a human Hovercraft, sailing across a placid bay on a gorgeous August afternoon.

Except that she was anything but placid. She dug into the slinky lyric—it must have been a kind of house anthem, because everyone was singing along with the choruses—responding to each real or implied sentiment in a way that would have done Balanchine proud. Hers was not so much a dance as a kind of kinetic reinterpretation of language, a gloss on the text. Byrne wondered what she could do with, say, Isolde's *Liebestod*.

Exactly when he realized she was taking off her clothes he could not be sure. Perhaps he missed the first crucial move, the wave of the hands behind the back, like a conjurer, the flick of the wrist that unfastened the hook from the eye, and began unzipping the zipper; at any rate, by the time she brought her hands back in front of her chest her dress had already fallen off her shoulders and she was lowering it, demurely, beneath her bosom.

Wild cheers and shouts from the crowd.

Abruptly, Ingrid pulled her top back up and smiled, to be rewarded with catcalls. In response, she smiled again and twirled around, looking over her shoulder and raising her skirt higher and higher. Although its progress could be measured in centimeters, Byrne had no doubt it was heading true north.

Prolonged approbation as part of her behind peeked out from beneath the dress.

"Isn't she beautiful?" Shannon sighed beside him, and he found himself answering, "Yes, she is."

The song—even in its ten-minute extended-play disco version—was nearly over, and so was Ingrid's dance. Her skirt had come up high enough for him, and everybody else, to see that she was wearing nothing underneath, and now she turned to face the audience and with the most gracious gesture lowered her dress to the ground.

Ingrid kicked the garment in his direction, and he caught it on the fly, occasioning a few jeers from the women. She spun around several times, pacing herself to the music, until, as it faded, she threw her arms into the air and stood revealed before all, naked as God, in Her infinite wisdom, had created her.

"Does she just give you the damnedest hard-on?" asked Shannon. She slid her hand between Byrne's legs for emphasis, but he pulled back quickly.

Ingrid came over to him, nodding her head to the applause as she walked. "Can I have my clothes back?" she asked. "Or do you want them? You might feel more comfortable."

"I don't think so," said Byrne, handing the dress back to her. "It's not my color."

"Then help me, will you?" she commanded. "I thought you were a gentleman." She kissed him on the cheek. A few of the women still watching her started to boo. Byrne felt like a black man at a Klan rally. He smiled and waved. "Thank you," he said, "thank you very much. 'My Girl,' ladies and gentleman."

"Look who's here," Shannon said.

It was Gunther, the big German he had decked the last time they met. Byrne's knuckles started to ache in sympathetic vibration.

"Good evening, Lieutenant," said Schiffen. Byrne found himself wishing his companions would not be quite so free with his rank. It was bad enough being a male.

"I hope I don't have to pop you again, Gunther," said Byrne. "Assaulting a police officer is serious business in our country." This time he wanted to get things straight between them right off the bat.

"My fighting days are over," said Gunther, affably.

"You know each other?" asked Shannon.

"Lieutenant Byrne knows everybody," said Ingrid.

"I don't have much time," said Gunther, "and this is not exactly the most congenial place for people of our, er, persuasion. But Ingrid has asked me to speak with you." He led Byrne away from the group, toward a stairway, and they ducked beneath it.

"I want to apologize for what happened the last time," he said. "I had a little too much to drink, and I mistook you for your brother."

"Don't worry about it," said Byrne. Schiffen was the second person in two days who had told him that; another spin of the wheel of fortune. But the connection between Gunther and the late Mr. Hines eluded him.

"No, seriously," continued Schiffen. "You may not believe this, Lieutenant, but I am a man of honor." They made an odd couple, squatting behind the stairway like two coolies waiting for a bus. "You have been to Ekdahl's flat?"

"Yes."

"And you have found the video?"

"Yes," he said.

"And you watched it?"

"What's it to you, anyway?"

"I'm the one who filmed it," said Gunther. "And now that I've told you that, I'm prepared to tell you a lot of other things in exchange for your word that you will not hinder me through the INS should I wish to return to your country from time to time. I still have much business here."

"You know I can't promise that if you're involved in something illegal," said Byrne.

"Not illegal, Lieutenant," said Gunther, "simply immoral. And highly profitable."

If there were something in the penal code against that, every Wall Street broker he knew would be in jail. "Talk," said Byrne.

Instead of replying, Gunther fixed him with a frank gaze. Byrne saw hostility in his eyes, mixed with pity. "I was just thinking of Ingrid," he said. "You find her beautiful, don't you? Maybe you've even made love to her?"

"Maybe," said Byrne, looking back at her. Clothed, she was almost more desirable than she had been naked. Her arms were thrown affectionately around her companion, and they seemed to be having a wonderful time. Byrne could feel his heart beating faster.

"So you know then that this supposed engagement between her and Tom is bullshit," said Gunther.

"Yes, I do," said Byrne. "He's not her type."

"No man is," said Gunther. "Although, granted, she's a healthy woman with healthy appetites. Her relationship with your brother is another one of her appetites, but this particular desire is not for sex, it's for money. Think of it as a business agreement."

"And that business is . . . ?"

"And that business is the same business that concerned your brother and Mr. Ekdahl and now concerns you," said Schiffen. "Welcome to the hall of mirrors, in which every shape and shadow is dangerous and unrecognizable, but in which the reflection you shatter may be your own." He took a long drag on a cigarette.

"I am not a good man, Lieutenant," continued Gunther. "I have made my living off the weaknesses of others—off the weaknesses of people like your brother, who made such an effective motion picture debut. I am not proud of this, but neither do I apologize for it, because that is the hand fate dealt me, and we Europeans still believe in fate. Because fate is a much more believable explanation for the things that happen to us all than your cheap rationalism."

"Not my rationalism," said Byrne. "Shit Happens, that's my motto."

"Shit happens," said Schiffen, "and this shit has happened to you. The problem is, you don't want to face it. You call yourself a detective, but this is one case you do not wish to solve, isn't it? Because you are afraid of what you might find out, because you lack the capability to understand God's capacity for evil, His relish of it. You think evil is something that, with enough good will, or presidential task forces, or white paper reports, or newspaper editorials, or class-action lawsuits, can be wished away; in the culture of know-nothingism there is no sin that cannot be forgiven, because in your childish American Weltanschauung *there is no sin*. But what does the Lord say? Is God kind? Does he forgive? 'And they shall go forth, and look upon the carcasses of the men that have transgressed against me: for their worm shall not die, neither shall their fire be quenched; and they shall be an abhorring unto all flesh.' Thus Isaiah 66:24. Has it ever occurred to you that there are some things that cannot be forgiven? Some transgressions that must and do have terrible consequences? Some prices that, in the end, have to be paid? This is what crime and punishment is all about, and if you do not believe that, then what are you doing in your profession? You have no more moral authority than the little Dutch boy with his finger in the dike, trying to hold back the flood. No wonder no one pays any attention to you.

You are an authority figure with no authority, a moral exemplar with no morals."

"Tell me about Ekdahl," said Byrne.

"I would rather tell you about Tom," replied Gunther. "For all his bluster, he is a weak man, especially around women. But weak men are often the most dangerous, for they act out of emotion instead of logic." Byrne could think of more comfortable places in which to discuss his brother's character, but this one would have to do.

"I filmed right up to the moment the girl died. I had no idea that was going to happen and neither did anyone else, except Ekdahl. I shut off the camera and came in from the other room. Tom was of course furious, but helpless; he was still not quite sure what had happened. The other girl was screaming in the corner over the body of her friend, but Ekdahl had already cleaned up and dressed. It was only a matter of time before the Moscow police would arrive and arrest Tom for murder. I heard Ekdahl say, 'Now you're working for me. Help me find what I am seeking.'"

"What is that supposed to mean?" asked Byrne.

"That I cannot tell you," said Gunther. "But it is clear they had some understanding. And it is equally clear that Tom had every reason to want Ekdahl dead. Whether Tom killed Ekdahl I can only suspect."

The big German stretched his arms skyward, arching his back and yawning. It was only a reflex, Byrne told himself, a reaction to the cramped conditions, but it looked for all the world as if he were beseeching heaven. He narrowly avoided conking his head on the stairs as he stood up.

"I've given you the key, Lieutenant," said Gunther, "and I've shown you the door." Byrne didn't bother to correct the idiom. "My conscience and my business dictated that I must. And now I am finished with you. I go back to Germany, where I am only half a human being. Unlike you, though, I accept my fate. Perhaps you should try that some time, Lieutenant; in the end, it really is less painful."

"Are you guys engaged yet?" said Shannon. From his awkward position, all Byrne could see of her was her legs, encased in fishnet stockings, and the hem of her black leather skirt.

"No," said Gunther. "In fact, we've decided to break up."

"I knew it was just sex," laughed Ingrid.

"*Auf Wiedersehen*, ladies," said Gunther. "Or perhaps I should say *Lebe wohl*."

"Wanna dance, Lieutenant?" said Shannon. She took Byrne's arm and dragged him onto the dance floor.

"You should have seen Eddie here—a vision of loveliness. The way that boy dressed would put any woman to shame. He was so good, even the dykes used to hit on him."

Byrne thought back to the row of women's clothes in Ekdahl's closet. Arms around each other, they slow-danced to a hard rap song. "You knew Ekdahl, knew him as Paine," accused Byrne. "You knew he liked to beat people, to scream something in Russian at them while he was torturing them. And yet you lied to me. Why?"

Shannon ran her hands down his back, and clutched his buttocks, pulling his crotch closer to hers as they swayed, not quite in time to the beat.

"Because you weren't ready to know."

"And I am ready now?"

"You tell me." Her face was close to his, and he could smell her breath, a mixture of toothpaste, alcohol and cigarettes. "True self-knowledge is a wonderful and powerful thing, but how many of us are ready for it?" She kissed him lightly on the cheek.

They were dancing very close together now, their bodies intertwining, her leg between his, her hands pulling him ever closer, hugging him ever more tightly. From over his partner's shoulder, Byrne could see Ingrid smiling at him. Or was it laughing?

"You're hot for Ingrid, aren't you?" she whispered. "Everyone is. Even me. But forget it. You can look, but you can't touch. Or maybe you can touch, but you can't really have."

Slowly, Shannon guided Byrne's hand down the front of her dress, over the curve of her breasts and down the flat expanse of her stomach. "Not everybody in here tonight's a lesbian, you know." His hand passed over her abdomen and, just below it, encountered a small but unmistakable bulge between her legs.

"Are we having fun yet?" she asked him.

"I am," said Ingrid, somewhere in the distance.

Chapter Thirty-seven
The Upper West Side
Wednesday, October 24, 1990; 10:00 A.M.

Byrne buzzed Dr. Sheinberg's apartment three times before he decided he'd have to find another way in. The doctor hadn't been seen at the morgue all week, which was not like him. Miss a day here and there, depending on the size of the binge. But not three days; never three days.

He was more certain than ever that Tom was the one who killed Ekdahl. It all fit: Ekdahl was Russian and Tom had recently been in the Soviet Union; Ekdahl was blackmailing Tom with the sex video; the video's apparent Russian locale; and they were both after the putative Oswald file, if such a thing really existed and wasn't another of Tom's red herrings. Not to mention Ingrid: Tom and Ekdahl must have been jealous of each other's relationship with her. Even the picture of his mother now made some sense: Tom obviously had it with him at some point and forgotten or lost it in Ekdahl's car. That business in the consulate Friday night had been a diversion—Pilgersen must have caught on to something—to put him off the trail and to give Tom some leverage. But what Tom didn't know was that little Frankie had some leverage of his own. Now if he could only get his hands on those bullets. . . . He was positive that the .38 slug in Ekdahl's belly would prove to have come from Tom's revolver. After a visit to Sy he could hand Tom's head to White on the silver platter of promotion. Captain of Detectives Francis X. Byrne, deputy extraordinaire to the new Police Commissioner J. Arness White, and his mother's favorite son: it sounded pretty good to him. It was payback time: for Mary Claire, for Doreen, for his whole damn life.

The only thing left to figure out was what hold Tom had over Sy that he could get him to bring the body up here. The beauty of this solution, however, was that he could ignore all the case's other complications as the coincidences and irrelevancies they surely were, including the various mafias and intelligence agencies. Dr. German was right: the simplest explanations were always the best. Now, at last, he had a handle on Occam's Razor.

He rang another bell, this one marked "Berkowitz," and pushed open the glass door when Berkowitz, whoever he or she was, let him in. "Bless you, my son of Sam," Byrne said to himself as the lock sprang. As he entered the elevator—there was no doorman—he could hear a woman's voice calling anxiously from the upper recesses of the stairwell. "Hello? Hello?" she said, curiosity mixing with fear in her voice, and then slammed her door safely shut.

Byrne rode to the sixth floor and walked down the hall to 6-J. It was quiet in the corridor, with only the sounds of a single television set intruding upon the afternoon stillness. At the other end a man was letting himself into his apartment, but he took no notice of Byrne's presence and said nothing as he closed his door quickly behind him and double-locked it. It was typical of New Yorkers that in the midst of one of the noisiest cities in the world they should maintain so faithfully the unwritten proscription against talking or even making eye contact in the hallways.

There was a mezuzah next to the door. There was a mezuzah next to almost every door. He rang the bell. It was the kind of doorbell that when you pressed in it went "ding" and you released it went "dong." Ding-dong. Ding-dong. Nobody home. "Sy?" he called out softly, but there was no reply.

He tried the doorknob, but of course it was locked. Even if you wanted to, even if you didn't throw the dead bolt, put the chain on and drop the metal bar, it was impossible to leave your door unlocked in New York. Neighbors just didn't "drop by," and the only unexpected visitors you were likely to receive would be very unwelcome ones indeed. For how many of the residents of this building had the same been true fifty years ago? He felt like he was intruding upon the Warsaw Ghetto.

There was a creak as the door to 6-H opened behind him and a female voice issued forth. "Is there a problem?" she inquired cautiously; Byrne noticed she kept the chain on.

"Hi," he replied cheerily. "I was looking for Sy Sheinberg. I thought he might be home, but there's no answer. Have you seen him?"

The door opened a little wider. Byrne apparently didn't look too threatening. He was, after all, white. "Not lately," said the voice. The name on the doorplate read M. AND M. KLOPFER.

"You must be Mrs. Klopfer," Byrne ventured. "Sy always said he had nice neighbors."

"I'm a little worried about Dr. Sheinberg," came the reply, still wary. "If he's going away he always asks Morty and me to feed his cat."

"Zelda," supplied Byrne, further displaying his bona fides.

"Zelda," repeated Mrs. Klopfer. She had unlatched the door and was facing him across a three- or four-foot safety zone. She might look old, but Byrne knew she could slam that door in his face and lock it in Olympic-record time. "Do you want to call? Maybe he's left a message on his answering machine, saying where he is."

"That would be very nice, thanks," said Byrne. "It's kind of urgent."

The door to 6-H opened to admit him and Byrne stepped inside. "Nice place," he said ritually as Marion Klopfer showed him the telephone. She was a small, dark-complexioned woman in her mid-sixties, with her gray hair tied back neatly in a bun. She had the slight trace of a central European accent.

It was a typical New York City apartment: a moderate-sized living room, with a tiny kitchen off to one side, and a single darkened bedroom whose doorway was visible across the room. The furnishings were simple and homey, with a couple of expensive paintings on the walls and the usual plethora of books. Byrne had the feeling that if he looked, he'd find old Pete Seeger records, pamphlets proclaiming the Rosenbergs' innocence and back issues of *The Nation* in the Klopfers' library. Byrne would bet a round at O'Reilly's that she hadn't left the perceived safety of her immediate neighborhood for years, maybe decades; like many New Yorkers, she had become a prisoner in her own home. "Do you know the number? It's unlisted."

"Yes, ma'am, I do," said Byrne, dialing. Sheinberg's phone rang four times; on the fifth ring the answering machine picked up.

"Hello, you have reached 227-4648. I'm sorry I'm not at home right now, but if you'll kindly leave your name and telephone number I'll be happy to return your call as soon as possible." It was Sy's baritone, all right, the words slightly slurred. Byrne expected a beep, but now the message continued in a language he didn't know. He hung up and turned to his hostess. "Mrs. Klopfer," he said, "do you speak Russian or Polish or would you know either one if you heard it?"

Marion Klopfer nodded. "I think I can still get around in both of them," she said. "I was born in Lvov, but I met my husband, Mordecai, in this country, when I was working on Seventh Avenue. He's American, but his people came from Kiev, so I know even a little Ukrainian. And Yiddish, of course. Not to mention some Hebrew." She dialed Sheinberg's number again and this time Byrne could hear it ringing faintly across the hall. "Hello, you have reached . . ."

Mrs. Klopfer was listening intently.

"It's in Russian," she reported. "It's a message for somebody named Sasha," she said when she had hung up. "Is your name Sasha? I don't know any Sasha, do you, Mr. . . . ?"

"Byrne," he replied. "Francis Byrne."

"You know where his office is?" she inquired. "Maybe he's there."

"Maybe he is," said Byrne. "I think I'd better head on over there right now."

"Not before we check on Zelda," Mrs. Klopfer said. "I have a key. He left one with us years ago in case of, you know, emergencies." She rummaged around in the bedroom and returned with the key to 6-J. Together, they stepped across the hall and let themselves in to the apartment of Seymour Sheinberg, M.D.

"What a mess!" exclaimed Mrs. Klopfer.

Some of the furniture was knocked over, although it did not look as if there had been a struggle. More like a rage. Make that a drunken rage, Byrne thought, as he spied the shattered whiskey bottle on the floor next to Sheinberg's armchair; the place reeked of booze. And, to his practiced nose, blood; shards of glass had blood on them, and as Byrne fished around on the floor, picking up the pieces, he came upon a single tooth. He hoped Mrs. Klopfer wouldn't notice.

"You'd better stay right here, Mrs. Klopfer," he told the suddenly anxious neighbor. "Don't worry," he added as an afterthought. "I'm a cop."

"I knew it all along," she said. "You think I let just anybody into my apartment?"

Byrne found Zelda where he half-expected to, in the refrigerator, where any self-respecting coroner would keep his patients. From the angle of her head, he judged that her neck had been broken. And Sheinberg's heart, too, he reflected. Zelda had been laid lovingly next to the milk on the top shelf, molded into a cozy little ball, as if she were sleeping. He closed the fridge's door reverently and went into the bedroom.

In contrast to the living room, it seemed to be in perfect order. The bed was made and apparently unslept in. Sy's not particularly extensive wardrobe—mostly sport coats, shirts and slacks; he never wore a tie—was hanging neatly in the closet, and in his dresser his socks and underwear were arranged carefully in their respective drawers. Only one thing was missing, and Byrne somehow knew it would be even before he looked. The pistol that Sheinberg had bought for self-protection after Amy Stevens had bled to death on his operating table because he was too drunk to suture properly, after the lawsuit, the publicity and the avalanche of anti-Semitic death threats, the Charter Arms .22 that he had always kept in the top drawer, was gone.

"Is everything all right?" called out Mrs. Klopfer from the living room, her tone indicating that she feared everything wasn't.

"Looks okay to me," said Byrne, returning to the front room.

Mrs. Klopfer was still staring at the disorder. "So where's Zelda?"

"I think she must be out," Byrne lied.

"Then what's that awful smell?" she asked, sniffing the air.

"Some meat in the refrigerator went bad," replied Byrne. "But I have to admit that I'm a little worried about Sy."

"You're worried? What do you think I am? He never leaves a mess like this. Oh, sometimes he drinks a little, and sometimes we hear him yelling when he's had too much, and sometimes he brings those colored girlfriends home with him, why he can't find a Jewish girl I'll never understand, and him a doctor, but you know his family all died in the camps during the war, and after what he went through we just leave him alone and never complain to the board, even though we could if we wanted to, it's our right under the bylaws. Thank God I got out in thirty-four, although the rest of my family was not so lucky . . ."

While Mrs. Klopfer was launching into her doleful family history, Byrne had picked up Sheinberg's phone and dialed his office number, but got only the voice mail. He hit the check-greeting button on Sy's answering machine. "Mrs. Klopfer, could you please listen to this one more time and tell me exactly what he's saying?"

She listened to the mysterious Russian words again, and shook her head.

"I'm sorry," she told Byrne. "It's been a long time." She shrugged. "I've tried to forget—"

"Just do the best you can," Byrne said. "Give me the gist of it."

She seemed to take that as a challenge. "You'll get more than just the gist." She drew herself up and listened once more. "Here goes. It says, 'Sasha: Now we do not have to fear a man with the rifle. This, as doctors say, is a quintessence.'" She looked at him apologetically.

"What the hell does that mean?" exclaimed Byrne.

"How should I know?" said Mrs. Klopfer. "Do I look like I work at the UN?"

"No, Mrs. Klopfer," said Byrne, "you certainly don't."

"Thank you," she said, with considerable satisfaction. "Those anti-Semites . . ."

Chapter Thirty-eight
Manhattan, Queens and Brooklyn
Wednesday, October 17, 1990;
5:00 P.M. and 8:00 P.M.

Out the window and onto the fire escape that leads down to the muddy backyards that separate the buildings on Carmine and Leroy Streets. His heels kick up the dust as he drops the last six feet onto the ground. Miserable little plots that host no growth, just dirt and stones and debris: like Moscow yards. He feels at home. The West Fourth Street IND station is just a few blocks away. The Italians always ride in cars.

Now Ekdahl feels pain, a pain in his abdomen that is like a fire below his belt. He has known pain all his life, from the time he was a boy, when Dad O'Brien would beat him with his belt; from the time on the Island. They had taught him to withstand pain, as if he needed to be taught that, but now, for the first time, the pain hurts.

In cars, so they will never think to look for him below the surface of the street. Riding around in wopmobiles on their big fat asses, they were slow and stupid, which is why they were losing to the Chinese, to the Jamaicans, to the Colombians, to the Russians—losing to all the groups tougher and hungrier and more willing to kill anybody and everybody in pursuit of their goal, which was and always will be money. Across Bleecker and up Sixth Avenue, it is an easy jog and nobody looks twice at him as he ducks into the southwestern entrance of the huge station, the underground crossroads of the Village, two levels of roaring, screeching, squealing trains that come and go in a shower of sparks, ferrying their human cargo through the stygian tunnels and into the eternal subterranean night.

Is he bleeding? A little; maybe it isn't so bad. But they said that the bullet that kills you is the one you neither see nor hear, and he has neither seen nor heard this one, only felt it, a single shot when his guard was down, one shot from out of the darkness, no word of warning, no comment, no smart remark, nothing. Just the obscene, unexpected spit of a pistol while his attention was elsewhere, and then the pain.

Here came the train, an E train that will drop him at Queens Plaza, where he can grab a cab and be at his destination within five minutes. The E train used to be a Jewish train, serving the shtetls of Forest Hills and Kew Gardens. Now it is a branch of the Orient Express, and where it crosses the number 7 IRT line, at Roosevelt Avenue, it resembles Hong Kong at rush hour. A blond, white male on the E train was starting to be a rarity and as Ekdahl looks around, he sees that most of the newspapers in evidence are Asian and most of the readers are women, who sit stolidly with their redolent shopping bags between their legs. How many chickens have died today?

Where is he hit? The pain is all out of proportion to the amount of blood, but it is endurable, and he can walk. It is a long way to where he is going, but the pain can be tolerated and the blood stanched; his car, the BMW the consulate gave him, is parked not far away. Within it, he is almost home. Almost safe. He just has to drive for a while.

The huge train rumbles into the station and Ekdahl hops aboard. For all the blather about safer subways, you still hardly ever saw a cop, even a dumb Transit cop. If he had been Bernhard Goetz, they would never have caught him. He would have smoothly sailed out of town, and certainly never would have turned himself in. Ekdahl was not in New York at the time of that incident, but he has read all about it; what Goetz did seems perfectly normal and understandable to him, if technically crude. Shoot first and ask questions later: the American way.

He is afraid. This is a new emotion for him. Not during the worst days at Sakhalin was he ever afraid. It must be the shock. He fumbles for the key, stabs it into the ignition and ignites the engine. The car is a stick shift, so he must use both hands to drive it. He would prefer to keep one hand pressed tightly against his abdomen, but he has no choice. He does not want to die in an automobile accident on the Brooklyn-Queens Expressway, his car ricocheting off the ugly concrete median and colliding with an unregistered vehicle belonging to a family of Puerto Ricans out for a spin, there to be found by some beat cop and cityside reporter, to have his injuries or death trumpeted across the pages of the Daily News *or* Post *tomorrow, fodder for the tabloid underclass.*

Where he is going is the last place any of Genna's goombahs is likely to look for him, even if they are Queens homeboys. It is amazing how comfortable he feels in New York, even in the outer boroughs, in the bridge-and-tunnel purdah that is terra incognita to most Manhattanites. He has made it a point to get to know the western sector of Long Island, the two fabulously irrelevant and overpopulated boroughs, the presumptuously royal counties of Kings and Queens. Tonight, in anticipation of his next appointment, and also as a precautionary measure, he has parked his car in Queens, near Calvary Cemetery, where Mother has said he will find what he is looking for.

The blood is seeping through his clothing, but surely the wound cannot be that serious. Why, then, does he fear? On the Island they had beaten him, and that had been the least of the physical torture. Were it not for the Light . . . He was invulnerable, as Mother had always promised, Achilles without a heel. But the gunshot, the bullet that he had not heard and of course had not seen, fired from the gun he had not expected, is causing him an anguish of the soul even more than of the body.

He instructs the cab to stop a few blocks from his destination. Pays the driver and walks down the quiet Queens streets. Queens, the "borough of homes"; the borough of squat, dumpy thirties apartment blocks was more like it. At once peaceable and appalling. Where is the life of the mind? And where the life of the soul, the great Russian soul? Here is the bell.

He cries out, and curses himself for his weakness. Can he not be true to Mother's ideal? Has he not heard, countless times, the stories of his father, how he survived torture much worse than any Vanya had ever experienced, survived and flourished, never breaking, never cracking, never giving in to his enemies? Has he not heard, on the Island, about his father's crimes?

How the very enormity of those crimes had given him the strength to persevere, to endure the direst provocations? And now he is so confused. The name . . .

A woman answers the bell. He searches for the resemblance he knows must be there. There is no time for a preamble. He pushes his way in the door, and as she steps back, he thinks he sees something in her face. Is it shock, fear or recognition? "I am Vanya," he says. She says nothing. "And I have come for the truth."

The Light is in his eyes; he has never been able to escape it. Even when it is dark, it still shines; even when he closes his eyes, when he thinks of Mother, the Light is still there, immutable and eternal. The Light is blazing behind his eyes, fracturing into hundreds of pinpricks, shooting like stars, soaring like eagles, glowing like a thousand godheads, drawing him onward, toward the eternal flame. But this Light is the light of Lucifer, the Bringer of Light.

"Sit down." She speaks in Russian, and her voice is calm and controlled, like Mother's. Mother, of course, is more beautiful. He sits. "Would you like some tea?" Some *chai;* "tea" in Russian, "life" in Hebrew.

Despite the pain, he manages to negotiate the side streets of Brooklyn without mishap. He could find Mother's house in his sleep. There is Brighton Beach Avenue, a left turn onto Brighton Fourth Street and he is home and staggering up the short driveway, through the door and into her arms. Even through his agony he can see her shining face.

"I have been expecting you," she says. "I have been expecting you for twenty-four years, and now you have come." Her voice has none of Mother's comfort in it, none of Mother's sweet music.

"My son," she breathes. "Can it be that you are hurt?"

"So my sister still lives. Is she well? Did they harm her terribly?" He is not sure what exactly she means, for Mother has always been well, could never be anything but well, at least as long as he lives. The woman bustles with the tea, setting the drink before him with a practiced hand, but not of course as practiced as Mother's.

"Can it be that you are bleeding?" There is concern in Mother's voice. She has her hand on his stomach, where his clothing has been dyed russet by the blood, the blood that yet surges forth and will not stop, though he might will it, though he command it, like Canute with the waves. But blood is only seawater by another color and just as disobedient as its oceanic cousin, and it comes and it comes and it will not stop because it has a life of its own and is taking his life away with it. His tears scald his face like molten lead and he can only hope that they will not burn her as well.

"Did they?" she asks, but just now he is not, God forgive him, interested in talking about Mother. He wants to know about his father, and this woman knows where he is. She will not sit, but instead wanders around the room, her hands pressed together as if in prayer.

On the couch there is peace. Mother is moving, not quickly, but deliberately. He hears her speaking on the telephone, talking warmly in Russian as his body grows cold. His body heat is evaporating, ascending heavenward. He can feel it, leaving him, no longer necessary, irrelevant to the further functioning of the universe. The thought that life can somehow go on without him he finds curious.

"There is so much to tell, but where do I begin? How do I begin?" Her hands are no longer praying; instead, they are wringing, as if she would somehow wring the truth from hands that would otherwise speak only falsehoods.

Mother is in the bathroom now, and he can hear the water running in the tub. The water of life. She is calling to him to undress and come to her, as always.

"You want to know where he is," she says. "But there's something else you need to know first." She has stopped moving about, stopped all her fidgeting. Her voice is calm and controlled and cold.

"Come, Vanya," he hears her saying. Her voice wafts from the other room, the small room near the back of the small house, and he can almost smell its perfume.

She draws near to him, and strokes his hair. "You look so much like her."

"Come to Mother," she commands and, instinctively, he obeys.

"Your mother was always more beautiful than I," Irina says. "When we were children, it was always your mother that the ladies would fuss over, always Natasha that everyone said would be famous, the famous dancer, the famous actress. Never me. Natasha. Even her name was more beautiful than mine."

Somehow, he has managed to pull off his clothes. Some of the blood has already congealed, and when he pulls his pants down the clots come off and the bleeding begins anew. He kicks off his trousers with a practiced motion; he is not wearing undershorts, because he never does. And now he is naked, walking into the bathroom, staggering, but making his way.

"I was so jealous," she says. "We all were, Vera and Marina and I. We were all envious of Natash', because she was the one who had been blessed by God, while we were just ordinary girls with an extraordinary sister whom God had marked. We would spend hours in front of the mirror, in our small flat with only one bathroom, hours trying to make ourselves up to be half as beautiful, half as radiant, as our sister Natalia, but we never could because God had made her perfect, and us he had made merely human."

He has reached the bathroom, where a tub full of warming water awaits him. Mother is there and, like him, she is naked. In ordinary circumstances, he might feel himself stirring, might feel that wonderful quickening that he could feel only in her presence. But not now.

"And so we hated her, even as we loved her. Did she ever tell you this? I doubt she has. Why should she? It was our problem, not hers. I knew I was not beautiful. How, I wondered when I was little, could we all have the same mother and yet each turn out so differently? But it was the luck of the draw, the spin of the wheel of fortune, that made each of us what we were."

She offers him her breast. "I give you life," she says.

"So isn't it ironic," she says, "that we all ended up here?" She pours him another glass of *chai*, of life, but she herself drinks from another container, whose liquid is amber. "All of us, in turn, made the journey across the sea, to take up and live out our false lives, to answer to others about what we did and where we went and who we knew and who we slept with, and we did as we were told because we were good girls, and nobody ever had to know what else we were."

He opens his mouth. On the table lies the Helper, shiny and beckoning.

She drinks the amber again. "And nobody did know. Not the husbands, nor the daughters, nor the sons. No one, except you, because you were the only person she trusted, because you were the only person she never betrayed, and even you do not know everything or else why would you be here? Do mothers ever tell their sons the truth? Why should we? Why would we?"

He slides into the water, with her nourishing breast still in his mouth.

"Until today I was not sure she was still alive. They told me she had died. Even when you were born I did not see her or speak with her, because that would have been a violation and in those days violations were punished very severely. Today, it's different. The war is almost over, and we have lost, and that is probably why you are here, to save yourself. I myself have been here so long I have practically forgotten what life was like on the other side, what the reasons were for my coming here, what in fact I am still doing here, except for the children perhaps, because children are something they can never take away from you, no matter how hard they try. Even when they are not yours."

He can feel her hand in his hair, one hand, the other washing his chest, washing his stomach, washing the wound that will not, cannot, heal.

"But I could sense her. Natalia and I were the closest in age, and we always had a special feel for one another. When they split us up, because our mother was a whore and a drunkard and thus an enemy of the state and of the people, she and I stayed together. Vera went to live with her father's mother, but Natasha and I went to the orphanage because nobody wanted to take care of us. And there we stayed until the state forgave us, and the Party came for us, and gave us life."

"Do not be afraid," Mother says. "The doctor will be here soon. I have called him, and he will come, to look after you, to heal you. He, who brought you into the world. With him, with us, you are safe."

She pours the last remaining dregs of the bottle into her glass. His own glass of tea is long since drained but she does not notice. "And trained us, and sent us here. To serve the great idea of the people." To his surprise, she lets out a loud, almost mannish, laugh. "And what was this great idea? To lie, to cheat, to deceive? To love someone and betray him? To employ our bodies as if they were our minds, to arouse and excite and seduce and abandon? To give of ourselves, to sacrifice our femininity, in the furtherance of—what? Of politics? Of ideology? Of the great idea of the people? Do you still believe in that? You, of all men? If you do, you are a fool. *Gore, gore, Rusi. Plac', plac', russki ljud!*"

Mother is weeping, silently, and with dignity. She is standing above him, exquisite in her perfection, frank in her beauty, innocent in her nakedness. Her hips are at eye level, and as he looks at her, he can see all the way to the locus of life itself. He places his arms around her hips, in order to draw her nearer. How fitting that this sight should also have been his first, the sight of those mysterious depths, that ineffable conduit, that endless, eternal passageway from this life to the next, whatever this life may be, whatever the next may hold. Even as they dim, he has eyes for nothing else.

"But was it not ever so? With our people? With all our sacrifices, what do we have to show for them? Is there something wrong with us, some deficiency in our brains or in our character, that we cannot succeed? Are we not smart enough? Do we lack courage? Or are we condemned to misery, our efforts futile, our actions laughable in the sight of God? We, who believed that religion was the opiate of the masses—is it thinkable that we are the sport of the gods, who punish us for our blasphemy?"

Her hands run down and along his body as she starts to shave him, stroking him in all the familiar places to make him beautiful once more. He loves the feel of steel against skin, only this time the feeling is different. Though she may kiss him, he can no longer feel the stimulation that used to send the blood coursing through his veins, the same blood that now colors the waters in which he reposes. The rapidly cooling waters, that once nourished and sheltered and protected.

"No, we cannot be wrong," he hears himself saying. "They have assured me that here I will find what I seek. And though I may yet serve the great idea of the people, so also do I serve myself, and seek to learn the truth. The truth that you, perhaps alone, know. The truth which I can get from no one else."

How cold the waters grow, despite the best efforts of his heart to warm them.

She is looking at him, fixing him with the judgmental stare that he has seen only in the eyes of a woman as she contemplates whether to go to bed with a man, whether to strip herself naked and reveal her most intimate physical secrets to him, whether to expose herself to his gaze and offer her body to his touch, whether to confer upon him the ultimate gift of herself. The same look he sees now in her eyes, the same assessment he feels in her gaze, the same weighing and assaying and appraising. There is nothing he can do to alter or hasten the process. "You have so much to tell me," she says, "and I have so little to say to you."

The razor glides over his skin, meeting no resistance.

"I am touched that she still had the photos; I got rid of my copies long ago. We had them taken one summer when we were teenagers, after we went to work for the People. In those days, the state still had enough money to send us on a Black Sea holiday from time to time. When that picture was taken, I was, I think, fifteen years old, and Natalia was seventeen. That was the summer we wore our skimpiest suits and felt the eyes of the men moving over our bodies as we walked on the beach, but always there were more eyes on Natasha than on me, more eyes caressing her than me, although I had my admirers, but she always had more, and better. As if we were animals, as if we were breeding stock, cattle that could make the plow move faster, hens that could make the cocks crow louder. Do you think we could not see them? Do you think we did not notice the lust, and the loathing in the eyes of the women? Do you think we did not revel in our power to corrupt and entice? But her power was always greater than mine."

Mother leans over him, sharing the bloody bath.

"What has she told you about me? How did she describe me? Or am I simply a phantom of her past?"

"Help me, Mother," he says.

His face has betrayed him. "I suppose I am. Natash' probably still lives, as she always has, in a fantasy world of her own device." She empties the bottle into the glass, and tosses it aside, Russian-style. It shatters loudly, satisfyingly, against the far wall. "You know," she says, "I pity you. I fear you as well, because I can guess what you have been through, and what you are capable of. But before whatever is going to happen actually does, you should know that, in every respect, you are her child. There is nothing of your father in you, only your mother. If woman born of woman could re-create herself, could give birth without intervention of the male, could split like an amoeba, could indulge in parthenogenesis, then that woman is your mother. She is a monster. And so, therefore, are you."

"I can help you, my son," she says. "I will help you." She is sharpening the razor once more.

He rises to his feet, in anger. No one may speak of Mother in this manner.

He is sinking ever deeper into the water now and he can feel his eyes closing in sleep. Her hands are once again upon his head, stroking him as she used to do when he was a child, and the water plays at his throat.

"No!" he cries. "I am here to learn from you the whereabouts of my father. I am here to learn the name of my father. Not the name he used in the Soviet Union, not the name of Idol he was given after his cowardly defection, nor Barman or Donor or any of the other names others gave him. His real name. Tell me this, and where he is, that I may find him!"

Her hands, as always, calm him.

"You poor bastard," she says with pity. "How they, and she, have deceived you! Have you learned nothing? Do you know nothing? Do you understand nothing?"

Slowly, gently, she pushes his head back, so that his hair is wet by the lapping water. She will wash his hair, just as she did when he was a boy. He can feel the warm water pouring over his crown, as if he were being baptized again. As if he were being christened, washed in the blood of the Lamb.

"No, I suppose not. It would be just like her not to know who your father really was. She would consider that somehow not important. That's why she was also so good at what she did. It is so easy to lie convincingly when you really believe. And your mother was always a believer."

His head is tilted all the way back now. Mother's breasts are again before him, ripe and full as the day he was born, and he opens his mouth to receive them.

"Mother is not a liar!" he shouts. But the woman is defiant, uncaring and unafraid. All his life, he has been used to fear, the fear that others felt in his presence, even when it disguised itself as curiosity or repulsion. He moves toward her, at once to threaten and, perhaps, to embrace. "My father," he demands. "Where is he?"

"My son," she says.

"Don't you mean *who* is he? Isn't that much more important to you? And do you really think that after protecting him all these years, I'm going to let a freak like you push me around?"

"My beautiful son," Mother says, kissing him.

"A freak and a monster!" Her voice enrages him, and so he puts his hand on her, just as he hears a door open. But his senses are engaged; his sixth sense, the one that warns him of danger, is busy, because it is focused on the danger from her, the danger that always attends revelation. And then comes the pain, spit from the unknown, like a fist in his midsection. And the face behind the pain, a face he has never seen before, but in it something familiar, something that makes him uneasy in his soul, because in it he can see nothing except himself. Not his face, and yet his face; not him, but him.

From far away, he can hear the door opening, and a low masculine voice speaking. He cannot make out the words, but Mother replies: "In here."

He turns, to flee, to run. Run from the only person who can do him harm, from whom he cannot flee, and that person is himself.

"He's in here."

Running from the man with the gun. Whence has he come? This specter from his subconscious, wished-for and yet not wished-for, this creature, this mystery, this doppelgänger, this man. Ecce homo.

He can feel the eyes running over his body, his naked body, like hands, only this time the looks of appraisal are more dispassionate, as if he were a whore in Times Square, and the touch impersonal, as if he were a piece of meat in the butcher shop on Little West Twelfth Street.

A cry, a groan and then he is out the window, which shatters into a thousand pieces as he crashes through, his blood marking every step. Out the window and onto the fire escape that leads down to the muddy backyards in this small corner of hell.

As if he were already in the morgue.

Chapter Thirty-nine
520 First Avenue, Manhattan
Wednesday, October 24, 1990; 5:00 P.M.

The cassette was lying next to the body on the operating table. Byrne put it into the boom box that Sheinberg always kept in his examining room and hit the play button.

"My Dear Friend Francis," came the familiar voice,

"The first thing you should know is that I am terribly sorry and embarrassed that you should find me this way. I can't be a pretty sight, not that I ever was. The worst thing about suicide is the shame and humiliation that you feel just before you die, and it's hard to think of anything more humiliating than checking out with egg all over your face. But so be it.

"I know you've been to see Jack German, and I can guess what he's told you. Although I loathe the man, I suppose I still have respect for Jack's expertise. He's not a bad shrink, as shrinks go, and sometimes I ponder the fate that made him rich and me a schmuck when in fact we're both schmucks in the sight of God. Whatever he said, it couldn't have been very flattering, although I'm sure you put up a good fuss in my honor, and I am really very sorry that I couldn't be more worthy of your trust and, yes, love. For I do know that you loved me, as unworthy as I may have been of that love.

"I assume too that, good detective that you are, you've found Gunther Schiffen, and probably Robert Brandmelder as well. Maybe you're even on your way to see Natasha in Brooklyn—you haven't missed her, have you? And of course you know Ingrid and your lousy brother Tom. So by now you've got all the pieces of the puzzle, of which this note should be the last, but perhaps I flatter myself. That's what happens when your name means 'key.'

"I don't mean to be indirect, or to dissemble. I've done enough of that already—hell, I've been dissembling all my life. Dissembling, deconstructing, and now decomposing. It's no more than I deserve, though. It's what we all deserve. Not just my clients here in the morgue, but all of us, from the cardinal and the grand rebbe of the Lubavitchers on down.

"Bitter, huh? (Did you find Zelda? Please give her a good Christian burial.) Well, fuck it. God gives the Jews the right to be bitter; the trouble is, we don't take enough advantage of it. Sure, I'm bitter. Bitter about the way this all turned out, bitter about the way it all began. I didn't ask for any of it. But, then, I didn't ask for Amy Stevens, either; I just got her. And she, poor thing, got me. Frankie, I know you've been known to take a drink or two in your life, so maybe you can cut me a little bit of slack on Amy. I wasn't as loaded as everybody thinks that night, but I did have a couple, and when she started fibrillating I was a little slow to react, and she died. She just died, Frankie; God took her home, as you sentimental Christians say. But maybe the devil dragged her down to hell. Did anybody ever stop to consider that possibility? Maybe the old goat-footed bastard himself snatched her away, not for the sins she had committed, but for the sins she would have committed had she been allowed to live. Preemptive punishment, as it were. Is it possible that God and Satan operate in tandem, good cop, bad cop, Yahweh and Beelzebub, working the same case, which is us?

"Speaking of Beelzebub, I got a visit from your brother Tom the other night. I knew he was allergic to cats, but really, did he have to? It was the same night you and I were down at that Irish rathole you like so much. Did you score with those two cop-shop groupies? I never got a chance to ask. I suppose you turned them down. You're a man of principle, Frankie, that's one of the things I always liked about you. That and your ability to keep up with me at the bar.

"Tom was quite insistent to learn whether I knew who killed Egil Ekdahl, but you'll understand in a minute why I pretended not to know. I wanted to buy some more time, for me and for you, because I know how much you'd like to put him away. I've been buying time all my life, and it has cost me far more than I could ever have imagined. All that I had, all that I earned, all that I ever would have, I should live so long. But time ran out for me, as it does for all of us eventually.

"Egil Ekdahl!—might as well use his real name, Ivan Yuriyevich Didenko, which I suppose is as close to a 'real' name as he ever had. Vanya. It's what his mother always called him, and I guess she should know.

"But I digress. (I apologize for rambling, but the only way I can face meeting my maker is with a little fortification. Plus that brother of yours packs quite a punch.) It's time to answer Tom's question, although perhaps not in the way you might imagine. I confess: it was I who fired the shots into Ekdahl's head, the coup de grace of a wholly repellent life that should have been ended before it began. And I had the power! I was God to Ekdahl's Jesus. I invented him and shepherded him into this world. Cursed before birth, malformed at conception, twisted by the devil and sent into the world as—what? An instrument of God's wrath, I think. Now I know how God feels. Except I can do something He can't: I can kill myself.

"I speak not against his mother, for I once loved her. Indeed, there was even a time I was her lover, although it is not something I am proud of. I had power over her, too, the power to make her do my will, and I used that power because it gave me pleasure. Something else I'm not proud of, but which I freely admit to you here and now, because I want you to know the truth.

"The truth! What a joke! We speak of truth as if it were some objective, quantifiable entity. Truth versus Falsehood, as if they were black and white. The life of the mind versus the lies of the mind. The difference between you and me, Francis, is that you believe in the truth, you seek it out, and once in a great while you may even find some of it. Whereas I always knew there was no such thing. I knew that the minute the first jackboots crashed through our door in Breslau, and all of my father's prayer shawls and phylacteries availed him nothing. The truth of the Torah was trampled underfoot and God was silent. Did He avert his gaze? Or did He just not give a damn?

"So the hell with the truth, whatever it is. I'm trying to put as much of it on this tape as I can, but of course I cannot help but lie to you. Often I felt like a father to you, Francis, and if a father cannot lie to his son, lie to him for his own good about the horrors that he will encounter on the road of life, then whom can he lie to? Greater love than this hath no man. Don't you suppose God lied to Jesus? Told him it wasn't going to hurt, told him the thirty-three years on earth would be a piece of cake, all wine, women and marriage feasts at Cana? How else do you think He suckered the carpenter's kid into this whole mess? 'This may hurt a little.' How many times did I tell a patient that? Knowing that it was going to hurt a lot? Knowing that it might even hurt so bad that the only way to cope with the pain would be to die? That was the beauty of working in this place, Francis: you didn't have to lie anymore, and it really didn't hurt.

"Of course, I still managed to find ways to lie. At Ekdahl's autopsy, for example. A lie of omission. My diagnosis was accurate—how could it not be, since I had been present at the destruction?—but I left out the little part about my involvement. I left out the part about how it was my finger on the trigger of the pistol that put those shots into his head.

"And present at the creation as well. Vanya was a beautiful baby, to be sure, but there was something wrong with him from the get-go. Something so wrong that as I cut the cord and gave him to his mother, I said, 'It's a girl.' Well, at first glance, it looked like a girl. You know how the genitals of babies are much larger in proportion to their bodies than those of adults? At a quick first glance, that poor schwanz of his didn't look much different from an enlarged clitoris, and at that moment, under those circumstances, when she was gasping for breath from the exertion, when she was covered with sweat and blood from her efforts to bring him forth, at that moment who is looking closely at such things? You have no children of your own, Francis, and so I doubt that you have ever watched a woman go through childbirth's agonies, but believe me if you ever do, if you and Doreen can ever get your act together, then I guarantee you that you will never be mean to your mother again. Not that you have been. I know how sensitive you are about her. About how you always wished that she could love you one-tenth as much as you loved her. But she couldn't, for reasons you'll soon understand, if you don't already.

"Vanya was never mean to his mother. Whatever else we can say about him, and we can say a lot, we can't say that.

"He was home when he died. Home with Natasha, who is Irene's sister. I assume you know by now that Irene had a sister; in fact, she had two, and one of them was named Natalia Medvedeva, living today among my people in Brighton Beach. Medved is the name she's currently using, because it sounds Jewish. It always helped if you could say you were saving Soviet Jewry—what an ugly word, *Jewry*—even if they weren't really Jewish, but the only temple half the crooks in Brighton Beach have ever seen is the temple of their victim just before they blow his brains out.

"I know you think your mother is Polish, Frankie, but she isn't. It was just easier for her and your father that way. Especially since his marriage to Irene would have meant that he had been married to *two* Russian girls, and sisters at that. Everyone would have thought he was a damn commie, although he was only doing his job.

"There were three girls in the family. Irina, your mom; Natalia, who is Ekdahl's mother; and Vera. Vera died before you were born, and she was your brother Tom's mother. You figured that when Irene cursed him and said he was no son of hers she was just kidding, but she was speaking the truth. He *was* no son of hers. He was the son of her sister. Which makes him, I suppose, not only your half-brother, but your half-cousin as well. I tell you, Frankie, your family history is more convoluted than that of the Wälsungs. (I always said you should get to know Wagner.) It's a complicated family you were born into, my friend, but then it's a complicated world. And what real difference would it make if you knew about it earlier? Still, now that it's come to this, you might as well know the truth.

"There's that word again. I've already warned you that I'll lie to you, right here in the Unofficial Suicide Apologia of Seymour Sheinberg, the chop-cock of the chop shop, which by the way I'll thank you to destroy. The official written version is on my desk, short and sweet. *To leave this life is, for me, a sweet prospect. I find nothing in it that is desirable and on the other hand everything that is loathsome.* Tom—and Kennedy assassination buffs—will appreciate the humor.

"There: the previous paragraph has a lie in it, which I think you can spot. I assume Jack German told you that my real name is Schlüssel. Siegfried Ishmael Schlüssel. Now I ask you, what kind of a name is that for a good Jewish boy? And yet it was mine. Siegfried, the doomed Wagnerian chump; and Ishmael, the first Arab, whose hand was against every man's and every man's against his. Wouldn't you change a name like that?

"His, by the way, is Rubenstein: Jakob Isaac Rubenstein, one of the truly evil men on this planet for whom no posthumous punishment could ever be enough, however eternal. This creep, who hides behind his lofty reputation and his respectable profession as if they could mask the ugliness of his soul. We were partners once, no twice, in some fairly ugly doings many years ago, and he has held that partnership over me all these years, that my silence about who he is and what he has done might be kept forever. Ishmael and Isaac, together again.

"We met at Theresienstadt. I don't know how much you know about the Nazi concentration camps, but maybe you know that Theresienstadt was the 'model camp' on the Ohre River just outside of Prague, the one the

Nazis kept spruced up, relatively, in case they needed to show it off to the International Red Cross and other such ineffectual outfits. It even has kind of a pretty name, Theresa's City, in honor of the empress, but the town itself was a grimy shithole, and the camp was the old German army barracks. Its Czech name fits it better: Terezín, as in terrible.

"At first, it was a kind of perverse old folks' home, where they packed the older Jews off to die, a Czech version of Miami Beach, where you had to be over sixty-five to get in. After a while, they added the Jewish veterans of World War I, who had been promised good treatment and who still had friends among their fellow soldiers. Jews who fought and died for the Kaiser, and Theresienstadt was their reward! Suckers! Pretty soon they were admitting other fancy-pantses, like the Jews who had been married to Aryans, the civil servants we call *Beamters* in German, members of the Reichsvereinigung, the Reich Union of Jews. And, can you believe, some rich Jews even bought their way in. Yes, sir, Theresienstadt was about as uptown as it got. No schnooks, schmegegges or Schmuyles allowed. Believe it or not, the camp even had its own currency, on which, no shit, was printed the image of Moses holding up the Ten Commandments. I can't remember whether 'Thou shalt not kill' was on there or not. But on January 10, 1942, they strung up nine happy campers for engaging in forbidden conversations or some such transgression, and by then all of us had pretty well figured out the counselors were not going to be our friends.

"Theresienstadt had only one exit, and that egress led directly to Poland, which led directly to Hell. Do not pass Go; do not collect thirty pieces of silver. The deal was that if you transferred all your worldly possessions to the Reichsvereinigung, you were supposed to be guaranteed in return food, shelter and clothing for life. The catch was that the food was going to be lousy, the clothing meager and your life wasn't going to last very long, but who knew? Not even those fat-cat Jews of the Reichsvereinigung, who all finally wound up there, after which the Nazis simply confiscated the organization's treasury. Pretty clever, when you think about it, getting the Jews to do their own dirty work, but I guess it takes two to tango. You Irish certainly know all about that; you've been dancing the same damn dance with the English for a thousand years.

"The way the camp was set up—it was Heydrich's baby, by the way, just before the partisans blew him to hell and gone—it had its very own SS command structure, which oversaw a Jewish Council of Elders, which was nominally in charge. The head honcho was named Jakub Edelstein, and his second banana was a guy named Zucker. Mr. Precious Stone and Mr. Sugar. There were Jewish guards at the camp, Jewish technicians and Jewish lawyers, of course. Theresienstadt was also home to a sizable artist's colony of poets, painters and musicians, who sang for their supper and cobbled up prettified works on order for the Nazi hierarchy. Jesus H. Christ, I remember we had readings of the poetry of François Villon and a staging of *Faust*—that was pretty appropriate, huh?—and performances of *The Bartered Bride* and the Verdi *Requiem*, and they were good, too. One poor bastard even wrote a children's opera for the kids to perform.

"Some of the braver artists and intellectuals secretly recorded the ugly reality in their spare time. Needless to say, this was frowned upon, and God help you if they caught you indulging in negative propaganda—i.e., telling it like it was. I remember a professor named Otto Unger, who fell afoul of one of the council members. They chopped off the fingers of his right hand, and sent him to Buchenwald, where I suppose he died. The man who turned him in, for 'agitation,' was Jakob Rubenstein. And, yes, it was I who suggested to Vanya what an appropriate payback might be when he visited the great Dr. German, although Vanya should have cut off his head instead of his finger. That would have been hitting him where he lived.

"Of course, I never mentioned to Vanya my own sordid role there. He got the same story you did. Studly Sy, cock of the walk, lording it over the Nazi scum and sporting the red, white and blue. What else could I say? And like any good cover story in the intelligence business, this one was ninety-nine point nine percent true; the only part I left out is what I was doing before the camp was liberated. I tell you, Frankie, there were times when I almost believed my own legend. You can't blame a guy for wanting to be the hero of his own life story, can you? Even when all the evidence is to the contrary.

"But you know what, Francis? I don't blame the fucking Nazis half as much as I blame myself and my fellow Jews. When they were choosing the weak, the halt, the lame and blind for transportation, 'for processing,' they said, who do you think picked out the lucky winners? We did. The SS told us to jump and the Council of Elders said, 'How high?' Inside the cozy little confines of our very own ghetto roamed no blond beasts—in fact, the SS was not even allowed inside the camp's walls. We did it to ourselves. And this charade lasted right up to 1945, when the SS finally took over because there were so few of us left. I'm sure you Irish can relate.

"But spare me please your sympathetic rationalization. Of course we had no choice. But didn't we? Couldn't we have just said no? Could things have been any worse if we had resisted? You know how I used to kid you about how dumb the Irish are, and maybe you are. Certainly, you're too dumb to know when to quit. Jews are a lot smarter than that. We're too smart to know when to fight.

"I'll give you an example. There was a rabbi in the camp named Leo Baeck, who was one of the few who actually knew what was happening to those who were 'transported.' It didn't take Wernher von Braun to figure out that once you left Terezín you never came back. We were getting reports, and we each harbored our own suspicions. But Rabbi Baeck found out in the summer of 1941 what was going on. A Gentile woman who had married a Jew voluntarily accompanied her husband; when they got to Poland, the couple was separated. She witnessed hundreds of Jews being herded into busses, which always returned empty, and she relayed the rumors that the busses were mobile gas chambers, all save one, which carried the Jewish grave diggers, who in turn were shot after they buried the victims. And the name of this place was Auschwitz.

"Rabbi Baeck kept this news to himself. Two years later, further proof came along in the form of a Czech Jew named Gruenberg, who heard the story from a Polish Jew who had escaped from Auschwitz. He decided to sit on this news, too. 'Living in the expectation of death by gassing would only be the harder,' he said. When in 1942 the Gestapo decided it needed Jewish *kapos* to help round up their co-religionists, the good Rabbi went right along with the recruitment drive. 'I took the position that it would be better for them'—he means the *kapos*; he means us—'to do it, because they could at least be more gentle and helpful than the Gestapo and make the ordeal easier. It was scarcely in our power to oppose the order effectively.'

"I admit that I don't quote this from memory. I had to look it up, because frankly I've been trying to forget it for fifty years. And I mostly succeeded. I think I really had convinced myself that I had not collaborated. But that was a lie. The truth was that both Rubenstein and I were on Zucker's staff. We were bright young men, little more than boys really, but smart and strong and somehow we managed to hang on. Being apprentice doctors obviously helped; we had access to what medicine there was and when we weren't using it on ourselves, we were helping our friends. Did we play favorites? Doesn't everybody? Doesn't God?

"I'll spare you the obligatory horror stories, although suffice it to say there were plenty of them. After I joined the ME's office, people used to ask me if it wasn't too disgusting working on cadavers, but after what I had seen at age nineteen, the morgue seemed like the Bide-a-Wee rest home. Things did become very hectic at the end, though, and this is where Brandmelder rears his ugly mug.

"I'm afraid the OSS was not terribly fastidious about which Nazis it denazified, and our boy Bob was one of them. Toward the end of the war, things weren't much better for the SS outside the walls than it was for us inside them, and so Jack and I struck up a deal with Obersturmbannführer Brandmelder, a tit-for-tat arrangement by which we scratched his back and he watched ours. He had a taste for Jewish girls back then, and it shames me to say we provided them. He would make them come into his quarters, strip naked and beg for a bowl of milk. And when they got on their hands and knees to lap it up like a cat, he would take them from behind, any way he wanted them, and if they cried out or complained he would shoot them through the head. And to think I vouched for this fucker.

"So when Vanya died, Herr Brandmelder owed me one, and I collected. I wish I could say that Jack German had something to do with Vanya's death, but he didn't—except that, in one sense, he made Vanya's life possible by helping me to escape the Nazi noose, and made Vanya's death inevitable by what he did to Natasha. Anyway, after Vanya was dead I made arrangements to dump the body on his property in Ramapo. I even drove it up there myself, in Ekdahl's car; I was wearing my autopsy gloves, of course. I covered the front seat with dark plastic, because he had bled all over the damn place as he drove home to Natasha that night, and I put his body, in a body bag, in the trunk. That was the brilliance of it: who's going to blood-test a body bag? Bob gave me a ride back to the city that night, which is why you couldn't find any evidence of another vehicle. The BMW was supposed to be sold off for parts. But betrayal never stops, and Brandmelder double-crossed me. I guess I should have expected no less. Instead of burying Vanya he called the state police, and they called NYPD and the rest you know. I half-bet that Jack put him up to it—he's really not smart enough to think up anything on his own—and then Jack sicced you on

Brandmelder. Although I beat him to it. I called Matt White and suggested you for the case. A cri de coeur, as it were. A preconfession, of which this is the fulfillment.

"Whoever did what to whom, I'm glad it happened this way. Sure, I could have kept the chess match going, and blown the whistle on Brand-melder and Jack, but what would that accomplish? I'd still be ruined, and at least this way I get to choose my poison. Plus, for the first time in my life, I get to confess. I always wondered what you Catholics found so attractive about confession, and now I know. And, depending on what you do about this tape, I get to fuck over Brandmelder and Rubenstein. The last laugh belongs to me after all.

"I don't mind dying here, on the slab. After all the time I've spent in these charming surroundings, it's home to me, and now that Zelda is gone and Rhonda is pissed off I really have nothing to go back to the apartment for. I won't have to see that yenta Mrs. Klopfer anymore, either, which thought certainly brightens my final moments. She's a little hard of hearing, and so doesn't know how loudly she talks, even to herself, and I had to listen to her mutter about the 'damn shvartzers' behind her door whenever I would bring one of my girlfriends home.

"You're probably wondering whether it hurts. Not Mrs. Klopfer's racism; my demise. I can't say for sure, because obviously I'm composing this letter before I get down and get busy, but I think the answer is going to be no. Before I start opening myself up—spilling my guts, as it were—I'll have so much booze and painkiller and pickle juice in my veins that I very likely won't feel a thing. I'll just start cutting, like a samurai warrior engaged in ritual seppuku, and we'll see how far I get before I have to stop. I always wondered what the Y incision felt like.

"Anyway, I won't feel the kind of pain Vanya felt. Not the pain from the gunshot wounds to the head, which I've already confessed to. But I didn't kill him. He was already dead when I shot him, just to confuse the issue a little, to make my show-and-tell for you and Mancuso a little more dramatic and believable. No, Vanya was bleeding badly when he got to Brighton Fourth Street, which is where Natalia lives. I jumped in a taxi right after she called and of course the Parsi or whatever he was didn't want to go to Brooklyn and I had to offer him twice the fare, as if he wouldn't get a pickup along the Boardwalk or over at Coney Island if he wanted to, except the dumb jerk probably never even heard of Coney Island, which is why they really should tighten the immigration laws, but of course they won't.

"He was in the bathtub when I saw him, and Natasha was washing him in the pink foam. I had a hard time taking him away from her, but eventually I managed to get him out of the tub and drained the water after I made sure there was no more blood in the body. I didn't need any more of a mess in the car. You might say I was doing you a favor, Frankie, trying to spare you some needless mystification, even as I was trying to create it by filing off his fingertips, a little something I had learned about at Vidnoya. To buy time.

"The message on my answering machine was for Tom. In Russia he goes by the name of Sasha, which is short for Alexander, which is as you know his middle name. It's what your father and his mother, Vera, used to call him when he was a little kid. The bit about the man with the rifle is a quote from a Soviet play by I forget who. Everyone was afraid of the men with rifles during wartime because, although you could never be quite sure which side they were on, chances are they wanted to shoot you anyway. Oswald's friend Golovachev used the line in a letter and the CIA twisted itself into pretzels trying to figure out if it had some hidden significance. It didn't then, but it does now. It meant that Vanya was dead.

"I realize you're a little too young to remember the Kennedy assassination, but I might as well conclude with this. After the war I joined the CIA as a medical officer and took part in the interrogation of Yuri Nosenko. Nosenko was a KGB officer who defected to the Americans a couple of months after the assassination and told CIA he had been in charge of the Oswald file during Lee Harvey's sojourn in the USSR. Basically, he said that KGB had had nothing to do with Oswald. That was an obvious lie, of course, but we could not be sure just how big a lie it was. The Russians have a saying: a lie has short legs. But this lie was wearing seven-league boots. We grilled Nosenko for years, broke down his story in many particulars, but never broke him completely. The son of a bitch was either the toughest monkey or the dumbest bastard I ever met in my life. And so, faced with the ineffable, the unknowable and the unprovable, what do you suppose we finally did? What we did later in Vietnam: we declared victory and pulled out. Nosenko got a whitewash and a contract, everybody who doubted him got sacked, and today he's working for us, how about that. Sometimes it's just easier not to know the truth. A proposition with which, I'm sure, you're coming to agree.

"Anyway, the old KZ-camp *shvitser* Schlussel—I'd dropped the umlaut by that time, too ethnic—the attending physician on the Nosenko case, saw an opening and he took it. I figured if Nosenko, whose two favorite things were booze and broads, preferably together, didn't respond to the psychwar we were waging against him, maybe he would go for a little R and R. I got the authorization for the girl if not the whiskey and brought Natalia in for him one night. They slept together, and that's the long and short of it.

"When Vanya came back from Russia, he was looking for Nosenko. Not to shake his hand, or give him a big hug and a kiss, but to execute him; that was what he had been trained to do on Sakhalin Island, once the authorities figured out what a wonderful monster they had on their hands. There's been a KGB contract on Nosenko since he defected, and as far as I know it's never been rescinded. But the U.S. government has been protecting him ever since CIA gave up and declared him kosher. The other agents the Soviets sent never got close to Nosenko. But in Vanya they had an agent with a more personal motivation: he wanted to kill Nosenko not only because he had been condemned to death, but for abandoning his beloved mother.

"And that's what this whole Oswald file business was about, a means to get at Nosenko. You had to admire the way Vanya set the whole multiple-identity scheme up, each name a reference to Oswald, right down to the initials of the last fake name he used: Lars Egil Ekdahl, LEE. What I don't know is whether he ever really had the file and if he did, to what use he intended to put it. Perhaps it began as a ploy to flush out Nosenko, but if you ask me, once he got here, in the bosom of capitalism, Vanya saw his chance to make a big score, which is why he was playing all those clowns—the Mafia, the CIA, the FBI, anyone who might have been a suspect in the Kennedy assassination and thus interested in the file—against each other. Five million dollars would have secured him and Natasha for life somewhere. I suppose the most charitable thing we can say over his grave is that he was corrupted by money and died for love.

"Now I have to warn you that Natasha isn't the most stable person you're ever going to meet. Until the other evening I hadn't seen her for twenty-some years, but even then she was never quite playing with a full deck. And that's what my old pal Jack German took advantage of, after she gave birth to the child: he had her declared insane, and institutionalized at Saint Elizabeth's in Washington. We had to; we couldn't have anybody know that we had introduced her to the nonperson Nosenko and what the result was. It was necessary; hell, it was a matter of national security. But Jack German didn't blink, didn't hesitate, to send her to the nut house. He's all head and no heart, always was and always will be. He even kept tabs on Vanya in his foster home in Bethesda; they called him Johnny in those days. Jack must have read you his notes of Johnny's psychiatric evaluation, although I bet he didn't tell you where they came from.

"That was right around the time Natasha and Vanya disappeared. She must somehow have plugged back into her old network—or maybe she was a double agent all along—because she got herself sprung and spirited Vanya off to Europe. We figured she'd gone back over to the Soviets, which she had, and that there would be hell to pay, which there was. Doubled, my ass—the girl was redoubled, back working for her real masters. Any way you slice it, it was an awesome display of tradecraft. With women you can never go wrong overestimating their capacity for treachery, or their stamina to keep playing the game long after the boys have tired of it.

"But there was a twist. She'd gone back, all right, but they fucked her; they didn't want her, they wanted the boy, they wanted Nosenko's son, and what they put that woman through in order to find him . . . Jeez, I thought the way we grilled Nosenko was bad, but his experiences on the Farm were, to mix my metaphors, a day at the beach compared with what happened to her. And to him. To Vanya.

"You have to feel sorry for the poor s.o.b., Francis, because we made him what he is today, which is now nothing. Yes, he was a sinner, but the original sin was not his, but ours. The joke's on us.

"And now for the last few details. The shots from the .22 came from my gun, which is in the drawer beneath the whiskey bottle; I'd appreciate it if you'd chuck that sucker into the river on your way out. What stumps me, though, is that other bullet, the .38. When you suggested on Sunday that perhaps they both came from the same gun, I decided to have a closer look. I ran them by ballistics and what do you know? You were right. Find the connection between Ekdahl and the body in the Dumpster and you've got your killer. I don't see any myself, but I guess that's why you're the detective and I'm the stiff.

"And now, my friend, it's time for me to go. I hate long good-byes, and this one is way too long already. I'm only sorry that I couldn't have said these things to you face-to-face. I tried to at O'Reilly's but when you showed me that picture of Jack and the Nazi, I knew it was just a matter of time before you'd figure the whole thing out—I really meant all those nice things I've said about your ability over the years, and if I've helped advance your career in even a small way, well, that's one good thing I've done in my life. And when Tom showed up at my place Sunday night with his brass knuckles and his bad attitude, I finally decided fuck it, let's do it. It took me two days of drinking, and on the third day I died again. Think of me as Jesus in reverse.

"Sorry I can't help you any further with the Ekdahl murder. Blame it on me if you want, or better yet, Tom, because I know you suspect it's his gun that's the murder weapon, but it's your call. This is one murder ol' Doc Sheinberg is still baffled by.

"Good-bye, Frankie. Live and be well. Do not judge your comrade until you stand in his place, as the saying goes. Words to live by. I just hope for your sake my shoes don't fit.

"Your friend, Sy Sheinberg."

Chapter Forty
520 First Avenue, Manhattan
Wednesday, October 24, 1990; 5:15 P.M.

Jesus, I thought he'd never shut up," said Tom. He looked at the body contemptuously. "Talk about spilling your guts."

"How long have you been here?" said Francis.

"Long enough to listen to this shit twice," said the elder Byrne.

They were standing on either side of an autopsy table in one of the lesser-used dissection rooms, deep in the bowels of the medical examiner's office, contemplating the body of Seymour Sheinberg, M.D., né Siegfried Ishmael Schlüssel, of Breslau, Terezín and New York, New York.

"Do you know what the Russian word for *dead* is?" asked Tom. "It's *ubit*, as in 'obit,' as in dead. Which he very much is."

Sheinberg was naked. A scalpel was protruding from his midsection, just below the rib cage, marking the northernmost point of his self-examination. A bottle of scotch—not his best, Byrne noted—stood nearly empty on the instrument table. There was blood everywhere.

"Congratulations, Detective Lieutenant Byrne, you've really distinguished yourself on this one," Tom said. "The bullets match. Now all you have to do is arrest the principal suspect and you're home free. Unfortunately, that suspect just happens to be you. How'd you do it, Frankie? I can't wait to read about it in the papers: 'Trigger-happy mackerel-snapper Francis X. Byrne, a known lush and hothead who's already been the subject of one departmental investigation, arrested himself yesterday in the death of Egil Ekdahl, 24, a law-abiding Danish diplomat and pervert.' And I can't wait to hear Doreen testifying at the trial, about your temper, and how you smack her around all the time, as the prosecution establishes prior behavior. Diplomatic assassination is the kind of crime they call the FBI in on, and I personally won't rest until I see you doing twenty-five years to life in Sing Sing, family ties or no family ties."

"I didn't shoot him," said Byrne. "How the hell could I? I never even saw him until after he was dead. But if I go then you're going with me."

"You talking to me?" said Tom mockingly. "About Pilgersen? You know, we still got a little inconvenience in this country called habeas corpus, and you ain't habe no corpus."

"That was him in the Dumpster," said Byrne.

"Burned beyond recognition; just another derelict, sleeping it off with a lighted cigarette. You can't prove a thing, except that your gun fired the fatal shot. Good thing for you the governor keeps vetoing the death penalty, buddy."

"I wouldn't be so sure about that," replied Francis. It was time for the trump card he'd been waiting all his life to play. "I've seen the movie: *Death and the Maiden*, starring Egil Ekdahl and Thomas A. Byrne. I must say you were terrific. But I guess a putz playing a putz can be pretty convincing."

"Where is it?" said Tom, his voice low and chilly.

"Somewhere safe."

"What do you want for it?"

"Not much," said Byrne. "Just the truth. Then I decide how we're going to play this one. Either that or we both go down. Brothers in arms till the end, just like you said." They faced off warily, on either side of the corpse. Byrne was vaguely aware of how ludicrous a location it was for a show-down, but life couldn't be like the movies. Besides, Sy would have appreciated the black humor. Irish versus Irish, as always.

Tom took out a pack of cigarettes and lit one up. "The file was always the key. No one outside the Soviet Union'd ever seen the damn thing. All the Warren Commission got from the Russkies was a couple of raggedy-assed documents that proved nothing except that Oswald was an anti-social dork who was always bitching no matter where he was. The big questions—about KGB involvement in the assassination, about Marina's bona fides, about the veracity of Nosenko's story—remain the big questions. Sure, you could say it happened a long time ago and half the people in this great land of ours not only don't remember where they were when Jack died, they weren't even born. But you'd be surprised how many people do care. You're too young to recall the Kennedy assassination, but for my generation it was a big deal. I remember when they made the announcement. The principal came over the loudspeaker and said something like, 'The president of the United States has been shot,' and we all put our heads down on our desks and said a prayer, although I vaguely remember that he must have said something about JFK's being hit in the head, and I thought, well, that's that, because unless you've got the skull of a nigger, head shots are the worst, and sure enough a half an hour later the principal got back on the horn and told us, 'The president of the United States is dead,' and I remember the girls in the class started to cry and that was the first time I ever realized—I know this sounds really crass, but it's weird what you think of at a time like that—it was the first time I ever realized that girls are really hot when they cry. Anyway, they were all bawling, and I guess somebody in charge must have figured out that no one was going to get any work done that day, it was Friday anyway, so they gave us the rest of the afternoon off and we all went home. So call it an obsession, but some of us are still fascinated. Mind if I have a drink?"

Tom reached for Sheinberg's whiskey bottle and took a long draught.

For the first time, Francis noted that his brother was wearing surgical gloves.

"Damn!" he exclaimed, setting the bottle back down. "You'd think he coulda brought some Bushmill's single malt instead of this crap. He might still be alive today. Anyway, the file. Ekdahl had put out a press release saying he'd copped it from the Minsk branch of the KGB, and was hawking it around like a program vendor at the Stadium. And we wanted it. When I say we, I do mean we. Everybody—CIA, FBI, even the Mob. Because who knew what the hell was in it? Everybody was scared to death. What confused the issue were his damn multiple identities: I had no idea when I went to Moscow that the KGB officer I met named Alik was working here in New York under the guise of Ekdahl, and the Mob didn't know that the man calling himself Murray Dutz was also the psycho Eddie Paine. And nobody knew about Ivan Didenko."

"Speaking of Dutz and the Mob," interrupted Byrne, "was that what that mess in the Village was all about? The late Special Agent Pavone in the coffee shop? And the three dead hoods on Carmine Street? I know you were there, because one of Genna's boys mistook me for you the other day." A thought struck him. "You were setting Ekdahl up, weren't you?"

"Sure I was," admitted Tom. "What was I supposed to do? He had me by the balls with that damn videotape. He wanted me to lead him to Nosenko, so he could kill him. But if my plan had worked, I woulda nailed Ekdahl and Genna together, plus I would have grabbed the file. It was worth the chance. My only regret is that when the deal went south Ekdahl didn't whack the don, too."

"So that's why you took your little European vacation: to get the Oswald file," said Francis. "Instead you wound up playing the costume party version of Hide the Salami instead. I didn't know your taste ran to S&M; nice going, dickhead. Who was the girl?"

"Some little whore. I forget her name. But you weren't there, Frankie; you don't know. You didn't see those girls."

"I saw the movie, Tommy."

"But you didn't touch them, Frankie, you didn't taste them, you didn't smell them. Do you know the sounds a woman makes when she's getting fucked? The same sounds she makes when she's getting killed. How was I to know he'd cut her throat? I wasn't watching. My attention at that moment was elsewhere. Look at the film and see for yourself. And spare me the moral judgments about my sexual appetites, will you? You think you're walkin' on the wild side because that girlfriend of yours is a part-time rug muncher, but that's her claim to fame, not yours."

Now he was getting mad. "Why'd you fuck Doreen?" Byrne blurted. "Why did you take Mary Claire away from me and break her heart? What'd I ever do to you?"

"Because they were there!" Tom retorted. "Because they were fuckable! Because you couldn't handle them! Because you were never around! Because it really does take two to tango!"

"And that made it all right?" shouted Byrne. "It didn't matter to you that I loved Mary Claire and that she used to love me?"

"You're the one who started the affair with Doreen while you were still married, pal, not me. I can't help it if she found out about it and came to me to drown her sorrow."

Byrne was glad he had his pistol with him. "And you got tired of her."

"I get tired of 'em all," said Tom.

There was no point in pursuing this any further. Tom was right: it was all his fault. "So there you were in Moscow, in your Frederick's of Hollywood handcuffs . . ."

"So there I was in Moscow, where I got fucked, as you saw. Then, surprise, we find out Alik is back here, in New York, hiding out as an illegal in the Danish consulate. And guess which little bird blew his cover? Ingrid."

Why was that not a surprise? "But what was in it for her?"

"Same thing that was in it for all of us. Money. And glory. Because her job was to make sure that whatever Ekdahl was up to, he wasn't going to succeed."

"Why?"

"Because the fabulous babe, my dear brother, is KGB." Tom paused to let his words sink in. "Despite your good looks, Irish wit and formidable brain power, the real reason Ingrid went to bed with you the other day was to find out how much you knew. There's no talk like pillow talk. She was Ekdahl's baby-sitter, because even after all they put him through they never could really trust him. The guy was nutty as a fucking fruitcake and even though he was their nut they couldn't be sure where his loyalties lay. In the end, of course, they lay with himself and with his mother, which is what cost him his life. If he had been a little less the dutiful son, if he had been a little more, a little more . . ."

"Corrupt, like the rest of us," said Byrne.

"Whatever," said Tom, "his scam would have worked, Nosenko would be dead and Ekdahl would be rich. Who's to say that wasn't the proper solution? There's still plenty of guys in the Company who're convinced Nosenko was a phony all along, guys like Pete Bagley and Dave Murphy, whose careers were sidetracked or wrecked by him, and who wouldn't shed a single tear at his demise."

"I still don't understand why this Oswald file is so damn important," said Byrne. "What could possibly be in it for everyone to risk so much?"

"It's important," explained Tom, "because it exists. Because it *may* exist. What's in it is utterly irrelevant. It is only valuable and dangerous because its contents are unknown. Who cares what the truth is? In the end, what does it matter for whom, if anyone, Oswald was working? What if it was the KGB? What are we going to do, retroactively declare war? Dig up Khrushchev and hang him? He's far more productive fertilizing a potato field, or whatever it is he's doing now. The point is to *get rid of it.* This business is only make-believe, a fantasy in which the truth doesn't matter so long as you can make the other guy believe. It's like religion, a belief in the unknowable, the unprovable, the ineffable. And we get to play God."

"And that's who you think you are? God?" asked Francis, picking up the scotch as if to pour himself a drink.

"And who do you think you are?" shouted his brother. "Saint Francis of Assisi? Bishop Sheen? The pope in Rome? Mr. Goody Two Shoes, who majored in empathy at Fordham and thought he was doing the world a favor by solving his two-bit barrio murders, when you know what? Nobody gives a good goddamn! The rules have changed, brother; Raskolnikov was right. Murder doesn't need a motive anymore; just pick some son of a bitch and off him because it feels good and so what if you're caught? You'll get a Jewish mouthpiece and he'll blather about victimhood because who knows victimhood like the Jews, they've elevated it to a fucking art form, that's their genius when you stop to think about it. *Kraft durch Schwäche,* Strength through Weakness, must be tattooed like a concentration-camp motto across the interior of their foreheads. Don't fight back, roll over like a dog and show your yellow belly and if the guy kicks you again it only goes to show how virtuous you are. What the hell kind of a way is that to live? That's the kind of thinking that led them to Theresienstadt and Auschwitz, places where all their lawyers and the psychiatrists and arbitrageurs couldn't save them because they finally ran up against a bully who enjoyed kicking them in the balls! You want proof, just look at this asshole."

"You make me sick, Tom," said Byrne. "You're a fucking bigot, and you make me want to puke." Tom never saw the whiskey bottle coming. It shattered against the side of his head and sent him to the floor, bleeding from a deep cut over his left ear. Byrne trained his gun on his brother, prepared to shoot. At this point, one more expended round wasn't going to make any difference.

"It's taken me this long," he shouted, "but thank God I can finally see you for what you really are—a goddamn gutless loser."

Tom remained on the ground. "Of course I'm a loser," he said. "We both are. Otherwise we wouldn't be here. We're losers because we're Irish, and the Irish always lose."

His anger subsiding, Byrne helped his brother up and sat him down in a chair. He grabbed a paper towel and tried to stanch the bleeding. The cut wasn't too bad, but he looked around for something to apply to the wound. Did they have antiseptic in the morgue? "Sorry I spilled the rest of the booze," he said. "You could probably use some right now."

Tom looked up. The effects of the blow seemed to be wearing off, and injury or no injury Byrne knew his brother well enough not to let down his guard. "Losers," he laughed, and pointed to Sheinberg's body. "You think I'm anti-Semitic, Frankie, but you're wrong. I'm not. I look at them, and you know what I see? I see us. I look at them, riding high right now—top of the world, Ma!—and I want to say enjoy it now, fellas. I don't hate Jews, Frankie, and God knows I don't begrudge them their moment in the sun. Because I know that it won't last. It never lasts for guys like us."

Byrne put Sheinberg's tape into the pocket of his sport coat.

"What about Brandmelder?" asked Tom. "And Dr. German? What are we going to do about them?"

"I'm way ahead of you," said Byrne. "I arrested Brandmelder this afternoon for making false entries on his application to enter the United States. He'll be deported, guess where; I've already been on the phone to the Israelis. And Jacob German killed himself by jumping from the window of his office this morning. He left a note that read, 'And they shall go forth, and look upon the carcasses of the men that have transgressed against me: for their worm shall not die, neither shall their fire be quenched; and they shall be an abhorring unto all flesh.'"

"What's that supposed to mean?"

"Isaiah 66:24," said Byrne softly. "I looked it up. The sins of the fathers . . ."

"What are you going to tell White?" asked Tom.

"The way I see it," he replied, "I have two choices, either one of which sounds like the truth. I can tell him that he was right all along about this being a gay sex crime. That Pilgersen and Ekdahl were lovers, and that Pilgersen accidentally killed Ekdahl in an erotic fit by cutting his throat while they were getting it on at the Rambone, shot him a few times to confuse the issue, and then drove his car up to Ramapo and dumped the body on the property of total strangers. That Ingrid Bentsen, his devoted personal assistant, followed at a discreet distance and parked on the main road to give Pilgersen an alibi and a ride home. That Pilgersen was suddenly recalled to Denmark—you're going to help me get his ticket punched posthumously by the INS or State—and that naturally Ingrid has followed. That the FBI in the person of Special Agent Thomas A. Byrne is satisfied with the resolution, since no international terrorism is involved. White and the department get a commendation from the Danish government, which you'll also see to, and with Flanagan gone, the mayor'll have no choice but to give Matt the job."

"What's the other option?" asked Tom.

"I can tell him that you did it. You had the means—my gun; the motive; Gunther's film—and plenty of opportunity, as Ingrid will be only too happy to testify in exchange for her sweet ass and a free ticket home. Sure, I lost temporary control of my firearm, but everybody will back me up when I say it was force majeure. And don't think that morphed video's going to do the trick, especially when you stack it up against your excellent adventure. In the end, Matt White and his faithful sidekick Tonto bust a rogue FBI agent and save the Republic. RIP, Thomas A. Byrne. The choice is yours, Tommy."

"What if Brandmelder talks?" objected Tom.

"Who's going to believe a Nazi war criminal, babbling in a cell in Tel Aviv?" replied Byrne. "And I don't think Jean or Jimmy are exactly unimpeachable character witnesses."

"And the Danes?"

"I hardly think they'll want to drag this through the press." Byrne stopped, pleased with his explanation. It was the Coloredo case all over again. Almost.

"How do you explain the fact that the bullets match?" asked Tom. "It was your gun that shot Pilgersen. And if you didn't shoot Ekdahl, then who the hell did?"

"I don't know," said Byrne, "and I'm not sure I care. But maybe the bullets *don't* match. Sy warned me he would lie, and of course he knew you might get to him first, so I choose to believe that statement was for your benefit. He guessed that you did Pilgersen, and he was trying to pin Ekdahl on you, too."

"Maybe," said Tom. "But there's one more thing: that picture of Irene you found in the car. What was that all about?"

Now there was something he hadn't considered, and couldn't explain. "It doesn't matter," said Byrne, trying to convince himself. "Nobody's going to care about an old photo. They're not even gonna know." That was a mystery he intended to keep personal.

"If you say so." Tom seemed satisfied. "What are you going to do about him?" He pointed to Sheinberg.

"We'll leave him just like we found him," said Byrne, turning away.

"Just like that?"

"What do you want me to do?" said Francis. Now it was his turn to shout; now it was his turn to grieve. "Stand here and weep? Say the Kaddish? Sit shiva? Don't you think Sy has had enough of death for one lifetime, that we have to give him one last wallow? Sy Sheinberg was a big boy, and took his medicine like the kind of man you say you admire. Listen to the tape again; is there one word of complaint?"

"I guess not," said Tom. "I also guess I like choice number one, especially since there's one tiny little detail you've overlooked. I assume you'd like your slugs back, just in case they really do match, but one of 'em's walked right out the door. You don't think I came here alone, do you?"

Now it dawned on Byrne what his brother was talking about. "Where is she?"

"Bingo!" said Tom. "You give me the videotape and I give you the featurette we made at the consulate and the mystery bullet. I go back to

Washington, you go back to work and Ingrid disappears. White makes commissioner and you get a promotion and everybody's happy."

It was a no-brainer.

Byrne opened his briefcase, where he'd kept the film since he found it, and they made the exchange. "She's at the airport, but you'd better hurry," said Tom. "Her plane leaves at eight."

"How do I know she's really there?" asked Byrne.

"You can trust me."

"But can I trust her?" asked Francis.

"Can you trust any woman?" said his brother.

Chapter Forty-one
Kennedy Airport, New York
Wednesday, October 24, 1990; 6:30 P.M.

I wondered how long it would take you to get here," she said. "We've got about half an hour before they call my flight."

"I'm not sure you're going to make it," he said.

"I guess that's what we have to talk about," she said.

In the unflattering lighting of the International Arrivals Terminal at JFK, he took a good look at her. She was wearing a pink jogging suit that concealed her figure; her hair was pulled back and looked like it could use washing. Her skin was flushed and there was a thin clear mustache of sweat on her upper lip. Her eyes were slightly dull, not shining, as they always had been whenever she and he had been together, and there was the hint of dirt under her fingernails. Byrne wondered for a moment whether she had changed her underwear in her haste, and then remembered that she didn't wear any. But he found he no longer cared.

"You're not going to believe this," she said, and tossed her head, "but I'm sorry."

"You've got a lot to be sorry for," he told her.

She chewed her lower lip pensively. "How much do you know?" The airport public-address system blared an announcement, which, like all airport p.a. declarations, was unintelligible. Around them, happy travelers wheeled oversized suitcases on little rollers toward their final destinations.

"Enough to put you away. I don't think diplomatic immunity extends to KGB illegals."

Her eyes widened in amusement. "Do you really think I had anything to do with Egil's death?" she asked.

"It doesn't matter," he replied. "I know you came here with orders to kill him if he stepped out of line and he did and now he's dead and you're on your way home. QED. Everything else is just bullshit to confuse the men—and the women, I guess—who are, or were, in love with you."

"Then I suppose you won't be needing this." She fished in her pocket and produced a .38 slug.

He reached for it, but she whisked it away, dropping it down the front of her jogging suit. "I know you, Francis," she taunted. "You're much too polite to feel up a girl in public."

"I might not be if I still cared about you."

"I told you not to rush me." She smiled. "If you had just given me a little more time . . . And now here you are, brandishing your handcuffs."

"If I had just given you a little more time," he replied, "you'd be halfway to Moscow."

"Which I will be soon enough," she said. "So you'd better make it snappy."

It was amazing how fast love could turn to hate, two sides of the same emotion, working the same case, which was him.

"I do have a couple of questions," he admitted. "Such as, why did you lie to me—you, who made such a big deal about me being honest with you."

"I didn't," she protested. "Tell me a single untruth I have uttered."

"You said Tom's story about Pilgersen was a lie."

"I said almost nothing about it was true; there's a difference. Pilgersen was no more KGB than you are."

"Then why did Tom shoot him?"

"Because he was on to us—on to me—and your chivalrous brother was trying to protect me. I think Tom loved me more than you did, Frankie."

"Although you never loved either of us," he declared.

"I would have thought Doreen could have told you that," she said. "I told you I wasn't making any promises. I just never told you why. It's not my fault if you didn't pick up the signals. Maybe it's about time you learned that words have meaning. That they have consequences. Words like 'I love you' and 'I'm going to kill you.' Words you shouldn't say unless you mean them. Words you have to be prepared to back up with deeds. Egil always was."

"And look what happened to him."

"Yes, but I had nothing to do with it. I really shouldn't care whether you believe me or not, but for some strange reason I do. After he left the consulate on that Wednesday, I never saw him again."

"Why not? You were supposed to be tailing him. And you let him go down to Carmine Street alone?"

"Tom was covering him, remember? But after the shootout Egil vanished. The next time I saw him was in those autopsy photographs."

"Where did he go?" he asked.

"I don't know," she said quickly. "No, wait." She glanced over at the check-in desk, but the agents were staring at their computers, ignoring everybody. "Maybe I do know. He told me . . . he told me he was going to see his aunt that evening. I didn't even know he had an aunt in the U.S., so I just shrugged it off as a cover story and forgot all about it. But maybe he did. He said his aunt lived in some place called Woodside."

That's funny, thought Byrne, my mom lives in . . . and then it all made sense. The prowler, the fingerprints on the dildo, Natalia Medved, of Brighton Beach, Brooklyn. Not far from Sheepshead Bay. Not far from JFK. Ekdahl's mother's name, according to Sy. His mother's sister. Mother's Little Helper. "Oh, Jesus," he said.

They both heard the desk person announce the boarding of Finnair flight 64 to Helsinki, departing at 7:05 P.M. The light of self-confidence was coming back into the bottomless fjord of her eyes. "I have to go now," she said, and stood up.

"Not until I get what I came for," he told her.

They were standing against a side wall in relative privacy, her back to it, his back shielding her from the rest of the transit lounge. She opened the zipper of her top and he caught a last, brief glimpse of her full, bra-less breasts. The bullet was nestled between them, the happiest projectile in the world. She fished it out and handed it to him.

"I hope you're satisfied," she said. "I hope this whole thing was worth it."

And then she kissed him, kissed him hard on the lips, and put her arms around him; in response, he moved his body close to hers and slid his hands around her back, one venturing under the waistband of her pants until it came to rest on her bare bottom, which got one last caress. Her eyes were brighter now, and he thought he could detect the faintest glimmer of affection in their wellsprings.

"It's all just a boy's game, isn't it, Francis? To you, to Tom, even to Egil. You all fight this secret war, and you think you're doing great deeds. You run around with your guns and your hidden cameras, like little boys with a secret clubhouse and magic decoder rings. Because it makes you feel big and strong and important; because it makes you feel like men.

"But we women know better. We know you're just showing off. We see right through you! Men are an open book, easily read and even more eas-ily manipulated. You think you can invoke things like national security, and preen about what goes on at the highest levels of government, and think you're impressing us. Well, I hate to be the one to break the news, but you're not.

"Look at the results! Do you know whether Brandmelder was black-mailing Sheinberg and German, or vice versa? You don't even know if there ever really was an Oswald file for sale or, if there was, where it might be right now. I could have it in my checked luggage for all you know. You're all just a bunch of jerks with too much testosterone, slink-ing around dark alleys and firing your guns wildly at phantoms. So Egil is dead, and I am leaving; are you really any happier?"

"What was in it for you?" he asked. "If you think this is all a boy's game, why did you join KGB?"

"I told you already: because I am a patriot. I would do anything to keep my country away from the West, away from all this shit, away from values I can't stand and people I hate. I don't give a damn about the Soviet Union, and neither did Egil. It's finished and so are you; what you Americans don't understand is that the game you're playing will eventually beggar you both. There's a price to pay, only you haven't got the bill yet. Because if you play it long enough, in the end you have nothing left: no trust, no beliefs and no certitude. But for us, for me and Egil, there was always one thing more important, for which we were really working, and that was our homes and our families. He had no home and I have no family, but we had each other. And now you've taken that away from me."

She kissed him again, this time lightly. "I really do have to go now. Good-bye, Francis," she said, and turned to leave. She clenched her right hand and raised it, whether in salute or triumph Byrne could not tell, leaning slightly toward the shoulder, the thumb at an angle over the fingers. *"Allt är klart,"* she said. "The job is finished."

"You forgot something." Something in his voice stopped her. "You're not going to Moscow, are you? You're going to Finland, a nice, neutral country. And from there you'll just disappear. I don't think your KGB bosses are going to like that. Are they, Gino?"

Andretti put down the newspaper he had been reading and stood up. There were two Soviet security agents with him, courtesy of Tom Byrne, and neither one of them looked very happy. "Come on, honey," he said. "Let's us take a little trip."

"I guess I forgot to tell you about this part," said Byrne. "But at least I didn't lie."

Chapter Forty-two
Brighton Beach, Brooklyn, and *Sunnyside*, *Queens*
Wednesday, October 24, 1990; evening; night

Brighton Beach was a neighborhood Byrne never went to. It was strange, alien, not his New York. He hated the sight of the old foreign men on the boardwalk, speaking softly to each other in the practiced low tones of conspirators; he hated the smell in the air, that smell his brother always told him was a Russian smell, a socialist-realist mixture of dried-in body odor and cheap perfume and strong cigarettes and disinfectant.

The part of Brighton Fourth Street he sought was a dingy lane running north off the boulevard, the wrong side of the tracks. South of Brighton Beach Boulevard were the grand apartment buildings, home to the middle-class Jews who had lived here before and after the war, who only wanted some peace and quiet and a view of the ocean before they died; the Striver's Row of Neil Simon country. To the west, rising like some Chinese Wall between Coney Island and Brighton Beach, were the projects, great ugly blocks of concrete that reminded the newly arrived Soviet Jews of the cheap apartment complexes they had gladly relinquished back home. To the north were the little cross streets, unimaginatively labeled Brighton First, Second and so forth, mixed-race no-man's-lands of Russians, Jews, blacks, Hispanics and whoever else was coming to America these days. To the east was the ocean, and nothing.

Brighton Beach, New York, the future of the United States in microcosm, like it or not. And here he was, parking his car in front of a small two-story house on the east side of Brighton Fourth Street, ready to wrap things up if he could, and go home. If he had a home to go to after it was all over. He wasn't feeling so clever anymore.

The shutters were drawn tight, and the little window in the front door had a heavy curtain pulled over it. There was no illumination emanating from within.

But he had the right place: the nameplate on the door read N.
MEDVED. He knocked; there was no bell. There was no answer, either,
but, faintly, he could hear the sound of music. Byrne knocked again, with
the same response. Nothing. He strolled around back.

The minuscule yard was landscaped in weeds and mud, and yellowed,
windblown newsprint was sticking between the slats of the cheap wooden
fence that separated the home from its neighbors. If there had ever been
any grass, he was sure it had never been mowed during the years of its
fragile existence. In this neighborhood, it wouldn't have made any difference.

"Who?" A voice out of the Brooklyn night. A voice with caution, perhaps fear in it. These days that was the rule and not the exception.

"Hello?" said Byrne, sprinting back to the front door.

As he stood on the small porch, he could feel himself being surveyed
by the inhabitant. He was being sized up, evaluated, weighed, judged; it
was like standing in the passport line of a hostile country, with your papers not entirely in order.

"Who?" reiterated the voice. The aspirant was hard, the vowel clipped.

"My name is Francis Byrne," he replied.

Silence for a long moment. "Come," said the voice, as the door swung
open.

It was dark inside the vestibule, so dark that Byrne at first could not
see anything. The sun had long since set, but there were no lights on, just
the flicker of a candle that rested in a holder, which was held by a hand
attached to an arm that belonged to the voice. It was a woman.

At least, Byrne assumed it was a woman; his eyes were barely functioning in the semidarkness and he could not get a visual confirmation.
"Come," repeated the voice, ushering him inside. It was low and resonant,
yet unmistakably female in intonation.

"Sit." The accent was strong, the words hard to understand. He sat on
an old sofa covered carelessly with an equally ancient handmade quilt. He
could see better now. But he still could not see the woman, for she was
draped from head to toe in a kind of monk's cloak, and her voice issued
from within its cowl.

"I am sorry so dark here," she said. "But I am child of darkness."

Her face flickered dimly, just above the candle's feeble light, the eyes
sensed and not quite seen, the rest of her simply a shadow.

"You are Natalia," he said.

"*Da,*" she said. "Natash'." There was a musty smell in the house, the smell of solitude, and of loneliness, and of despair, and death.

"Irina's sister," Byrne said.

"Irina's sister, and sister of her sister, and sister-in-law of your father twice over." The recitation was almost biblical. "And more." Like Irene, she pronounced the word *sistra.* It is the Russian word for "sister."

His sight was adjusting to the gloom but it still was difficult to make out anything but shapes. How could she see? Byrne supposed the cane that rested by the side of her chair was meant to help her navigate, and he began to wonder if she was blind.

"It pleases me to make your acquaintance again, after so many years," she said. Even without the accent it would have been hard to distinguish the words; the woman must have a speech impediment.

"Do you know song I sang him on night we met?" she asked abruptly. "Old Russian song, about beauty of Russian girls."

It didn't seem to bother her that there was already music playing in the background. She rose unsteadily to her feet, and swung the cane in time with her singing, like a conductor. She sang:

> *Is it not she who comes down to the river?*
> *Looking intently at the water*
> *With her eyes so bright*
> *She bends over the water;*
> *She looks down and wonders:*
> *"Could this be me?*
> *"Perhaps this is only a red dawn*
> *"That is flaming in the sky*
> *"Which is reflected in the river?"*
>
> *Oh, there must be a reason*
> *Why Russian beauties are famous!*

But the words were in Russian, and so Byrne did not understand them.

"This was favorite," she said, returning to her chair. "And was also favorite of son."

"It is about your son that I wished to speak with you."

"*Pryikrahsnaya,*" she said, and tried to clap her hands. "*Horasho.* My son," she said.

"Your son."

"Is dead. *Ubit.*"

"*Ubit.*" He remembered that, at least.

"You are policeman?" she asked.

"I am," replied Byrne.

"There is nothing more to know," she said. "He is dead, and now is nothing. No one, nothing, *nichevo,* and I too am *nichevo.*"

As she was speaking, his pupils had widened sufficiently and he had a chance to examine her more carefully.

As any woman would, she felt his eyes on her. "My son thought I was beautiful, and I was, famous Russian beauty as beautiful as flaming red dawn that lights sky in east."

Byrne produced the photograph of his mother and Natasha that had caused him so much wonderment and squinted at it in the gloom. "Yes," he said, "you were very beautiful." Her face was still buried deep within the folds of the cowl, but Byrne could sense her eyes on him, and so he handed it to her. Natasha, however, made no move to take it, and he rested it gently on her lap.

"To him I was always beautiful," she went on. "He honored me above all women, venerated me as son should venerate mother. And they took him from me!" She began to weep. "What crime did I commit? Why they always take from me? Why?"

Why? Two hours earlier, he had been sitting in his mother's living room, mouthing the same question. It used to be his living room, long ago. This was the house he had lived in, the house he remembered, and if home really was the place where they had to take you back when you came, then he supposed he had the right to call this place home.

Certainly, it was more home than the half-empty flat where he lived now; more home than Doreen's apartment at the corner of West Fourth and West Tenth, the next best thing to Waverly and Waverly, more of a home than the apartment in Sunnyside he used to share with Mary Claire, before he found out about her affair with Tom, the affair she had been carrying on for months and that after a while she conducted brazenly because after all he was never home. And when he did find out, when things were irrevocably ruined and Mary Claire told him she didn't love him anymore and wanted him gone, he had confronted his brother, asking him to do the right thing if he really loved her and Tom just laughed and said, "You can have the bitch back, I'm sick of her," and then dumped her. Any place was more of a home than that.

"Why, Mom?" He was trying to keep his emotions in check, the way she always did. But mothers always sensed tears.

"It was for your own good, Francis," she said. She had always been cold to him, and now she was like ice. "I knew this day would come," she continued. "It's just that I thought it would come later, is all. Because, despite everything, I never hated you."

What kind of thing was that for a mother to say to her son? "I thought you loved me, Ma," he said. "I always loved you."

"I'm sure you did," she replied. "That was the way we wanted it, your father and I."

Was she afraid of him now, just a bit, as he had always been of her? Was that fear he saw in her eyes—fear, an emotion close to his heart and, aside from anger, his best friend? "What did I do that you should treat me like this?" he asked.

"You were born," she said simply. "That's your crime. And now you're going to do the time."

She put her arms around him, something she almost never did. When he was a small child, a little boy, he used to lie in bed at night and wish so hard that she would come in to hold him before he drifted off to sleep that he would sometimes start to cry, just to get her attention. "Shut up, ya sissy!" Tom would yell at him, from the bunkbed above his, but it was hard to stop once he started. "Crybaby, crybaby," came the taunts from above, and either she would hear them arguing or she wouldn't and either she would open the door to the boys' bedroom and peek in or she wouldn't, but she never, ever, came over to him, never held him, never kissed away the tears and told him it was all right, there was nothing to be afraid of, lying there in the darkness, because now he knew that the sleep of reason produces monsters, and there was everything to be afraid of.

It felt good to be in her embrace, even if it was elusive and ephemeral. "I can answer a lot of your questions," she said, "but if I could answer Why, then I would be God. It's the hardest question there is, Francis, and you've been asking it practically from the day you were born. No wonder you wanted to be a detective. Maybe someday you'll learn that nobody ever really has an answer to it. Not even your mother." She patted his back gently. "Not even me, little boy."

He pulled back and looked at her; perhaps for the first time in his life, he could see her for what she really was. Neither madonna nor whore, but only a woman.

She was talking to herself now, more than to him, performing a monologue she must have rehearsed a hundred times. "I know the nuns taught you in school that we are all creatures endowed with free will," she said. "But do you really believe it? You, after all your *experience in the streets? Aren't some people born to be bad? Born to kill? Born to die? And who chooses them?"*

"God chooses, Mother," he said.

"Then that makes Him no better than Satan," she said bitterly.

Byrne could hear the woman's labored breathing from within the confines of her mufti. "I don't know why," he said. "You have to help me. You have to tell me what happened." Now he had to know. He had to understand everything.

"He was bleeding. Do you have any idea what is like to see son in this way? Bleeding life away, and yours as well? How can you possibly understand what woman, what mother, feels?"

The music that he had heard when he arrived was still playing, faintly, in the background. The recording was old and scratchy and Byrne could just barely make out the singer's words.

> *And if I thought he would*
> *If I thought he would try to go*
> *Then I would sigh,*
> *No, I'd cry*
> *Yes, I'd lay me down and die*

She noticed that he was listening. "Is called 'Honey Man.'" The *h* was heavily aspirated, Russian-style, a combination of *g* and *h* that started in the throat: almost *Ghunny Man*. "I like old songs best," she said. "I have known this song since I was little girl. In Russia we had few recordings from west and we listen over and over again. In those days I do not understand words, but I feel them. I feel how sad she is, singer. I feel sorrow."

"It's a sad song," said Byrne.

"When you are Russian, there are only sad songs," she said simply. She paused, then continued. "It makes me think of him. He was bleeding, shot. I try to help him. I fear he die."

"Sy told me. Dr. Schlussel. And he is dead, too." He still hoped, improbably, that she was talking about the .22 slugs, although he knew she wasn't.

There was a long pause before she spoke again. The song was still playing in the background.

Yes die,
If I should lose my honey man,
Oh, Lordy, that man!

"But Vanya not dead," she said. "Bleeding from stomach, but not dead."

Byrne swallowed hard, and asked: "How did he die?"

"How he die?" Natasha was saying. "He die in my arms. Like baby."

Byrne caught a glimpse of her hands as they shot from her sleeves and began to tear the photograph he had given her into small pieces. Without ever looking at it, she shredded it slowly and carefully, until the picture had been completely destroyed. The sight of her flesh was just beginning to register in his brain when she reached toward her face and took down her cowl.

"You were very young when your father passed away, Francis," his mother said. "And I must say you took it very well. Even back then, they wanted me to get you counseling to help you deal with the trauma—I forget whether they used that word in those days—but I refused, because that's the way your father would have wanted it. Your father always got what he wanted."

She was sitting in her customary chair but for the first time in memory the television was switched off. "I'm sure that you know by now that Tom's mother and I were sisters. You probably think it strange that two sisters should marry the same man, but believe me back in Russia such things are not at all unusual. If a man found a good wife and mother, and if she suddenly died, then it was only natural for him to look in the same place for a replacement, and that's more or less what your father did after Vera died."

"And did Dad love you as much as he loved her?" asked Byrne.

"No," she answered simply. "He married me, but he always loved somebody else. How do you explain love? How do you even explain physical attraction? It's hard for a woman to understand that a man can feel love for more than one woman, or that he can he love one woman and lust after another. I've finally figured that out, but back then I hadn't."

"She was very beautiful," said Byrne, producing the photograph he had taken from Ekdahl's car a lifetime ago. This time around she evinced more interest in the picture, taking it from him and examining it carefully.

"Yes, she was," she agreed. "But this is not Vera; this is Natasha." There was the hint of a laugh. "When we were little everyone always argued whether Vera was more beautiful than Natasha, or vice versa. No one ever said I was in the same league. Of course, Natasha was also a whore. There was no one that Natash' wouldn't sleep with if she thought it

would do her any good. After we came over, CIA used her as a honey trap, the kind of pretty thing they would dangle to make some poor bastard come across when all else failed. It's amazing, Francis, what a man will do to get a woman in bed, or say to her once there. People think that women are the ones who have to be seduced, that when a woman gives her body she also gives her soul. Bullshit! Women have been faking it ever since Eve told Adam the earth moved for her, too. But men—put a desirable woman in front of them and there's nothing they won't do, say or admit to. The toughest guy breaks down in the presence of a good-looking woman. The problem is, after a while they tire of even the most beautiful girl—they develop an immunity to her, and so you have to change or up the dosage. It's all sadly predictable, and women like Natasha have been making their fortune off this fundamental principle of human nature forever."

Byrne took back the photograph.

"Vanya showed me this picture the night he was here, the night you came crashing in like Sir Galahad. His mother had given it to him, so that he could see what I looked like, and told him that I had the answer to the central question of his short life."

"Then why did he have his hands on you?" asked Byrne.

"Why did you shoot him before you had a chance to find out?" His mother's voice was flat and dispassionate; it was like she was talking to a stranger. "You and your goddamn temper. When you were little, I could never decide whether your temper or your smart mouth would get you into more trouble when you got older. Now I know."

And at last he knew who killed Egil Ekdahl. "I thought he was trying to hurt you," said Byrne lamely.

"He wanted to know where his father was." She looked across the void at him, and suddenly he realized that all their lives they had been strangers to each other, two parties bonded accidentally, yet separated by a wide gulf of feelings and experience. This is why she had never come in to comfort him when he was crying; it was not that she was cruel, or that she wanted him to suffer. It was that she just didn't care.

"He was looking for a man named Nosenko," she went on. "A Russian. A defector. A spy, whom Natasha entertained as a pleasure girl one night and told him was his father. Who knows, maybe she even believed it. By that time, she was so crazy that she could have convinced herself of anything. And who was he to doubt her? If you can't believe your own mother, who can you believe?"

The creature who sat opposite him, in the weather-beaten rattan chair, looked to be a thousand years old. The skin had been flayed off the hand that was extended toward him. Her lips had been pared away, which is why it was so difficult for her to speak. The cane that rested at the side of the chair helped her maneuver on the two broken feet that had never quite healed. Both her ears were missing. Her hair, what was left of it, hung in wispy strands around her disfigured face, and her eyes bulged because the lids had been removed and there was nothing else for them to do except to stare at him, reproachfully.

Whoever had done this to her had done his job well, decorticating the facade of the woman and leaving only the irreducible essence beneath. It was like looking at a creature who wore her muscles and sinews and tendons on her exterior; shorn of her skin, devoid of all cosmetic device, she had been stripped nakeder than any man could ever strip her.

"Here is where he died," she said simply, pointing to her tortured breast. "Here, where he was always welcome. Where he was always loved. Where he first tasted life."

"*Your father wasn't always a policeman; he was CIA, which is how he met me, and how he met Sy Sheinberg. They were both working the Nosenko case; your father was one of the deputies in the Soviet Russia division, and his career went down the tubes along with everyone else's who disbelieved Nosenko, and after he left the Agency, the best he could do was catch on with the NYPD. And I went with him; they made me.*"

"*Who made you, Mother?*" he asked.

"*The Soviets, of course,*" she replied. "*You don't think my sisters and I were real defectors, do you? It was an unbelievable coup: to have direct bedroom access to the deputy chief of the SR division. Angleton suspected everybody of being Sasha, his famous mole, but he was too much of a chauvinist pig for it ever to occur to him that Sasha might be a woman. Or two or three women.*"

"*Didn't they ever suspect?*" he asked.

"*You probably think CIA is staffed by supermen,*" snorted his mother. "*Well, it's not. They are only human, like the rest of us. And like all humans, they are capable of not seeing whatever it is they don't wish to see. When it comes to security, the U.S. is as vulnerable as anyone else. In 1960, a man named Bernon Mitchell defected to Moscow, taking a big chunk of the National Security Agency files with him. Here was the fabled NSA, an electronic-surveillance outfit so secret that the joke was its initials stood for 'No Such Agency,' and they hired this man Mitchell who had admitted to six years of 'sexual experimentation' with dogs and chickens. But they wanted him, and so they did not see. Just as, in this moment, you still do not see.*"

He had to ask her. "What was Ekdahl saying to you? It sounded like Iubin, or something like that."

"*The last words he spoke to me,*" she said, "*were Ya lyublyu vas. In Russian that means, 'I love you.' He was thanking me, not threatening me. Because he had come to the* end of his long journey at last. I told him who his father really was, and where he was. Not hiding out under some CIA cover, but in the cemetery, just down the street. At Calvary. Not Nosenko. Robert Byrne."

And then he knew. Knew then what his namesake Saint Francis the Assisian knew, what Father Dignan also knew: that there is evil in the world, and there is good, and that they are simply two halves of the same whole, that one cannot exist without the other, that one gives meaning to the other, that they define each other, and that the holy man must exist in and of the world, and not apart from it, that he must pluck his sainthood from the dung heap of evil in his soul.

"I think your father saw something of Vera in Natasha," she continued. "They looked very much alike, and I think also he felt sorry for her. But I don't really know. As I said, how can you explain passion?"

Do not judge your comrade until you have stood in his place. Until and unless you have walked a mile in his shoes. . . . It was all coming clear to him now. "Are you saying," asked Byrne, "that my father was also Ekdahl's father? That he was my half brother?"

To his surprise, this brought forth a bitter laugh from Irene. "You still haven't figured it out, have you?" she asked. She let out her breath in a rush. "There was no way she could have raised you; her profession, shall we say, wouldn't have allowed it; the Company wouldn't have allowed it. There's nothing more useless than a pregnant whore, and so she gave you up."

"Natasha was my mother?" he gasped.

"But she came back for Vanya," Irene told him. "She couldn't lose two sons. That would have made her even crazier than she already was. You were adoptable, movable, fungible, and I was barren: a perfect match. But he was deformed and nobody cared about him; and anyway by then, a decade later, she was too old for CIA. They didn't give a damn what happened to her. So she had nothing to lose. She used our old Soviet network and kidnapped him from his foster family, and made her way back to Russia. That was another nail in your father's coffin, because her cover was blown then, and after that it was just a matter of time before his fate caught up with him. As now yours has you."

She kissed him on the cheek, a kiss of farewell. "Welcome to the world, boy. I've been waiting a long time to lay down this burden. Today, at last, I am free."

"Good-bye, Mother," he said, but Irene did not even look up as he left. She had put the television back on. "Look at it this way," she called after him. "You're half legitimate."

"Or only half a bastard," he said.

There was no television in Natalia's house, just the ghostly voice on the old phonograph, singing its endless sad refrain.

Yes die,
If I should lose my honey man,
Oh, Lordy, that man!

Natasha stood, letting her cloak slip to the floor. The pieces of the photograph fluttered away, forgotten and irrelevant. Beneath the robe she wore nothing.

"My son," Natasha said. She stretched out what was left of her arms, and puckered her lipless lips. "Come to Mother."

Chapter Forty-three
Brighton Beach, Brooklyn
Thursday, October 18, 1990; 12:30 A.M.

Now he is safe, safe in the warmth of the water, safe in the warmth of her arms. He feels the liquid cascading over his brow; she is pouring it, just as she always did when he was small, just as she did when she took him away for the first time and washed him and bathed him and made sure everything was clean because after all she was his Mother.

Her voice is far away, farther away than it has ever been, even when he was on the Island, where a sinner like him had been transformed into a saint. A sacred trust is bleeding away and he is powerless to stop it.

She is stroking him now, pushing back gently on his forehead. This is what she always did when he was little Vanya, push back on his forehead or tug on his long curls in the back, either way he ended up in the same position, his eyes heavenward, but there was no religious significance to

the gesture because it was only a way of preventing the soap from stinging his eyes even if she promised no more tears but he didn't really believe it because when you got right down to it there were always tears.
"Mother," he says. "*Ya lyublyu vas. Lyublyu bezmerno.*"

He is lying on his back in the water, across her knees. His head is back
as far as it can go, and now he can look into her eyes and see all the way
to heaven. A heroic deed of unprecedented prowess, he had promised:
the death of the man who had caused her so much pain. And now,
through no fault of his own, he had failed. Surely, this could not be just.
The thought, suddenly upon him, enrages him. He opens his mouth, but
no sound comes forth. He has spoken his last words.

"*Ya lyublyu vas*, Vanya, my beautiful son," she is saying, half-singing, as
she caresses him. "But how they have deceived you."

He can feel the water upon his cheeks now, as it rises higher. What if
it should spill over the side? Mother would be very angry then. But she
is in the tub with him; she knows what she is doing. Mother always
knows what she is doing. She is shaving him with the razor he always
brings along. He can feel the sharp edge of the blade as it slides
smoothly over his skin. Soon it will be time for him to rise from the bath
and for her to dry him with the rough towel that imparts such a delicious tingle to his skin.

But he cannot rise. And now, he notes, he can no longer see.

No matter. She is holding him tight. The back of his head is against
her neck, the Inca bone pressed into the concave hollow of her neck.
And he is slipping away from her, leaving her, betraying her, as he said
he would never do. He hopes she will not be too angry with him.

And now comes a pain in that Place, a pain of such ineffable sweet-
ness that he wonders how he has lived without this pain all his life. It is
not like those other pains, the pains he felt on the Island or, worse, the
pain he felt when he was separated from her. This is a different pain, a
good pain, a pain that puts an end to the evil, useless thing with which
God has cursed him. It is a sharp, sudden pain, and then it is gone and
with it all his troubles are gone.

The water is even redder now, *krasny*, for in Russian the word for
"red" is the same as the word for "beautiful."

Her voice is in his ear, singing softly. With his blinded eyes he sees
clearly that it is not a tub he lies in but a river, the river of life being ir-

rigated by his passing. Could this be me? he wonders. Or is it only the red dawn, flaming in the sky?

"It could not be allowed," she says, bending over the water, looking down, still weeping, instrument in hand, "for I loved him once, too. And those I love, I love forever. As I love you."

She kisses him passionately upon the lips. With a sudden stab of joy, he knows that the father must be very near. The light is burning brighter and more fiercely than ever as she draws the blade, lovingly, across his throat.

Acknowledgments

A book of this scope cannot be written without the help of a great
many people. A huge debt of thanks is thus owed to Steve Tilley, cura-
tor of the JFK Collection at the National Archives in Washington, D.C.,
who kindly guided me through the thickets of declassified documents.
Despite the many unanswered questions that still surround the Kennedy
assassination, there can be little doubt that Lee Harvey Oswald, on his
own, shot President Kennedy that day in Dallas; whether earlier in his
short life Oswald had connections with various intelligence agencies,
however, is a very different matter. I am therefore grateful to the orga-
nizers of the thirtieth-anniversary conference on the assassination, held
in Dallas in November 1993, and in particular to Jo Rae DiMeno, for
exposing me to the points of view of the dissenters. And thanks as well
to Ben Loeterman, whose PBS documentary *Who Was Lee Harvey Oswald?*
is a brilliant unraveling of Oswald's tangled web.

In Moscow, my *Time* magazine colleagues John Kohan, Jay Carney and
Felix Rosenthal were extremely helpful. Providing assistance as well were
Sergei Butkov, Berlin correspondent of the *Komsomolskaya Pravda*, and retired KGB Colonel Oleg M. Nechiporenko, whose own excellent mem-
oir *Passport to Assassination* is his firsthand account of meeting Oswald in
Mexico City in 1963, shortly before the assassination. In Scandinavia,
valuable suggestions about the character and motivation of Ingrid

Bentsen were made by my friends Ole Sørli, Benedicte Adrian, Ingrid Bjørnov and Inghild Aasen.

In Germany, thanks go out to my late friend, mentor and colleague, Franz Spelman, and to Wolfgang Robinow, two Jewish men who were evicted from their Austrian and German homelands when the Nazis came and who returned with the American army, the OSS and the CIA after the war, there to stay. While neither of them resembles Seymour Sheinberg or Jacob German in the slightest, their experiences and perspectives, so different from those of American Holocaust survivors, were poignant and valuable background material in the creation of the characters.

The great American author Paul Horgan was unflagging in his encouragement for this first-time novelist, who rang him often with stupid questions and annoying worries. His death in March 1995 has left American letters much the poorer.

Apologies are in order to the Danish government, whose exemplary diplomatic service most emphatically does not harbor such characters as Egil Ekdahl, Ingrid Bentsen and Nils Pilgersen.

Finally, thanks to my dear wife, Kate, and our beloved daughters, Alexandra and Clare Walsh, for their love and support.

Any and all errors in fact and judgment are entirely the fault of the author.

October 18, 1996
Lakeville, Connecticut

Notes on Sources

The fictional story of Francis Byrne and Egil Ekdahl takes place within overlapping historical contexts and I have endeavored to be as accurate as possible in their reconstruction.

The internecine warfare that nearly destroyed the CIA is admirably detailed in David C. Martin's seminal *Wilderness of Mirrors*, Edward J. Epstein's *Legend: The Secret World of Lee Harvey Oswald* and, most recently, in David Wise's *Molehunt*. Yuri Nosenko really was held as a prisoner of the CIA for more than four years; Nosenko is today a contract agent for the CIA, living somewhere in the United States, and still under a death sentence from the KGB. Sasha, meanwhile, was never found or, if he or she was found, never recognized.

The Sakhalin Island prison camp and the account of Vanya's tortures and subsequent insanity are drawn largely from *Communist Control Techniques*, a recently declassified CIA document prepared by the Technical Services Division in 1956, as well as *The Official KGB Handbook*, a samizdat pirating of an internal-security KGB document translated and published in English after the collapse of the Soviet Union.

The sections relating to the KGB in general and its "illegals" program in particular were kindly vetted by former KGB officers with personal knowledge of the Nosenko case, Lee Harvey Oswald and the illegals program. In my fictive account, a Soviet illegal may have attained the level of consul general; in fact, according to KGB sources, an illegal once rose as high as ambassador to the United States.

All documents regarding the Kennedy assassination and the Nosenko case referred to or cited in the text are real, and have been drawn from the JFK Collection at the National Archives in Washington, D.C. Donald Jameson's comments about defectors are as he uttered them, with some small modifications.

Oswald was an opera fan, and opera plays a large role in this story, as either text or subtext. Most obvious are the references to Tchaikovsky's *Eugene Onegin* and *The Queen of Spades*, while Mussorgsky's *Boris Godunov* figures in the action as well; in each case, the words are by that most beloved of Russian poets, Pushkin. The poor translation of Yeletsky's aria from *The Queen of Spades*, which Ekdahl hears on the radio, was made by Oswald and was found among his effects after the assassination, as was Natalia's "Russian beauties" song. The cryptic letter from Dir. Wennström of Sweden warning of the mysterious organization with a distinctive sign is just one of many oddball letters received by the U.S. government in the wake of the assassination.

Dr. German's assessment of the young Ekdahl's character is based on the psychological examinations of Lee Harvey Oswald conducted in New York City by Dr. Renatus Hartogs and Evelyn Strickman. The medical details of Ekdahl's autopsy report are drawn from the actual autopsies on both President Kennedy and Oswald. Assassination buffs will also recognize many other peripheral names and details buried in the text.

The account of the Malchiel Gruenwald–Israel Rudolf Kastner libel trial uses as its authority Israeli journalist Tom Segev's definitive *The Seventh Million: The Israelis and the Holocaust.* Among the many other sources for the story of Schlüssel, Rubenstein and Brandmelder I would like to single out Hannah Arendt's *Eichmann in Jerusalem* and Nora Levin's *The Holocaust: The Destruction of European Jewry 1933–1945.*

The Mezhdunarodnaya Hotel in Moscow was, in 1990, exactly as described here, as were the *Alexander Block* and the Ismailova housing projects.

The description of Ekdahl's pornography collection is both accurate and, if anything, tame. The "Amazing Microvideo," shot originally for medical purposes, is for sale at the price advertised.

Angelo Genna's pungent and colorful dialogue was inspired by FBI wiretaps at the Ravenite Social Club on Mulberry Street in Little Italy, Manhattan. "John Rawlston" was one of the aliases used by Filippo Sacco, better known as the flamboyant mobster Johnny Rosselli. His story is detailed in the book *All-American Mafioso*, by Charles Rappleye and Ed Becker.

Places like the Rambone and the Hunt Club really do exist in contemporary New York, where they attract large and enthusiastically participatory clienteles.

Lee Harvey Oswald's KGB file is now the property of the former Soviet republic of Belarus and remains in Minsk, still classified top secret.